Archon:
Gift Of Light

L. S. Quail

For my sons, Cruie and Jax.
And for my stepson, Logan
I love you all!

Table of Contents

Note from the Author

I want everyone to know that I apologize for the first edition. Ashamedly, it wasn't my best work, and it most certainly wasn't what I wanted to present to my readers and hopeful fans. That's why I am offering this second edition publishing.

I hereby promise to you; from now on, all works I publish, professionally or independently, shall be presented to you as it should be; clean, as error-free as possible, and edited to the best of my abilities or with a professional if possible..

I have also changed the Prologue of this book because I, personally, was not too happy with it. I hope this brings about a more exciting read for all of you, including those of you that have purchased the previous copy in the past.

I want to thank you all, and I hope you enjoy reading this book and much as I have enjoyed writing it.

If you would like to visit my website, please visit http://www.lsquail.com to learn more about me and other works in production, or if you would like to read my shorties (short stories), please visit http://www.shortstories4u2share.com where you are asked to Read! Like! Comment! Share!

Have fun and remember... SMILE!
L. S. Quail

Prologue

"As we've come to know...

and as it has been, the Circle of Darkness wages war against the Rings through the Circle of Light and all of Terra-Earth. As the Circle of Light believes in peace and love through the power of knowledge for eternal life within the Spirit Realm to be with our creators, the Rings, after their life within the Earthen Realm.

"The Circle of Darkness believes all creation should only exist to serve as commanded. No love. No peace. All the Order of Terrans should only know the knowledge of servitude or a painful and agonizing death to further serve upon the Plane of Hell. In so, the Circle of Darkness delivers upon the Order of Terrans his very own Order of Demons led by a King of the Order of Demons created from his own black heart. This King is named Liche. So vile, so ferocious and despicable is this Liche that no army from any league can stand successfully against him. He carries with him a foul weapon of death he calls Poison, a sword created from a fang of the Circle of Darkness. Liche's duty is to torment and force all leagues from the Order of Terrans to serve and obey only the Circle of Darkness.

"In their despair, the Rings would not allow their precious Terra-Earth to be forced to live in torment, so they gave the Circle of Light a gift and the Circle of Light called this gift 'Archon.'

"Archon's purpose is to protect Terra-Earth from Liche and the Order of Demons to allow us all to live, love, gain knowledge, and thank the Circle of Light for giving us all this so that we will be with the Rings in death. As the gift of Archon was given to the Circle of Light to put upon TerraEarth, the Circle of Light gave Archon a gift of his own to defeat Liche. Archon calls it 'Flare.' It is a weapon that carries the flames of the Circle of Light. No Terran may wield it. No demon can stand up to it.

"Archon and Liche use their weapons to slay one another. Their battles are hard-fought. Sometimes Liche slays Archon, but Archon returns in a new form from the Rings. Stronger, more powerful, and more determined to protect Terra-Earth from Liche and his Poison. The Circle of Darkness never fully rules Terra-Earth because Archon serves the Circle of Light with the power of the Rings. Thus, Light always triumphs over Darkness.

"It is also said that one day, a final Archon will come to fight the most powerful Liche ever put-upon Terra-Earth by Darkness. That battle will decide whether we, the League of Humans, and all other Leagues that remain will be free within the brightness of the day with the Circle of Light or if we should serve in eternal damnation within permanent night ruled under the tyranny of Liche and his master, the Circle of Darkness."

"When will this Eternal Archon come to be?" a young voice asks.

"We will only know this when that time comes. This knowledge is given to us by the Circle of Light for us to cherish," responds the professor.

"So says the Circle of Light!" responds the class.

A voice shouts, "*Peasant!*"

I

he entire room jumps. Some scream. Some curse. Some do
both. The professor is also startled into a jump. Everyone turns
just in time to see the overly tall, brown-headed, boy standing at
the doorway turn nose-first into the door. His blood paints the
door, and he falls to the floor with his legs crossed and his
hands on his lap. Blood continues to flow from his nose as he curses,
"Damned hard oak!" to himself. Aside from his nosing the door,
everyone knows he is the "peasant" someone has just called out. His
breeches are a patchwork of material that has continued the length to
cover his entire toned, long legs. His pale, yellow tunic resembles the
same materials used to cover his lean, muscular body. His dirty,
calloused, hands show the hard work he puts into caring for his land.
His brown eyes show his distaste for the "damned hard oak" door.

Another man, in silver robes and carrying a tall staff with a
hawk carved at the top, steps over the boy. He reaches down and
snatches him to his feet, shaking him the entire way up.

"What in the Light's name"—Professor Dahlmür pauses—"Eh .
. . Eh. . . Eh. . . is going on out . . . Eh. . . Eh. . . Eh. . . here?" His
stuttering causes some of the students to giggle and mock him.

He ignores them all and walks to the scene, "Eh . . . Eh. . . Eh. .
. why is my class being disturbed?"

The man, frantically trying to hold the boy up to keep him from
passing out again, smiles and puffs out his chest and chin then
gallantly answers, "I found this peasant watching your lecture from
the door. I apologize for this. . . *disturbance* and will punish him
appropriately, Professor Dahlmür."

Professor Dahlmür looks at the boy and hands him a
handkerchief for his nose, "Clean yourself up, Young Master . . .
Eh. . . Eh. . . eh?" He shakes a finger at the boy, trying to cue him
for his name.

"Rodin," the boy says.

"Rodin," he then cues him again, "Sir."

"Sir."

"You see, Professor Widd—"

"Wide."

"Wide, yes. You see. . . Eh. . . Eh. . . Eh, Professor Wide, I was asking, why are *you* disturbing my class?"

A bout of confusion displays over Professor Wide's face, "What?"

"Well, Master. . . Eh. . . Eh. . . Eh," Professor Dahlmür cues him again.

"Rodin."

"Rodin. . . Eh," Professor Dahlmür quickly corrects him, "Sir."

"Sir."

"Yes. . . Eh. . . Eh. . . Eh, Master Rodin here was waiting, ever so patiently, I might add," Dahlmür begins to speak frantically, trying to rattle Professor Wide, "was waiting to. . . Eh. . . Eh. . . Eh, clean my boards and desks as I have. . . Eh. . . Eh. . . Eh. . . asked him."

A student chuckles, "Yeah, right," and the class giggles back.

Dahlmür stares at the student and clears his throat at him. He picks up his staff beside the door and taps it to the floor. *Snap! Snap! Snap!* Large sparks ignite from the large quartz crystal at the top, causing the room to become silent. He faces Professor Wide, "Now, where was I?"

Rodin fills him in, "He was disturbing your class."

Dahlmür remembers, "Oh, yes! Eh. . . Eh. . . Eh," he looks at Rodin, "Sir."

"Sir."

"Yes. . . Eh. . . Eh. . . Eh. . . You were saying?" Dahlmür looks at Professor Wide for a response.

Professor Wide is startled and befuddled, "Yes, well I. . . You see. . . well, Rodin here—"

Rodin cuts in, "Master Rodin."

"Yes, Master. . . I mean. . . " he turns at Rodin, "You be quiet!"

Rodin smiles, "Sir."

"Sir." Then Professor Wide realizes something, "Oh, dammit all to Darkness! Just. . . Never mind! I'm leaving!"

"But what about my nose?" Rodin asks.

"Shut up, peasant! Before I have you thrown in a stockade!"

Professor Dahlmür is displeased, "All because you interrupted *my* class. Now time is up, and I was not finished yet. You owe me an apology as well."

"I will not!" Professor Wide fires back and turns on his heels, throws his chin up, and marches away.

"I do not like him," says Rodin.

"Nor do I, Master. . . Eh. . . Eh. . . Eh..."

"Rodin, sir."

"Yes," he looks up at his nose, "Master Rodin, please go to the far corner over there and sit." He turns his gaze at the puzzled class.

The boy that commented earlier hisses at Rodin as he passes by, "Stupid peasants!"

Rodin stops and stares at him, "We hate you too, Vil," then he proceeds to the far corner as asked.

Vil stands, "Did you just speak to me, peasant? You will *never* speak to me. You will only listen and follow as I say! You worm!"

Rodin laughs at him, "I guess I missed that lesson, Vil!"

Fury rises into Vil's cheeks, "I will kill you, you worthless peasant!"

Dahlmür starts to speak when a shorter boy with straight blonde hair, blue eyes, and distinguished robes stands and faces Vil, "Shut up, Vil!"

"What did you call me?" Vil approaches the boy, towering over him just inches.

"That is your name. Right, Vil?" he stands between Vil and Rodin with his arms folded across his chest, glaring up at him.

Vil looks down at him with disgust and snickers at him, "And just who the hell do you think you are, new guy? Are you some peasant-lover?" His comment gets a few laughs from the class.

The boy smiles at him, "You will bow and address me as 'You're Majesty' or 'Prince Byron,' Vil!"

Vil's face is overcome with astonishment, "What?" he says in confusion, then the rest of the class jump and fall to their knees, bowing at the boy. Dahlmür leans on Vil's shoulder, forcing him to do the same as he taps his cane to the floor.

Snap! Snap! Snap!

Rodin goes to a knee but does not bow, "I think he likes doing that with his cane, *You're Majesty.*" Rodin smiles as he emphasizes the Prince's title.

"I think so, too, Master Rodin." Prince Byron smiles at Dahlmür and motions at the class to rise, "Except you, Vil. I don't care if you are from the Class of Lords or not. Remain to bow until

I say otherwise, and you will repeat after me." Vil remains bowing. Heat begins to redden his neck, "I apologize, Master Rodin."

"What?" Vil looks up at him, puzzled, "No!" The class gasps.

"What did you say? I don't think I heard you. And bow!" The boy stomps toward him and begins to circle him, "I could give a *damn* who you are, but in this kingdom, I am Prince Byron! And you will do as *I* say!" He leans into his ear, "Is that clear, Vil?"

Vil whispers something in response as the rest of the class watch in shock, except Rodin, who is smiling at the spectacle.

"What?"

"Yes, Your Majesty!"

Professor Dahlmür taps his cane again, *Snap! Snap! Snap!* "Pardon me, Master Byron, but. . . Eh. . . Eh. . . Eh. . . I really must release the class."

Prince Byron looks around at the others calmly and places a hand on Vil, "Yes, of course, Professor Dahlmür. You may. Lord Vil, the next time I hear a whisper of you treating anyone within *my* kingdom with the malice you did here today, I will most certainly have you locked up in the stockade in the center of town. Is that clear?"

Vil whimpers to him, "Yes, Your Majesty."

Professor Dahlmür begins to usher everyone out as Prince Byron walks up to Rodin, places a hand on his shoulder, and asks if he can look at his nose. Rodin looks at him in confusion and allows him to take a look. Just then, Prince Byron places a hand in front of his nose, and it begins to glow. Rodin flinches in surprise and feels his face tingle as the pain and numbness subside. His nose stops bleeding and surprisingly feels as if he had never smashed it into the door at all. He reaches up and feels around his nose and face while looking at Byron in amazement.

Dahlmür walks up and inspects his face and grumbles his approval. For a moment, Rodin looks at the two of them suspiciously. Nobody in the class has ever done anything out of kindness for him or any peasant that he's known. Especially a prince. Rodin can only remember one person, but that was the day a group of trolls tried to invade the village through their farm. He hasn't seen or heard from that person since. Still, this is very unusual and unexpected.

"What is wrong, Master Rodin?" Professor Dahlmür asks.

He looks at him humbly, "I'm still waiting for one of you to yell at me or throw me out by my feet."

"What?" Byron asks, amazed to hear his statement, "I would never do that to anyone. Especially not to someone that doesn't deserve that kind of thing. How do you know Lord Vil anyway?"

Rodin looks down at his feet as he digs his toe into the floor. It isn't a memory he wants to revisit. He remembers the day all too clearly. The day his parents died.

A young Rodin is at home, getting himself and his then twelve-year-old little brother, Logan, ready for supper when his father bursts through the door. His father is panic-stricken. His eyes widened, and his face covered with dirt and sweat from working the soil on that hot day as he puts his back to the door while muttering, "Oh, Light! Oh, Light! Please! No! They're coming! They're coming!"

His father grabs a nearby trunk and drags it against the door, blocking somebody from coming in. His mother becomes frantic, begging him and asking him to explain what is going on. Rodin's father runs to him and his brother and quickly shoves them out the window.

His father pleads for Rodin's mother to come to the window while screaming, "Trolls! A whole army of them! Coming this way!"

His mother doesn't believe him. She begs him to calm down and tries to bring Rodin's brother back through the window as she explains that there are no trolls in this side of the kingdom.

Bam! The door slams as if something heavy has run into it. The trunk slides slightly away, and his father races to push it back. Suddenly, the door is thrown open, and a horde of small, angry, gray, trolls rush in with knives and tiny axes. They scream in fury and snarl at everything around them, baring horrid, broken yellow teeth as they rush in, causing frantic havoc.

Rodin's mother screams and tosses Logan out of the window. Rodin hears the bone in his brother's arm break when he hits the ground as he jumps out after him. His brother screams in pain. His mother screams in terror. His father screams in the fight against the trolls.

One ugly little troll makes it to the window opening, but that is as far as it can go. It becomes obvious to Rodin that his father has found his hand ax and uses it to remove the bottom half of the troll's body at the stomach with just one blow. The sight is putrid.

Rodin screams in terror. He picks up his screaming brother, and they run. Behind him, more screams erupt from the house. He turns and sees trolls climbing over one another in a rush to get into the house. The sounds of screaming trolls soon take over the sounds of his mother crying in agony. His father stopped yelling before she did. The trolls are torturing his mother in the most painful of ways by the sound of her constant screams.

Rodin carries his crying brother over his bony shoulders, forcing his long legs to take longer strides a lot quicker. He soon loses balance and falls to the ground at the road.

A man on a horse suddenly stops just before trampling him. Rodin yells that the trolls are killing his mother and father. The man laughs in disbelief and wants to know what has happened to his brother until he hears Rodin's mother let out her final scream. The huge, bulky man leaps down from his horse, grabs his sword and shield, and heads into the house.

Another rider rides up to Rodin and Logan. Instead of asking what is going on, he tries to force his horse to walk over them. When the horse refuses, he curses at the two and threatens to kill them for blocking the road. The man who had run off into the house screams a battle cry, and the sounds of trolls dying in screams and screeches echo out. The rider sits on his horse and curses the man for making him late. He states that he doesn't have time for the man to fight trolls in a peasant's house. He cries out for him to leave them and let the peasants handle them, but it was no use. The sounds of the metal blade and the metal shield hitting various parts of the house mixing with shouts of triumph and screams of troll agony breaks through the silence of the night.

A woman and a girl from the next farm rushes to the street where the three of them stand as they cry that more trolls are chasing after them. The rider realizes that he is the only person there with a sword. Of course! Why would peasants have swords? He pulls his sword and fumbles with a horn that dangled from his saddle. He blows the horn as best as he can.

Rodin sees that the girl is his longtime friend Millette and her mother. When her mother realizes that Rodin's brother is in pain, she grabs him and takes him to a ditch covered in brush on the side of the road. Her father isn't with her. He stayed to protect the house.

The road fills with village peasants. All of them scream about trolls invading their homes and how somebody stayed behind to fight them.

The rider blows the horn again frantically trying to make the call seem dire with quick and loud blows. He fears for his own life and keeps ordering the peasants to form a circle of protection around him. They all scream and curse at him as they tell him to fight to save the village.

Rodin doesn't care what is going on around him. He can't stop holding Millette and watching his home, where the man is still fighting the trolls.

Finally, help arrives in the form of more than twenty knights on horses. Each ask the peasants what is going on until they realize the severity of the situation and split up to attack the groups one by one leaving behind five. The rider orders them to circle around him and kill any troll, or peasant, that gets too close to him.

It takes a few hours, but the invasion is over. All homes are clear of trolls. They report that some of the peasants that had stayed behind didn't survive. Some had been skinned alive. Some report that they suffered horribly. That is when Rodin knew his mother met the same fate and knew that the screams he had heard were his mother in agony as they skinned her before she finally died. Rodin collapses in anguish while clinging to Millette. Her petite frame collapses with him as she shares in his agony with the death of her father.

He never sees the man that killed the trolls in his home again, but the rider, he finds out from the men circling him, is Lord Vil. He tries to take the credit as the hero of the battle, but Rodin or any of the other peasants call him a hero. They all know he had blown the horn to save himself. They curse him when the event is over. Some throw dirt and rocks at him. None respect his title. When his father, Lord Noler, arrives, they accuse him of not raising his son heavy-handedly. When the lord hears what his son has done, he strips his sword from him and promises everyone that he will be punished. The next day, he forces Lord Vil to help dig the graves of those who died so that he can learn and share in the peasants' pain. Unfortunately, this only makes him loathe them even more. His loathing makes them lose all the respect they have for him, and they never refer to his class when addressing him again. When they see that Lord Noler had tried to change his son, they respect and pity him for it.

Rodin spends the year learning how to care for the farmland that is left to him and his brother. In trying to learn on their own, they have become behind on the collection of taxes through harvests, and once again, Vil has shown up with men. He has come to take his family's home by force, without any negotiations. He believes that any peasant that is unable to provide the necessary harvests for taxes deserves to die so that someone else who can provide can work the land. In anger and desperation, Rodin grabs his father's ax and throws it at Vil to keep him from entering his house. Vil moves out of the way as the ax soars through the air, missing him, and landing into his horse, killing it instantly.

Since Vil has no sword, he cannot retaliate as the peasants from surrounding homes gather and swarm the three men he had brought with him. Again, to save himself, Lord Vil blows his horn. No men arrive to save him. Instead, his father came to discover the problems his son has caused. He sees Vil's dead horse and grunts. He looks down at his feet and announces a pardon to Rodin and his brother. He dismisses the men and asks the crowd for someone that will be able to teach him how to farm and care for the animals on the land since Rodin's father has died, his knowledge of farming is limited, and Lord Vil has given no sympathy for them.

Many step up to offer their knowledge. They all share in teaching not only Rodin but also one another what they know. This helps solidify their small peasant town. From now on, nobody goes without want, and they protect one another when needed. Together, they share songs and poems about how much they all loath Vil and that Lord Noler is, undeservingly, cursed with such a wretched son.

After telling the short of the story, Rodin sees compassion in Prince Byron's eyes. Prince Byron looks as if he can cry. Professor Dahlmür seems a little more than furious than expected. To change the subject, Rodin hops up and offers to clean Professor Dahlmür's boards since he isn't going to be doing anything anyway. Prince Byron offers to help, but Rodin refuses because he doesn't want Professor Dahlmür getting into any trouble if anyone is to see their prince cleaning boards alongside a peasant. Prince Byron laughs at this and proceeds to dunk wet rags into the bucket and slops it against one of the boards as soapy water runs all over his feet. Rodin laughs at his awkwardness and begins to help.

It doesn't take long for them to finish. Professor Dahlmür invites Rodin back again tomorrow, and Rodin agrees. He makes his way out of the school after receiving his day's wage and quickly walks into town. He watches as lords and knights go around on their horses, looking over all the vendors on the streets. Some motion their approvals to their servants or squires to purchase whatever the vendor is selling them. Rodin wonders if life would have been better if he had applied to be a servant instead of being the school janitor for what little bit he brings home. Today, it's just eight copper coins. Hardly enough to get the mead and pheasant he wants to bring home for him and Logan to celebrate his first day. Luckily, it leaves him one coin that he will store under the plank under his father's—*his*—chair.

Rodin knows Logan will be surprised to see the bounty for tonight's feast. The pheasant is the smallest, but it is only him and Logan eating it.

He is making his way to the path leading to his house from the main road when he hears Logan scream. Immediately, he drops everything and runs for the source of the sound. Logan screams again, and Rodin follows the scream to the shack beside the house nearest the trees. He hears loud clanging and what sounds like a bad imitation of a wolf sound made by someone with a high-pitched voice. He relaxes, thinking that Logan is playing with his friends.

He casually starts walking to the door until Logan screams desperately for help, and he sprints headlong in fear for Logan's life.

He pushes one of the double rolling doors to the side and finds nothing. Logan isn't making a sound anymore, which makes it difficult for Rodin to find him quickly. He crawls around the equipment, searching for him. As soon as he feels it is safe for him to break the silence, he calls for Logan, "Logan! Are you in here?"

"Rodin!" Logan calls back, "You better get up here quick!"

Rodin runs for the steps leading to the loft. He races up, skipping a few steps as he climbs, and sees Logan hunched over something squirming under him, a bloody machete lying beside him.

"What in the Darkness are you doing?" Rodin asks him breathlessly.

"I hurt it, Rodin! Please help it!" Logan sounds like he is crying.

"What is it?" He walks up to look over Logan and sees a giant spider on his lap. The spider is light brown and hairy all over. It has a black stripe that runs from its face between its two sets of smaller eyes on the sides of its head to the tip of its abdomen.

Rodin begins to slowly approach Logan while keeping his eyes on the giant spider, "Logan, why are you holding that spider on your lap?" he asks as calmly and quietly as he can.

Logan gazes up at him with tears in his eyes, "I didn't mean to hurt it, Rodin. I didn't know they were only chasing a fox into the shack. Please help it, Rodin," he pleads to him.

Rodin looks at him and figures out that Logan must have attacked it and injured it with the machete. *Wait, did he say* they? "Logan, you said *they*. Where are the rest of them?" He grabs a pitchfork and starts searching around him.

Logan looks at him, surprised, "Put that down, and I'll tell you."

Rodin shakes his head in refusal, "No, Logan. You need to put the spider down and come with me back to the house, where it's safe." He looks around him, scanning the area, watching for any movement, his muscles tightened and ready to react at any moment.

"No, Rodin." Logan continues to coddle and rock the spider as if he were doing the same for a pet, "You need to get the healing pouch and help it."

Rodin begins to feel anxious and impatient with Logan, "Logan, I'm telling you now put the spider down. Tell me where the others are so we can safely get out of here!" He kicks a garden rake. When it crashes against the wall, Rodin swings the pitchfork at it. He hears what sounds like a child giggling at him. "That wasn't funny! Now let's go!"

Logan looks at him with a response shown with sad eyes, "That wasn't me. Now help it. Please?" he is begging.

"No! Now . . ." He pauses. He quickly surveys the attic with his pitchfork. *If that wasn't him laughing, then who was it? We need to get out of here now before more come to attack us,* Rodin thinks to himself.

Rodin starts swinging at every creak he hears. He steps back into a bunch of leather straps hanging from the ceiling. It startles him. *Spiders!* He turns and swings fiercely at the straps. The pitchfork tangles into the straps and becomes caught. Rodin is trying to pull it free when the handle breaks away from the fork and sends him backward. The back of his legs hit an old wooden cartwheel, causing him to land squarely on his back, knocking the wind out of him.

He groans as he tries to catch his breath, "Damned hard oak!" he forces himself to say. He opens his eyes, and his vision is slightly blurred. He keeps blinking to clear his eyes, and through the ringing in his ears, he hears the child's voice laughing at him again.

"I said it's not funny!" he grunts at Logan.

"And I said it's not me!" Logan shoots back.

As his vision clears, he catches movement on the ceiling directly overhead. He turns his head, trying to make out the object into the light. *What the hell is that?* The light in the attic isn't strong enough to fully light the open space above, but Rodin can only make out the movements of the thing above him. Suddenly, the *thing* starts to drop toward him. *Spider!* He tries to jump up, but his position on the rickety wheel makes it difficult for him even to sit up.

Oh, no! I'm stuck!

Rodin tries desperately again but slowly stops as he watches the spider in his clearing vision hang a few feet above him, *laughing* at him. Heat rises in his face, and he becomes angry over the fact that he is being laughed at by a giant spider.

"That's not funny! Dammit!" he hollers at the spider.

It swings and drops down beside him, laughing uncontrollably like a child being tickle-tortured.

Rodin groans and is finally able to pull himself up, freezing for a moment, and tries to regain his balance. The spider jumps up and starts . . . *barking* at him. Rodin looks at it with unamused curiosity. *That spider actually thinks it's a wolf. And it's barking at me!* He stomps the ground at it. The spider yelps and jumps back frantically, barking even more.

Rodin's curiosity holds him still. He is amazed to see that the spider is protecting Logan and the other spider on his lap. *I can't believe I'm going to do this,* he thinks to himself. He motions to the spiders and Logan, "Just... wait right here. I'm going to get the healing herbs from the house."

Rodin climbs down and leaves the shack. Rodin shakes his head the entire walk back to the house. *I still can't believe I'm doing this. I'm going to save a giant spider. Blessed Rings! What am I doing?* He finds the herbs in a pouch inside a pantry beside the iron woodstove and makes his way back to the shack, still shaking his head and mumbling disbelievingly to himself. He climbs back up and watches the spider that barked at him console the other as Logan coddles and pets it.

This is crazy!

Rodin calls for Logan's attention, and the spider jumps up and runs toward him. It yips at him excitedly and guides Rodin over to them. Rodin hands the pouch over to Logan. Logan dumps a handful of the various herbs and flower petals into his hands, spits a glob of saliva into it, and starts massaging it into a wet green mush.

Rodin shakes his head at him, "You're supposed to chew it."

"I know." Logan continues to knead it and spit on it, "I can't stand the taste. It's very nasty. Smells too." He makes a sour face and continues working the pulped mass until the smell is stronger.

Rodin watches him spread the gooey mixture onto an amputated end of one of the spider's legs. The spider nips at him and shrills in pain. The healing herbs begin to steam and harden over the wound. *I bet Prince Byron could have healed him better than that stuff,* he mockingly thinks.

The spider stops shrilling and stands up awkwardly. Rodin can see that Logan has somehow severed one of the spider's first sets of legs behind its head at the knee. At first, it falls, temporarily forgetting that the leg is missing.

Logan smiles at the giant spider and comes to his feet. He reaches over and pats it on the head. The other spider barks in excitement. "I'm really very sorry about chopping off your leg, but you did try to bite me," he rubs over its abdomen, "Please forgive me."

Logan crouches down next to it, and the barking spider runs up to them and whines as it rubs against Logan's knee as if to beg him to give it the same attention "Okay!" he responds, "I'll rub on you too."

The hurt spider nips at the barking spider, trying to draw it away from them, but the barking spider nudges it's partner back and causes it to fall. The barking spider begins to laugh at the fallen spider as it kicks around, trying to right itself. Logan stands up and scolds it, "Hey! That's not nice!" The spider laughs again.

Rodin shakes his head at them in disbelief, "I . . . Uh . . ." He tries to think of what he wants to say about all this.

This day just keeps getting weirder.

"You know what? I'm just going to go back to the house and start cooking the pheasant I brought home for supper. I'll just leave it to you three to do . . ." he waves his hands at them "Whatever." Rodin shakes his head and climbs back down to go to the house, picking up the pheasant and jug of mead along the way.

I can't believe this. I don't know what to think. I hope Logan doesn't want to keep them as pets. Rodin chuckles at himself as he figures out he's been muttering and shaking his head to himself the entire time it takes him to prepare supper.

He finishes by placing the plates, forks, knives, mugs, and cloth napkins on the table set for two. It has been this way since his parents' death. Rodin prepares dinner and sets the table for Logan and himself. It was hard for him to only see two settings in the beginning. Sometimes he chokes back tears at the sight of the other two chairs that are not set for his mother and father, only faking strength in front of Logan. Rodin also remembers how his brother would cry when he saw the empty chairs never to be filled by them again.

These memories almost cause Rodin to erupt again. He pauses to regain his composure so Logan will not see him and ruin his spirits. He sits and waits for the pheasant to finish cooking and remembers the kindness the two people at the school have given him earlier in the day.

By the time supper is ready, night has fallen, and the temperature outside grows colder even though Rodin's outlook about tomorrow grows brighter and warmer. He opens the door, steps out, and calls for Logan. Logan quickly appears and runs for the house, laughing all the way.

Rodin sees the two giant spiders following close behind him, "Whoa!" he puts a hand in the air signaling the three of them to stop and points at the two uninvited guests, "No!" Rodin says, shaking his head furiously, "Sorry, but this house is for humans only! No spiders allowed!"

Logan looks at him in protest, "Awe! C'mon, Rodin! Please?" he begs, "They'll behave. I promise." Logan puts his right hand up and places his left hand over his chest, "They really are good spiders. And they're my friends."

"Really?" Rodin crosses his arms, "Then what are your friends' names?" he smiles at him. He mimics the same expressions his father used to give him when he was little as he tried to convince him the same thing about a lynx kitten. He failed his father's test, and that was a good thing since later on that night, the mother showed up to track down her kitten. She had terrorized and killed half the chickens. The only reason she didn't kill the rest was that the kitten had treed itself and the mother had to rescue it. If Rodin had kept it then, half the animals could have been killed by the mother.

"I'm waiting!" he says.

Logan points to the spider that is jumping and barking with anticipation and replies, "That's Mutt." then he points at the injured one, "And that's Biter. I call them that . . . Well, as you can see, this poor fella thinks it's a dog. And that guy tries to bite." Logan looks at Rodin for a moment and adds, "At least it didn't invect me with venom, Rodin."

"*Inject.* And that makes it all the better?" Rodin comments. He throws his arms in the air in defeat, "Fine."

Logan laughs as Mutt barks and runs over to Biter, nudging it enough to make it lose balance and fall. Mutt laughs at Biter as it clumsily stands back up. Biter jumps at Mutt, and the two start to wrestle around. Biter is not going to let Mutt push it around.

Rodin shakes his finger at them, "And none of that! Not in my house. And if either one of you does. . . whatever it is you do, in this house, I'll get that pitchfork and stick both of you."

Mutt barks in reply. Rodin puts a hand to his face and uses his thumb and middle finger to rub his temples, unsure how to handle the situation. *I guess that's a yes. I do hope this doesn't mean they want to stay. I don't think I can handle this. What do I feed them anyway? I'm sure as hell not going to start feeding them live rabbits.*

Logan runs inside, and Rodin grabs the door, motioning for Biter and Mutt to go in, "Get in. I'm not heating all of Terra-Earth," one of his mother's favorite quotes. He's always thought the comment is silly, and he's never thought he'll be repeating them.

As Rodin and Logan begin to eat, Rodin talks about his first day at the school. Logan listens and eats quietly. Rodin explains how it takes him and three others all day to sweep and clean the floors. He explains that the school is so vast that he never knew it was three stories in some regions of the school. He tells him about how students from faraway kingdoms, lordships, and towns actually live there in the area towers around it. Rodin is in charge of keeping one section of the school clean as well as one of the three towers.

He laughs as he says, "And they pay me eight coppers per day to do this! No wonder the rest of the town fights for these jobs.

People are cooking for the kids that stay there. Some people do nothing but run errands for the headmaster. There are people that clean and keep the grounds. Some people clean the horse stables and feed the horses. There are even people who do nothing but go around to classrooms and ask the lords who study there if there was anything they need for them to do. Of course, we are all glad that we don't have to wait on Vil because he keeps his house servant with him at all times. He is such a horse's ass."

As soon as he says that, Mutt begins to laugh out. He falls over from his laughter. *Do they know Vil?* Rodin shakes his head at them. *They can't possibly be laughing at Vil. They don't even understand what I'm saying. Do they?* Rodin turns back to Logan but keeps his eyes on the two spiders in the corner.

Logan watches them in the same manner as he asks Rodin, "Do you get the feeling they know what we're saying?"

At that, Mutt jumps to his feet and grunts a confirmation.

"Great," Rodin remarks, "That's all we need. Smart giant spiders." He puts his head into his hands and rubs his temples more profusely. Mutt laughs at him.

"Oh boy," Logan responds, crossing his arms on the table and laying his head down, "I'm sorry, Rodin. I didn't know they were intellectant."

Rodin looks at him, confused, "What? You mean *intelligent?*"

"Yeah. That. I didn't know those two were smart. Well, anyway, tell me more about today." He raises his head and watches him as he pushes his plate of bones away.

Rodin refills his mug and then pours a little more for Logan. *Since there are no adults, we drink what we want when we want.* Rodin lifts his cup to Logan, and Logan lifts his back to him. He drinks a few gulps and puts it down. *Wow. Better than the homemade stuff. I think tomorrow I'll get the more expensive mead.*

I'm going to take a couple of silver with me and stop after I finish my work.

Rodin ponders the thought for a few moments, and then Logan snaps at him, "Hey!" he snaps again, "Hello, Rodin! Are you listening to me?"

Rodin's thoughts leave him, "I'm sorry. Oh, you wanted to know about my day? Well, I met a really nice professor named Dahlmür. He has a bad stuttering problem. He helped me out when I got busted for listening to his lesson on the stories of the Archon."

Logan sits upright, smiling with interest. The Archon stories have always interested him, "Oh! Did you learn more stories?"

"No. It was about how the Archon came to be and how the Circle of Light and the Circle of Darkness doesn't get along."

"Awe, man!" Logan expresses his disappointment.

"It's okay, though. I liked the way he told it. He really knows how to tell stories. Anyway, I got busted, and somehow, I smacked my nose into the damned hard oak door. I don't like those damned hard oak doors. And then Dahlmür sent me to the back of the room. Then Vil was there as a student, and he started calling me names and threatening me."

"What did you do?"

"I insulted him. And that made him so much madder that he threatened to kill me. He was red and shaking all over. You'd have laughed if you saw him. And then this boy stood up and started yelling at Vil. Vil started threatening the boy, and he asked the boy what his name was so that he can tell someone that he was threatening a lord. And you know what the boy said?" he asks excitedly.

"What?" Logan gets excited in anticipation.

"*I am Prince Byron!*"

"No way!"

"Yes, way! And everyone dropped down and bowed, except Vil."

"Oh, wow! How stupid!"

"Yeah, I know. And Dahlmür walked up and forced Vil to bow to Byron. Byron threatened to put Vil in the town stockade the next time he sees him treating anyone like that again."

"That is so great! I can't believe that. I wish I could meet Prince Byron. I bet he would be fun to hang out with."

Mutt starts barking excitedly at Logan and Rodin. They look at the spider curiously. Mutt starts chirping and squealing at them. Biter squeals at Mutt. Mutt turns its attention to Biter. They communicate with each other in a series of grunts, chirps, and squeals. Rodin and Logan quietly watch them with enchantment.

Logan whispers, "This all so faxinationing, but what do you think they're arguing about?"

"I have no clue. I'm just as *fascinated*," Rodin corrects him, "with the way they talk to each other. I guess by the way Mutt is acting, they want to tell us something, but they're trying to figure out how."

"I guess we'll never know."

"Guess not."

Rodin stands, dumps the remainder of his pheasant into the garbage bucket beside the door, and places the dish into the wash bucket. He grabs his mug and downs the mead. He grabs the jug and pours the remainder between the two of them, "If you can't handle the mead, then see if they will possibly want it. If not, dump it."

"I'm a little sloshed." Logan lays his head down onto his arms again, "I think my stomach is a little upset."

"Eat the rest of the bread to soak it up then drink some water. I'm going to sit outside for a bit before I go to bed. I want to get an early start on the cows before I have to go."

Logan waves a hand up at him, keeping his head down, "That's fine. Go. I'm going just lie here a few minutes to make sure I don't die. If I don't, then I'll clean up."

Rodin smiles and grabs his father's pipe and some tobacco. He opens the door then stops and motions at the two spiders, "Time to go . . . wherever."

Mutt and Biter jump up and walk over to Logan. Mutt jumps onto the table and grabs Logan's mead and carefully carries it out with Biter staying close behind, "Please bring that back when you guys are done with it. I can't believe I'm letting you guys take my mug. I can't believe I'm even talking to giant spiders at all. This has been one mixed-up day."

Mutt giggles back at him. Biter stops at Rodin's feet and lays his half-leg onto his shin, "I'm sorry about your leg. I'm glad to see you will be all right." *What am I saying? Damned mead!* He shakes his head and sits on the chair next to the door as he watches the two giant spiders leave through the woods that run alongside the house.

I can't believe how this day went. I meet a professor. I meet a prince. I piss off Vil. And I make friends with giant spiders. He chuckles at his thoughts and looks at the stars above, "Circle of Light, I pray you are sharing good signs and knowledge for us. Otherwise, this will end up being one bizarre day."

With that, Logan busts out of the door, throwing up beside the house. He groans, "No more mead!" and throws up some more.

Rodin snuffs out the pipe, smiles, and pats Logan on the back, "Goodnight, little brother." He enters the house, leaving his brother to his hangover.

The day starts the way it usually does, only a little earlier. Rodin quickly cares for the three cows and milks them as they feed. He stops now and then to pour the milk into a larger bucket. Rodin also stops to drink some for himself. He grabs his sack of grain and tosses handfuls in front of the large chicken coop. Rodin peers in as about thirty of them scurry around. He notes that he has to tell Logan to gather the eggs inside. He pulls the ox by its yoke and leads it to the pile of hay he picked for it. He picks up a large bale of hay onto a cart and hooks it to the yolk so Logan can run the feed to the steers. Rodin makes a note to himself to stop by the butcher after work to offer one of the steers out and see how much he can get for it.

After everything is done, he goes to the house. He grabs some cheese and what little bread Logan hasn't eaten and calls it breakfast. Logan comes down, and he reminds him to make butter and cream and gather the eggs. He also tells him to feed the steers another bale of hay so they will be good and fat by the time the butcher comes to negotiate a price. Logan, obviously still hungover, grunts his acknowledgment and walks out the door. Rodin walks to the chair over the hideaway floorboard and proceeds to gather some coins for the day. After replacing the chair, he heads off for the school.

Along the way through town, Rodin watches the hustle of the street vendors pulling their vending carts out from their small shops. The smell of fresh bread, honey cakes, roasted meats mixed in with roasted nuts, charred wood, the iron worker's coal fires, and the brewer's steam all bring him to life. In the center of the square is the stockade fountain. The stockade is in the center of a waterfall fountain, where the person in it can be easily seen. Most of the time though, it's a peasant.

Today it's empty, so the fountain isn't running. Rodin smiles as he pictures Vil locked up in it. Rodin suddenly realizes someone is standing beside him, "Picturing your future, peasant?" *Great! It's Vil!* "By the end of the day, you will be there."

"Yup, on the other side over there, where the manure cart goes through, grabbing a handful to throw into your wretched face, Vil." At that, he turns on his heels and runs for the schoolyard, knowing it will take Vil a minute to process that and another minute for him to find his horse to chase him down.

II

"League of Rogue. League of Gia. League of Sas. League of Humans. These are the four main leagues that make up the Order of Terrans. We all dwell on what is called the Plane of Terra-Earth.

"There are different orders on the Plane of Terra-Earth. The Order of Animals. The Order of Terrans. The Order of Creatures. Do not confuse the Order of Creatures with the Order of Demons. The Order of Creatures was created by the Circle of Light. They are as intelligent as we are. They have their own leagues and kingdoms as we do. They share knowledge as we do. All other orders were created by the Rings except those created in the Plane of Hell by the Circle of Darkness.

"The Order of Aquatic Animals and the Order of Aquatic Creatures reside in the Aquatic Plane. Beware, the Order of Demons also has leagues that possess the power to live there as well. The Order of Birds and the Order of Winged Creatures belong to the Aerial Plane. Demons live here as well.

"The Plane of Hell. It is where all leagues of the Order of Demons are created. The Circle of Darkness resides in this plane as ordered by the Rings.

"All four of these planes make up the Earthen Realm. The stars. The moon. The sun. They are outside the Earthen Realm. That place is called the Spatial Realm. It is where the Circle of Light dwells to watch over us all. The Rings reside beyond the Spatial Realm called the Spirit Realm. The Rings created it all. They care for it all.

"This knowledge is ours, given to us by the Circle of Light to cherish," says Professor Dahlmür.

"So says the Circle of Light!" the class responds.

A voice shouts, *"Peasant!"*

Again?

Rodin's nose, once again, smacks into the door. Stars appear and explode before his eyes as he grabs the door for balance. His feet clumsily kick the bucket of soapy water, spilling its contents everywhere. He loses traction and lands flat on the floor, banging the back of his head against the solid door. Rodin grunts in pain, "Damned hard oak! Damned stone floor!"

He hears the class moan, reacting to his pain. A set of hands grabs him by the arm, and instead of helping him to his feet, they jerk him to his feet. He tries to see who it is, but balls of multicolored lights dance before him. His ears ring too much to distinguish the muffled voices yelling at him. He slips again and falls onto his back, knocking the wind out of him, "Oh, Light, please. Stop trying to pull on me. The floor is too slick."

After a few moments, he finally hears the voice of Professor Wide and Professor Dahlmür arguing above him. Another set of hands jerks him up once again. His vision starts to clear, and he sees Vil pulling him up. Rodin kicks out his legs as if he were slipping, and his foot lands into Vil's shin, knocking his leg out from underneath him. Vil hits the ground chin first, and Rodin lands on top of him, "Oh, man. I'm so sorry. My head is spinning so bad I can't see straight." He takes the opportunity to try to get up as Vil groans and rolls onto his back.

Faking dizziness, Rodin drops on him again with a knee. From the sudden groans and wincing from the male students in the classroom as well as Vil's sudden high-pitched, breathless squealing, Rodin knows his knee has found its mark. Rodin privately smiles to himself. He gets to his feet. As tall as Rodin is, he lumbers over Vil. He bends down to him and apologizes once again. He offers no help to Vil. Instead, Rodin stumbles over him, kicking him in the chest as he walks over him, "Ooh! I'm so sorry, Vil." Rodin begins to taunt him, "Does it feel good to get your ass kicked for no damn reason? A Lord like you deserves one every once in a while! Maybe then you'll learn to respect people and not classes, you—"

Rodin rears a foot back, but as he does so, Dahlmür bumps into him and knocks him into the classroom, "I'm sorry . . . Eh. . . Eh. . . Eh, Master Rodin. I know Master Vil has. . . Eh. . . Eh. . . Eh caused you great pain without any provocation, but I cannot allow you to. . . Eh. . . Eh. . . Eh. . . Retaliate," he leads Rodin to an empty seat and offers a handkerchief for his nose. A few students laugh and talk out, and Dahlmür taps his staff to the floor. *Snap! Snap! Snap!* He nods at Prince Byron, motioning him to attend to Rodin, "You sit here, Master . . . Eh. . . Eh. . . Eh. . . Rodin. I'll tend to this outrage," and he taps Rodin assuredly on the head with the quartz at the top of his staff.

Rodin calms down. A peaceful swoon flows over him. A wide smile crosses his face as he feels light as a feather. *I feel fine. My nose hurts, and it's bleeding, but I feel just fine. Oh, look, here's Byron. He's going to make my nose feel so much better. He's such a nice prince.* He gives Prince Byron a friendly nod. Byron looks at Rodin as if he had grown a third eye. The class watches him as they point and laugh. Snap snap snap!

Professor Dahlmür argues with Professor Wide who had shown up out of the blue as he shakes Lord Vil, but Rodin can't make out a word they're saying, "Hi, Prince Byron. I like you. You would make such a great friend. Too bad, you're a prince."

Prince Byron looks at him, puzzled, "What's wrong with me being a prince?"

Rodin smiles at him some more, "Oh, you know," he clumsily puts a finger to Byron's chest, "You're a prince"—then he points at himself— "and I'm what Vil calls a lowly 'peasant.'" Rodin looks at him and pouts, "Don't you just hate mean ol' Vil?" He turns to Vil and smiles at him, "You're so mean, Vil. You're ugly, *and* you're mean."

The classroom erupts into laughter. Vil's face turns bright red. He rushes at Rodin before Dahlmür realizes he's gone and knocks Prince Byron to the floor violently. He grabs Rodin and begins beating him in the face.

The biggest boy in the class, obviously a knight's squire, grabs Lord Vil and tosses him across the room, shouting at him, "You will *never* lay your hands on the prince again!" The boy pulls a long dagger from his belt, "Time to pay the price!"

Prince Byron and Professor Dahlmür stop him as Professor Wide tends to Lord Vil, "No! Please stop!" Professor Wide begs, "Please, Master Slindee! Stop! That *peasant* started this mess! Kill him!"

Rodin rises back to his seat, bleeding profusely, with a huge smile, "Who, me? I was just here doing Dahlmür a favor!" he looks at Professor Dahlmür, "Sir."

"Yes," Master Slindee confirms, "I was there when he asked Master Rodin to stand by his door because he had a chore for him. He wanted help with cleaning the boards and his floor. Master Rodin agreed happily. There was no reason for Lord Vil to attack him as he did. Nor you, for that matter. If anything, you should be punished for allowing Lord Vil to act this way. I'm tired of seeing you allowing him to treat all the commons who work here poorly and lowly!"

Master Slindee sheathes his knife and gathers his belongings, "I'm leaving this school. My father will hear of this. Sir Galla is the best knight around, and I wanted so much to be taught by him! Sadly, I can't. My father will pull his funds in the morning after I return."

Professor Dahlmür grabs him by the shoulder, "Now, now, Master Slindee, please sit," he taps Master Slindee on the forehead with the quartz of his staff.

Rodin points and giggles at the squire while his face is covered with blood and welts, "Uh-oh, Master Slindee, you're going to feel good now."

Just then, Master Slindee looks at him with the same goofy grin, "I feel good, Master Rodin. I'm sorry he hit you." He looks up at Prince Byron, "I'm sorry I didn't stop him from hurting you in time."

"Enough!" Vil stands, hissing at Professor Wide as he shoves him to the side, "I don't care who gets in my way! I will kill that damn peasant!" He finds another student's dagger, draws it out, and lunges for Rodin.

Prince Byron steps between them, and Professor Dahlmür slams his staff to the floor. Hard. The sound of his voice echoes throughout the room and through the hall as if it was amplified, "I will not tolerate this madness any longer!" he wails. Smoke billows from around the staff and surrounds Lord Vil, "You have committed a most heinous act here today, Lord Vil. You have interrupted my class. You have attacked the helpless school staff. You assaulted a prince and a headmaster! Your actions will not go unpunished. You will spend the next two days in the town stockade!"

Rodin smiles, "Wow, he's loud," he whispers at Master Slindee and Prince Byron. *Boy, I sure do wish he would break this spell. I want to be angry. I want to beat Vil. I want to— Oh, that quartz is really shiny!*

"I *am* Lord Vil! I will not be ordered around by a common professor! You will not treat me like I'm that"— he points at Rodin, who's calmly being healed by Prince Byron— "peasant! You *will* remember your place!"

Byron quietly signals to the other students that at that very moment, it is their cue to leave. *Quickly.* He pulls Rodin by his chair to the farthest corner away from Professor Dahlmür and calls for Master Slindee to join them. He says to them with wide eyes, "Not good."

Dahlmür's face becomes red as sapphire. He raises his staff high above his head. With both hands, he slams the floor with it. *Boom!* Thunder crashes as swirling storm clouds erupt from the now-black crystal at the top.

Students and staff begin mumbling as they gather in front of the door. Some scream in terror and run away at the site. Others are too terrified to move or take their eyes off the events unfolding in the room.

Dahlmür's voice explodes, "You will never talk to me in that manner! You will bow in respect to me! I am not just a mere professor who just traveled into this town! I am King Saul's wizard! King Vaniir and Prince Byron bow before me! I answer to *nobody*! You will address me as Grand Wizard Dahlmür! And for your insolence, I banish you! Now off to the stockade with you!"

A human-sized tornado forms, and as Vil turns to run, it surrounds him. He screams in horror as he violently spins around. Instantly, he vanishes with the tornado.

Dahlmür turns to Professor Wide. His face fumes with anger. He touches the now-clear, quartz-again crystal to his forehead. A sense of serenity passes over his face.

Master Slindee looks at Prince Byron and Rodin as they whisper in unison, "Uh-oh."

"Due to your inabilities to take control of this academy, you will not be headmaster anymore," Professor Dahlmür calmly states with a sigh.

Professor Wide looks at him, offended, "You have no authority here."

"I do, Professor Wide, and you too are hereby banished from this school. You can either walk away or be shown out in the same manner as Lord Vil."

With that, Professor Wide slowly gets up, keeping an eye on Professor Dahlmür, gathers himself, and starts for the door. He turns to Dahlmür and sneers, "I will return with Lord Noler. As will Lord Vil. You will be relieved as a professor at this school. That *peasant* will be punished." He turns to Master Slindee, "Your resignation will be accepted. You will not be knighted under Sir

Galla's tutelage." He looks over at Prince Byron, who finishes healing Rodin, "I'm sorry, Your Highness, but your mother will hear about your actions."

Dahlmür calmly replies, "No, they won't."

A massive bear of a man walks into the room. He lumbers over toward Professor Wide. To Rodin, his arms are as big as logs. His chest is more significant than any barrel that he's ever seen. His head is bald, and the hair on his chin reaches the top of his gut. Immediately, Master Slindee kneels before him, and the man places a hand on his shoulders, "Stand, Slender. I've been told of your actions here today, and I'm here to tell you that I am most displeased." Prince Byron stands, and the man kneels before him, "Forgive me, my prince. I heard you were present also. I've come to enforce a proclamation that has been made today."

Dahlmür walks calmly toward him, "And what proclamation would that be, Sir Galla?"

Sir Galla remains bowing even before Professor Dahlmür, "Grand Wizard, it is the proclamation that you have made here today. I'm here to offer my services as a knight formerly Head Knight of King Saul's court. I will follow your command if you wish."

Rodin, still wearing a goofy grin, says to Sir Galla, "Forgive me, Sir," he bows low at him, "I recognize you. You are the man that entered my home and attempted to save my mother and father from the trolls. You protected us from Lord Vil's wrath against us. *You* of all people under the Light receive my deepest gratitude. I never had the chance to thank you for what you tried to do that night for my brother and me. Please accept my gratitude," Rodin chokes back tears. Some escape him and fall to the floor below.

"Young Master, no thanks is ever needed. My duties since I retired are to the teaching of squires and protecting the Lordship of Langdoline. That includes the Class of Commons."

"That's enough!" Professor Wide looks at them in disgust. He waves at the people left gawking at the door, "Shoo!" and they scatter away. "I'm done here. I'll be returning tomorrow to take care of the business we spoke about."

Everyone rises and looks at Professor Wide. Sir Galla starts toward the professor, but Professor Dahlmür stops him, "No need, my friend. What he doesn't realize is that when I banish someone, they really are banished." Professor Dahlmür walks toward Professor Wide, using his staff as a walking cane, "You see,

Professor—or rather, just Master Wide, because that title no longer belongs to you— you see, neither you nor Lord Vil will be able to step foot onto the grounds of this school after today. By nightfall, if you have not left, you will simply be thrown off. And when I say *thrown*, I mean that in a literal sense. The spell will lift you from your dirty feet—"

Master Wide scoffs at him, "Dirty feet?"

"and you will be thrown out the nearest window, and you will not land until you are clear of the grounds. *Hard.*"

"I do not believe you."

Professor Dahlmür smiles at him, "You may test this at any time if you would like, but you will be hurting after your first attempt. To be honest, I don't care what you do."

Prince Byron walks toward Master Wide, "By my command, as the prince of this land . . ."

Master Slindee smiles and looks at Rodin, "He's a poet!"

Rodin smiles back and nods, "And he didn't know it."

The comments catch Prince Byron off guard, and he lets out a quick snicker, "I hereby command you to leave and never return." He turns to Sir Galla, "Please, Sir, see this man off the grounds. Straight off. There is nothing in his office that's of any importance to him. So, please do not delay."

Sir Galla bows his head, "Yes, Sire." He turns to Master Slindee, "Slender, please accompany me. You and I will talk about your coronation after."

Master Slindee stands up, and Professor Dahlmür taps him with the cane. *Hey! Why can't I get this spell taken away from me? Oh, shiny!* Master Slindee stops and turns to Prince Byron, "Sire, I ask that if I do decide to stay, will you two please be at my coronation?" he looks away, ashamed for asking.

"It would be a great honor to me."

"I will," Rodin says loudly, "as long as you will be my friend and not treat me as an underclass."

"Master Rodin, I will be proud to be your friend. You deserve my friendship. My teacher has always taught me that"— he points at Sir Galla— "the Class of Commons deserves more respect than what the kings and lords give them." With that being said, the two grab each other by their right forearm and embrace.

Prince Byron looks at them, "I would very much like to be in your friendship. I may be a Prince in Class, but as my father reminds me, I am *still* human."

Rodin gives him a wide, still-goofy grin, "If I weren't under this spell, I would be crying," tears flow down his cheeks. The three newfound friends grab one another's forearms and embrace one another in a circle.

"And the gift will be given to one deemed most worthy within his circle," Professor Dahlmür mumbles quietly.

Sir Galla's eyes widen, "Oh my!" he says as if he has just realized what Professor Dahlmür is saying.

"Please, Dahlmür, *sir*, take this stupid curse away from me," Rodin pleads to him.

Master Slindee and Sir Galla escort Master Wide out and through the halls. Sir Galla's voice echoes all around, "No, Master Wide, there is nothing for you that way. The door is this way. Do not make me carry you like a sack of potatoes. Prince Byron and Grand Wizard Dahlmür have made their decree very clear. Now let's go."

Suddenly, Master Wide screams, "Put me down! No! Let go of me! Her Majesty will hear of this! Put me down now!"

Sir Galla laughs, "Slender, he kicks like a girl! And he screams like one too!" Sir Galla's hearty laughter echoes everywhere.

Dahlmür looks at his feet, and sorrow fills his face, "I am so sorry about all this. My prince, Master Rodin, please forgive me. Prince Byron, I did not mean to overstep my authority here in your kingdom, but as Grand Wizard, I have a duty that I am bound by oath to uphold. And yes, Master Rodin, I release you," he taps Rodin on his head.

Instantly, Rodin feels normal. He looks at Professor Dahlmür, "No. I started it. I'm sorry. I lost my temper with Vil. I really shouldn't have done that. Thank you for stopping me. Dahlmür, Sir, are you really *the* Grand Wizard?"

"Yes, I am," he smiles at Rodin and winks at Prince Byron.

They look at him in amazement. Prince Byron speaks, "Why are you here, Master?"

He gathers them together and leads them out, "That is business between me, your father, and some select others. The matter, for now, is too trivial for a young prince and young commons such as yourselves. Go out and enjoy the rest of the day. Don't trouble yourselves over the events of today any longer. I believe you can still catch up with your friend, Master Slindee, along the way."

Rodin and Prince Byron look at each other as if they were plotting some mischief. They laugh and run off after Sir Galla and

Master Slindee. Rodin says along the way in laughter, "We need to ask him what the whole '*Slender*' thing is about."

"Oh yeah," Byron remembers. They race ahead. With Rodin's height and long legs, he easily outruns Prince Byron. They run out of the building and catch up to Sir Galla. He has Master Wide hanging over his shoulder. Master Wide is not amused or thrilled with his current situation. He rests his head in one hand that he props into Sir Galla's back.

He sees the pair and hisses at them, "You wait until your mother finds out, boy!"

Sir Galla stops and turns, swinging Master Wide like a ragdoll on his shoulders, to see Prince Byron and Rodin behind him and smiles at them. His smile is wide and full of teeth. In the sunlight, Rodin can make out the age lines in Sir Galla's tanned face. His cheekbones seem to meet his eyes when he smiles. His broad nose protrudes from his mustache. His whiskers are full of sand color and gray, peppered with darker shades of brown. He has a white streak in his sideburns from his hair to his jawline. His build doesn't reflect his age. He is all muscle in his chest and shoulders. His tunic can barely contain his upper body.

With all those muscles, Rodin wonders how the man has such a huge belly. Rodin asks Prince Byron if he can be a gia instead of human as tall as he stands. His pants alone will be a perfect tent, but Rodin isn't willing to camp out under the seat of the oversized man's pants. From behind, his shoulders stretch as long as Prince Byron is tall. The hand holding Master Wide onto his shoulder is enormous. It's big enough to hold Master Wide by his entire head.

Rodin touches Master Slindee's shoulder, signaling him to slow down so they can talk, "We were wondering. Is Sir Galla a gia?"

Prince Byron nods in agreement, "He's big."

As he continues ahead, Sir Galla laughs heartily, "Did you know that gias can hear an elk's heartbeat before they can see it?"

Startled, Rodin and Prince Byron stop in their tracks. They stare at Sir Galla for a few moments, until Master Slindee smiles at them and pats them on their shoulders, "Part gia, actually. He's very short compared to his father."

The two shake their heads in agreement and start to continue on until they both freeze in wide-eyed realization, *"His father?"*

Prince Byron grabs himself, sympathizing with his mother's apparent pain.

Rodin comments, "Oh, that poor woman!"

Sir Galla chuckles a comment, "My mother says that she handles my father nicely."

Their jaws drop to their chests, and they stare at Sir Galla. Master Slindee looks at them in the eyes, "Now think about his birth," and he runs to catch up with him. Rodin and Prince Byron drop as they imagine the pain. Rodin winces. Prince Byron whimpers.

From his position, Master Wide looks at Sir Galla's back in surprise, "My Rings, man! A human birthed you?" Sir Galla laughs, and they reach the wall of the school.

As Rodin and Prince Byron run to catch up, Sir Galla lobs Master Wide across the threshold of the school grounds. He wails as he flies through the air, landing yards away. Sir Galla turns and smiles at them, "I don't trust him for about as far as I can throw him," he breaks out in a jolly laugh.

The three boys laugh in return astonished at the distance he is tossed. Prince Byron turns to the knight, "Sir, if you don't mind, I'd like to invite Master Slindee with us to go into town."

Rodin looks at him, startled, "Us? You're going with me into a peasant town?"

Sir Galla smiles, "Fantastic idea. I think you should go, Slender. Be sure to see Coleman and ask about my boots, please."

"Yes, sir," Master Slindee replies. He looks at the two of them, "Shall we go?" They agree, and the three of them wave at Sir Galla and head off.

Rodin eyes Master Wide, who walks dutifully back toward the school ground's entrance after dusting himself off while mumbling something about someone being "rude" and how he will show "them." Frantically, Rodin signals them to stop and watch, waiting in anticipation for Professor Dahlmür's spell to react.

"Do you think the spell is immediate?" Rodin snickers.

Prince Byron grins from ear to ear, "Oh, I hope so!"

Master Slindee stands against a tree, "I've got to see this."

On a mission, Master Wide steps beyond the threshold. Disappointment appears on three boys faces. When he is a few yards in, the ground shakes and suddenly thrusts upward and out in a long, slender form, catapulting a shrieking Master Wide over ten yards into the air and over twenty yards back. He lands hard into a tree with an, "*Oaf!*"

The three of them acknowledge his pain and howl in laughter. Rodin laughs so hard he falls to his knees. Prince Byron falls flat to the ground, holding his stomach. Master Slindee laughs so hard he turns, undoes his pants quickly, and relieves his bladder while holding tightly to the tree with one hand. Rodin sees Slindee and points him out to Prince Byron. They laugh so hard they find it hard to catch their breaths. Rodin drools uncontrollably.

Prince Byron begs them to stop making him laugh, "My stomach hurts."

When they finally calm down, Master Wide gets up, wobbles, takes a few steps, and falls facefirst to the ground. The laughter begins again just as hard.

III

They enter the town and begin looking around. Master Slindee looks at everything in amazement, "Wow! There are more shops here than in Maitland! That's where I'm from."

Rodin looks at him, astonished, "Are you serious?"

Prince Byron smiles, "Rodin doesn't know that this is a major hub town between the four surrounding kingdoms," he looks at Rodin and explains, "This town is where major trades happen. That's why we are the Trade Kingdom. My father oversees all trades between all kingdoms that wish to make major exchanges and need a mediator to negotiate the terms. Even King Saul comes to negotiate trades. He'll leave Anglon Island, bringing with him as many ships as it takes to carry whatever he's selling and paying with."

"But why does he need a mediator when he's the League King?" Rodin asks. "He can command any price he wants to pay or make them pay."

Byron plainly states, "Well, when you want to rule a kingdom fairly and want to receive the same courtesy in return, you go through my dad. This way, you don't look like an ass, and any kingdom he trades with will be a little friendlier when he needs an ally."

"Well, that makes sense." Rodin freezes the moment he steps into the square. He sees that the fountain is running at full stream. The splashes and the running of the water echoes around the shops, intensifying the noise. There in the center, inside the stockade, yelling, screaming, and cursing at everyone that walks by, is Vil. His face contorts from his anger. Sweat pours around his face, or is it from the moisture coming off the fountain? His hair hangs damp and limp over his face, covering his brow. He looks around at all the people ignoring him and screams furiously for someone to set him free. The roar of the water drowns out most of his screaming. He's been yelling for so long his voice starts to crack.

Master Slindee sees him and laughs, "Let's go see how he's doing!"

Prince Byron grabs his arm as Master Slindee starts to make a run over to the fountain, "No. We do not speak to or acknowledge anyone in the stockade. The person in that particular stockade is in there for the most severe punishment. They're to see how we will all move on without them because of their actions. We do not have corporal punishment. Most will spend some of their lifelong sentences in there from time to time as proof to them that they will never be a part of this world again. The roar of the water echoing around the square is to drown out their cries and pleas to the people around them so that nobody will have to feel the need to console them for what they've done. We don't mock them, because they are receiving enough punishment as it is from all this. As we move around the square, you must never look at him. You look past him if you have to look in that direction."

"It's been like that for a long time," Rodin adds, "That stockade's been there since before Prince Byron's father was born."

"Okay." Master Slindee turns his gaze away from Vil. He looks at the two of them and smiles, "Look, guys, if we're going to be friends, call me 'Slender.' I hate titles unless it's necessary. Between the three of us, it's not."

"Okay, *Slender*," Rodin mocks the name, "Only Dahlmür calls me 'Master.' You guys don't do that. I've never been a 'Master' to anyone."

"And you two may call me, 'You're Majesty.'" Prince Byron smiles and puffs out his chest as he forces himself to stand taller than the two of them, failing miserably, "You're too tall, Slender, and, Rodin, you're too damn tall."

Rodin steps up to him, looks down at the top of his head, and puts a finger in his hair, "Did you know you have a bald spot right there, *Byron*?"

"What?"

Slender looks over, "Oh yeah, you do, *Byron*."

They walk away, chuckling, leaving Byron rubbing the top of his head, "No, I don't! Really? Where? Hey! Where are you guys going? Get back here and show me where!" he chases after them, "And it's '*Your Majesty!*'" As he says it, someone bows and greets him. He bows back in return, welcomes them, and runs off to catch up with Rodin and Slender.

I see you! I hate you! I will kill you! All three of you! Why can I not hear you? Can you hear me? I'm calling out to you! Peasant! Prince! Squire! Hear me! I'm calling for you to hear me promise to kill you!

Look at you. The three of you stand there, talking. Yes, tell the tall, fat one who looks my way. I'm right here, fatso! Come, step right up so I can stab you straight into your heart. I know you want to.

Oh, look, the peasant is mocking you, Poor Prince. See how he towers over you and laughs at you? I do. I see it very well. Doesn't he deserve to die for his mocking of a prince? Indeed, he does. He should never tower over you like that. He should crawl on his knees when he is around you. He's a peasant! And aren't peasants so lowly? They're dirty! They stink! They wallow in the same dirt and filth as the animals they keep! They don't deserve to be called humans! I will kill him because of his filth and rid Terra-Earth of all his kind! Mock me, will you? Mock your prince who rules over you, will you? You're nothing! I will kill you!

Now, the squire mocks too? Look! He laughs. He stands over you and laughs. Do you allow this? You're no prince! I will kill the squire and kill you too! I'll kill the squire just to hear a fat pig squeal. I will kill you just to listen to a prince beg for his life as he falls to his knees before me! And why not? You're no prince! He's no squire! He's not human!

Run! Run because I'm coming to kill you! Run!

Byron catches up to Rodin and Slender at a vendor's cart, breathless, "Not funny." They chuckle in response.

"Hey, I know this cart!" Rodin points out.

An older man walks up to the cart with a huge smile, to their delight, "Your Majesty! Good to see you!" he comes around to Byron and gives him a huge hug then turns to acknowledge the other two boys, "Master Slindee! Or is it 'Sir' yet? No, that would be soon. I know. Master Rodin! I was just by your farm this morning! Please allow me to give you the offer I made with that marvelous young brother of yours. He turned me down. Told me I was offering him too much money for all those eggs and tried to throw in one of your cows for it. I offered him more money to take the cow, but he said he wouldn't dare steal from a mindless man such as me!" he laughs and hugs on Rodin, "You've done well by your mother and father with him, Master Rodin. Very proud of you."

Rodin beams at him, "Thank you, Mast— I mean, Coleman."

"Always a pleasure, Master Rodin. Your Majesty, you've got an odd circle of friends about you. A squire. A peasant. Your mother, the Queen, will be most displeased with you," Byron raises a finger to interject, but Coleman continues with a wave, "but I know you're just like King Vaniir. '*Everyone is looked upon equally in the eyes of Light,*' so says the Circle of Light. Enough of that. Let me take care of you, and then I will get to them."

Byron says to him, "My friends and I came to see you since we haven't seen or heard from you in so long. We worry about you."

Coleman smiles and looks over the three of them, "Friends?" His smile softens as a tear glistens in one of his soft brown eyes. He quietly mutters, *"And the gift shall go to the one deemed most worthy within his circle."*

Slender begins to ask, "Why does everyone say that?"

But before he can finish his sentence, Coleman speaks up, "Now, Master Rodin, my offer is five gold, twenty-five silver, ten coppers, and these two bear-fur coats, which I made sure to size for both of you ahead of time, for the whole barrel of eggs, broken and all, two pigs, traps, the cow, and five chickens. Please take it, Master. I will not pay less. What do you say?"

Slender's jaw drops at the outrageous offer he's given Rodin. Byron tells him that he will be a fool to let an offer be turned down. Rodin looks at him and says shamefully, "Would you please take back three silver for two pairs of boots?"

"Done! Thank you so, very much!" Coleman laughs and hugs him, "Now, Master Slindee, please tell Sir Galla that I have the boots he wants. Ready and waiting. Oh, and I do have something for you that your father has bought from me and wants me to give to you." Coleman circles onto his carriage, parked behind him, and climb in. He rattles around the inside, and the carriage shakes from side to side, "Where did they go? Oh! Here they are!" He emerges with a shield wrapped in a blanket and a sheathed sword wrapped in a cloth, "Your father said that this is a gift to you in congratulations of your coronation as a knight! He is very proud of you. He wants to see you with it during the ceremony that he and your mother will be sure to make."

Slender unwraps the sheath and pulls out a long double-edged, two-handed sword. The brilliance of its blade blinds everyone. Slender looks at it in awe as he swings it around to get a feel for it. In Slender's big hands, it is practically a single-handed sword. His swings are controlled and fluid. There's virtually no weight in the blade to slow him. It is balanced perfectly. There is a hilt in the form of fire flowing toward the blade. It looks magnificent in his hands. At the bottom of the handle is a bright blue crystal. He smiles, "Wow. I can't believe how comfortable it is in my hand. It's almost as if the sword is doing the movements, and my hand follows. It's beautiful. What's its name?"

Coleman smiles back at him in satisfaction, "I'm glad you know that a sword of this caliber has a name. It shows that you are a truly remarkable swordsman. Its name is Chill. By your command, it will blow a wind so cold that it will freeze anyone in its path. During the heat of battle, the blade will start to freeze anything it comes in contact with until it is frozen to the point that it breaks like ice. Ordinary swords, shields, armor, and even flesh are no match for it." He turns speaks at the sword, "Chill, meet Master Slindee. If you will have him, he will be your partner."

The blue crystal flashes and the metallic flame on the hilt fold down, engulfing his hand. Ice forms around his hand, freezing it to the handle.

Coleman smiles and hugs a confused Slender, "She has accepted you!"

Byron looks at Slender, confused, "Isn't it cold?"

Rodin touches it and pulls away, confirming how cold it is.

Slender looks at him, "No. It's actually a warm sword to me. I love it! Chill is a brilliant name for it." He sheathes the sword back into its sheath, and the ice retreats. The flame returns to its original position.

Rodin reaches for it, "May I—"

Coleman grabs his hand before he can touch it, "No, don't!" he cries, "As long as Master Slindee and Chill are bonded, that sword cannot be touched by anyone. It is very sensitive to its owner." He signals Slender's attention to the shield, "Please, Master Slender, I want you to meet Mortar." Then he speaks to the shield, "Mortar, will you have Master Slindee and Chill?"

Slender pulls out a shield made of thick steel brushed to a finish instead of a polished shine. In the center of the shield is a large red crystal held in place by thick cords of steel that wrap from top to bottom crisscrossing their way throughout the frame. The shield is large but again feels light in his hands. He puts his arm through the strap and grabs a steel handle. He begins to swing the shield around.

Before he can perform a ground block, Coleman warns him off, "No, don't!"

"What?" he asks.

"Mortar has unique gifts as well. If you perform a ground block, it will raise a wall of rock, or whatever surface you're on, that soars up to four yards high and four yards in both directions, protecting everything behind it. If you pound it on the ground or what have you in a fashion that you were directing a blow, it will send a tremor through the ground until it reaches your enemy and catapults him or them into the air and away. Mortar cannot be dented or scratched by ordinary weapons. It can block even the biggest boulders catapulted at you."

The three of them laugh, looking at one another, remembering what they have recently seen with Master Wide. Slender refocuses on Coleman, "Yes, sir."

"What do you say, Mortar?"

Mortar starts to vibrate in his hand and rumble. The handle that he is holding wraps around his wrist to hold itself in place and the strap tightens to his arm. Slender pounds the back of the shield as if to test its strength, and the shield rumbles again, "I think Mortar and I will get along very well. It's a great shield and very powerful. Handsome too."

Byron looks at it closely, "I'm afraid to touch it."

Coleman says, "Good. Don't. While he's wearing it in battle, it will pound itself into any enemy that gets too close to him."

Rodin smiles in amazement, "Wow. I change my mind. I want magic boots."

"My friend"—he places an arm around Rodin and pulls him in close—"you are magical indeed. You've made friends with the two greatest people I've ever met. That, Master Rodin, is something I cannot sell you or buy for myself at any price." He turns and presents himself to Byron, "My Prince, I'm sorry to say that I can only offer you my blessings today. I bear no gifts at this time. I will, however, have one for you at the feast in a few weeks."

Byron steps up to him and hugs him, "Dear Coleman, just you being here is a gift to me." He lets go and bows to him, "Welcome to Trade Kingdom and the town of Langdoline!"

Coleman returns the bow to Byron, "I thank you, Sire! Until we see each other again. Master Rodin, I will be by there in the morning."

They smile and wave as they leave the man to his business. They are fascinated by Slender's gifts.

Rodin suddenly remembers that he has to pick up dinner and mead for him and his brother. He tells them that he has to go when Byron stops him, "Wait. Rodin, I want the three of us to feast together in your house if that's okay with you so that we can celebrate our friendship."

Slender's stomach growls, and they look at him, "I would love a feast right now. Will there be mead?"

Rodin looks at him, looking disappointed, "I can't. I'm only a peasant. I can't afford a feast until the Yuletide feast. I only have what is on hand from the farm," he says, lying, knowing full well that he has a huge cache of coins back home.

Byron smiles, "I got it."

Slender looks at him, smiling, "Oh wow, a feast with a prince! This will be great! I hope there's going to be mead."

Rodin quickly catches up, "Wait! Are you sure you want to be seen in a peasant village?"

Byron looks at him, "Rodin, it's going to be just fine!"

Byron walks into a bakeshop. Rodin slows and enters cautiously. He has never actually been *in* any of the shops since he buys the cheaper stuff sold outside. *This place smells remarkable!*

The small, skinny lady behind the counter becomes shocked to realize that Prince Byron is her customer. She looks at Rodin and quickly runs up to him and pulls him toward the door, whispering into his ear, "Please, Master Rodin, play along. You and I will talk in a minute. That's Prince Byron!" she begins to shriek and yells at him as she winks and smiles at Prince Byron, "Shoo! Go! You're not supposed to be in here! Go outside and make your purchase!"

Rodin plants his feet to the ground and stops himself before the door, almost laughing with delight, "It's okay, Agatha! They're with me!"

She stops, suddenly feeling confused, "What?"

Rodin turns and escorts Agatha back to the counter, "Prince Byron, Master Slindee, meet Agatha. She's the best baker in town." Rodin comes back around, ducking below the low ceiling, and stands next to Byron.

Byron reaches a hand to her. When she reaches out to him, he places her hand to his forehead.

"Pleasure to meet you, Miss Agatha."

"Pleasure to meet you too, Miss Agatha," Slender confirms.

"Oh!" she blushes in embarrassment, "It's *Lady*, please. My husband is actually out to buy some cream and eggs from your brother right now, Master Rodin."

Rodin looks at her, feeling a little embarrassed himself, "Agatha, please, just *Rodin*. It's fine. And he'll get plenty. I promise."

"Rodin, thank you so much," Agatha says graciously.

"No, Agatha, thank you and David for sharing your knowledge and helping in the past."

"We should all share in the knowledge we have to help others learn and become better," Agatha says.

"So says the Circle of Light," they all recite.

Slender looks at them, puzzled, "I'm new to this town, ma'am, but I'm wondering, why is it that Rodin here receives and gives so much gratitude from everyone? Except for Vil, of course."

Agatha smiles at Rodin and reaches over and touches his arm, "You see, Master, Rodin here lost his mother and father a few years ago from a terrible troll invasion one night. His farm was in shambles. The poor dear didn't have anything. He only knew what little tending he could do for his farm. Because Rodin's father had such a huge land and helped provide so much for Millington Village, we all decided to give back by sharing with him everything we knew." Agatha begins to tear up, "We all knew we were doing a service to a friend's sons who needed us, but we didn't know that in return, they would give back so much more as they do."

She begins to lose her composure and begins to cry, "Rodin has been sent to us by the Light. He had shown us the true meaning of blessings when we shared our knowledge with him and his brother. We beg the Light every day that he gives Rodin blessings of his own. He deserves so much." She runs around the counter and grabs Rodin around the waist. Her small, fragile frame clings to him, and she shakes and cries on him.

Rodin hugs her back, "You, David, and Joe deserve so much more than I can give."

Just then, a man barges through the door, grumbling, "Huge spiders! And he keeps them as pets! That boy is loony! Kindness pours from him, but he's loony for having giant spiders as pets! Did you see that one barking at me? I could have sworn the stump-legged one was going to bite—"

He looks up and sees Rodin standing under the low ceiling with his wife curled around him, crying, "Rodin, my boy, how are you? Look, Joe, Rodin is here! And so is . . ." he bows quickly to the floor. Another man walks in just about the same time, falling over David, and immediately bows down. David says, "My Prince, it's an honor to serve you."

Byron looks at him, raises his hands, and says, "Please, Master David, I presume. Your beautiful daughter was telling us about how well the town prospered with the help of Rodin here."

Slender looks at him with a smile, "And Rodin says that you and she are the best bakers in Langdoline."

He smiles at them as Agatha laughs, "Prince Byron, stop. Please, that's my husband."

David laughs at them, "Well, leave it to Rodin to tell the truth. And leave it to the son of King Vaniir to insult *me* and flatter my wife!" he bursts out laughing.

Joe grabs a few baskets. He bows and smiles at them. Joe grabs Rodin by the arm and touches his head to Rodin's shoulder, smiles, and carries the baskets out. He waves at everyone and closes the door.

Slender looks around at everyone, "He's awfully quiet."

"Master . . . uh?" David reaches a hand out to greet him.

"My name is Slindee. I'm currently a squire under Sir Galla. I'll be knighted in a few weeks by him. I've only been at this school this year so that I can be taught by my father's longtime friend. Now we're here to buy bread for a feast between new friends, one of whom we're finding out, is more worthy of a large feast than a small. I guess His Highness and I didn't know that Master Rodin was a great deal more respected than anyone in this kingdom."

David shakes his head and laughs at Master's Slindee's long-winded speech, "Actually, my young squire, nobody on Terra-Earth is more respected than young Master Rodin here." He looks at Rodin quizzically, "But did you know your brother has giant spiders running around with him?"

Prince Byron looks at him, surprised, "Giant Spiders? Do you know where they came from?"

Rodin looks at David, "Yes, I do. I had no choice. He hurt one."

Byron tries to interject but goes unnoticed, "Hurt one? How? Is it alive?"

"I put some healing herbs on it, but it lost a leg."

"Healing herbs? Lost a leg? Which leg? You know, they need their legs to jump. Are you listening to me?"

"After that, he begged me to keep them. I said no. He cried. And now we have giant pet spiders. I know I'm a sucker when it comes to Logan. And Millette, but that's another story."

"Wait. Who? A girl? You didn't tell me you have a girlfriend. Is she pretty? Is her sister pretty?"

David smiles, "Well, Master Rodin . . ."

"Dammit, why isn't anyone listening to me? I thought I was the prince here. You know, royalty? Hello?"

"You really do have a soft heart. Your brother too. He sold me an entire barrel of eggs and a casket of cream and a bucket of butter for only four silver! What? That's unheard of! I should have paid more!"

"Wow. That is cheap. You should have charged him more. You really aren't all that great with this whole bartering thing, I've noticed."

Rodin smiles and continues to speak with David, "We have too much! Thankfully, Coleman has agreed to take the other barrel of eggs, some pigs, a cow, and some other things with him."

"Oh yeah, I take that whole bartering thing back now. You made out like a bandit with him. You're not even listening to me, are you? Your prince is speaking, and you're not listening. What is going on here? Slender, will you help me out here?"

David's eyes light up, "Oh yeah, Coleman is in town, isn't he? Now I see why. You're probably going to get a whole lot more from him. Still, we do thank you for the eggs and the cream. We know you practically gave it to us. Joe is out there separating it all out. Now"— he claps his hands together— "what was it you needed?"

Rodin hears Byron mumbling at him. He asks, "What? Did you say something?" Slender laughs at Byron.

Byron shakes his head in disbelief and sighs, "Unbelievable! We're here for two loaves of bread. I'll be paying for it."

Agatha replies, "If it is going to be for all three—well, four, if you count Logan—then they're free," she bags two loaves of fresh bread and gives it to Slender, who smells the aroma from it and gives them an approving smile. The trio smiles and leaves.

"I can't believe you didn't hear me the whole time. I'm a prince! I should be heard when I'm speaking."

Slender bumps shoulders with Rodin, "Why is he mumbling to himself? I can't understand a word he's saying."

Rodin looks at Byron and talks to Slender from the side of his mouth, "I think we need to watch over him. They say the crazy ones are the ones who talk to themselves."

Byron growls in frustration "Ugh!"

"I think he just lost in his own debate. I think Professor Dahlmür needs to know so he can figure out how to cure him," Rodin says, giggling at him.

"I'll let Dahlmür know in the morning. In the meantime, where do we go from here? I'm starving. Can we visit that shop over there? I hear they have great roast beef!" Slender says as his stomach rumbles out again.

Byron, obviously miffed, yells back at the two of them, "Not funny! You asses!"

Rodin smiles, "You know, for someone who's going to be a ruler, you sure do speak softly." Rodin turns to another store, "C'mon. Logan is waiting at home. I want you guys to meet him." They wave to Agatha and David, who walk out to join Joe.

There you are again! Where did you three go? Tried to hide from me, didn't you? That's okay. You will never be able to hide from me. I will find you wherever you go. I'll be everywhere you go. I'm watching you!

Why are you so upset, Prince Herring? That's what I'll call you. Prince Herring. Because you are as mindless as a fish! Look at you, swimming around without a care in the world, like a mindless fish swimming in the lake in search for nothing in particular. When the time is right, I will snag you on my hook and pull you to my feet just like a fisherman does with his catch. Then as you flop around helplessly, gasping for the air of freedom, I will skin you and gut you. Mercilessly!

Hide, Prince Herring! I'm trolling for you! Hide! Ha ha ha!

IV

When they arrive at Rodin's farm, Logan runs out excitedly to meet them, "I made a lot of money today, and I got rid of so much stuff too. Hi, I'm Logan! You must be Prince Byron. Rodin told me so much about you. You, though, he never spoke about. You must be new. My name is Logan. I am Rodin's little brother. Not because of my height, because, let's face it, Rodin's very tall for his age. Well, he's pretty tall for any age. But anyways, as I was saying, he's my big brother because he's a few years older than me, and that's okay, because he does a very good job teaching me. Why, this is the first year I've been allowed to take care of the farm all by myself. I do a good job too, I must say. Hey, did you know we have giant spiders living with us now? They are very nice. I named them. Mutt and Biter are their names. You'll know why I named them that when you meet them. I love those guys. They are so talented too. Mutt made me a silk shirt! Did you know that giant-spider silk is very, very strong? It really is. Something smells really good. Is that roast beef? Are you guys coming for dinner? That's frantastric! I think I said that right. Well, anyways, if you are coming for dinner, then I need to go set the table properly. Is that mead? I swore off mead. None for me! I get sick from mead. But that's okay. I'll just drink some milk. Come inside! Our home is yours! Make yourselves comfortable. Rodin, I'm going to go get Mutt and Biter to meet Prince Byron. I can't believe you're really friends with a prince. I'm so excited!"

Byron, Slender, and Rodin look at him in utter exasperation. They watch him leave and breathe in relief.

Byron looks at Rodin, "Wow."

Slender asks, "Did he even breathe?"

Rodin shakes his head in exasperation, "I think Millette gave him sugar candy again."

"Tell her not so much next time," Byron responds.

"Yeah." Slender starts laying out the table, "I noticed something on the way here. Rodin and I carried everything. Byron carried nothing. What happened?"

Rodin shoots an answer before Byron can open his mouth, "Our Prince had to carry his ego. It's so big we would never have had the strength to carry it."

"Oh, ha, ha," Byron says, "I paid for it all. And that mead better be the best I've ever tasted as much as Barry bragged about it."

"Well, if it's the total opposite of the cheap stuff that I bought in the past, then it should be very good," Rodin says.

Rodin sets the roast beef, a serving fork, and a carving knife onto the carving board and places it onto the table. He places a butter dish at the end of the board to catch the juices. He places everyone a spot and looks around for more mugs and flatware. He's never had to set the table for more than Logan and himself and, occasionally, Millette. After a quick search, he finds everything, including another board and knife for the bread. Luckily, Logan has made a vegetable stew for lunch and left it in the kettle over the fire. Logan must have thought that it would have made a great leftover for dinner.

Rodin is thankful.

Logan returns and sits in his chair, disappointed, "Mutt and Biter must be out hunting. I was hoping you'd get to meet them. My head is killing me. Millette brought me some sugar candy. I'm sorry I didn't save you guys any. I ate it all because Rodin really doesn't like sugar candy. Don't know why. But oh well, more for me. I like it that way. Millette makes really great sugar candy. I'll make sure to ask her for some for you guys next time. I mean, I hope there will be a next time. I hope we don't disappoint you guys. Rodin is known to be kind of boring sometimes, but whatever. Millette seems to not think he's boring. All she does is stare at him. She's weird that way. Rodin likes her. He thinks she's pretty. Who thinks girls are so much fun anyway? They're so boring! All they want to do is cook and clean. She even had Rodin cleaning and hanging the wash a few days ago. He's weird, too, sometimes. Anyways, I'm starved. Is dinner ready?"

"Wow." Byron exclaims.

"I swear I didn't see him breathe the whole time!" Slender points out.

"Logan, go outside and drink some water. You ate all that sugar candy, and it's driving us insane," Rodin points Logan toward the door. Reluctantly, Logan goes out the door and gets some water as the three of them finish setting up the table.

Logan returns as soon as they are done. Automatically, Logan goes to his chair, and Rodin goes to his at the end of the table. Byron moves to the head of the table, and Slender moves to the chair opposite Logan. As soon as Byron and Slender start to sit, Rodin and his brother look at them nervously and mournfully. They freeze in midmotion and look at the two brothers.

"What's wrong?" Byron asks.

Slender asks, "Did we do something?"

Logan quietly answers, "Mom and Dad used to sit there."

Rodin looks at them, abashed, and just as quietly answers, "We're sorry. It's just that . . ."

A flood of emotion overcomes him. Rodin swallows back the tears. Memories of his father telling stories of his past. Reminding them of their chores. Reprimanding them for what they've done that day. His mother sitting and laughing at them as they try to entertain or tell their own stories of the day or reprimanding Rodin for picking on his younger brother because he's littler than he is. She tells him, "You should be watching over him, not beating up on him." Everything that made his family what it was before they were torn away from them so violently by the trolls.

He sighs and looks up to avoid looking into their compassionate eyes and continues, "Nobody has ever sat in those chairs since the troll invasion."

Byron slowly steps from around the chair, "I'm sorry. We didn't know—"

"No, no," Rodin shakes his head and regains his composure and gives Logan a quick nod of approval, "Please sit. It's not something we were trying to stop. Those chairs are meant to be sat in. Those spaces are meant to be taken. We are happy, actually, to see those spaces filled by our friends."

Slender quietly replies, "My friends, I'm honored that you've allowed me into your home and to dine with you." He grabs his mug and places it into the air and pronounces, "To our new friendship! May we share in teachings and knowledge. May we share joy and pain. May we share victory and defeat. May we share only love."

They all hold their mugs in the air, "So says the Circle of Light."

"I didn't know you were such a poet," says Byron.

Slender takes a chunk of bread and shoves into his mouth whole. He chews on it and swallows then responds, "My father taught me that whenever we brought new knights and squires to eat with us."

"Wow, Slender, you must have had a lot of guests each year in order for your father to repeat it so much for you to be able to remember it," Rodin says jokingly as they all sit and begin eating.

Byron laughs. Logan giggles. Slender squints his eyes at him with a smirk, "Oh, ha, ha."

Logan sits up and asks Slender, "Where did your parents come up with the name Slender?"

Slender giggles and swallows more of his food to answer, "Actually, my name is Slindee, after my father's father. Sir Galla started calling me Slender because even though I'm big compared to most knights, I'm still slender compared to him. So now everyone calls me Slender. I like it."

"Oh, so you're learning to be a knight?" Logan asks.

"Yes, I am," he pushes his chest out as he boasts.

Rodin looks over at Byron, "Isn't someone going to be looking for you? Nobody knows you're here."

Byron wipes his face with a napkin, "Actually, my father and mother are out of town. He had to mediate some kind of royal meeting between King Saul and the King of Bolt. I'll be all right."

"Okay," Rodin replies with apprehension, hoping Byron's right.

A few moments later, someone knocks at the door. Logan excuses himself and answers the door, "Hi, Millette!"

Rodin stands at the sound of her name jarring the table as he does and nearly tipping the table over. Slender and Byron look behind him curiously. A beautiful figure of a young woman their age enters the dining room. Her hair is long and black as velvet. Her wardrobe fits perfectly around her curves even though it is made only of wool. Her black eyes sparkle in the firelight.

Rodin greets her with a hug, and they kiss. Logan rolls his eyes at them. Byron and Slender stand in surprise and fascination like hungry wolves. They recompose themselves as Rodin introduces her to them.

"Your Highness! What brings you to our village?" she asks as she curtsies to him.

"I'm here with Rodin. We met at the school, and we became friends. You must be cold," he motions for her to take his seat, "Please sit by the fire."

She smiles and bows, a little embarrassed, "No, Sire, please. I just came by to let Rodin know that tomorrow, he must go to the town hall. The surrounding villages need to choose a Common's Leader for King Saul's upcoming visit. Millington's casting a vote for Rodin to go represent us."

Rodin is shocked to hear this. Everyone else looks at him, impressed, "Way to go, Rodin!"

Embarrassed he waves them off, "Thanks. When?"

"Noon. I will bring Thornrose for you. Do you want Mom to bring any nice clothes?" She looks at him and snickers, "Never mind. None of Dad's clothing is going to fit you." She smiles at him sweetly, ignoring the others around them. She grabs him by the hand and pulls him through the house, "Let me get some measurements. Mom and I will make something quick that will make you look good." She says it loud enough so everyone will know her intentions. As soon as they enter his room, she pulls him close to her and smiles into his eyes, "I've missed you these past few days," she says as she pulls him down to her to kiss him.

Rodin kisses her and smiles back at her, "I've missed you too. How much longer until the Yuletide Celebration? I want to announce our engagement so much. I love you."

"I love you too. Just hold me and kiss me for a few minutes longer. I already know your sizes," she snickers mischievously at him.

"I know," he obliges her with kisses for just a few moments longer. "Okay. We better go back. I'll walk you to the door," he kisses her again then leads her back, beaming.

"I'm sorry to intrude, and now I've got to go." Millette starts for the door then turns suddenly, "Oh, my Prince, I forgot, since your father is away, they've asked for your presence as well to mediate. I guess you haven't gotten word yet."

"Oh," Byron answers, startled by the notion of having to be Mediator, "I'll be there before noon then."

She curtsies and thanks him on her way out the door. Rodin follows her out a few steps and pulls her toward him. They kiss again. She pulls away and cradles his cheek as she looks up into his eyes. She smiles, "I better go. You have guests. I'll have something for you before you're done with the chores tomorrow." She kisses him one more time, turns, climbs onto her horse, and rides off with a wave.

Rodin turns toward the door, his smile wide and his face glowing. As he enters the doorway, he hears a lot of footsteps and laughing going from the window back to the dining room.

Why, those bastards! I guess I've no secrets with those guys.

He returns to his seat and starts eating as if nothing has happened. Byron, Slender, and Logan try to stifle their laughs. They grunt and clear their throats as they watch over Rodin, who ignores them while eating.

"Uh . . . hmm hmm," Byron starts, "So, Rodin, she's such a beautiful girl. Is she, by any chance. . . uh"—he clears his throat to keep from laughing—"single?"

Rodin grabs some bread and bites a piece off nonchalantly, "Actually, she is seeing someone. I think she said something about marriage."

Slender joins the conversation, "Oh, wow. I hope she's not making a huge mistake with the guy. You know, marriage is a huge commitment, what with costs of the wedding itself. Having to cater all those people. And then she would have to move in with the guy. Does she know him well?"

Rodin nods, "I think she says she's known him all her life."

Byron shakes his head, "No, he means, does she *know* him?"

Rodin shakes his head, "Oh no, she doesn't *know* him yet. She's waiting until they get married."

Logan looks at him curiously, "Well, that would be a terrible disappointment for her."

Rodin looks at him curiously. *Oh, now I've got to deal with this?*

Byron says, "What do you mean? I'm sure he would be able to make her happy. He can provide for her. I'm sure he can make his home a place where she'll enjoy herself for the rest of her life."

Slender chuckles, "No. What he means is, she will be disappointed to know how *lacking* he will be the first time."

Rodin shakes his head in confusion. *Wait, did he just say . . . ?* Suddenly he understands. He laughs and tears pieces of his bread and throws it at them, "You bastards!" They all laugh at him.

The evening becomes night as they continue their bantering and eating. The four boys are fast becoming the best of friends as the night goes on.

I now know where you live, Trash! I know who your family is. And now I know with whom you love most. I could have killed her, Trash. It would have been really easy. She was right in front of me, and she never knew I was there. Next time, your woman, Trash, may not be so lucky. When I do decide to kill her, you will see it. You won't be able to do anything about it. I will kill her slow and painful. You will be helpless. It will be your torture. When I finish her, you will watch the other trash you call a brother die the same way. How does it feel? I'm going to kill them, and you can't stop me! I said, how does it feel, Trash?

Oh, look! Its Piggy and Prince Herring! Well, now the gang's all here! If I had known, then the games would have already started. Lady Trash first. Brother Trash second. Then Piggy. Then Trash. And then you, Prince Herring.

Your death is going to be so sweet! I can hardly contain myself!

Ha ha ha! Eat! Enjoy your meal! Celebrate your last days! I'm coming to kill you all!

Spiders! No! Run away! Stay away from me!

There's a loud noise outside the door, and Slender reacts instinctively, grabbing his new sword and shield, which lie within reach. Byron jumps and pulls a short sword tucked behind his back under his tunic. Logan runs to the other side of the house and returns with his father's hand ax for Rodin and a small bow fixed with an arrow for himself. Cautiously, they move toward the door. A scream unlike any they've ever heard comes from the side of the house. There's no window to look out, giving them no choice but to run outside and face it. The four of them run out, covering one another and watching over one another as they make their way to the side of the house where the scream has been heard.

Byron points toward the tree line by the river, "Look! He's running!"

Logan immediately fires an arrow at the shadowy figure just as it enters the trees. He misses. Barely. The arrow embeds itself in a tree just next to the intruder's head. Rodin runs into the house, grabs a couple of torches lying on the fireplace mantle, and immediately lights them. He runs out and hands one to Slender, who leads the group forward quickly and cautiously.

Suddenly, Rodin hears barking. *Mutt is back? Where are they?*

Rodin scans the ground around them, looking for a sign of the giant spiders, and sees their silhouettes running not far beside them. He motions at Logan, and he notices them too.

"Try to surround him, Mutt!" Logan commands.

Mutt jumps ahead and into the treetops. He disappears into the darkness. Biter launches himself to the other side of the group and into the trees.

We're creating a gauntlet.

Rodin signals for everyone to spread out. They break the line and go into opposite directions. Slender commands them not to go too far and to signal when they find him. He doesn't want them to attack in case he's dangerous. They agree and enter the trees.

Rodin carries his torch ahead of him. He has to slow down to avoid tripping and falling. He realizes that he's the one with a torch, not his enemy, and that makes him vulnerable. He may be signaling to the assailant his position, allowing him to sneak up on him and kill him. As soon as he reaches the river's edge, he dips the torch into the water, extinguishing its light. He stands a moment to allow his eyes to readjust to the darkness around him. He begins to make his away alongside the river, searching for clues of the invader. He relies on the knowledge passed down to him by his father from the days he went hunting in these woods just across the river. He remembers the tree he and his father chopped down to make a bridge just thirty yards to the south from where he is standing. That bridge is also behind the shack. It's a great place for someone to think they can sit in and hide or to cross over the river and get far away from here without being found.

He hears the sound of Slender trudging through the brush. He too douses his torch. He joins Slender and whispers for him to wait for the others and points at a footprint in the bank's mud leading in the direction of the shack and the bridge. As soon as everyone gathers, they plan their next move, then they quickly and quietly move on. As if the spiders understand the plan, they resume their position among the treetops.

When they get to the point of the trail that splits between the bridge and the shack, the footprints disappear. No more signs of the direction of the figure. Rodin suggests that this means the person must have gone into the water to try to get across, but that means that he's most certainly dead.

"That river is too violent for even Sir Galla to swim," Rodin explains. He moves into the grass line and points out horseshoe prints sunk into the soil.

"But I didn't hear a horse!" Byron exclaims. Mutt and Biter chirp and grunt out. "And neither did they," he says, pointing at the two above.

"Well, he had a horse, and he got away," Slender remarks. "Today was his day."

As they return to the house, Slender says to Rodin, "You should have been a knight. I mean, the way you took control back there. You would've made an excellent knight's commander. You actually taught *me* something."

Rodin reminds him, "Thanks, but we didn't get him."

They emerge from the trees muddy, disappointed, and defeated. Biter jumps down and lands awkwardly on his seven legs. Mutt laughs as Biter falls, and he lands gracefully beside him. Mutt gives Biter a couple of elbows and laughs when Biter falls toward his bad side. Biter gets up and shoves Mutt back, chirping and grumbling at him. They walk back to the safety of the house. Each of them walks quietly, lugging their weapon of choice on their shoulders in disgust for having been defeated so easily and without notice before it was too late.

Not this time! It is too early in the game to reveal myself to you. We will play soon. When I say we, *I mean* me. *When I say* play, *I mean* torture. *Because I will torture all of you, including those disgusting spiders Brother Trash calls pets! I will use their silks to tie you all in place. Yes! You won't be able to escape my web!*

Go inside! You will be safe! For now. I will be watching you. I'm watching you now. Can you sense me watching you? I'm right here! I'm behind you! Look! Turn around! I'm waving at you! Hi,

Piggy! Look over here! I have something for you. It's a spit to turn you over the fire with! Mmm. I so love bacon. Ha ha ha!

V

Logan leads them inside as they put their weapons away.
Rodin places his ax on the trunk against the wall behind the
door as a precaution. Slender puts his shield and sword on
Rodin's chair in the living space by the fire. Byron
reemerges from the dining room, carrying three mugs and a
fresh jug of mead. "Care to join me."

Rodin grabs his pipe and carries a chair and a lamp toward the
open door, "Sure. Let's go outside." He speaks up for Logan to
hear, "Will you be okay, little brother?"

Logan responds, "Go ahead. I'm going to clean up and go to
bed. Too much activity in one day for me!"

"We'll be right out here." Mutt and Biter follow out behind
them. "The spiders want to join us," he says.

"That's fine. I'm just going to disapose everything and clean the
dishes. Did I say that right?"

Rodin smiles at him and says, "It's *dispose*! And thank you."

They all chuckle at Logan's struggle with big words. Rodin sets
his chair down with its back against the house and uses the lamp
fire to light a piece of kindling to use as a match. Slender and
Byron set their chairs, forming themselves into a small circle
surrounding the lamp. The chilly breeze is cool enough for them to
wrap themselves up in their coats. They sit for a moment, waiting
for someone to complain about the cold. They chuckle at one
another and agree to make a small fire in the yard to gather around.

Rodin grabs some logs from the side of the house and starts
forming a pile. Slender pulls a long log from the other side and
places it in front, meaning for them to sit on it. Byron comes out of
the house with some burning kindling and places it under the logs
to begin their campfire. They sit, Byron in the middle, on the log.
Rodin relights his pipe. Slender goes back and grabs the mead and
mugs. He hands them out, giving two to Byron so he can pour for
them. He sits back down and takes his mug from Byron. Mutt and

Biter make a sudden break for the woods. Rodin figures their night is over.

Byron pulls out a knife and slices his hand. He picks up his mug of mead and allows the blood to drip into it. He passes the knife and mug to Rodin. Nervously, Rodin looks at his hand and back at Byron. *Are we making a blood oath? I don't think I can cut myself. This is gonna hurt.* He pulls the sharp blade over his palm. The blade stings as the blood comes up in a thick line in his hand. He squelches back the pain and then allows his blood to flow into the mug.

Slender wastes no time. He grabs the mug and the knife, cuts into his palm, and allows his blood to flow effortlessly. Byron takes the blood, wipes his knife in the grass, puts it away, and holds the mug into the heat of the flames, "The fire represents the light given to us by the Circle of Light. The heat of the flame represents the warmth given to us by the Circle of Light. We ask the Light to use the heat to merge our blood so that we may each drink on our oaths as brothers. We will trust one another. We will protect one another. We will treat one another equally. We will share our experiences no matter how painful or joyous. We will never leave one another, and we will share our knowledge with one another. The light of the fire will represent the Circle of Light's witness to this oath. So says the Circle of Light."

"So says the Circle of Light." Rodin and Slender quietly confirm.

The three of them drink from the mug to honor their oath. To Rodin, the liquid seems a little too warm to have been in the fire for that short of time.

I think the Circle of Light actually touched this mug.

At that thought, the fire grows bright. The flames shoot all around them. All three of them are startled and frozen with fear as a ring of fire burns into the ground around them and rises into the air. There isn't any heat coming from the flames, but none of them want to risk rushing through the fire to get out. A ball of light forms in the center of the campfire, and it begins to glow and sing. The light grows in intensity. Suddenly, it explodes, showering sparks all around, and extinguishes the circling fire. Soon, the night returns, and the campfire remains. They are frozen in shock.

As soon as their eyes adjust to their surroundings, they see three men on horseback before them. By the looks in their eyes, they've just witnessed the phenomenon themselves. Rodin comes to first and rises to greet them. Then Slender and Byron follow him. They are all speechless. Not a word is spoken.

Professor Dahlmür can only dismount and walk toward them with tears in his eyes. Sir Galla and another man, both whimpering themselves, dismount, and all three bow down to the ground before Rodin, Slender, and Byron.

Slender finally finds his voice and whispers to his companions, "What was in that mead?"

The three of them are dumbfounded as Professor Dahlmür and his crew finally calm down. The stranger with them quietly recites, *"The gift will be given to the one deemed most worthy of his circle."*

Byron speaks out and demands an explanation, "What does that mean? We've heard that all day. Not once has anyone told us what that means. Now, I demand to know. Talk!"

This is the first time Rodin's actually seen Byron press his authority as prince outside the conflict between him and Vil. He pokes Slender and nods at Byron, who tries to show that he has authority here.

Slender grunts his agreement.

Sir Galla steps up to him, "My lord, we're sorry to be rude, but unfortunately, we are bound by oath not to say anything without your father present. It is *he* you must ask."

"I will," he responds, unsatisfied with his answer.

Rodin steps between them, "To Darkness with that! I want to know what in bloody blazes happened just now. As someone that was just in it, I want to know now, or everyone can start leaving!"

Slender agrees, "Answers would be nice right now. And if any of you say that we have to wait on King Vaniir to come back, I will personally use Chill to freeze your asses!"

Byron stands beside him, "Not if I don't behead them first."

Defeated, the three men look at one another. The stranger motions them back to the log. Professor Dahlmür taps the ground with his staff, and three boulders rise from the ground. They each choose a boulder to sit on. For the next few minutes, they all sit, staring into the fire, not making a sound. The silence is deafening.

Finally, Professor Dahlmür speaks, "What you did was make an oath of brotherhood in witness of the Circle of Light. What you do not understand is that the three of you are now bound together by blood for as long as you shall live. The scripture you hear also refers to the promise of a gift to be given to the one who is deemed worthy by the Circle of Light. We cannot explain what this gift is because King Vaniir has sworn us to never reveal this to Master Byron and his own circle until the time comes to present the gift or until he speaks of it himself. All I can say is that, Master Byron, you have been chosen by prophecy to give this gift to either Master Rodin or Master Slindee. One of them will bear the gift, while the two of you, sworn by the oath, will stand with him until his end. That display was the Circle of Light's confirmation of your oath, and the three of you have sealed it in blood. You cannot go back on your oath. None of you. If you do, death will be the least of your punishment."

The three of them sit on their log, taking in what Professor Dahlmür has just told them. Rodin's face is blank. *What do we do now? This would be so much easier if we knew what this gift was, wouldn't it? Did Byron really not know what he was doing? I mean, I've never heard of a ritual like that before? Where did he get that? I have no idea how this is going to affect Millette. Millette! Can I even tell her about this?*

Rodin turns to Professor Dahlmür, "Dahlmür? Sir? I've got a question," he pauses, trying to think about how he wants to ask, and what exactly it is he's asking, "Is this something that is to be kept secret? I mean, what do I tell my brother and future wife? Or what will the three of us say to anyone?"

Sir Galla speaks up, "Well, for one, if I were the three of you, I wouldn't allow a certain class to know about a brotherhood between people of different classes. That will cause problems. Two, don't *ever* mention the gift or what was witnessed tonight. That would only destroy you."

Slender stares into the fire, grumbling, "These answers are pretty thin. I still don't understand what's going on."

Bryon tosses a stick into the fire, "You're not the only one, brother."

Rodin rubs his temples with one hand and holds the back of his neck with the other, "Oh man, Byron, you're not going to believe what happened. I think I just woke up from a dream!"

Everyone chuckles at him, and Byron lays an arm on his back, "What was in that pipe? Because we all had the same dream."

Rodin shakes his head and smiles, "Dammit!"

Slender looks over to the stranger, "Hey, I'm sorry"—he extends a hand to him— "I haven't been introduced. I'm Master Slindee. I'm studying under Sir Galla to be a knight. I will be coronated in just a few weeks."

The man is tall and handsome with his dark hair, dark eyes, and tan skin. The total opposite of the others, who are rough and tough-looking. The man smiles wide, a row of white teeth gleaming, and takes his hand, "Nice to meet you, Master Slindee. Master Rodin," he shakes hands with Rodin then bows to Byron, "Prince Byron. My name is Master Lawrence. I have come from Graystone Kingdom to deliver you a message. I've forgotten the urgency of the matter with all this. A report"—he pulls a scroll from his saddlebag— "from King Matterhorn. 'I have been saddened to send word that has been delayed over time due to recent events. We have received reports that there have been sightings of the League of Troll armies spreading throughout several kingdoms, towns, and villages. I have the unfortunate news to tell you that I can personally confirm these reports to be accurate and true.'" Rodin stands in surprise.

"'Just recently, we've lost several villages to the east and almost all villages to the south. I have conversed with King Fulst in the Bolt Kingdom. He has had a very recent attack in the village of Durham. Please be aware the Durham Village borders your kingdom to the north and that these trolls are attacking peasant villages along the way. The destruction is absolute. They leave nothing but skinned bodies of men and dead women and children. Although one report from Durham shows that a female rider and her horse were skinned to death as well. We have absolutely zero reported survivors.

"'We have offered assistance to Bolt Kingdom, and they have accepted. Jointly, we are offering our assistance to Trade Kingdom as well. If you require it, we will provide. Signed, His Majesty, King Matterhorn.'"

Byron, Slender, and Rodin stand and stare at him in disbelief.

Byron falls to his knees and looks at Professor Dahlmür. Tears roll down his cheeks. His chest heaves quickly, "My father and mother went through Durham! They were going to mediate a deal for King Fulst! Please! Did they make it?"

Rodin and Slender immediately surround him. They lay their hands on him in anticipation of shock, but Professor Dahlmür looks at him calmly and assuredly, "Yes, Master Byron, I'm surprised you didn't know that your mother returned the night they left. She was overcome with an illness and returned home. Your father sent word the day he arrived safely."

Byron breathes relief and lowers his head to catch his breath, "Thank the Light. Boone never told me. I would have checked on her. I'll see her in the morning to make sure she's feeling better."

Slender asks, "Professor Dahlmür—"

Professor Dahlmür interrupts him, "Master Slindee, please. As long as we are out of the school, I am Dahlmür. Sir to you, Master Rodin."

Rodin looks at him and smiles snidely, "Yes, Dahlmür," no *"sir"* added.

Sir Galla laughs at him, "Not from that one, Dahlly!" he says and pats him on the back.

Dahlmür smiles, "Most certainly not, I see." He returns his focus to Slender, "As you were saying?"

"I was going to ask why you and Sir Galla were here."

He strokes his long, stubbly chin, "Well, we got a little worried about Master Byron, and we also needed to see Master Rodin about the urgent matter of the trolls. We just got lucky to have found Master Byron and Master Rodin together in the same place. Unfortunately, we weren't expecting a spectacle."

Rodin looks at Sir Galla, "How can I be of service to you, Sir Galla?" he bows to him.

"As you've heard, we have troll problems. As you have experienced before, they attacked from the river beside your land. We want to avoid this from happening again, so with your permission, Master Lawrence and I would like to head a small detachment to make camp upon your property. We will not interfere with your day-to-day doings, and we will provide for ourselves."

Rodin sits for a minute to think about what it will be like to have knights and soldiers on his land. *I have plenty of room on the land. They can be set up at the other end in the clearing hidden from the road and the house by all the trees. Also, it will keep Logan safe.*

Before he can answer, Slender poses a question, "May I join the detachment, sir?"

Sir Galla smiles, "I knew you'd ask. I've already gotten permission from the headmaster to allow this detachment to be treated as training exercises, and I shall grade everyone accordingly."

Rodin is shocked at the assumption that he will agree. *Well, I guess I have no choice.* "Well, since the decision has been made, you can set up your men in the clearing two hundred yards off to the south there"—he points toward the clearing hidden from the trees—"beyond the trees, just twenty yards in, where there's a clearing that borders the river. There's no visible line of sight from here or the street, so those men can work in secret and have open access to fish, fresh water, wild potatoes, and the winterberries that grow in that field. I'm not harvesting that field this season, so they will be left in private."

Sir Galla nods in agreement, "I understand."

"Also, since harvest is over and I have no need for the equipment, my brother and I will move the equipment from the shack beside the house to the barn. You, Lawrence, and Slender can use it for yourselves. Also, if I hear that any of those that camp in the clearing has offended, interfered, or harmed in any way anyone around this village or the shopkeepers that trade with me, at any time, I will personally use my ax to drag their heads off my property. Also, as far as I'm concerned, you three may use the house if needed. Welcome," he reaches out toward Sir Galla to shake his hand to settle the agreement.

Dahlmür stands and interjects, "Now, hang on!" he turns to Prince Byron, "Mediator, do you feel these terms are fair to both parties?"

Byron is startled at first then smiles, "I believe Master Rodin's terms are sound. How say you, Sir Galla? Can you agree to follow the terms?"

Sir Galla stands and addresses the court, "Mediator, Master Rodin has offered many terms for our protection of his house and village. I've never been asked to conduct such a matter in such secrecy as this. It is, in a way, preposterous."

Sir Lawrence stands, "I object! Master Rodin has actually provided everything the people in the camp would need. He's offered them food, fresh water, a cleared space sufficiently large enough to gather without interference from the forest, and another advantage Sir Galla has not considered."

Byron raises the question, "And what would that be, Master Lawrence?"

He smiles at Sir Galla, "A location to use covertly to watch from all sides without being detected by any impeding enemy."

Sir Galla raises his eyebrows in amazement, "You are correct, Master Lawrence. I did not fully consider that particular advantage," he laughs and turns to the mediator, "In that case, all terms are agreed!"

"Then, by the power vested in me as mediator and as witnessed here tonight by Master Slender, I say the agreement has been made, and all terms are hereby accepted. Including the part about the ax thing. If that happens, I'd like to see it."

They all laugh as Rodin and Sir Galla shake hands, and Dahlmür closes the subject with a shower of sparks from his staff. *Snap! Snap! Snap!*

When things settle down, everyone decides to end the evening with a final round of mead. Rodin pours some for Slender, Byron, and himself, and the gentlemen offer to pass the jug around. As soon as it's done and the night has been toasted, Dahlmür extinguishes the fire, and everyone but Slender heads to stay in the town inn for the remainder of the night.

Slender thanks Rodin for his hospitality and immediately assumes a position on a cot in an unused room. Rodin is grateful Slender has volunteered to stay, because the recent news of the trolls will have kept him awake all night as he patrols, paces, and searches out every movement and noise the entire night.

VI

"R*odin!*"

Rodin jumps from the bed and into a stupor, his arms reaching immediately for his hand ax. *Where is it? What's going on? Who's there?* All these thoughts race through his head all at once. The only word available to him is, "Yes, Dahlmür! Sir!"

"Brother, there's a girl here to see you!" Logan exclaims, "Her name is Helana. I'll leave you two alone. I won't tell Millette."

Rodin rubs his eyes, trying to clear the sleep from his vision, "Tell Millette what? Who's Helana? And what does she want?"

"I'm Helana."

Rodin freezes. He suddenly realizes she's in the room with him, and he's just jumped out of bed like a madman. Even worse, the cold air reminds him that he's very cold and naked. He can't focus to find something to cover himself. He searches frantically around, at the same time watching the woman in the room with him. Her hair is golden and kept in an elegant braid. Her frame is very curvaceous at the top. Her smile is broad and beautiful. Her blue eyes sparkle. If Rodin were any other man, he would have chased her down in an instant.

I can't believe Logan did this to me. Wow, she's gorgeous! Those are bigger than Millete's, and Millette is big! Oh shit! Where's my blanket?

"Oh! Good morning!" she cries. She turns her head and laughs, "Early riser!"

"What? Oh man." The cloud clears, and he's finally able to find and wrap the blanket around himself, "Do you? I mean, hi, I'm Rodin. Pleased to meet you."

"Obviously."

"Huh? Oh, can you? Would you mind?" He points toward the door as he breaks out into a sweat.

"Why go now?"

"What? You can't . . . I mean, Millette would . . . you really . . . I don't want." He stops to catch his breath.

"Right. Slow down there. I'm only picking with ya. I'll be in there," she gives him a wink and a seductive look as she walks out the door. Before she closes the door, she comments, "Whoever Millette is, she is very lucky," then she shuts the door behind her.

Rodin freezes midstride. He mutters to himself, "I am so in trouble! I'll kill that boy!"

Rodin hears Slender's voice, "Good morning, miss!"

"Oh, whoa, fella! Sheath that thing!" It's followed by Logan laughing as she states, "Too many snakes in this village for me!"

"Sorry, miss. Let me put some pants on."

"Please!"

When Rodin emerges from his room, Logan is lying in a chair and very red in the face as he tries really hard to breathe from his laughter. Rodin walks up to him and punches his leg, "Jerk!"

Logan laughs so hard he barely manages an, "Ouch!" as he rubs his leg.

He looks at Helana quizzically, "I apologize for my brother, but why are you here?"

"It's okay. I'm here because my father sent me to go with you to the meeting today."

"And just who is your father?"

Slender asks another question, "And why is he interested in a common's election meeting?"

"My father wants me to inform all villages about the troll invasions and volunteers the king's men for protection camps in their areas. He wants you to push for these services because if one village is lost, we can all lose."

Rodin nods in agreement, "I understand. Now, again, remind me, who's your father?"

"Grand Wizard Dahlmür," she replies. She shakes Rodin's frozen hand and smiles at his shocked expression, "My father admires you. He doesn't know how to handle you, but he admires you."

Slender says, "I'm Slindee. I'm going to be coronated as a knight next week. How does he feel about me?"

She looks at him as if she were trying to recall a memory, "I don't know who you are. Do you know my father?" She turns and winks at Rodin on the way out, and Logan chuckles at Slender.

Rodin snickers, "She's joking, Slender."

Slender realizes and nods, "Damn, she's a beauty. And she knows how to be a real smart-ass. I like her."

"I do too." Rodin knocks Logan on the top of his head, "Do that again *ever*, and I'll let the trolls have you."

Logan stops smiling and looks at him in seriousness, "What trolls? Have there been more attacks? Not around here, right?"

Rodin looks out across the field, "Not right now. Slender will fill you in. Coleman is coming with a deal I made with him. Slender, can you help him? I really have to get these chores done as quickly as possible and then bathe before Millette gets here with the clothes she and her mother made."

"I sure can. Can we talk about everything from last night?"

Rodin stares at a bewildered Logan, "Let's wait."

"Okay. Let's go clean out the shack, Logan, while our brother gets to his business."

"What do you mean *our brother*?" Logan walks out ahead of him, "And why are we cleaning out the shack?"

Rodin smiles as he puts on his coat and heads out to get started. *So much to do in such short time. I woke up too late. And that Helana is beautiful. I better watch out for her around Millette. She's going to get me in trouble.* Before long, Rodin has caged enough chickens, filled enough pails of milk, and gathered enough hay to feed the bull to have them ready for Coleman. As soon as he finishes all the chores, Millette comes carrying clothes for Rodin.

She steps up to the porch and hands him the clothes with a kiss. *She may not be Helana, but she is perfect.* Rodin takes the clothes and escorts her into the house. Millette sets the clothes on the table and stares at him.

"What?" he asks.

"What went on here last night after I left? There was a huge light show coming from here. Mom and I saw it. We started to get worried."

Quickly he searches for an answer as Slender walks past the front window, "Well, Slender is going to be knighted soon, and we were celebrating."

She looks at him, confused, "And all those lights and explosions?"

"Sir Galla and Professor Dahlmür came by to celebrate with us. Dahlmür provided the fire and explosions. He is a wizard. He can do those kind of things."

"Okay. I understand that. Now"—she presses him against the table and looks right into his eyes—"who's that gorgeous girl that was here this morning?"

Sweat rolls down his face as he tries to swallow, "Was she gorgeous? I don't . . . I mean . . . I wouldn't . . . who are we talking about?"

She kisses him and laughs, "It's okay, my love. I've already met her on my way here. She says that I am very lucky to have you. She said she's interested in someone else anyway. She said that you were a gentleman. I told her that you are a fabulous find, and she agreed."

He breathes a sigh of relief, "Oh, thank the Rings."

She turns and walks out with a water pail in her hand, "She said that I am going to be extremely pleased on our wedding night!" Rodin just about trips over his own feet, "And I told her that it will be *you* who has to be prepared when that night comes," he hits both knees to the floor.

Behind the house, he draws his bath. When it's done, he checks the temperature and climbs in. He relaxes for a few minutes. The chill in the air makes the wet areas of his body not in the water freeze. He sighs and climbs out. He grabs his towel and wraps it around his waist as he goes back around the house and into the front door. As Rodin enters, he stops and looks around at his unexpected guests. *Why me? I just want a bath.* "Good morning, everyone. Sorry, it's cold outside. I want a blanket to put over the washtub as I bathe. Is that fine with everyone? Okay. Great. I've heard you and Millette have met. Hello, Byron. You look like hell. Logan, my breakfast better be done by the time I get out," he speaks as he goes into his room and grabs a large blanket, "Slender, you better save me some. Millette, my darling, I love you."

He sees his scrub brush on the table beside Millette. He walks up to her, kisses her, and grabs the brush. She smiles back at him. That's when he feels a sudden chill around him.

"Oh, hey! It's Mr. Happy, and he is happy to see you, girl!" Helana cries.

Logan bursts out laughing as he runs out of the house with his towel. Rodin drops his head in disgust. He shrugs his shoulders and raises his arms in defeat, "Why not?" Rodin kisses her again then walks up to Byron and kisses him on the cheek too. Byron yells and scrubs his face with his hands and yells at him to get away. Slender jumps from the table and flees out the door as soon as Rodin looks at him.

Helana yells at him, "Take that dancing snake out of here and get washed up!"

He winks at Millette and walks out the door, laughing.

Rodin finally settles into the tub. He throws the blanket over himself, making a tent to keep in the warmth. Rodin takes his time pouring warm water over his shoulders, down his back, and over his chest. He remembers how when he was very young, he could have easily dunked his whole body into the warm water all at once. Now he needs a bigger tub. Well, for Rodin, it will have to be a much bigger tub. He scrubs away the dirt from his chores and the sweat from all that he's done this week. He begins to feel renewed the more time he takes.

If I were Byron, I would never leave the comfort of a good, warm bathtub. I wonder if they have a special place in the palace, or if he has to bathe outside too. He is just about finished when someone pulls the blanket up and crawls in. *Millette. Sweet, beautiful Millette. I love you. You've done so much for me. You've looked out for me. You've made sure that Logan and I have been well since the most horrible day of our lives. You allowed me to help you during your loss. You and I have shared so much emotion, comfort, pain, and knowledge. I am so blessed by the Light with you. I love you.*

He pours out all this in a single kiss with her.

She pulls back from him with bliss, "If you don't go soon, you'll be late."

"I know," he stands as she takes a towel and starts drying him off.

"No, no, no. Let me do that. You go," he grabs the towel from her as she laughs. "I don't want Mr. Happy to get any ideas before our wedding night."

She laughs again and crawls out. She turns and talks to the blanket, "She's right. I will be very pleased that night." She walks away. He blushes.

Rodin pulls the blanket around him and drapes the towel over his wet head. As he walks into the house, he notices his audience has gotten larger. *Really?* He nods at Sir Galla, Master Lawrence, and Coleman as they introduce themselves to Logan and Millette, pausing long enough to see Rodin as he is. Of course, Sir Galla is being very gentlemanly about his introduction to Millette. Rodin closes the bedroom door behind him and sheds the blanket as he works his hair with the towel. As he dresses, memories of those days that brought Millette and him together flood back.

Before the horrible events that tore their families apart, Rodin and Millette were inseparable. Their mothers got together daily to discuss the scuttle of the town, and their fathers always spent their times away from their work bringing the two families together. Rodin and Millette would run out to play in the secluded fields or run through the woods on the other side of the river. This was before he and Logan became closer as brothers. The woods were always an adventure for them, especially in the spring, when the new flowers bloomed and the trees started blooming fresh greenery. There was one tree in particular they climbed and sat in, telling their stories. They told each other their secrets, and that was also where Rodin and Millette had secretly discovered their differences as boy and girl.

They had grown to the point that they became candid about everything. They kept no secrets. As a young boy, Rodin discovered that she had a birthmark in a very conspicuous spot. Back then, he always thought it was the most amazing birthmark since neither he nor Logan had birthmarks themselves. As he thinks about it now, he realizes it's not the birthmark but the place on her body that really fascinates him. They've watched each other grow over time in those woods. One day, they both came to realize that they needed to stop sharing so much between themselves. Modesty had become a part of them.

After many years of knowing each other and meeting under the tree, they decided to never do the things that adults did. He asked her to marry him. She, of course, said yes. They knew when they wanted to be married. They talked about it all the time in that tree. They talked about it in the clearing. They talked about it in their homes. Still, to this day, they've never stopped talking about it.

The day her mother found out was a day they thought they were alone. They were both lying in the grass after coming back from their errands in town, and they were talking about the people they were wanting to see there and how the wedding was to be the most beautiful the town had ever seen. Both knew that it would never happen that way, but that didn't stop them from talking about it. That was when her mother came running around the house and just about tackled Rodin in a fury of hugs and kisses. They knew immediately that they would be married to each other just as they wanted.

The days since the troll attack never stopped them from falling deeper in love. With the two of them looking out for Logan and she and her mother watching over him, it just couldn't make them any closer than they already were.

After dressing, Rodin goes into the living area of the house, where the current congregation has gathered. They comment on his appearance as well as laugh at his appearance. He shrugs at everyone humbly and asks Byron if he is ready to leave. Byron nods, and they begin to say their good-byes. Rodin bows at Sir Galla, and Master Lawrence places his right fist to his chest and his forefinger and middle of his left hand to his forehead and bows to him. Rodin looks at him quizzically as he bows the same way. *The Common's Bow? That's just as a peasant should bow.* He smiles at Lawrence and waves at the rest of them as he leaves.

Suddenly, Helana is up and out of her seat, "Oh, wait! What am I doing? I'm supposed to go too."

She offers Rodin a ride on her horse with her, but Rodin shakes his head and straddles onto a horse brought by Millette, "She already brought Thornrose for me."

She shrugs, "Oh," then she turns her horse and begins to trot away.

Byron trots up to her on his huge mount. Rodin admires its beauty. The horse, Warsaw, is large. He reeks royalty. His beautiful black velvet coat with a bright white stripe from his nose to the top of his head where the mane begins. Warsaw's mane is long and very silky black. He trots with his tail raised high. This horse knows that it is a regal beast just by the way he holds his head up. Warsaw prances fluidly as he gallops. *Remarkable,* is all Rodin can think about this animal.

Thornrose is short but wide and muscular. Even though Millette keeps her, she belongs to Rodin. Rodin is very proud of Thornrose. She's hardworking, strong, full of stamina, fast, and very intelligent. Thornrose can work for hours in the day, pulling the various carts and carriages around the farm and through town before she begins to slow down. Millette does very well to give her the sheen her coat needs to make her look very beautiful. Her tail is wrapped in ribbon at the top and in the middle to keep it well-kept, allowing a hand's length free to whip. Her mane, well groomed and cleaned, flows like feathers in the breeze. Her white markings show no sign of her hard work in the dirt of the fields or the dust from the barn.

He can keep his horse. I'll keep Thornrose over royalty any day.

Helana's horse, however, is the smallest of the three. White with gray spots freckled all over. Shade is obviously built for speed. His body is streamlined, thin, and very well-muscled in his legs. His mane is kept short to keep out of his rider's face. Gray and white, it still billows in the wind. His tail is long and plush. Shade looks to be poised and ready to sprint at any moment. His ears flick about, perched high on his head, always alert. Each of them admires their horse. Their horses obviously admire them.

"Are you staring at my horse's backside, brother?" Byron's voice snaps Rodin back to reality.

"Huh?" he smiles. "I was noticing just how Warsaw's backside resembles yours."

Helana laughs out loud. Byron looks at him, taken aback, "Really? Have you seen her and hade here? I noticed a hint of resemblance in the nose."

"Hey!" she immediately covers her nose. Rodin has to admit, it does sit wide and long on her face. It makes her look good, but long and wide.

"What?" Bryon smiles at her as Rodin laughs out loud himself. Byron reaches into a pouch on his saddle and pulls out a carrot, "Would you like one?" he offers to her as he snickers. Rodin can't help but laugh wholeheartedly at the joke.

"Why, you!" she flicks her hand and flips the carrot out of Byron's grasp onto the ground.

Shade stops and picks it up. He begins to eat it himself, grunting in delight.

Byron leans over to face Shade, "Your welcome." Shade knocks into Byron's face and rubs his cheek against him. Helana rubs the side of his neck and giggles.

Rodin rides up alongside Byron, squeezing him to the middle. He looks across him to Helana and asks, "What is Dahlmür like when he's not teaching?"

Curious, Byron looks at her. She smiles, "Well, there are some things I can't talk about when it comes to who he is, but my father loves to observe people. How they live. How they react to situations. He watches how people interact with others. He hates people that think they are superior over others, no matter what class they come from."

Byron laughs and knocks elbows with Rodin, "Yeah, Rodin and I witnessed that trait yesterday."

She turns to look at them, "I wondered why he was so upset yesterday. It has been a long time since I've seen him so pissed off."

Rodin smiles, "Oh, he was pissed, all right."

She asks, "What happened?"

Byron answers, "Lord Vil had the nerve to insult Grand Wizard Dahlmür of King Saul's Court."

She raises her eyebrows in understanding, "Oh! So everyone knows him now." She shakes her head and shrugs, "So that's how that boy ended up in the stockade."

Rodin says proudly, "Yup."

She nods and then shakes her head as she contemplates it, "My father only uses his title when it is necessary. I've got to say, though"—she turns to them—"the three of you have really captured his attention. Especially you, Rodin. He says," she mocks her father "'That boy is going to be great. A great what? I don't know. Right now he's a great pain in my ass. Curious. Very knowledgeable. But a pain in the ass indeed. Helana, you need to watch him. He's going to be great.'"

Byron laughs, "Who? Rodin? A pain in the ass?" Comically, he smacks Rodin on the shoulder, "Are you a 'great pain in the ass', brother?"

Ashamed, Rodin looks down at the back of Thornrose's head, "You know me."

Byron laughs, "More like a great pain in Vil's ass. That boy tried hard to make Rodin miserable, but just like my brother, Rodin wouldn't let him." Byron pats his shoulder as he praises him.

"I noticed something else," she begins, "This village and most people in town hold you and Logan in high regard." She turns to look at him, whipping her braid over her shoulder. "Why?"

Rodin smiles, "They do because our family has always opened our farm to the people. My family has the best piece of land in the kingdoms when it comes to farming. My farm doesn't dry out even in drought. There is a huge underground water lake. When the river floods onto my land, it brings up all its minerals and deposits them into the soil. It only floods one week a year. It's just me and Logan. So why should I be greedy and keep it to ourselves?"

"My father invested his life into turning this farm into the supply farm of the kingdom. He told me a long time ago to never hoard the bounties for myself, 'Help and feed our friends, and they become our family.' He never knew how true his words would become. His father horded everything. My father gave me the knowledge to open it up. People come and share my land for their own crops."

"Not all those chickens are mine. At least not at first. They noticed how well we tended chickens and worked cows and bulls that they just started trading them for their piece of land each season. I have asked them to stop and that they didn't need to trade me any more, but they won't, and I'm overflowing. I'm grateful to share with them. Especially since they've shared so much knowledge with us."

This even impresses Byron, "Your model of village farming should be shared everywhere. This village has learned and offered so much for one another, the town, the lordship, as well as the kingdom. This village's family model will be something I will share with my father. We need more like this."

Helana looks over to Bryon, "I think that would turn this kingdom into a model kingdom for the entire League."

As they enter the center of town, they make their way through the bustling people. The fountain roars as they skirt by it to take the road on the right to the meeting hall. They do not look in Vil's direction. Helana was told of their stockade tradition, apparently, because she purposely never looks in his direction. Rodin waves and smiles warmly at a few people as they call his name. When they notice Byron, they bow or curtsy as they welcome him. Helana tells them how impressed she is of the hospitality of the townsfolk. They arrive at the hall and dismount from their horses. They tie them off and head in.

Look who's just rode into town! It's Prince Herring and his trash! Who's that with you? She's new. Ha ha ha!

Fantastic! More to kill. Oh, what a sight you are! Beautiful. Well-shaped. I love devouring beauty. I will devour you.

Ha ha ha!

You missed me last night, Prince Herring! You were so close, Trash! I was right behind you in the woods, but oh, you just couldn't find me. Ha ha ha! I could have killed any of you if I wanted to, but what would the fun in that be? I want to kill you with a grand audience! A king should watch as his prince is destroyed in front of his eyes. The town will cheer as I destroy your trashy friends. Then they will recoil in grotesque horror as I soil your beautiful new friend. The piggy will squeal! You will die! Then your kingdom will belong to a new master. From then on, all kingdoms and all leagues will be mine*!*

I promise you! Are you listening, Prince Herring? I will kill you! I will kill you all!

VII

As they enter, they notice people milling about. There are groups gathered everywhere around the meeting hall. Each town's representatives and leaders as well as curious folk from their areas huddle together, carrying on discussions among themselves. Some in seriously heated discussions. Others just idle chat.

The Overseer of the meeting looks up from his bench and spots them as they walk down the main aisle. He gasps as he recognizes the prince of Trade Kingdom. He stands and immediately pounds his gavel onto a sound block and announces, "His Majesty, Prince Byron!" Everyone immediately stands and turns to them.

Silence.

"Now that's an entrance. You are very well respected in your kingdom, Sire," notes Helana.

The Overseer clears his throat, "Young Lady, neither he nor his father, the King, gives us any reason not to respect them."

Byron raises his hand, "Please. Thank you, Overseer. Please have a seat and carry on. We know we are early. Don't let me interrupt your discussions before the start. I'm just going to prepare for this gathering as Mediator. This lady is Professor Dahlmür's daughter. She is new here and has been chosen to be my adviser in his absence."

The Overseer bows to her, "Very well. Lady Adviser to the Mediator, we welcome you."

"Thank you, uh, Master . . . ?"

"Durestes, my lady."

"Thank you, Master Durestes," she bows back with a smile.

Rodin watches from the side to keep the attention away from himself during Byron and Helana's moment. The Overseer then recognizes him, "Master Rodin!" He stands and walks toward them. He gives the Common's Bow to the two of them, pardons himself, and gives Rodin the Common's Bow.

Rodin smiles and returns the gesture then offers his hand, "Great to see you, Master Durestes. I wasn't expecting to be a representative of my village, but I'm honored to be chosen. I wish it could have been you."

Master Durestes shakes his head, "No, son. You are a fine choice. I wouldn't be able to be Overseer and represent our village without anyone suspecting favoritism." He pulls Rodin to the side, "Besides, you are highly favored to represent our kingdom as Common's Leader. To be honest, when your name was mentioned, everyone else stepped down. You, Master Rodin, will be Common's Leader, and we will work hard to give you the knowledge you will need, Light willing."

Rodin steps back and shakes his head, "But, Master, please. I can't, I mean I am most gracious, but I'm sure Master Stewart is a better choice. That's who I was going to advise the votes for."

Master Durestes's eyes water as he smiles, "You have no idea, do you? Master Stewart was the one who named you."

"What?" This is shocking to Rodin. *I can't lead. I don't know how. Master Stewart chose the wrong person. I'll announce my withdrawal during the meeting.* He smiles and nods to Master Durestes and finds a seat with his village folk. Millette's mother is there as well as a few others. At this moment, he can't begin to recall their names. His mind is racing. He doesn't want the job, yet everyone thinks he's perfect for some reason. Byron and Helana try to speak to him, but their words go unnoticed.

This is happening way too fast, he thinks to himself. Rodin has never tried to lead anything or anyone. He's always glad to share his fortunes with everyone. He will even give the shirt off his back if it means to help them out. *Why am I being picked? Who will tend the farm and my brother as I represent them? I want to marry Millette! How can I be a husband to her if I'm gone all the time? This has got to be a mistake!*

Suddenly, Lady Suzette, Millette's mother, stands and hugs him, "You will be fine. I'm proud of you, Rodin. Millette is very proud. Don't worry about anything. You will be a fine representative and a fine husband. I love you, son."

Rodin leans into her embrace and smiles, "Thank you so much, Lady Sue. I love you too," and he does. This woman has shown him just as much love as his mother. He will be lost without her love and support. She's raised them all without any regret. Not once has she spoken a bad word about them, nor has she ever raised a hand against them. Since that day, she has been Logan and his mother.

It isn't long before the gavel hammers down onto the sound block again, and the meeting is called to order. Byron sits to the side in the Mediator's Box, Helana sitting to his right. They've put on their appropriate robes for the meeting. Byron is wearing his red robe, and Helana is in a pale yellow.

The Overseer cries out, "All rise!" and the room stands without any voices, "Let us give thanks and ask for guidance, strength, and knowledge to direct this hearing to make wise decisions for the benefit of all the League of Humans today. We ask that the Circle of Light allows sound judgments to pass through us today. We thank the Rings for giving us a loving guide in the Light. We ask the Light to allow the Mediator to help us in our path for the best decisions and knowledge. So says the Circle of Light."

Everyone utters in unison, "So says the Circle of Light!" Everyone sits.

The Overseer clears his throat, "Before we begin, we would like to most graciously acknowledge our Mediator," then swings his hand to introduce the Mediator, "Prince Byron, welcome!"

The crowd stands and claps. A few cheer and whistle. Byron stands and waves at everyone. He motions for everyone to calm down, "Please sit. I'm honored to be here. My father has told me so much about these meetings. He enjoys being Mediator to you all. The Class of Commons is the closest-knit group of people that I've ever seen. I always thought that kings were petty and knights were overly boisterous. Then one day, my father took me to witness a lord meeting. I learned that day that there are such things as dragons." Everyone laughs.

"He says that the best knowledge comes from observing the common man. Their discussions and stories are real. So much knowledge is passed around from one village and town to the next in this very room. He says that one day, the Light will bless me to receive that vast knowledge and that it will astound me. So far, I've already learned so much just being around one of you. I've made a close friend. Professor Dahlmür has asked me to keep a low profile and not to allow anyone to know how close we have become over just three days. I have realized that no matter how hard I try, my secret will come out."

"I am truly thankful for my new friend that I call brother. He has a huge heart, and from what I've seen, the Class of Commons in the Trade Kingdom respects and adores him. The last few days have taught me that nobody goes without notice in this town. You people are also the most accepting class when acceptance is least deserved. You also accept my friendship when other classes look upon it as unnatural or unbecoming of a prince like me. Thank you all for accepting me and for accepting my friendship with this person without judgment. I'd also like to thank you, Rodin of Millington, for accepting me into your brotherhood and allowing me to see the Class of Commons from the inside."

"Hear, hear!" the Overseer cries.

The room echoes back and gives an astonished Rodin a standing ovation. When the crowd calms down, the Overseer announces to Prince Byron, "Understand, Your Majesty, we know what would come if anyone learns of your friendship with a member of our Class. That is why it is a secret kept to ourselves that isn't even discussed with one another. We love and respect you, Your Majesty. The lords need not know what they haven't been told already."

"Thank you, Overseer. Thank you all."

They begin with business. The meeting goes on for hours. They recall the previous meeting's discussions and speak on those discussions still left open. Rodin begins to nod as the recounts begin to drag on for what seems like hours. When they call to close the accounts, they begin the new topics. A few of the group leaders from the other villages discuss their impeding needs. The Overseer hears the remarks, others offer to overcome their remarks in some way, and the Mediator accepts both sides to the agreement.

Soon the questions come forth, "What are we doing to protect our villages?" and, "How are we to provide for the services that the knights and their soldiers provide?"

Rodin, now fully awake, stands to reply, "Sir Galla himself has made my farm his command post. If each village would like, you may follow me home to barter with him an agreement. Fortunately, he may not require much since I have already offered him so much from myself. I'm sure if the Mediator would understand our urgency of the matter, he may follow us to mediate such discussions that can take place in Sir Galla's headquarters." Rodin looks at Byron.

Helana smiles at Rodin and whispers something to Byron. Byron nods and announces, "This will be acceptable! I will be there after this meeting is adjourned. What say you, Nigel of Brickmeyer?"

The man who has raised the question stands and faces the Mediator, "Mediator, I accept."

The Overseer addresses the congregation, "The Mediator and Nigel of Brickmeyer have accepted Master Rodin's terms for a resolution. Does anyone object?" The room is silent. "All in favor say 'Aye'!"

The room responds, "Aye!"

The Overseer proclaims, "It is done! After the conclusion of this Commons Council, if you would like to barter terms for the protection of your respected villages, please follow Master Rodin to see Sir Galla." He bangs the gavel, "Next order!"

Lady Suzette stands, "In keeping with everyone's time, I move that we discuss the topic that is most important, the choosing of Commons Leader of Trade Kingdom for the League Gathering in a few weeks!"

The room grumbles their agreement to the new topic. Rodin slumps down. He doesn't want to be chosen. As a matter of fact, he doesn't even want to be at the gathering. He wants to plan his wedding with Millette and move on with his life. *Why can't I just live my life my way? Just me and Millette? I let everyone have access to my land. Why can't I get married, make babies, and die of old age without doing this?*

Rodin sighs with his head between his knees while Lady Suzette rubs her nails on his back.

Why me?

The Overseer bangs his gavel, "We hear your request, Lady Suzette of Millington. Do we have a second on this notion?"

Many hands go up, "I second!" two people respond at once.

"Then we call to order the leaders of each village to stand. Nigel, for whom do you cast your vote?"

"Rodin of Millington, Overseer!" Nigel calls.

"Rodin of Millington, you have been nominated. For whom do you cast your vote?"

Rodin stands and quickly cries, "Stewart of Alding!"

The congregation grumbles at him. Some call Rodin's name. The Overseer bangs his gavel.

"That is a vote for you, Master Stewart of Alding. What say you?"

A man in the front row dressed in clothing more fitting of a lord than a peasant stands, brushes his hair to the side away from his eyes, and answers as he turns to face Rodin, "Overseer, I'd like us to go ahead and call the vote. Master Rodin of Millington."

The Overseer addresses the mediator, "A call to the vote has been made. Needless to say, Master Rodin has been granted the majority lot of the votes. Mediator, do you accept our vote?"

Byron stands, "I have heard two votes cast for Master Rodin of Millington and one vote, voiced by Master Rodin himself, for Master Stewart. Before I accept the terms and approve the lot, are there any other nominations?" Byron pauses and waits. He looks at Rodin with a smile and winks. When no other names are called out, he laughs. "I have been to too many lords meetings. In a meeting of five lords, my father and I would hear over thirty names and eighty disapprovals!" the crowd laughs, "Now, I hear two names, and one of the people nominated is trying to cast a lot for someone else! What kind of blessings has the Light given me today?" everyone laughs and claps at Byron's point, "I hereby accept this congregation's majority nomination with overwhelming joy and refreshing pride. Congratulations, Master Rodin of Millington! You are hereby Common's Leader!"

The congregation stands and cheers for their nomination. Rodin stands in outrageous disbelief. He shakes his head and stares at Byron and Helana. Lady Suzette pats his back and hugs him. She places a kiss on his cheek and ushers him to the front of the congregation. He faces Helana and pleads to her with his expressions, hoping she'll get the picture and make someone change their mind. Byron leans into Helana and whispers into her ear. She grins and brings the sleeve of her robe over her mouth.

The Overseer slams his gavel as hard as he can onto the sound block, and everyone quiets down. He chuckles, amused at the congregation, "I haven't acknowledged our vote yet." Everyone else laughs with him, "By the authority vested in me as Overseer of the congregation of the Class of Commons of Trade Kingdom, I hereby accept the nomination of Rodin of Millington and pronounce him Common's Leader for our kingdom. Master Rodin, you will be just fine!"

"Speech!" people cry.

Without warning, Rodin's mouth begins to move, and words flow from him. *What the hell? Helana!* "Thank you, everyone! It is true that I have been very reluctant to accept this nomination, but I feel that I will do my best to represent you all in a positive and intelligent manner." He eyes her and squints angrily at her as she continues to control him, "I love this kingdom. I love my village. You people are my family as well as Byron." Byron elbows her, and she wheezes, making Rodin's voice wheeze as well, "I mean Prince Byron. I will humbly do my duty to represent each and every one of you. Thank you for your confidence in me. All of you!"

The crowd laughs and cheers. They all know the real "Rodin" behind the making of that speech.

Rodin gives up and gives the Common's Bow as his thanks to everyone.

After the meeting, Rodin saddles his horse as he speaks with a few of the leaders about following him to meet Sir Galla. Some need reassurance that Sir Galla is genuinely concerned for their villages' safety and not just for the lordships in the area. Sir Galla is certain that it has only been the villages being targeted by the invading trolls. Byron and Helana appear in the doorway and join their group. The crowd bows and accepts them to join them. As they all talk and trot into the center of town, they notice the sudden quiet in the center.

"Lord Vil has been released today!" Lady Suzette exclaims.

They all look at the stockade. Lord Vil is no longer locked into the blocks. The fountain has been turned down to a quiet trickle.

Rodin grumbles his disapproval, "I guess I better be ready for my punishment outside the school soon."

"*Peasant!*"

VIII

D *ammit!*

"Stop right there!" Everyone turns their attention to Lord Vil, "You can all leave! Your trashy leader can stay!" Everyone gasps as they spread out, revealing their leader in the middle.

Vil's face turns white as Prince Byron smiles at him casually, "You know, Lord Vil, you must really love that stockade," he calls out at the top of his lungs. *"Guards!"*

Three men appear seemingly out of nowhere. They draw their swords and gather to their prince, "Yes, Your Highness?" they respond.

Prince Byron points at Lord Vil, "Which of you witnessed what this man did?"

"I did, Sire!" a soldier in leather armor steps forward, "I alerted another guard to retrieve a Knight already, sire!" The man bows to him.

"What's your name, Master?" Prince Byron asks.

The man holds his bow, "Master Theodore, sire."

"Master Theodore, what exactly did he call me?"

Vil yells at him, "I didn't call you anything! Now you're acting like a damn fool!"

Again the crowd gasps. Rodin says to Helana, "Did that moron just call the Prince a fool?"

Helana laughs, "Sounded like that to me." She turns to the guard, "As the Apprentice Adviser to the Throne and new to the traditions in this town, I must ask you, Master Theodore, what you and your staff would do about it."

Master Theodore draws his sword. The other two guards stand with him and face Lord Vil, "Lord Vil, you are hereby under arrest for publicly insulting the crown!"

Lord Vil stands erect and begins to sweat as all the blood leaves his face entirely, "Oh shit," a puddle forms around him, and the front of his pants turns darker when wet.

"Make way!" a voice cries out, "Lord Vil, I am here to formally take you in!"

A Knight rides in on an all-black horse. His armor is brilliantly polished. A lightning bolt from a sun is etched into the shoulder shield of the armor, "Prince Byron, I am Sir Matthew. If you would allow me, I will escort him to the castle for his punishment."

"No, actually, take him to his father. Explain to him what has happened." Prince Byron points to Master Theodore, "Take Master Theodore as my witness."

Sir Matthew bows and motions for Master Theodore to apprehend Lord Vil and follow him, "I will do just that. Lord Norel will not be pleased to hear that his own son has insulted the crown. He might lock you up himself. With those nasty pants on you too. Do you know you stink, Lord Vil?"

Insulted, Lord Vil tries to recompose himself, "How dare you!"

Sir Matthew laughs, "How dare I?" He looks around at his men, laughing, "Indeed!"

Lord Vil reaches behind his back to grab his short sword, but Master Theodore is quicker, "I don't think so, prisoner. That will be enough!" Lord Vil is shocked at how quick the soldier's movements are. He struggles against him to fight for it back but is unable to best him. Lord Vil spits at him—rather, he tries and fails miserably. He manages to make the spit dribble down the front of his shirt.

Everyone laughs, and Sir Matthew asks, "What the hell was that?" He shakes his head and waves them away. He turns to Prince Byron's group, "Sire, I shall handle it from here. Sorry for this idiot's attitude."

Lord Vil hisses, "Idiot?"

Byron laughs, "It's okay, Sir Matthew. Take care of it then reward your men accordingly for me."

Sir Matthew smiles and bows, "Will do, Your Highness." He turns and leads Master Theodore with Lord Vil in tow out of town on the northern road.

Rodin comments quietly, "I guess he was released too soon." He turns and looks up at Byron, "Slender would have loved to see that."

Byron chuckles and whispers to Rodin, "I hope he tries to go to the academy grounds tomorrow."

Rodin chuckles at the thought, "Oh yeah!"

Helana moves ahead, "Let's get moving, Sire. We don't want to keep everyone too late."

The group moves on, following her and talking about the events of today. Rodin suddenly remembers those events and lowers his head. He is not prepared to take on these responsibilities. He doesn't even want them. Much like the responsibility of caring for his land, home, and brother, all this is just thrown at him without warning. He should have known this is going to be a bad day. *One thing is for sure, seeing Vil get arrested, again, does make it all a little easier.* He smiles at the thought. Luckily, he can remain in his thoughts without anyone noticing. The leaders of each village have been talking Byron's ears off. It makes him smile more knowing that, on the inside, Byron is not interested in speaking about political affairs with anyone.

Helana trots up beside him, "They are just enamored by him."

Rodin smiles, "It is because he is actually talking *to* them and not *at* them."

She looks at him, "Why didn't you want to represent your class at the gathering?"

Rodin sighs, "I just don't want the attention. I just want to live in peace without worrying about whether or not I'm making decisions that impact us in a good or bad way. I'm not a politician like my father."

"Everyone obviously thinks highly of you. Including Byron. As I said before, my dad does too. Just take it slow. You'll be great." Helana digs her heel into Shade's side, and he gallops forward to catch up to the group.

Rodin shakes his head and stares at the back of Thornrose's neck. He is left to his own thoughts again. *Well, I hope someone tells that idiot Vil to watch out. If he keeps trying to start fights with me, he's just going to keep ending up in the stockade now that I am Common's Leader.* Rodin smiles, looks up, and makes Thornrose catch up quickly.

Trash Leader now, eh, Trash? Well, aren't you special! I don't care. I will still kill you. You can make that fatso king piggy, and I'll still gut him just to hear him squeal.

Prince Herring, I'm tired of you mingling with Trash and all his trashy friends. I think I will kill you soon.

How soon, you ask? Very soon. And I hope that beauty with you is there too! I want to devour her! She's so beautiful.

She's begging me to devour her. I'm coming for you, Beauty!

Oh! I just thought about something. I can make Piggy squeal as I devour Beauty and you cry in anguish over Trash's dead body with his trashy woman and trashy brother! Oh, what fun! Soon, Prince Herring! Yes, very soon!

They all arrive at Rodin's farm. As soon as they all reach the house, Sir Galla steps down from Rodin's front porch. He greets them all with open arms and bows to Byron. Some of the village leaders are shocked to hear that what Rodin has told them is true. The equipment that was inside the shack has been neatly laid outside and covered to protect it. Somehow, a woodstove was brought in, and the shack is accommodated with a chimney. The shack is now a working headquarters in such a short time. Even Rodin is amazed. He looks back to the trees that lead to the clearing and sees smoke rising above the treetops, proving that the other soldiers and knights have already made camp. They are gone for just half the day. These men obviously know how to prepare for anything at astonishing speed.

Sir Galla says to them, "I see Master Rodin has invited everyone to meet with me about the arrangements he's made on your behalf."

Master Stewart looks at him, "So Master Rodin was doing his job as Common's Leader before he was chosen." Everyone nods their heads in agreement.

"Common's Leader? Master Rodin, I am honored to be at your service, my lord."

Rodin jumps back, "I'm no lord!"

Sir Galla smiles, and Byron speaks up, "In the League Gathering, you words are more valuable to the kings than that of any knight or lord. You represent the Class of Commons. You are the people of the League of Humans, my brother. No matter how poorly any lord may speak of the Class of Peasants, they do not represent the Class of Commons. As a matter of fact, in our kingdom, you are not labeled Class of Peasants. You're labeled Class of Commons and are held in respect, which, as future King, I am working toward helping remodel in other kingdoms. My father has taught me to be that King."

Even Master Stewart is surprised to hear this. Master Durestes bows to Byron, "May the Light grant you knowledge to guide you in your quest, Your Highness."

Master Nigel clears his throat and interrupts, "I hope you can change the minds of future lords, such as the nasty one we met in the town square. What was his name, Lord Vil? Nasty child. His father deserves a stern talking to."

Byron interjects, "His mother, actually. His father plans to help me in bringing about change."

"Then may the Circle of Light guide him to bringing about change in his son as well."

Master Durestes looks at Sir Galla with a smile, "Sir Galla, my friend, looks to me like we are seeing the young do what we set out to do in our youths. May the Light bless us all with mindful young minds such as these."

Sir Galla nods and laughs, "Indeed!" He swings an arm over Master Durestes's shoulder, "Come! Let's talk about our dealings with these trolls."

Byron looks at Rodin and smiles, "Sir Galla," he calls to him.

Sir Galla pauses, "Yes, Your Highness?"

"I am going to take Common's Leader Rodin, Master Slindee, as well as Lady Helana and Master Logan with me to see Wizard Dahlmür at my palace. Please conduct your meeting without us. We are confident they will accept your terms made with the Common's Leader."

"Aye, Sire." Everyone bows their respects and bids them farewell as they go to Sir Galla's headquarters.

"Go get our brothers while Helana and I speak, brother."

Rodin stands still for a moment, "On one condition. Will there be food?"

"And wine, not mead."

Amazed, Rodin whispers, "Wine," and a smile crosses his face. He takes off for the house, yelling for Logan and Slender, "We're going to the palace! Let's go!"

Slender is the first to go out, "Oh, I've been dying to go to the Trade Palace! Will there be food?"

Rodin says, "And wine!"

Logan breaks out, "I don't want wine, but I'll eat the food!" He stops and looks at Rodin excitedly, "Oh, Rodin! Look! Master Coleman came by and made his trade. You have boots!" He points to a pair of boots on the porch, and Rodin is quick to put them on. Logan takes off from the porch, "Watch this, Rodin!"

Rodin laces his new boots as he watches Logan. Logan takes a runner's stance and is suddenly gone. A trail of dust rises, leading to the end of the path that leads to the road. Rodin freezes in awe. Logan waves then bends at the knees. Suddenly, he is high in the air and landing in front of the house, all smiles. Rodin jumps up and meets him in disbelief.

"Took me a little bit to figure out how to control my jumps," Logan explains, "Let's see what yours can do!"

Rodin runs, but nothing happens. He jumps but barely makes it a few feet from the ground. *Maybe if I stomp the ground?* He stomps. Nothing. He puts his arms up in surrender.

"I'm sorry, Rodin," Logan says with disappointment.

Slender says to him, "Yeah, I was really hoping for something myself. But you have a bearskin coat!" he reminds him about it.

"Oh yeah!" Rodin rushes over to grab the larger of the two coats thrown over the porch railing. He puts it on and throws up the leather hood, "Well, I guess we'll see if maybe it's a protection of some kind." He turns to them and sees them looking all around him in wonder, "What?"

Byron and Helana walk up, and Helana says, "Go let lover boy know we're ready."

Byron searches around, "Where did he run off to?"

Logan and Slender point at the porch. They look at the house, and Byron asks, "What's he doing inside?"

Slender responds, "He's not."

Rodin realizes what is going on. *I'm invisible!* He sneaks behind Helana and smacks her behind. Then he smacks Byron's as well.

"Hey!" they shout as they jump in surprise and rub their behinds.

Rodin laughs and drops the hood. Everyone looks at him and laughs. Rodin says to them, "Master Coleman so got his payment."

Helana, not amused, punches his shoulder, "Touch my ass again, lover boy, and I will tell your future wife."

Byron looks at Rodin, "Whoopsy!"

Slender retrieves his horse, and Logan jumps onto Thornrose with Rodin. They make their way to the road. Once on the road, they head north to Trade City, where the palace lies.

IX

A fter a few hours' travel, the sun is setting, and they reach the city. Because of the lack of light from the setting sun, there's really no view of the castle. They can see the silhouette of the walls and the shadows of the towers as well as lights from the main castle house windows from the firelights within. Logan is barely able to contain his excitement as they draw closer. As a matter of fact, he begs Rodin to stop so he can relieve some of his excitement in the nearby brush.

As they ride closer to the castle's bridge, Rodin makes out the silhouettes of two guards at the gate. He looks behind himself at Logan and smiles. Logan looks at him in question, "What?"

Rodin whispers as he pulls back behind the rest of the group as he shushes Logan, "Just sit there. Let your arms go and don't act like anything is out of the ordinary." Rodin throws on his hood and instantly vanishes.

Logan chuckles, "Oh man, they're going to be astroniksed to see this."

"It's *astonished.* Now just be quiet and sit there."

As they pass over the bridge and through the main gate, the two men on guard welcome Byron and the others. When Logan enters, they stare in amazement as Rodin, still invisible, steers Thornrose into a twirl, backs up, twirls again, and then proceeds as Logan sits in the saddle without any hands on the reins. The two soldiers drop their spears with a loud *clang.* The others turn to see what's going on. Helana shakes her head. Byron and Slender stifle a laugh. Thornrose speeds up to catch them.

"That's hilarious, brother," Slender tells the invisible Rodin.

Byron leans toward Rodin's place in the saddle, "Those two will never look at Logan or your horse as normal again."

Helana rides past and snickers, "I can't believe they fell for that."

Rodin decides to keep up the charade. They continue riding in through the city. There are more markets and inns than he thinks he's ever seen in his town. Prince Byron explains that this area is actually called the Trade Commons. "The Class of Commons has decided to live and earn their living within the city walls. Most of them don't know that they get a majority of their supplies from you or the town," Byron explains.

Rodin lowers his hood and looks around. People quietly move about in the evening, closing down markets, pulling their carts, and extinguishing their torches that light the outside of their shops— some doubling as homes. The loudest voices come from the nearby inn. Rodin has heard of the city inns. "They are the city brothels as well," he remembers hearing someone at the school saying. He doesn't understand what goes on inside. His mind pictures women running naked around the inside of the inn while drunken men chase them down. He pictures orgies and sex splayed throughout the inn. Curious and at the same time repulsed by this, Rodin steers Thornrose in the direction of the inn, intending to get a peek inside. He tries to redirect Thornrose in a way that makes his direction seem natural and not intentional. He doesn't want his friends or Logan to know what it is he's trying to do.

As soon as he's in view, he cranes his neck to get a look inside. He sees a table with men sitting and playing cards. Money lies in the center of the table, and the man facing the entryway seems to be winning. A woman with huge breasts and dressed in a scanty dress with knit sleeves hangs on him while blowing onto his neck and playing with the curls in her long black hair. The man seems to be concentrating more on the cards than the woman's bosoms, which seems to Rodin are about ready to spill out of her dress. The man grabs a mug and pours the contents down his throat as he lays his cards faceup to the other three men in front of him. The men throw down their cards and start screaming. One man stands screaming and cursing as he throws his chair to the side, trying to intimidate the man who won.

The winner calmly sits and watches the man throw a tantrum and motions with his hand for the loser to hand over his winnings. The one throwing the tantrum instead spits on his lap. The woman is obviously disgusted by the scene and begins to yell at him for his disgusting habits. The winner sits emotionless and motions for his winnings again. The sore loser pulls a short sword.

From Rodin's vantage, he can see the man who won calmly place his hand under the table and pull a miniature crossbow loaded with a deadly dart from the side of his leg. Again he motions for his winnings. The man screams more obscenities and throws the table over, causing the other two cardplayers to scatter and curse at him. The sore loser rushes at him, and the woman screams and jumps away.

The winner suddenly points the crossbow and fires. The sore loser falls back and lands faceup, a wooden dart sticking out of one of his eyes.

Logan is fascinated, "Wow! Did you see that guy? He was so awesome! He just sat there and waited without moving. He didn't even falink when that guy pulled his sword at him!"

Rodin corrects him, "*Flinch*, and yes, it served the bastard right for being such a sore loser."

Logan sits up, and Rodin moves along, "That was a damn good shot. Rodin, do you think I could ever be that good of a shot? I know Dad was a good shot, but not like that."

Rodin shrugs and speeds up to catch with the group, "As long as you practice. You have to be patient and learn how to use that kind of weapon with a steady hand. That guy practiced really hard to be that perfect. If he hadn't, he could have just as easily killed someone else by accident, and the other guy would have killed him for sure."

"Then I guess I better practice, then. Hey, what kind of weapon was that anyway? A crossdoe? A croftdoe? Bowfin?"

"*Crossbow*," Rodin replies, "Where the heck . . . bowfin?"

"Sorry. I didn't know," Logan mumbles.

Rodin catches up to everyone. Helana and Slender look back at them, smiling. Byron glances back with the same smile. Logan asks Rodin, "What's up with them?"

Rodin shrugs, "Ahdontkno."

Byron speaks up, "Are the local brothels your thing now, brothers?"

Logan speaks out, "No. This guy won at cards. This other guy got mad and pulled a sword at him like, 'I'm not paying!' And the guy just looked at him and stuck his hand out real cool like, 'My money.' And the other guy was all, 'Bullshit! I'll kill you!' And the other guy was just sitting there like, 'I don't think so.' And the lady with him was like, 'Ah! He's got a sword!' The man was all, 'So?' And *thunk!* Shot him right in the eye with this tiny bowfi—I mean crossbow! And the guy fell back and landed faceup with a small dart sticking out of his eye!" Logan breathes, "It was so cool."

Slender shakes his head in disbelief, "You should really learn how to slow down when you talk. You give me a headache just trying to keep up."

Helana laughs.

Rodin chuckles, "S'okay, little brother."

They continue onward to a huge horse barn. Two guards stand at the entrance. They bow to Prince Byron and recognize Lady Helana. Byron introduces Master Slindee, Master Logan, and Common's Leader Rodin. They each recognize and bow to Rodin. He awkwardly makes a Common's Bow back to them, knocking his head between the ears of Thornrose, who grunts in reaction. He isn't used to the sudden recognition of Common's Leader just yet, he explains to them as he rubs his head then rubs Thornrose.

Several men and a small woman run up to them and offer to take their horses into the stables for them. Byron hands the reins down to one man who praises Prince Byron for allowing him to do such a job. Prince Byron hands a silver coin to each person that accepts the reins from each of them. The woman curtsies, and the men give the Common's Bow. Rodin returns the Common's Bow to them. They immediately recognize the new Common's Leader and offer their congratulations to him. The woman looks at him in anxiety and pulls him to the side. Rodin follows and questions her.

She looks in Slender's direction and whispers, "Can we speak in private, my lord?"

Rodin acknowledges, "Yes, but please don't call me lord. Master Rodin will do."

"Yes, Master. Please follow me out. I don't want to disturb the squire."

He looks at her, perplexed, and follows her out. Two of the men join them. They speak out, "Don't listen to her, my lord. She doesn't know what she's talking about, that one. She's loony, she is."

The young woman is disturbed by this and looks shamefully down at her feet. She timidly responds, "I should thin tha' Common's Leader should know wha' goes in Commons City. I thin he should know 'ow the knights are treatin' us."

The man that's spoken out puts a dirty finger to his lips, "You oughtn't speak like 'at bout 'em knights. 'Ey jus' followin' 'ey orders."

Rodin stops them, "Wait. I am the Common's Leader, and I am very good friends with Prince Byron. If something is wrong, then you tell me now. I won't go without knowledge of wrongdoings among us Commons."

The other man sweats and becomes nervous, "I don tink I cahhs for twubewl, Syah. I means, dese felluhs claim dayh's pwotetin' uhs, buh dayh's wohtin' coppahs we cain't payhs 'um."

The man's broken gibberish makes Rodin's head spin, "Who's taking your money? What are they protecting you from?"

The young woman responds, "The knight 'ere, Master. They want us to pay coppers we don have ever week. If'n we don, they trow us out the city. My father's shop was sold to ah other fella from the harbor town cause 'nee couldn't pay they fee. They say it a new tax that everyone's 'quired to pay to the city guards."

Byron, Slender, and Helana step out. Slender addresses them, "Pardon me, Masters and Lady. What tax is this? In the Class of Knights, there is no tax for our services. We Knights offer our service out of our own free will. Our nobility holds this in the highest regard. I promise this is not something sanctioned by Sir Galla."

Byron bows to them, "As prince of this kingdom and ruler of this city, I beg you to tell me who these unworthy knights are."

The young woman pleads, "Please, Sire. If Lord Rodin of Millington, Common's Leader, says to trust you, then I will tell, as long as my father isn't made patsy by these persons."

The man who speaks the better of the two asks, "Will you please not name us, my lord?"

The other man begs, "Pwease, Syah! I got chiwdwen tah feed."

Byron nods, "Agreed. And, my lady, your father will get his shop back. Plus some."

The woman jumps for joy, "Yes, Sire. It's Sir Gawlton, Your Highness. He and his four followers."

Slender shakes his head shamefully at his feet, "I hate that he has done this to you. My deepest regrets, lady and sirs."

Helana pulls up her staff and whispers into it. She slams the ground. *Snap! Snap! Snap!* Green clouds form in front of them. Byron says in fascination, "Just like her father."

Five men, drunk and slobbering, appear from the clouds. They look around in confusion, their hands holding mugs that aren't there anymore. The biggest of them drools and squints at the woman, "Hey, Fannie, what the hell are you doing here? I thought I kicked your family's asses outside the gates last week? Get out! Or I'll run you through with my sword!"

The other four draw their swords at everyone. A man in a black leather outfit screams, "Nobody movesh! You're all going to be drone out of thish shitty by your ashesh!"

Slender pulls Chill, "By order of Prince Byron, lay down your weapons!"

Sir Gawlton laughs, "Yeah, bullshite! Prince Byron isn't ordering me to do shite! Squire, quit being a fool and take this for your payment in advance," he tosses a small pouch to Slender and tells him, "I order you to take that sword and run those two men through. Then take that harlot there, have your way with her, then dump her naked filthy arse outside the walls and into the moat."

Byron steps in front of the men, "I'll tell you what I'll do, you morons," he states.

"Moronsh? Do jou hear what that ash jush call ush? I'm gonna shlishe hish froat!" The drunkest soldier points his sword towards Byron and runs at him as best and as straight as he can. An arrow pierces his arm, and the man drops his sword and falls to his knees, looking at the arrow in confusion, "Ow! Shomebody shot me!"

They all turn to see Logan with another arrow notched and drawn, waiting to release. He swings his aim across each man and says, "Anybody care to limp? You've threatened the Prince. You've disgraced the Class of Knights. And you have treated the Class of Commons poorly as well as embazzizzled money with false taxes."

Rodin corrects him, "*Embezzled.*"

Byron holds up a hand to Logan, "Drop your swords and remove your Knight's Badge. You five are hereby discharged from the Class of Knights."

Sir Gawlton drunkenly laughs, "I will arrest you for impersonating the prince! You're under arrest!" He raises his sword toward Prince Byron.

Snap! Snap! Snap! Everyone turns and sees Dahlmür standing behind the drunkards. He raises his staff and yells at them, "Insults to the crown will not be tolerated! Stealing from the Commons with fake taxes is a crime against Trade Kingdom! Your Prince has handed you a sentence!" A flame rises from the stone of his cane as the white quartz turns bright orange, "Kneel before the crown!"

The men suddenly sober up and realize the person they have been insulting really is Prince Byron. They fall to their knees. The injured man continues to hold his arm, trying to steady the arrow. They plea for their Prince to forgive them. They apologize to Fannie, asking for her forgiveness. The Commons man with the

horrible speech impediment runs to one of the men beside Sir
Gawlton and kicks him square on his protruding jaw. The man's
eyes roll back, and he falls backward, unconscious. Everyone looks
at the man, impressed with his efficiency at knocking the man out
with one blow. Fannie spits at Sir Gawlton.

Helana speaks out with her staff held up, "Your punishment is
banishment. In your banishment comes disgrace!" Her blue stone
turns a pale red. She forms a shape in the air and continues, "You
will be marked! The mark of your disgrace will be recognized
everywhere you go. Nobody will recognize any titles to you.
Nobody will want to be seen with you."

The men scream in pain and hold their hands to their necks.
The smoke rises between their fingers, and the smell of burning
flesh fills the air. When they remove their hands, a naught symbol
is burned into their skin, permanently disgracing them.

Slender looks at Gawlton, "Gawlton! Remove your armor!
Remove your Knight's Medallion! All of you!" Slender raises Chill
at them, and frost flows into the men's direction from its tip,
"Now!"

Rodin and Logan whisper to each other. Logan points to their
fellow Commons. At first, Rodin shakes his head then shrugs.
Wizard Dahlmür calls to him, "Lord Rodin, as leader of the Class
of Commons what is your punishment?"

Rodin replies, "If it pleases you, Dahlmür, sir, relieve these
men of their burdens."

Byron looks at him, puzzled, "What?"

"Their purses look extremely heavy, brother. Logan was
pointing out how big they are, and I agreed. Come to think of it, I
really don't think they can handle the load of any of the coins they
keep within their own barracks. Please show them pity and allow
these three to take on their burdens and redistribute them to those
that gave it all to them. And for their hard work, I think Fannie and
her friends here deserve an extra few coins themselves."

Wizard Dahlmür smiles at Rodin in agreement with his point,
"Yes, my lord, it is done." He smashes his staff to the ground, and
pouches of copper, silver, and gold lie before them. He remarks,
"My, that is such a heavy burden to carry. Thank you, Lady Fannie.
Gentlemen."

Wide eyes of joy and smiles shine across their faces, "Thanks,
my lord, we'll take care of this right away! The people will be

overjoyed!" Fannie cries. They grab all the pouches and immediately run out to distribute their newfound wealth.

The four men help remove the unconscious man's armor and pendant. They create a pile of their belongings between them. "Swords!" Slender cries, and with horror, they throw their swords into the pile. Their shame flows as tears in some of their faces.

Prince Byron circles them and kicks dirt at them, "Feeling lower than a peasant now aren't you?"

Each man whimpers, "Yes, Your Highness."

Byron bends down and looks at Gawlton, "What made you think that you would get away with this? Especially since I have been working so hard to earn the trust of my people while my father is away. I am ruler in his absence. I make the laws! What made you think I would not find out? I walk among these people every day! I attend the academy where many Commons are employed. Including the Common's Leader! You disgust me! Get out of my kingdom! Stay away from Trade Common's villages! If any knight, soldier, lord, or commons catches you within the limits of Trade Kingdom, I will have your heads! Do I make myself clear?"

The men almost break into crying, "Yes, Sire!"

"Go! Now!" Byron stands and draws his sword at them. The men get up and run, dragging their unconscious comrade with them.

With a satisfied look, Byron turns to Dahlmür, "Remind me to have their faces posted among the villages and towns in the morning. And post them in the Knights' barracks as well as the soldiers'. Please, Master Dahlmür."

Dahlmür bows, "Certainly, Master Byron."

Slender asks, "How did you know something was going on?"

Helana walks up, "I called him."

Rodin points out, "You know. The three taps on the ground?"

Slender responds, "Oh, yeah."

Logan smiles at all of them and says to Rodin, "Big Brother, I think I like your new friends. You guys have the best fun."

Rodin says to Byron, "Were we having fun?"

Byron shrugs, "That arrow shot was pretty cool."

Slender says, "Oh, yeah! You can really shoot!"

Logan acts as if it were no big deal, "That shot was nothing."

Dahlmür says to Helana, "That mark idea was rather remarkable. I'm proud of you, Lana, for doing it well."

She smiles, "Thank you, Father."

He changes the subject, "That Logan boy can teach these archers a thing or two about shooting."

Logan grunts, "Did he just call me 'Logan boy?'"

Helana agrees, "I think it can be arranged. Make it more of an accident so they can keep their pride."

Rodin perks up at this, turns, and points a finger at Helana, "No."

Logan jumps in excitement, "When? Yeah! I'll do it! Come on! I can intructicate them!"

Rodin corrects him, "*Instruct*. And no!"

"Awe, man!" Logan kicks up dirt and stones.

Helana waits until Rodin's back is turned then whispers to Logan, "Gimme a couple of days."

Without turning around, Rodin yells, "I heard that! No!"

Slender and Byron place their arms over his shoulders and laugh.

Dahlmür pauses to see how really close the three of them have become over a matter of a few days. He admires how they can bring out the best of one another without trying. What bothers him most is how their friendship will hold when the gift is given to either Master Slindee or Master Rodin. Master Byron can't be the one chosen because it is he that has created their circle with his blood. Master Byron doesn't realize that he has been prophesied as being the one who must create the circle to have the one most worthy to receive the Light's gift. Dahlmür hopes that in return, its being passed to one and not the other doesn't ruin their brotherhood. He couldn't stand seeing another brotherhood broken because of it again. This brotherhood has so much more going for them. They have truly accepted one another. No class. No titles. Just one another. But Rodin does seem to draw their attention without intent. Rodin is truly the center of their circle. Does that mean he's the one that is worthy?

Helana interrupts Dahlmür's thoughts, "Who do you think it is?"

Dahlmür's turns to her in disappointment, "I don't know. The two of them are just so worthy enough to me. Slindee is a fabulous warrior. Brave. Honorable. He's also very kind. He loves everyone. He loves Byron and Rodin even more. He treats Logan as his own little brother. He fights to protect the people he loves."

"And Rodin?"

Dahlmür shakes his head in amusement, "He is the most *peculiar* boy I've ever met. He cares for everyone—except Vil, of course. But there is something about him that makes me wonder why he's been blessed into this circle of brotherhood. I can't understand it. He wants nothing to do with glory and recognition. He just wants to be the best husband and brother. He wants to provide for everyone and wants no reward for it. He's perfectly happy to receive his fair share, but everyone keeps giving him the rewards and recognitions."

"Have you seen how he reacts when he's recognized?" Helana says, "He was named Common's Leader and absolutely refused it. He didn't want it, but everyone gave it to him anyway. And without hesitation, he has already done so much just because he would have done it without the title anyway. It's as if they know. They know he is meant for greatness."

Logan interrupts them unexpectedly, "Master, my brother is great. The Common's Prophecy says that 'the natural-born son of the new village where this prophecy is found will be chosen for a gift most precious. He will be the last to receive this gift and will live forever from it. He will form a large circle of brotherhood for himself, and they will be his army to be with him for as long as he lives.' Our village is not that old, Master Dahlmür. My father found the scrolls in a small cave on the other side of the river on our land the year after Rodin was born. He took those scrolls to the Common's Council, and they saw the scrolls for themselves. These scrolls were examined by secret societies and wizards to determine whether or not the prophecy in them was genuine. After the troll invasion, as the scrolls also foretold, they found the prophecy to be genuine, hid the scrolls away, and decided that it would be kept secret even from our villagers so Rodin will not find out. They will let the Light guide him.

"Look at him, Master. He has no clue. I only know because my father has given me this knowledge over and over before the trolls took him. He told me to make his life simple for as long as I can because eternity will make his life complex and, oftentimes, painful. I saw my father again last night. He said, 'The time has come. Rodin will now fulfill his destiny given by the Circle of Light.' When I awoke, I saw the blessings the Light had given to the three of them as it had blessed me at the same time. He is my big brother. The other two are also now my brothers through their blood oath. They may not know that I am within their Circle of

Brotherhood by the Light's blessings last night, but that doesn't mean I don't love them and won't do for them as I have done for my own brother." He looks at Helana and smiles, "And I won't tell Byron that you think he's cute."

Dahlmür pauses and looks at his startled daughter, "You think Master Byron is . . . eh . . . eh . . . eh . . . cute?"

"What? No! Well . . . maybe a little . . . but . . . he's Prince Byron and I'm—"

Dahlmür looks at her sternly, "Indeed."

Logan laughs and sticks his tongue out at her. She starts after him, and he takes off, leaving a trail of dust behind.

Helana looks at her father with a look of serious curiosity, "Do you think what he said is true?"

"I guess we're about to find out. We have Aranae's children summoning us," he points ahead.

X

odin, Byron, Slender, and Logan reach the front doors of the palace. The two soldiers standing guard snap to attention and recognize their prince. Prince Byron nods and greets them. He introduces Master Slindee and Common's Leader Rodin. The two men give Rodin the Common's Bow and welcome their lord as well as his brother, Master Logan. They turn to Master Slindee and salute the squire. One man offers congratulations on his upcoming coronation. The other man recognizes him and congratulates him as well.

When they are all satisfied with their welcomes and pleasant exchanges, they begin to enter the palace.

Dahlmür calls them, "My prince!" they all freeze and turn to him, "We have company. Our presence is required elsewhere." He points off into the shadows behind a set of well-trimmed hedges leading to the yard beside the palace.

They follow the path around the side in curiosity. Dahlmür has yet to tell them who it is they are meeting. They hear a sudden rustle in the trees, and Logan points up, "Mutt!"

Mutt greets them with a bark and jumps down on top of Logan, knocking him to the ground. Logan laughs and accepts his greeting as Mutt mocks, licking his face, panting, and barking while wagging his abdomen like the tail of a dog.

Rodin walks up and scratches Mutt on top of his head between his center medium eyes. He puts a hand out, "Slender, Byron, meet Mutt. I guess you've already met him, Dahlmür, sir, and I guess you have as well, Helana."

Dahlmür, Byron, and Helana look at one another guiltily. Dahlmür responds, "Yes, Master Rodin. We three have."

Slender looks at Mutt curiously, "I think I had too much to drink, but did I see two giant spiders last night? This is one of them that Logan was going on about. Right?"

Rodin nods, "Yes, and Biter was there with Mutt last night. Where they went after that is beyond me."

Byron clears his throat and looks at Mutt, "So you've accepted names for yourselves?" Mutt jumps off Logan and comes to Byron. It squeaks and grunts at him. Byron nods and says, "I've known their mother my whole life. They aren't giant spiders. They're young girachnids."

Slender, Rodin, and Logan freeze for a moment when they realize what he's just said. Rodin stares at Mutt. He examines him to see if he can spot the youth in Mutt's form. *Girachnids? They're huge! And this is a youngling? Oh, wow.* A sense of awe passes over Rodin's face as he walks up to Mutt and lays a hand on his head. Logan rubs his abdomen. Slender bends down and rubs one of his legs.

The thought of Mutt growing to be over sixteen feet tall is so inconceivable to them at the moment.

Logan smiles and hugs him.

They hear the approach of several horses. Mutt barks excitedly as the others draw their weapons. Dahlmür turns calmly. He looks as if he's expecting them. Biter runs around the corner, squealing and grunting at them. He trips and falls from instability. He is still trying to get used to seven legs instead of eight. Logan jumps up and runs to Biter, who greets him nonchalantly. Byron approaches him as Biter bows to him clumsily.

Logan introduces him, "This is Biter."

Biter runs up and pretends to nip at Byron. Byron smiles.

The men on horseback appear. Sir Galla, Master Lawrence, and Master Coleman greet them. Dahlmür approaches the men with open arms, "So, it is time, my brothers."

Coleman climbs down from his horse and embraces Dahlmür, "We are short one."

Dahlmür remembers, "Ah, yes. His father. Allow me."

Slender asks Sir Galla, "Time for what? What's going on, Sire?"

Just then, Helana steps between Rodin, Logan, Byron, and Slender with her arms out, and a green cloud forms in front of Dahlmür. Byron looks at her and motions at Dahlmür, "What's he doing? What's going on?"

Helana says nothing. She looks over her shoulders as she continues to keep them back. The green cloud grows thicker, and Byron's patience wears thin, "Tell me. Now!"

Rodin points at the cloud, telling Byron, "Look! He's summoning someone."

Byron looks in recognition of the boots and clothing and says in confusion, "Dad?"

King Vaniir appears as if he were expecting to be brought to this spot at this moment. He looks at the men and laughs, "Brothers!" They gather in an embrace.

Confused, Byron steps toward them. Immediately, Rodin, Logan, and Slender bow to their king. King Vaniir acknowledges them, "Oh, stop! It's just us. Stand! You are all welcome to drop the pleasantries around us alone," he points a finger at Logan, "Except you!"

Logan bows in surprise, "Yes, sire," he replies humbly.

King Vaniir lets out a boisterous laugh, "I'm kidding, boy! I welcome you all." He surveys the boys and stops at Byron. Then he looks at Biter and Mutt, "You two have names now? Good!" He looks at his son then to his feet and speaks softly to him, "I'm sorry, Byron, I never told you any of this. I'm sorry to all of you. The three of you have been given a blessing that will change your lives."

Logan steps forward and replies, "If it's the prophecy, Sire, I've kept them secret as I've been sworn to do by my father. I know of it. My name is Logan, Sire. This is my brother, Rodin. He doesn't know."

Rodin looks at him, surprised, "What prophecy? And how do you know the word *prophecy?*" With a scared look, he turns to Slender and Byron, "I don't know what's going on, but we need to go, brothers. Now." He starts to walk off, but he is stopped by Biter and Mutt.

Vaniir looks at Logan, "So you are the one who has been watching over the chosen? I was never told who it was. You also know the rest of that prophecy, then?"

Logan bows to Vaniir, "Your Highness, I am, and I want you to know that I am not ready for my role. I'm too young. My brother may have given me so much knowledge over the years, but I am still learning."

Rodin looks between them, "Too young for what? What is going on?" He begs Coleman, "Master Coleman, please tell us."

Lawrence walks up to Logan, "I was his age when we were first chosen then cursed." He turns to Dahlmür, "He is very much like me."

Slender asks Helana, "Will you tell us?" She shakes her head in silence.

Byron looks around at all of them, "Somebody? Please!"

Mutt and Biter squeak and walk away toward the back side of the palace. Vaniir points to them, "We have to go and see Aranae now, son."

They all follow the young girachnids. Helana and Dahlmür light up the darkness with their staffs as they all lead the boys to their answers.

Oh, look! King Herring is here! Everyone is here! Now I can kill you all before the gift is passed on to one of you. Which one of you is it? Who gets to be killed before they can be accepted by the Light? The despicable Light! My master will destroy the Light's world, and I will destroy the Light's chosen! I hope it's Piggy! It would be so much fun to skin a piggy chosen one. Ha ha ha!

I'm not worried about the trash being chosen. He is so filthy. His brother too. Oh, look, another trash! Oh, you are the old one, aren't you? Three trashes! I love killing trash. I'll kill you too, Old Trash! Ha ha ha!

I know! I'll kill the gift-giver! Yes! But I don't know where she is. I'll follow you. Yes. Lead me too her, spiders! As soon as you lead me to her, I will kill her!

Oh, a wizard? Beauty's father? Oh, this will be great! He can watch me devour Beauty as well. Then he can die with her. I am going to enjoy killing the supposed "most powerful wizard on Terra-Earth." I will laugh at you as you cry and watch me devour her, then I will kill you too.

Oh, a big piggy! Big piggy. Little piggy. All in a row. Who will squeal the loudest when I chop off your toe?

Ha ha ha! You're all here! This is fantastic! My master will be so proud of me. I will kill the gift-giver, the king, and

Prince Herring, Big Piggy, Little Piggy, Beauty, Not-so-Powerful Wizard, Old Trash, Little Trash, Trash, Baby Spider 1, and Baby Spider 2! And I don't know who you are yet, old man. I'll just call you Creepy. You look creepy. I'll just kill you for being so damn creepy.

Ha ha ha! I will kill you all!

They turn the corner while Byron asks his father, "I thought you said we were going to see Aranae? Why are we going this way?"

Vaniir shushes him, "Be patient, Byron. You'll see." He turns his attention to Logan, "Logan, I was told of the scrolls your father found. As a matter of fact, he and I read them together. He didn't tell me that it was his children that were prophesied. If I had known he even had children, I would have taken you into my home not long after the invasion. I guess he didn't want the prophecy to be affected by any action that could have altered the process. It could have had disastrous effects."

Logan nods and responds, "Yes, sire, I know. My father said the same thing."

Rodin grumbles at them, "We still want to know what the hell is going on, for the Light's sake!"

Slender growls, "That's just putting it lightly."

Logan asks quietly, "Sire, my brother and I would like to know what my father's name was. From where did he hail?"

Rodin does want to know. It is something that he has never been told. Nobody he's asked can tell him. He only knows him as Bale of Millington. His family name is never told. Their mother was only known as Colleen of Millington. He speeds up so he can hear Vaniir's answer.

King Vaniir is a billowy man. Jolly too. More so than Sir Galla. He laughs at them for their curiosity, "Your father founded Millington Village when he left Anglon. He was a very noble man with the belief that everyone should live the life of a commons. He worked to have the Class of Peasants be recognized as their former Class of Commons and bring honor back to its Class. Many men retired with him with the same ideals. He was a very knowledgeable man. Very brave for his convictions. I knew him because he had been a student under Master Lawrence's tutelage. Master Lawrence introduced us. He made his proposal of creating a village where everyone lives, learns, and thrives off one another within the kingdom. I saw his convictions and told him to choose an area and make it happen to the best of his abilities. And he did!" Vaniir laughs, "Wow, how fast it happened. Trade Kingdom became the most prosperous kingdom in all the League! Then one day, he came to me with the scrolls. As soon as I saw them, I told him to find people within the Commons Council, which he formed by the way, and have them help him hide them until the time was right. I guess the time is right, and Master Durestes will be turning them over to us soon.

"Anyway, during these times before his death, I did come to know his name. Your family name is Ganders. Bale Ganders, born in the Yawn Lordship. Your father was the second-born son to the Lord of Yawn in the Anglon Kingdom. He joined the royal army because he didn't want to have a life that was based on the Class of Lord's rules and lifestyle. He wanted to live the honorable life as the Class of Commons. Be very proud of your heritage, sons. It is the most honorable family name," he pats Rodin on the shoulder and pulls Logan into a tight embrace.

This is a lot of knowledge for Rodin to comprehend. *My father was a lord? He founded our village? He had it made! We could have been lords, but his sense of pride got him and my mother killed!* The thought of living in another kingdom as a member of the Class of Lords is unnerving to him. His father is stupid for choosing a life like this. *He should have considered how his children's lives were going to be affected. Of course, how could he have known? He never actually lived as a peasant. He was a lord! He ruled over his own territory. He didn't have to suffer the life of a peasant. Working day to day just to earn enough taxes to pay the lord of his land. And all the coins under the floor? That was what he could have used to take his family home to reclaim their places in the kingdom. I don't want commons honor! I want Logan and me to live as we were supposed to have lived! It was our destiny! He took that from us!*

Rodin can't stand it anymore, "Forget this! I don't care who is summoning us! I don't care how honorable my father's intentions were!"

Everyone stops and stares at him. Byron looks at him and asks, "Brother, what are you talking about?"

Rodin points at him, "Did you know?" Tears begin to run down his cheek, "Did you know all this that your father has just said about my family? I'm supposed to be lord! My brother too! We were supposed to be living the lives of the Class of Lords, but my father's stupid sense of nobility and pride got our mother and him killed, and we were left living and surviving as Class of Peasants! People sneer at us! They treat us like trash! They even call us trash! Look at Lord Vil! He's proof of this. My brother and I suffered humility and hard labor just to serve Lord Vil's lordship! What do we get for our blood, sweat, and tears? My mother is dead! My father is dead! Our names were lost! Our titles lost! Now all of a sudden, we are to fulfill some kind of prophecy? Did you know this? Tell me now, brother, because I cannot wait to hear this."

Slender steps toward Rodin calmly, "Rodin, please calm down."

Rodin screams at all of them, "Tell me now!"

Dahlmür begins to shuffle forward, "Master Rodin, you have no idea what is really going on. This prophecy is something that cannot be stopped any longer. Too much has already happened. Too much has already been fulfilled. We have to go—"

Logan yells, "No! I never wanted to be a part of any of this! I don't want to be the answer to a prophecy! I didn't ask to be a part of any of this! I don't want my brother to be a part of this either! I want my answer. I want it now, Prince Byron!"

Byron looks at his father, "No"—tears fill his eyes—"I didn't know. To hear it was painful for me also, brother. I don't know what's going on either. If it were up to me, I'd send us all home and plan how we could reclaim your lordship, but I am just as much a puppet as you are at the moment." Byron walks up to Rodin and embraces him, "Let us just face our puppet master and reclaim your lives afterward. I promise we will, brother. Slender will help. We're brothers through our oaths. That is what we do for one another no matter what everyone else wants us to do." Byron releases Rodin and looks around at the other men and stops and stares at his father. After a moment of contemplation, he tells him, "After this nonsense is over, I want his lordship given back to him, Dad. Whether it is here in Trade Kingdom or Anglon. I will order it so."

"I don't think Rodin has anything to worry about anymore," Lawrence says.

Coleman points to a large tunnel running under the palace, "Aranae has a gift for you, Master Rodin. Let us go and receive it."

Before Rodin can protest, Logan throws his arms around him, "I love you, big brother. Believe me when I say that I do not regret my life. You've made it the best life anyone could give me. Now let's go retreat your gift."

Rodin looks at him, smiling, as he clears the tears from his face. *The little bastard.* "*Receive,*" he rubs Logan on his head. He whispers curiously just loud enough for Byron and Slender to hear, "Why aren't you as scared as we are?"

Logan smiles wide and says, "Because we are going to live forever. And while you three are fulfilling your destiny and saving Terra-Earth, I'm going to be king." He turns and runs off to the cave, leaving the three of them standing there speechless.

XI

They all enter the cave with Dahlmür lighting the way from the front and Helana lighting the way from the rear. Byron slips back to talk to Helana. "Hi," he says.

She smiles shyly at him, "Hi."

He smiles and fumbles for words to say, "So are you going to be staying here in Trade?" he manages to ask.

"I wasn't planning on it," she responds.

"Oh, you have a home to go back to?"

"No."

"Oh well, where did you plan to go from here?"

She laughs softly, "I wish I can say. Prophecy and all."

"Right." He pauses for a moment to think more about what he wants to ask her, "I was wondering . . . well . . . I was wondering if you had someone somewhere waiting for you."

"You mean you want to know if I'm available?" she so bluntly puts it.

"Um, yeah," he smiles at her, "Yeah, I do. Are you?"

"Only if you know somebody that's interested," she asks him quietly, "Are you interested?"

Her question makes him flustered, "Yes." He pauses a moment and adds, "I am interested. I'd like to be your boyfriend, if you'd have me."

She looks at him and says, "I've never had a prince ask me out before."

He states, "I've never asked anyone out before."

"Well then, the answer is yes. I would like to be your girlfriend." She kisses him on the cheek then whispers, "You better catch up. We're falling behind."

Byron blushes, "Huh? Oh yeah." He begins to run ahead then turns and kisses her on the cheek. They blush at each other, and he runs.

When he catches up, Rodin leans over to him, "Way to go, lover boy."

Slender adds, "You got a hot one there, brother."

Helana's voice calls to them, "I heard that!"

They laugh as Byron looks back at her, still blushing. She smiles at him. He returns her smile.

Dahlmür announces, "Mater Byron, if you don't mind, when we are done here tonight, I'd like a moment of your time in private."

Byron stops short as well as his heart. He's unsure what to say. He clears his throat, "That would be fine, Master Dahlmür."

He sees Logan smiling and mouthing, "Busted" at him. He stomps at Logan, and Logan runs to be with Coleman, giggling along the way.

Rodin looks at the back then to Byron and back again and says, "I don't know why I feel like someone is following us."

Byron looks back into the pitch-black behind Helana and whispers to Slender, "Is it just me, or does it seem like the darkness is closing in around us?"

Lawrence tells them, "It is Aranae's spell. Only the light from Dahlly's and his apprentice's staffs can show the way through the caverns. Anyone outside the lights will be thrust into total darkness."

Helana adds, "If either one of us should be separated too far, nobody will be able to find their way in or out."

Galla states, "Just ask the three poor fellows that ventured in here a few days ago." He pauses for a moment then adds, "If we ever come across them again."

Vaniir says, "I thought I told you guys that I wanted those three men found."

Helana says, "Sire, my father and I searched the entire cavern. There are too many tunnels to search in such a short amount of time."

Lawrence explains, "It is too late for them now. They have already succumbed to the darkness. They have been in this enchanted darkness for so long that they've become blind. Their pupils are so dilated that their entire eyes are black, making even a single candlelight burn their vision. This cursed blackness carries nothing but sound, so their hearing can pick up the slightest noise. They are probably hungry and dying of thirst."

Vaniir says in sorrow, "Those poor souls. Two of them have probably eaten the third already."

Byron and Slender look at each other in fright. Logan runs and throws his arms around Rodin, holding him tightly.

Coleman says, "You know, we should really start keeping our voices down. They may come after us and snatch one of us for their next meal."

Vaniir turns and motions for Byron to come closer, "Stand close to me, son." Byron quietly walks up beside him. Byron's face is ghost white, his eyes wide and searching out into the darkness.

Slender draws Chill, and Galla warns him, "By the time you get the chance to use that, one of us will be gone." Slender shrugs and keeps it out anyway.

Helana speaks softly, "Father, how much farther is it? I thought we were supposed to have taken that last tunnel."

Dahlmür stops, causing everyone to stop with him in confusion. He looks around with his staff shining at the surrounding walls, "I think your right. If that's the case, then we are lost."

Logan whimpers, "What do you mean *lost?* We can't be lost!" He begins to shudder in Rodin's arms.

Rodin looks around at everyone and surveys the severity of the situation and notes how Lawrence and Vaniir continue to smile and look at each other. Rodin catches on and relaxes. *Oh, here we go. Scare the young ones. I'll play along.* He stifles a laugh.

Just then, Dahlmür puts up a finger to signal everyone to be quiet and whispers quietly, "I hear something."

Slender and Bryon nervously look around. Logan whimpers again. Rodin shakes his head and pretends to look around in fright, overdoing it a little. Suddenly, they all hear a noise. Everyone freezes. Rodin realizes that the men are now serious and this isn't part of their game. Dahlmür commands Helana to turn down her light. She does, and everyone is on alert. Logan loads an arrow onto his bow. Rodin wishes he has his ax. Swords are drawn from their scabbards. Sir Galla bangs his head on the ceiling as he draws his sword, "Oaf!" Master Lawrence pulls a cat-o'-nine-tails from his hip. They all scan the darkness, poised and ready.

Click! Everyone turns toward the sound. *Click!* They turn the other way. *Click! Click click click!* The sounds draw closer, and more join in. They tighten themselves into a bunch. Everyone frantically tries to seek out the source. The clicking noises become overwhelming. Confusion among them sets in. Their tight gathering separates as each of them pursues the noises, hoping to catch the intruders.

Suddenly, two large forms drop from the ceiling, screaming and barking at them. They all turn and scream in fear. Rodin drops to the ground, taken by surprise. Logan shoots, and the form swings in midair, just barely dodging the arrow. Mutt and Biter fall to the ground, laughing at their successful game.

Logan runs up to them, "You guys scared me!" he yells. The young girachnids continue their laughter.

Slender comments, "Dammit! Now I have to change my pants!"

Rodin rises from the ground, swallowing hard to keep his pounding heart in his chest. He yells obscenities at them in between breaths.

Byron and Helana separate from each other and exchange bashful glances. Byron asks her while rubbing his head, "You okay?"

She nods, almost laughing at herself, "Yes."

Vaniir and Galla walk up to the hysterical spiders and look down at them angrily. Vaniir says to them, "Not funny!"

Lawrence laughs, "Yes, it was! They turned the game around on us, and we fell for it! I find it hysterical!" He laughs even harder, "You should have seen your royal face, Vanny!" He mocks Vaniir with a look of horror and screams.

Out of frustration, Dahlmür interrupts them. *Snap! Snap! Snap!* Then he clears his throat, "If we are done . . . Eh . . . Eh . . . Eh, brothers, we have business to attend."

Coleman agrees, "Yes. Let's get to it. Aranae is waiting." He turns to the laughing spiders, "Lead the way, you pranksters."

Biter clumsily stands while Mutt continues his laughter. Biter kicks at Mutt and chirps and squeaks at him. They get up and run to the front of the pack. Their feet click on the hard stone surface with their *fifteen* steps. Lawrence chuckles and congratulates them for a well-played game. Mutt barks and laughs his thanks.

Rodin and Byron come together with Slender, and they suddenly stop and look at Slender. Byron backs away with a look of repulsion. Rodin does the same while fanning at him.

Slender puts his hands up, "What? I told you I have to change my pants! Don't blame me!Blame those two."

Mutt makes a squeak sound, "Pew!"

Biter grunts, "Blech!"

Helana shouts, "Awe, dammit! I'm standing downwind!" Logan, Coleman, Lawrence, and Vaniir chuckle at her. She says bitterly, "Blessed Rings, it's not funny!"

Dahlmür announces, "We are here!" He taps his staff to the stone floor, and the light opens up all around them.

They stand in an immense cavern. At the far end, an underground spring flows in from more than ten yards above and cascades down in the form of a beautiful waterfall filling a pool that is at floor level below the opening. The sound of the falls echoes all around them. Rodin finds it strange that the falls aren't as loud as they should be with the amount of water that is constantly flowing.

After spotting the waterfall and the pool, Slender takes off running, "Pants first, scenery second!" He jumps in the pool.

Helana says, "Oh, thank the Rings!" as she exaggerates being able to breathe.

Logan gazes around in wonder and asks, "Wow! Where are we?"

Vaniir tells him, "We are under the castle. This is the home of Aranae. This is also the place where the gift will be given."

Byron and Rodin ask at the same time, *"What gift?"*

Galla responds, "Let's go to that area over there"—he points to a cluster of boulders laid out in a circle on the far side near the falls—"and we can now formally discuss the answer to that question." As they begin to walk, Galla calls out, "Slender, hurry!"

Helana yells, "Yo! Hey! What did we talk about this morning? Girl here, little fella!"

Slender slips his wet and cleaned pants back on, blushing, "Sorry. I forgot you're not one of the guys!"

Helana says, "Yeah, one of us might find that weird," she tips her head to Byron and continues, "Besides, I'd be ashamed of myself if I were *one of the guys* after Rodin was showing off what his girlfriend is getting on their wedding night."

Rodin blushes. Slender stops midstride and asks Byron, "Wait"—he points at her—"did she just call me *little* fella?"

Byron chuckles, "Yup." He pats him on the shoulder.

"Dammit!" He shakes his head in defeat.

"No more of that, please!" Coleman cries. Then he finds a boulder to sit on.

Rodin is still fascinated by the chasm. The walls are streaked in multiple shades of tans and grays. A few streaks of blues and yellows accent the colors. The chasm is too dark to see a ceiling.

Rodin wishes for Dahlmür's staff to light up the entire chasm so he can actually see the corners and far walls. He sees a slight glow above the center of the boulders. A soft blue light emits from within the darkness. He stares at it as he tries to figure out what it is that's glowing.

Vaniir steps up and looks at it with him and says, "It's the Blessing Stone. That stone glows blue until the Light shines itself upon the person that he deems worthy. That stone has been there for centuries. It is how the gift-giver is shown who the worthy one is." He wraps an arm around Rodin as the others come together to view it with them in fascination. "It will shine tonight onto you," then he adds, "We hope," and walks away.

Rodin looks at Byron and shakes his head defiantly, "I don't think I want this *gift*, my brother."

Slender says to him, "I don't think I would want it either. Whatever it is seems to me to be too much weight than anyone is willing to carry."

Byron looks down at his feet shamefully and says softly, "I didn't know I was passing on anything. I wish I had answers, my brothers."

Rodin looks over to Logan, who sits on a boulder forming the circle. He pets Mutt and Biter as he waits for everyone patiently. *He knows. He knows everything and didn't tell me anything. How could he do this to me? I never kept any secrets from him. I trusted him. I gave him everything I had. Now he keeps secrets from me?*

Byron sets a hand on his shoulder and looks at Logan with him, "I see it in your eyes, brother. He is holding this secret from you. You didn't even know he had a secret this big. Makes you wonder what else he isn't saying. As in, how does he know he will be king? And how will he become king?"

Rodin's face reddens with rage. Slender places a hand on his other shoulder, "They are all holding back secrets, brothers. Don't just blame him. Byron, your father knows everything too. Probably more than Logan. Dahlmür and Helana know. Obviously, Galla, Coleman, and Lawrence are a part of all this as well. We're left in the dark. They may as well have left us in the cursed caverns we went through on the way here. That is how far in the dark we are."

They stand and watch all them talk and joke in their circle while sitting on the boulders. Helana and Dahlmür sit facing away from them. Logan is seated next to Helana. Beside him are three empty seats representing their places. Lawrence laughs as Galla tells a story while balancing his half-Gia frame onto the comparatively small boulder. Vaniir strokes his beard and laughs with them. Coleman points at the spiders as he talks to Logan. They act as though nothing that is very important is really going on. The three of them stand and watch as they remain together to comfort one another's concerns.

Finally, the spiders chirp, and the group stands. Lawrence calls to them, "Rodin, Slindee, Byron, it's time."

They look at one another with worry. They are in this together, and they will see it through together. They resist the urge to refuse to join them. All three are helpless to resist anymore. There are no questions to ask that the others are willing to answer. They've never felt so vulnerable before now. They silently join the circle.

Rodin looks around to figure out what it is they are supposed to do. Nobody is looking in their direction. They all stare at the ground. Slender and Byron look at him with fear and anticipation in their eyes. Then Slender looks past him, and his eyes widen in astonishment, and his jaw drops. Byron notices and looks in the direction Slender is looking, and his expression is as if he were not expecting to see someone. Rodin looks at them in confusion, then he realizes something is behind him. He slowly turns his head, and a look of horror comes over his face.

A girachnid! Larger than any spider Rodin has ever seen or heard tell of steps out of the dark corner and into full view. Its lumbering legs are like tree trunks with massive fibers extending from all over. They are the color of various shades of browns and grays. On top of them is a body so large it can crush a house if it falls on it. Rodin will have to climb a house just to look into its tremendous face. The fangs are as big as Rodin. It's deep black eyes vary in size from as big as Slender's fists to the size of wagon wheels. A white spot is painted on the bottom of its enormous abdomen in the shape of the sun with a yellow halo around it.

Scared beyond belief, Rodin wants to back away, but his feet are planted in place. He looks at everyone else and sees that only he and Slender are the ones scared at the moment. Even though Logan has never been here before, he seems excited to see it. He smiles at it as if it were a new friend that he is glad to meet. He happily waves at it. Byron bows to the girachnid as well as the others, leaving Rodin and Slender to stare in awe.

Vaniir introduces them, "Gentlemen, meet Aranae. She is the only remaining adult girachnid. She and the two younglings are all that remain of her League."

She looks at Rodin, and he is immediately blinded by a blue light that emanates from her forward small sets of eyes. When his sight returns, he sees Slender and Logan recovering from the same effect.

"Can they hear us now?" a voice calls out.

"I don't know, but I can't wait to tell that little boy how much I want to bite his leg off and see how he likes it," another responds.

"He said he was sorry. You did try to bite him, you know," the first voice says.

Rodin and Slender look around in confusion. Slender says curiously, "Who's saying that?"

Logan shouts, "I told you I didn't mean it! I said I was sorry! He's right. You did try to bite me. I did heal you. Please forgive me."

Rodin turns to him, "Who are you talking to?"

Mutt and Biter step up from beneath Aranae. Mutt looks at Rodin, "He's talking to us. We like you. You are very brave to accept us. We could have been trying to eat your brother, but you let us in your house. Biter likes you too. He said that he hates that you had to meet us like that."

Biter says, "Why did you help me?"

Rodin shakes his head in disbelief. Slender's jaw drops. Rodin responds, "You were hurt. If you were really all that dangerous, I would have killed you."

Mutt laughs like a child, "Oh, you mean like you tried to do with that broken pitchfork right before I dropped down at you?" he laughs again.

Slender says in disbelief, "Talking spiders."

Biter looks at him, "Hey! We're girachnids! Not common spiders, Stinky-Pants!"

Mutt laughs, "Oh yeah, you were so funny!" He rolls on the floor, laughing hard, "Stinky-Pants!"

Another voice chimes in, this one sounding like a mature woman, "Enough, you two. We are here for other reasons." Aranae looks over them, "I apologize for my children's behavior. They are only a year old."

Coleman says to her, "Such is the joy of motherhood, my lady. You must teach them while they are young, or else, it would not be a cherished life if they were to mature without love and knowledge."

Aranae turns to him and responds in kind, "They are my cherished ones."

Vaniir speaks to her, "My lady, we have brought the four of them here tonight. The oath has been made. They've all accepted. We are ready for the Light's gift."

Rodin, Slender, and Byron repeat aloud together, *"What gift?"*

Aranae looks over them for a moment then turns to Vaniir and Galla, "You never told them?"

Lawrence steps forward, "As you know, my lady, it is that time. They weren't taught or told about it. They do not know. We didn't know until last night." He looks at Byron.

She sighs, "I figured out that time was upon us when these two hatched and when Byron was born. I guess the rest of you haven't bore young? This young girl must be your daughter, Dahlly. She looks just like you," she turns to Helana, "I'm sorry, child." Helana smiles as she fends off a laugh.

Dahlmür grunts, "I see you have adopted a sense of humor in your child-rearing." Lawrence manages a chuckle.

Galla speaks up, "The prophecy stated that we would find worthy apprentices. I didn't know mine was fulfilled until the day I met Slender. I mean Slindee."

Slender turns to him, "Apprentice for what? Am I not your squire?"

Coleman speaks up with a finger raised, "I have no apprentice." He points to Vaniir, "Vanii here has two. The boy and his own son."

Dahlmür interjects, "That is true, but Byron can't be the healer and king at the same time. So naturally"—he points to Logan—"the boy is his real apprentice."

Logan crosses his arms and scolds Dahlmür, " *The boy* is named Logan," then he adds, "Dahlly."

Dahlmür adds, "Sir."

"Hmph!"

Dahlmür finds it amusing, "Not like his brother."

Coleman shrugs, "I hope the time for me is soon, brothers."

Byron and Rodin look at each other in confusion. They congregate around Slender. The three of them cross their arms with a stern look on their faces. They've had enough.

Byron says, "Stop! We were promised answers. We want them now!"

Rodin adds in a quiet voice, "Please."

Slender nods in finality of the question, "We're not doing anything more until somebody starts talking. If not, I'll just grab Chill and freeze you all."

Galla states, "Didn't we just go through this outside?"

Helana says to her father, "I think it is time we tell them, Father."

Rodin agrees. "I think so too."

Aranae sits in the middle. Her long legs fold under her body. Rodin still has to look up to her. She invites everyone to sit as she begins to explain what is going on.

I made it! That cavern was nothing. I live in the darkness. My master trained me in the darkness. It is my home. I can see through it. I have no need for your precious light. Now tell me where the chosen one is!

Who is it? Speak up! Who's the chosen? What is the big spider doing here? Why are they speaking in gibberish? They don't make sense!

Trash! Speak in human! Prince Herring, why are you clicking? Piggy, why do you have your sword?

Are you getting ready for war? Are you going to kill one another? You can't! I'm supposed to kill you all. You can't kill one another! It was my promise, remember? Master would be happy, but it would make me mad.

Where is the gift-giver? Is it Creepy? I would have never thought it was him. He's so creepy. It might as well be him. The Light would make it so they wouldn't think it was him. I know you now, Gift-Giver! Creepy! Creepy GiftGiver! I know you! I will kill you!

I'm ready! Get rid of the ugly giant bug and its little roaches! It's time to kill!

Aranae begins to tell them, "You have been blessed. The Light has prophesied that the children born under the gathering of the Circles will be chosen to become the Light's chosen. The firstborn will be the one to form a brotherhood of his own. This oath will be sealed in blood as witnessed by the Light. The Light will give one of them a gift. The gift will be given to the one deemed most worthy within his circle.

"This gift is the gift of the Rings. The gift of Archon. The champion of all Terra-Earth. Those within his circle will become his army. The firstborn will be his healer. His strongest brother will be his commander.

"Many more will join him. They too will be born under the same signs. They will come from the Order of Terrans and the Order of Creatures. They will all be brothers and sisters by the blood oath under the Light's witness. Their leagues will teach the Archon.

"They will train him how to fight. Teach him how to survive. Teach him how to live. They will teach him how to love. Archon will use this knowledge to receive the Light's weapon. Then, he will face the leader of the Order of Demons, Liche, who will be reborn, and Poison will be received by him again. Before Archon can defeat him, everyone will suffer again under his rule. He will raise new armies and create new leagues to bring Terra-Earth to suffer.

"You, young prince, are the firstborn under the event of the gathering otherwise called the eclipse. You have formed the brotherhood under a blood oath. Now it is time for the Light to choose the Archon."

Rodin stands and speaks to Aranae, "What about the scrolls? Everyone says it is me, but you say something else entirely. You act as if this chosen one hasn't been named yet"—he points around at Logan, the four men, and Helana—"but these people say that *I* am the chosen one. What is going on? Who are we to believe?"

Aranae looks at Vaniir, "What scrolls?"

Vaniir starts to explain the scrolls when Slender interrupts, "Are you saying that all this is because you all have no clue what's going on here? You say prophecy by the scrolls, and she says prophecy by the Light. Either you have an actual prophecy or you don't."

Galla begins to speak when Byron erupts, "I was born under an eclipse! How does that make *me* the one that starts all this? How do you know *I* was born first under this eclipse? It could have been a morpher or a merfolk for all you know! Maybe a rogue or a sas! Hell, it could have been Rodin!" He looks at his brothers and realizes they are staring at him solemnly, "What?"

Logan tells Byron, "Rodin *was* born under that eclipse."

Galla says, "So was Slindee."

Byron looks at them. They stare at one another in wide-eyed realization. The three of them are brothers under the eclipse.

Dahlmür leans in and says to them calmly, "The three of you must take the oath again. This time with your *sister.*"

Helana stands and looks at him, startled, "What? You mean *me?*" She steps back. Her breathing becomes sporadic, "No. Father, this can't be. You never told me. I don't want to be his brother."

Dahlmür tells her, "It is true, Lana. You were born under the eclipse. Second to him."

She begins to cry, "No! I don't want to be his sister!"

Dahlmür asks, "Why not?"

She looks at Byron and tries to fight the tears, "I want to be his *lover,* not his sister!" and she breaks. She rushes away and sits by the pool to cry alone.

Rodin is furious. *Damn them! They have ruined our lives! Logan fell for this? Did they tell him all this, and he believed them? Is this a spell he's under? How did she not know? Her father tricked her too?*

Hey! I've come to kill you! Stop fighting and face me! Hey! Trash! Piggy! Herring! I'm right here!

Dammit! You call yourself a wizard? You don't even realize I'm out in the open! I'm coming to skin a herring, and you can't even sense me! Stop making the beauty cry and turn to face me!

Big Piggy! Turn and draw you sword! I want to fight you until I grow tired of you and stab your heart! Turn around!

King Herring!
Big Trash!
Creepy!
Giant Bug!

Somebody! Hey!

Aranae steps out of the circle furiously, "How am I to know who gets the gift? I can't repeat the curse that was placed upon us all those years ago! *Somebody* better figure this out!"

All of them begin shouting and yelling at one another from their places. When Aranae moves out of the center, Rodin notices the symbol of the Circle of Light on the floor, surrounded by the stars representing the Rings. He points them out and furiously calls to Dahlmür to explain it all. Dahlmür is more concerned with arguing with his crying daughter, who refuses to take the oath as she screams in tears. Byron is yelling at his father. Logan yells at Rodin. Slindee yells at Galla and Lawrence. It is a chaotic scene. The young girachnids join the madness as well. Coleman tries his best to calm the situation, but nobody is listening.

Suddenly, there is a cry from the cavern they've entered. They all become silent. Aranae withdraws into the shadows, as well as Mutt and Biter. Weapons are drawn. Slowly, they all gather together, forgetting their prior threats to one another. They all approach the cavern, prepared for a fight.

A faint blue light illuminates the cavern's walls and grows brighter as it gets closer to the chasm. They freeze and stand at the ready. A lone figure enters.

"Vil?" Rodin says to him.

Vil looks around the chasm in confusion, and his eyes fall on them. He fixes his gaze onto Rodin and angrily replies, "Lord Vil, you trash!"

Rodin tries to shake the anger swelling back into him. *I swear to the Light I'm going to kill him!*

Rodin turns and walks back to his place in the circle of stone seats, "Keep him away from me before I sink my teeth into his chest!" He throws himself down onto his place and watches them, red-faced.

Byron asks, "What are you doing here?"

Dahlmür steps forward, confused, "More importantly . . . Eh . . . Eh . . . Eh . . . How did you come to be released from the stockade?"

Vaniir looks at Dahlmür in surprise, "The stockade? How did he get there?"

Galla responds, "He put him there for threatening Prince Byron."

Vaniir turns to Vil, "You threatened my son?"

Dahlmür responds without taking his eyes off Vil, "Yes, and I . . . Eh . . . Eh . . . Eh . . . Placed a curse on him while he was in the stockade. He wasn't supposed to . . . Eh . . . Eh . . . Eh . . . Be released until tomorrow morning."

Slender says to him, "We thought you released him this afternoon. He insulted Prince Byron again, and Sir Matthew escorted him to his father. I guess his father didn't punish him."

Byron looks at Vil with anger growing in his eyes, "How did you get out of that stockade, and how did you get here?"

Lord Vil gives them an evil grin, "It doesn't matter. Let's just say that I have some pull in much higher places."

Lawrence walks up, ready to crack his whip at him, "Do you have something you'd like to share with us, Lord Vil?"

Vil laughs in amusement, "Oh, now my Class is recognized! The man who comes from the Class of Peasants at least recognizes his superiors!" He gives an evil laugh at them.

Galla repeats Byron's question, "What are you doing here?"

Vil looks at him and answers snidely as he tosses a light stone in the air and catches it, "I'm here because I wish to be here. I followed you idiots here. At first, I got lost. Then I found this light stone, and then I followed your voices to this place. You were all really having an intense moment there. I didn't mean to disturb you. I only want to kill that piece of trash over there for his insolence toward me as my right as the Class of Lord, then you can carry on with your bickering," he looks at Helana and adds, "and your crying." He smiles coyly at them as Helana starts at him with her sword drawn from her staff poised to kill.

Rodin stands and cries out, "If someone doesn't shut him up, I swear to the Rings . . . " His body shakes as he tries to control his anger.

Logan draws back an arrow, "I will nail you to the wall with this if you go near my brother, you sorry son of a—"

Vaniir interrupts, "Language, boy!"

Vil turns to Vaniir and mocks a bow toward him, "My King, I ask that you allow *me* to rid you of this trash that surrounds you."

Lawrence's temper flares, "Why, you insolent little bastard." He flips his whip, and all nine tails hit the floor at once. *Crash!* Flames flash up.

Vil continues to address King Vaniir, "If you don't, I will!"

Vaniir looks at him, astonished, "How dare you!"

Vil responds in amusement, "How dare *I*? How dare your son to surround himself with such filth. How dare *he* allow a peasant speak to a lord in the way he does. How dare that common *professor* put me in a stockade! How *dare* you allow this in your in your own damn kingdom!" He foams at the mouth as he shouts, "Rings be damned if *I* will allow a king to let a peasant address me in any manner other than lying on the ground so I can scrape the dirt off my boots with his face! Rings be damned if *I* will allow *you* to unjustly rule this kingdom!"

Rodin stands and begins to run. *I've had enough! I'm going to kill him!* As he steps through the center of the circle of seats, a blinding light flashes into his face. *What's happening?*

Vaniir is no longer amused. He says calmly, "Dahlly, return him to the stockade."

Dahlmür acknowledges his command and smashes his cane to the floor. *Boom!* Vil is once again transported to the stockade.

They all calm down. Relieved to be rid of Vil and his threats, they look at one another with satisfaction. Everyone suddenly realizes a bright light is shining behind them. They turn and see Rodin in the circle being blinded by the light shining from the Blessing Stone. The emblem of the Rings on the floor glows all around him.

I'm blind! I can't see! Where is this cursed light coming from? It hurts! Rodin tries to force his eyes open to see beyond the light surrounding him so he can retreat, but it is too intense. So intense, in fact, that it even affects his hearing as well. Garbled voices yell at him. *What's going on?*

Everyone rushes forward in awe of the scene. Logan, Byron, and Slender repeatedly ask them what's happening, but nobody is answering. Aranae crawls from her hiding place and walks to Rodin, fully erect. Everyone except the three boys drop to their knees in praise of the Rings and the Circle of Light. Aranae bares her fangs behind Rodin.

Logan screams.

Byron cries out, "Brother! No!"

Rodin can't move. His feet seem to be stuck in place. He can't hear even though he could have sworn he's heard Byron call to him. *Is Logan screaming? He's in trouble! I must save my brother!* He tries desperately to see, but he is blinded. The light causes him pain.

A shadow is finally cast over him. He opens his eyes just in time to see Slender point up behind him.

Too late!

Pain.

Can't breathe.

Black.

Silence.

XII

"**W**elcome, Rodin. You have been chosen. You are very blessed. The Rings hold you in the highest regards. They have told me to give you their power."

"Who are you? Where am I?"

"You are with me. Do not fear, my child. I want to show you your history. Learn. Take in my knowledge and become your destiny."

Circle of Light! "I trust you. Please show me."

Images flash.

A boy. Younger than Rodin.

His name is Arik.

He boldly steps forward. Instantly, he is transformed into a white figure. He holds a sword. It's much bigger than any sword Rodin has ever seen. Thick. Strong. Heavy.

"Is that Flare?"

"That's before I gave Flare to Archon."

The image flickers to Arik the Archon defeating Liche and the earliest demons. They look like devils. They were the first League created in Darkness's Order of Demons.

"I've never heard of the first Archon stories."

"It has been so many centuries that the stories became distorted. Some entirely wrong in many ways. Watch."

Another image flickers.

A new boy.

A sas named Muk.

Wearily, he steps forward and is transformed. His sas body is surrounded by a swirling mass of the cosmos, with stars swirling all around within him. He wields a brass club with a spike protruding from the end, with a gleam like a star at the tip.

He battles with a new breed of demons, the League of Trolls and the League of the Undead. He crushes them all.

Another flicker.

A young woman.

Her name is Tara. A Rogue.

She accepts her gift. She is transformed into a warrior clad in armor that emits light like the flames of the sun. She draws twin daggers.

The Order of Vampires is born. This time led by Liche. Fast and agile. More so than Tara. He pulls an iron claw and wears it in battle. In his speed, he slices her neck. Her head falls.

Flicker.

A young boy.

A Morpher. He is Ariston.

He steps forward. His body is changed into bright white scales of a dragon with the wings of an angel. He draws a sword so bright it lights the world.

"That is Flare?"

"He is the first Archon to receive my gift."

A battle between Archon and Liche flashes. Archon raises Flare and brings it down, slicing Liche from shoulder to hip.

Flicker.

"How many Archons were there?"

"Many."

This time the image is of five men standing in a circle.

"What is this?"

"A new prophecy to the legend of Archon as told by the Rings. I created a new Order of Creature to give the gift by the new prophecy's nature. Watch."

He knows four of them. The fifth looks vaguely familiar. "That's Vaniir! Lawrence! Coleman! Dahlmür! That's Galla! Who's that?"

"Vil."

"As in Lord Vil?"

"He is a descendant. Just watch."

A girachnid steps forward. Aranae. She pushes Vil to the side. She approaches Lawrence. He shakes his head. They point to Vil. She refuses. She points to Lawrence, who is basking in light. He shakes his head and points at Vil. Reluctantly, she sinks her fangs into Vil. He becomes a lighted figure that fades. Vil is nothing but a formless black figure without a weapon.

Light engulfs them all. A voice cries, *"Because Archon was created by your choice, you are cursed! You will forever live to* serve the prophecies of the gift. Until I have given you worthy apprentices born under the gathering of the Circles, what you call an eclipse, where the one that fulfills the proper prophecy will be chosen, only then you may rest in the Realm of Spirits with us. This false Archon will fall because of your own choice to refuse our prophecy."

A battle between this Archon and Liche leading the Order of Orcs. Liche carries Poison and strikes Archon. Archon perishes.

Flicker.

A Gia.

A woman named Centuria.

The four stand in a circle around her. Aranae steps forward. She gives Centuria the gift. She transforms into an Archon with four arms. Three arms hold knives. The other holds Flare. Archon battles Liche. Liche is defeated.

Flicker.

"So many Archons."

"Yes, my brother is forever trying to destroy my beloved Orders."

A woodland.

A boy named Vine.

Again, the four are there, presenting him to Aranae. She, again, gives him the gift. He is transformed into a body of vines with thorns and blossoms that radiate light like a prism.

He faces a horde of demons. He defeats them easily.

Flicker.

Another Gia.

Zenith is his name.

Three of the four men look tired. Lawrence is not with them. Aranae looks as though she is just going through the motions. She steps up, bites him, and leaves.

He transforms. Archon is now a massive form made of lighted crystal and stone.

He raises a hammer made of light.

"That is Flare?"

"Yes. It takes the shape of the Archon's weapon of choice."

"I was always told Flare was a sword."

"As I said, some stories are distorted and wrong. Keep watching."

Liche appears with Poison again. He rides a lizard-like creature with wings. Archon's battle is hard-fought. He slays Liche.

"That was the lineage of Archon before you."

"Why do the prophecies say that I will live eternally?"

"You are the final Archon. You are destined to form your eternal army through the oath I will witness through the blood."

"But can I love? Can I have a wife? Millette and I are to marry. I love her."

"You can marry. Your fellow brothers and sisters can marry."

"Byron and Helana?"

"Your oath can also be served by marriage under my witness."

"I will tell them."

"Do you accept my gift, then?"

"I don't understand why the Rings have chosen me."

"You are blessed."

"Why?"

"It is not for me to question the Rings. They gave me the gift of Terra-Earth and all those that dwell upon it. I love everyone."

"I do not understand why I am blessed, but I will not watch others suffer. I want peace and honor for everyone. Including all classes."

"Only my League of Humans has such things as Classes."

"I wish to end the separation of Classes between us to end our wars, to live as one. I want all Leagues to live as one Order. No more wars. No more hatred."

"That makes you worthy."

"Then I accept."

"Awaken, Rodin, and arise as the Eternal Archon!"

"Rodin!"

XIII

"**I**s he awake?"

"Will you back up and let me see?"

"He's my brother."

"He's our brother too, little brother."

"All of you, back away!"

"Dahlly, check on him."

Rodin opens his eyes and smiles as he sees Dahlmür, "You guys are *old!*"

Dahlmür laughs at him quietly, "And you are so *peculiar.*"

Byron shouts, "He's awake!" Logan yelps for joy.

Slender looks down at Rodin, "You worried us, brother. I thought you were going to sleep for days."

Rodin looks at him, startled, "Days? How long have I been out?"

Lawrence says to him, "Ten days."

Byron looks down at him, "You look so cool!"

Logan squeezes by him, "Hi! I missed you! I'm so glad you're okay. You look really cool. Your body is covered in these giant, silvery, webby thingies that just flow around and around and around and around. You look very cool. Millette is worried about you. We told her you were sick. She's here with us in the palace. We're actually in the palace! Isn't that cool? I'll tell her you're awake, but she can't see you because you might be cantancherous. I know I said it wrong, but whatever. Did you know that there are people that serve us? I'm treated like royalty! Well, probably because I'm King Vaniir's aprehentis. I know I said that wrong too, but you know what I mean. I'm going to be King because you are Archon. Isn't that cool? Well, I better go tell Millette that you're awake now. She's been crying about you. She really loves you. You didn't tell me you were getting married in a few weeks at the festival. Now that's just mean. I'm your little brother! You're supposed to tell me everything! Well, I better be there. I love you, big brother. I'd kiss you, but you look too weird. Bye! I love you!" And he's gone.

Everyone is stunned. Galla leans down to Lawrence, "Did he breathe?"

Rodin shakes his head, "Will somebody please tell Millette, no more sugar candy!"

Slender says, "Believe me, I will."

Rodin tries to sit up, but Byron holds him down, "Whoa! You better lie there for a little bit. You just woke up."

Rodin says to him, "You're the one that looks tired. What happened to you?"

Byron smiles and shakes his head, "I'm okay. Besides, I'm your healer."

"My healer? From what?" Rodin asks.

He responds, "Aranae bit you to give you the gift. She had to sink her fangs in pretty far. It is my duty to heal your wounds as you become Archon. For the first couple of days, it was just Dahlmür and me. The process is tiring, but you should be proud of my work."

Rodin replies jokingly, "Ten days? I don't know how good of a job you've done to keep me under for ten days."

"Oh, ha ha!"

They all laugh at Byron.

Rodin spots Helana. He looks at everyone and asks, "Can I talk to Helana and my brothers alone, please?"

The four men stand. Coleman points to the door, "Gentleman, I think that would be our cue." With that, they leave, closing the door behind them.

Rodin calls to Helana, and she joins him. He grabs her hand then grabs Byron's. He looks at them and smiles, "I saw the entire lineage of Archon. I spoke with the Circle of Light!"

They respond in fascinated gasps and draw in closer as he continues, "There were so many before me. You wouldn't believe the Leagues that became Archon. I'm sure, by now, they've explained their curse to you guys. I just want to let you know that I have a special message from the Circle of Light to you, Helana, and to you, Byron."

Helana looks at him curiously, "What message?"

"You don't have to take the oath of brotherhood to be a part of our circle."

Byron is surprised, "What?"

Slender asks, "How does she join us then?"

"The same way Millette will join us," he looks at her and smiles, "By marriage."

Helana bursts into tears, "Marriage?"

"Yes."

"I'm going to get married?"

"To Byron, if you'd like."

Helana becomes overly excited, "I'm getting married!" She leans over to Byron and kisses him, "I love you!"

Byron is stunned, "I'm getting married?"

Slender pats him on the back, "Congratulations, brother!"

Helana dances around like a giddy little girl. "I'm gettin' married! Oh, my Rings! What am I gonna wear? Oh, wait! Who's gonna to be there? What are we gonna eat at the wedding feast? Oh, my Rings! I'm gettin' married! I've gotta tell my father! You better tell *your* father! We're gettin' married!" She bolts out the door, screaming, "I'm gettin' married!"

Byron is still stunned, "I'm getting married?"

Rodin asks him, "Are you okay? Maybe you should sit down."

"I'm getting married?"

Slender laughs, "Here, brother, let's sit," he pulls up a chair for him.

Byron sits, "I didn't know I was getting married."

Rodin says to him, "Breathe. Take deep breaths. You'll be okay. Be happy, my brother."

"Why am I getting married?"

Slender says, "Because you love each other."

Still dazed, Byron replies, "Yeah. Okay, I love her. I mean, I do. I'm in love with her. Helana is a beautiful girl. She's funny. She laughs at my jokes. She loves me too. I'm going to get married?"

Rodin and Slender laugh. Suddenly, they hear laughter coming from behind the door. Galla bursts through with an arm around Dahlmür. Dahlmür has a look of loss and confusion about him.

He mutters to everyone, "My little girl is getting . . . Eh . . . Eh . . . Eh . . . Eh . . . Married?"

Galla's laughter is jolly and celebratory, "Be proud of your daughter, Dahlly! She's becoming a fine young lady! She will be a wonderful wife!"

Vaniir is escorted in by Lawrence and Coleman, "Vanii, please calm down!"

Vaniir is red with anger, "Calm down? My boy is getting married! He's too young for marriage! Dahlly, please talk some sense into them."

"My sweet, precious little girl is getting . . . Eh . . . Eh . . . Eh . . . Married."

Coleman states, "They are hopeless."

Lawrence looks at Byron, "Congratulations, son!"

Byron looks at him with a blank expression, "I'm getting married?"

Slender says, "He's been like this ever since he found out he's getting married."

Lawrence asks, "Found out? You mean he didn't know?"

"Nope."

Dahlmür says to Byron, "My baby girl is getting . . . eh . . . eh . . . eh . . . eh . . . married."

Byron responds, "I'm getting married?"

Dahlmür presses the quartz of his staff onto Byron's arm. *Bzzt!*

Byron doesn't flinch, "Ouch."

Rodin shakes his head, "Will somebody please make them stop? I've got a headache."

Slender laughs at him, "You're the one that suggested it."

Rodin replies, "I take it back."

"Too late now, brother."

After a few hours of dealing with Vaniir, Dahlmür, and Byron, as well as trying to slow down an overexuberant Helana, they all come to terms and try to deal with the pressing matter of the Archon. Slender has brought Rodin a mirror so he can see himself.

Rodin didn't realize he is in Archon form because it feels as natural to him as his normal self. Now that he can see himself, Rodin is in awe of his face. Logan is right; his body is covered in what seems to be a massive weave of spider webbing that constantly flows about his body, changing directions and patterns. His face has no features. He has no nose, brow, mouth, cheekbones, or ears. It is plainly the featureless shape of an odd-shaped ball on his neck. His normally brown eyes are now yellow beads of light in a bed of a black void that cuts across his face where his eyes should be. He watches the beads move up, down, and around as he moves his eyes and head around. They don't sit in an eye socket like eyes do. The beads of yellow light are just there, floating in dark nothingness. He looks down at his hands. They are the size and shape of his hands, but the same webbing flows about. He asks Slender to help him to a larger mirror, and he obliges him. Rodin stands in front of the mirror without anything covering him up. His body has no anatomical features even though Rodin knows he's naked. Archon is not a suit. Rodin's entire body *is* Archon.

This is just too weird. I really am the Archon. He smiles at himself even though his featureless face doesn't take any shape to indicate a smile. *I'll work on controlling that.*

After Rodin spends a few hours of sitting on the floor in front of the mirror staring and studying himself, Byron and Slender sit down beside him to watch. "It's just so weird," Byron states. *Weird* is the only word any of them can use to best describe it. To use any other word aside from *cool* will be an understatement.

Slender pinches his forearm, "Can you feel me doing that?"

"I can feel that, but just . . . not as if you were pinching. It just feels like"—he shakes his head—"I don't know, but I know you're pinching my arm. What does my skin feel like?"

Byron and Slender rub his arms, then his shoulders, "It feels like skin, and it looks like a bunch of webbing flowing around and over one another, but it feels like . . . " Slender tries to describe it.

"But it flows. As if I've got my hand on top of the water of a fast-flowing river."

"Yeah. I can feel the ripples and the movements as well as the curves and the direction of the flow of it all, which constantly change. You'd think I'd feel the many different strands bulging and crossing over and going under each other, but I don't. It's just . . . weird."

"But so cool."

"Yeah."

Rodin looks at himself and shakes his head, "Cool."

Slender tells him, "You sound weird too."

"Really?"

Byron says, "Yeah. You have a deeper, raspier voice, like you're talking with sand in your throat."

"I don't hear it. To me I sound like my voice."

Slender nods, "Yeah, but we hear different."

Byron chuckles, "Your eyes are cool. Scary, but cool. I really love your eyes."

"Thanks, sweetie. You're too kind," Archon mocks a female voice.

Slender laughs.

Helana eventually joins them as they talk more about his features. She enjoys his eyes as much as Byron does and says that she can fall in love with him just for his eyes, but her heart is already taken. She hugs onto Byron as the two of them kiss. Slender and Rodin laugh at them and ask the two lovers to knock it off.

Dahlmür and the others interrupt, "Okay, you kids can stop admiring one another now."

Vaniir laughs, "Stand up, Master Rodin, and let me have a look at you."

Rodin stands as the men look him over. Dahlmür grasps his hands and pulls them up to inspect them. They look at it curiously. Dahlmür places his palm over the back of one hand and looks at the others in puzzlement, motioning them to do the same.

Coleman holds one hand and rubs Rodin's forearm, "Weird."

Lawrence does the same with Rodin's other hand, "Cool."

Rodin says in annoyance, "The two words of the day today."

Vaniir says, "We need to get him down to Aranae today. Only she can help him control it. He has to be able to regain his natural form and become this form at any given moment."

Coleman states, "That is his natural form now."

Dahlmür agrees, "Yes, but after breakfast. I'm famished."

Lawrence looks at Rodin, "Are you hungry?"

Rodin tilts his head at him, "Apparently, I haven't eaten for ten days. So yeah, I'm starving."

Coleman snickers, "Come. Let's go get you something to eat."

Vaniir mumbles, "If he can. He has no mouth."

Rodin replies, "I better, or else, I'm going to be the Eternally Starving Archon." Lawrence laughs at his joke.

Dahlmür sighs, "Let's find out." He opens the door wide enough to stick his head out, "My dear lady, will you ask the kitchen staff to gather breakfast for us all?" He starts to shut the door and remembers something else, "Oh, and fetch that young lady . . . Eh, Millette as well as Master Logan and ask them to join us. Thank you, young lady, you're very kind."

Rodin asks, "Do you think that's a good idea?"

Vaniir replies, "We'll find out."

After what seems to Rodin like hours, there is a knock at the door. Rodin scrambles to hide as Byron answers. He opens the door to allow servants with a couple of large trollies full of food and another full of dishes, flatware, napkins, and mugs to enter the room and begin setting up the large table to the side. They continue their conversations, ignoring the servants, while Byron explains the setup with the head servant. When the servant is done, he leaves the trollies to the side and asks that they call on him when they are done and he will be pleased to clear the table for them. Byron thanks him and hands him a silver coin as he asks that they aren't disturbed during their meal except to let in Logan and Millette.

There is another knock at the door. Byron opens the door slightly to peer out then pulls it all the way open to allow Logan and Millette in. Millette looks around the room, timid and confused.

Logan trots in and spots the table, "Oh, good. I'm starved!" He chooses a seat and sits down.

The servant looks over to King Vaniir, "Your Majesty, there is a messenger out in the guest room, awaiting to serve you a message from King Saul, I believe."

Everyone freezes for a moment. King Vaniir replies, "Thank you, Master Walton. Tell him I will see him when I'm done with my current meeting. It won't be long. Oh, and, Master Walton."

"Yes, sire."

"Please tell Master Boone and Master Daniel that I want to see them along the way to meet this messenger so they can give me an update on my wife's condition. Tell them that I will not take kindly to a negative response. If you catch my meaning."

"Yes, sire, I completely understand." Master Walton looks at everyone in the room, "Do any of you gentlemen and ladies need anything else from me?"

Byron replies, "No, Master Walton. We thank you very much." Master Walton bows to them and excuses himself out the door.

Byron tells everyone, "He is the best person we have in his position. I think he will make a good replacement for that hateful toad that Mother hired."

"I do too," Vaniir agrees.

Dahlmür taps his staff to the floor. *Snap! Snap! Snap!*

Galla yells at him, "Confounded, Dahlly! Will you stop that?"

Slender grins and says, "Helana likes to do that too. Annoying."

Helana looks at him in spite. Black smoke swirls around her hand. Her staff appears, and she taps the floor in quick succession with her staff as well. *Snap! Snap! Snap!*

Slender remarks, "See what I mean?"

Dahlmür stands in the center and motions everyone to give him his attention, "I believe that we have a confession to make to Lady Millette."

All at once, everyone realizes what he's talking about and turn in Rodin's hidden direction. Millette looks in that direction also in confusion. Logan sighs, "Millette, please sit down. You're gonna be on the floor if you don't."

Slender mumbles, "That's puttin' it lightly."

Helana shows her to a chair, "Sweetie, I know you're not going to be ready for this, but trust me, girl, you will be happy for him and be proud of him."

Millette begins to breathe heavily as she panics. "What's wrong with Rodin?" She looks in his direction and cries out, "My love, please, what's going on?"

From behind the drapes, Rodin responds, "Please believe me when I say I didn't want anything to do with this. I didn't ask for it. It just happened. Well, until I accepted it in the end. Remember, it's still me. I love you, my darling Millette."

She tilts her head in confusion. "You sound different. Dear, are you still not well? I'm here to take care of you."

"Oh, you have no idea." Rodin steps from behind the drapes slowly.

As he emerges, Millette jumps to her feet and cries, "What have you people done to him? Logan, why didn't you stop them? Why didn't you come and get me from the beginning? I could have done something to save him!"

Helana steps up to her. "Please calm down."

"Calm down my ass! Stay away from me!"

Rodin walks up to her and hugs her. Suddenly, she is calm. Confused over what just happened, Rodin looks at Dahlmür.

Dahlmür rushes up and helps him lower her to the chair. Dahlmür says to him, "It's you. You have a calming effect on those you are trying to comfort."

Rodin nods to him then says to Millette, "Please, we are going to tell you everything. Eat and listen. I promise all your worries are for nothing." He bends down to kiss her then remembers the lack of lips to do the job.

Rodin is surprised. It takes less time to explain everything to her than he's expected. They tell her everything, from the prophecy to the moment Aranae bit him, in the amount of time it took them all to eat. Apparently, Rodin's need for food allows a mouth to form on his face to let him eat. Everyone else finds this amusing. Lawrence expresses his disappointment in the so-called Eternally Starving Archon jokingly.

Millette listens with quiet intent. Finally, Millette asks, "Rodin, does it hurt?"

"No," he says.

"Will you be like that from now on?" she asks.

"I hope not," he says.

"Will you hold me?" She begins to cry.

Rodin comes around to her, lifts her up, and embraces her. "For as long as you'll let me." Millette bawls in his arms.

After few moments, Dahlmür says to her, "My lady, we must go now. We have to meet Aranae to have her begin training him to control his form and to becoming a true Archon."

Vaniir stands. "She can join us. She is a part of us as much as everyone else is. She will be a member of his circle by marriage soon anyhow."

Helana remarks, "That's true! That's how it is going to happen for me and Byron!"

Dahlmür rubs his temples. "Don't . . . Eh . . . Eh . . . Eh . . . Remind me."

Byron raises a question. "How do we sneak him out? It was easy to get him here because it was late at night. Now it's early afternoon. People are everywhere."

Logan jumps up. "I know!"

He runs to a chair and grabs the fur-skin coat. "This is his."

Slender points out. "Oh yeah, Coleman, you recognize that!"

Coleman looks at it and grins. "Perfect."

Logan helps Rodin put it on. As soon as he throws the hood up, he disappears. Millette chuckles at the sight. "Oh, the trouble you can get into with that."

Rodin responds, "I never thought of it that way." Then he grabs her behind and squeezes.

She jumps and shrieks then laughs at him. "Behave!"

Helana says "Don't you dare!" and covers her behind.

Rodin circles Logan and sets him on his shoulders. "Shall we go like this, little brother?"

He laughs as he tries to balance himself. "Can we go past those two guards from last night?"

Byron cries, "No. They'd quit!"

Slender laughs. "Awe, man!"

Vaniir agrees. "Please put him down. Dahlly would have to come up with an explanation why he's levitating him when he isn't."

Dahlmür agrees. "Especially if I have no reason to."

Logan is disappointed. When Rodin puts him down, Logan reaches into his pocket and pulls out a piece of Millette's signature sugar candy.

"No!" everyone cries all at once.

Slender tears it from his hand. "I'll take that."

Logan is baffled. "What?"

Millette laughs. "He's been eating too much again, huh?"

Slender states, "I swear he doesn't breathe when he eats these things." He inspects it and nibbles a piece off. "Oh wow, that's good!"

She tips her head at him, "Thank you. Just don't go eating the entire piece all at once. It has the same effect on everyone. There's a reason it's called breathless sugar candy."

Slender inspects it and shrugs. Before he can put it in his pocket, Byron snatches it out of his hand. Slender yells at him, "Hey! That's mine!"

Byron says, "No. This is his, but he's not getting any more today. Since I am the prince, I will eat it." With that said, he slips the entire piece into his mouth to everyone's surprise.

Rodin pulls down his hood and says, "Didn't you hear what she just said?"

He swallows. "No. What?"

Rodin looks at Byron then looks at Helana and shakes his head. "Unbelievable."

Vaniir says, "If you start running off at the mouth, I'll put you out of *my* misery."

It doesn't take long for the candy to take effect. On their way to the tunnel within the palace that leads to Aranae's chasm, Byron begins to run around, dance, talk to everyone he passes, and grab Helana and kiss her repeatedly. He puts everyone except Logan in an unpleasant disposition.

Logan watches him in amazement and laughs at him.

"You're worse," Slender reminds Logan as he continues to instigate Byron.

As soon as they enter the chasm Aranae greets him and is surprised with Byron's actions. "What is with him?" she asks. Millette is immediately horrified and screams. Aranae asks in amusement, "What is with her? Who is she?"

Rodin holds Millette, and he offers her comfort and tells her everything is all right. A state of calm is instilled in her. This confuses Rodin.

Byron happily answers while dancing around with Biter and Mutt, who are amused with Byron's willingness to play with them. "That's Millette. She's Rodin's fiancé. They're getting married soon. So are Helana and me. We love each other. Isn't she just the most gorgeous girl in all of TerraEarth? You're the most gorgeous girachnid in all of Terra-Earth. I always love talking with you. My dad still doesn't know about all those times I came down here to see you, but I guess he knows that now. By the way, Rodin is here with us. He's invisible. That's why you don't see him. Hey, brother! Let your hood down! He likes being invisible. He plays tricks on people. I love him like a brother. Logan and Slender too. I hope Rodin is the best Archon the world has ever seen. He will be. I just know it. Your kids are cool. Mutt and Biter. I love them. I'll tell you what? I'm going to go and sit over there while you and the old guys—don't tell them I called them old—talk. I love you, Aranae. Bye now."

With that, he walks to a boulder and sits down. Seconds later, he is lying down, out cold and drooling.

Aranae looks at everyone. "Did he breathe?"

Millette looks around in confusion as Lawrence, Logan, and Slender laugh and the others express their disgust. Rodin realizes that they've all been speaking Aranae's language and Millette hasn't understood a word of what's just gone on.

Aranae realizes this situation also and immediately flashes her spell to her so she can understand. "How do feel now, little lady?" she asks.

Millette is startled. "I'm fine. Thank you . . . um . . . I'm sorry." She shakes her head in disbelief. "I don't seem to understand. I'm scared and calm all at the same time."

Aranae stands up, lumbering over everyone. "That's okay. Archon has that effect on everyone when he wants to calm people down." She looks around in search of him. "Now, where is that boy?"

Rodin suddenly understands. "Oh." He lowers the hood, and Archon appears next to Millette, wearing his fur coat. "I'm right here, my lady."

Millette looks at him in her confused state. "You're Archon." A tear flows from her eye, "You, Rodin of Millington, my soon-to-be husband, you are Archon." She stifles her crying. "Please. I want to see you, Rodin. I want to see if this is true and not some trick or dream."

Archon lowers his head. His expressionless face looks at her feet as he grabs her hands to his chest. "I don't know how."

Dahlmür interrupts. "My lady, we have brought him here because Aranae not only gives the gift but also trains him how to use it."

Vaniir joins him at his side. "We brought you here because Rodin has expressed his deep love of you. His heart longs to see you every day. We've seen it in his eyes when he speaks about you. He loves you, and we want you to remind him how much you love him."

Lawrence gently tells her, "We have to go. Rodin—or rather, Archon—must stay for the next few days in seclusion with Aranae."

With horror of what this may mean, she asks, "Seclusion? Why?" Archon turns to him, wanting to hear the answer as well.

"He must if he is to learn how to discover and control his abilities."

Aranae says to her in comfort, "No worries, my dear. He will learn quickly. I can sense that from him."

Millette wipes away the tears from her face as she tries to laugh at Aranae's last comment. "Oh, he's a quick learner, all right. He always amazed me and my mother at how fast he learns things."

Aranae laughs reassuringly. "He'll be just fine. You'll see him in no time. If you'd like, come by in two days to check up on him."

Millette becomes more and more accepting of everything going on. Even more so than Rodin expects. *She understands what's going on? How can she be so accepting of this when I don't even know how to handle this? I don't want to be alone here. I want someone to stay with me. I'm scared out of my mind. What am I going to do?* His face expressionless, Archon grabs Millette and holds her. "I love you, my sweet darling Millette. Please stay and be with me."

Millette looks at him calmly. "You will be fine. I see that now. These people love you. Not as much as Logan and I do, but they love you. I will return in two days, I promise."

He wants to kiss her but can't. "Okay." Reluctantly, he releases her.

Logan steps up to her and grabs her arm and happily tells Archon, "I'll come back with her. I have to make sure you're being taken care of. Gotta look after each other, big brother."

Slender says to him, "If I can get Prince Drool to join us, we'll be back too." He motions a look in Byron's direction as he begins to snore.

Galla slaps a large hand on his back and hovers over him, saying, "No worries, Archon. Your friends are with you." He turns to Aranae. "My lady, he's all yours."

Helana goes to wake Byron. She is steaming about his behavior. She begins to poke him. Nothing. Then she starts pushing on him. Nothing. Furious, she raises her staff high above her head, "I swear. If he doesn't wake up, I'll leave him." She slams it to floor beside his head. *Boom!*

Everyone jumps. Even Aranae cries out, "Whoa!" and Byron is horrified as he hits the floor.

Helana helps him up. "Eat that candy again, and you'll be single."

He wipes the drool from his face. "I'm sorry. That candy is evil. Logan, how do you eat that stuff?"

Logan laughs. "I love it. Why did you take it from me? I had some more if you wanted some. I ate the last of it. I'm sorry you didn't get any, Helana. I think you'd like it. Millette makes the best candy—"

Slender quickly covers his mouth, and everyone breathes a sigh of relief. "Joy! Now you left us with this little hyper guy!" He pushes him to the entrance to corridor. Logan struggles to say something, but Slender is not letting go. "Breathe, Logan! Just breathe! Holy cow!" Logan decides to give up and waves at Archon.

As everyone follows them out, Coleman stops to tell Archon, "Archon—"

"I'm still Rodin."

"Not in that form, you're not. You must remember that." He smile assuredly to him. "Please learn from her. Aranae is willing to share vast knowledge to you from the Archons before you. As long as you work from that knowledge, you will exceed all expectations, and you will be the greatest Archon who ever lived."

Archon bows his head in agreement. "Yes, Coleman. Thank you. And please watch over Millette and Logan for me."

Coleman looks at Slender and Logan. "Logan will be just fine. As far as Millette is concerned . . ." He motions at her. Helana wraps her arm around her and starts talking to her cheerfully. "Well, girls, stick together."

"I see," Rodin observes. Coleman puts a hand to Archon's shoulder to reassure him and walks away, leaving him and Aranae together alone. Even Mutt and Biter leave, escorting Byron and the others.

Aranae lies flat to the floor to look Archon eye to eye (to eye to eye to eye . . .). They stare at each other for a few moments, sizing up their situation. The sound of the falls from the spring fills the quietness. They remain this way for a long time. Archon takes comfort in her gaze. As he watches her, his body begins to tickle. He finds the feeling mesmerizing and soothing. Soon, he feels a chill in the air. He looks down at himself and sees his bare feet. He wraps the fur tighter around himself. He's Rodin again.

He whispers to her, "I'm sorry, my lady. I forgot to bring clothing with me."

She laughs at him quietly. "It's quite all right, little one. I'm used to it." She pulls back from him, but he continues to lie there, "That feeling you just had, remember it. Use that feeling any time you want to regain your human form. You and I will sit this way for a while longer to see how well you hold before your true form returns."

He is startled. "This is my true form."

"Not anymore, little one. You are Archon now. This form is Rodin. Your former human self. You use this form to hide your true form from others when it is not necessary for Archon to be there. You will come to know your true self."

"My lady —"

"Others have called me Aranae. Please call me Aranae."

"Yes . . . Aranae. Why do we have different forms?"

Aranae laughs and responds, "It is all based on your heart and your ferocity toward evil. You are so kind and gentle. That is the comforting effect in your voice that was able to calm your lady friend down. But your form is the most ferocious I've ever seen. You can command your body, and that . . . I don't know . . .

webbing? . . . to do whatever and become whatever you want. It can be your weapon and your protection. You are the most versatile Archon. It can make you quick and agile. You can climb with it. It can catapult you great distances and into great heights. It's amazing what I am seeing from your form. Your training won't be difficult, because this particular form actually wants you to control it in every possible way. It is . . . weird."

"But you gave it to me. Through the bite you gave me."

"No." She sighs as she scratches her head with her front leg. "I gave you the power to become Archon. The Rings blessed you with your form. I cannot choose who becomes what. I've seen Archons that could only wear the form. Some only use that form for protection. Others use their form to allow them to be fierce in battle. Even they could not revert to their former selves." She tilts her head at him, "You are given the ability to control every aspect of your form. That is a beautiful gift. We will take this knowledge and use it in every possible way. Okay?"

Rodin smiles at her. "Yes, my . . . I mean Aranae." Archon returns a moment later. "That didn't take long."

"No, it didn't, but that's okay. Bring yourself back."

Archon stands there for a moment. He tries to concentrate. After a few moments, he is frustrated and shakes his head. "I can't."

"That is quite all right, little one. You were able to do it once. You will be able to do it again. Soon you will master it well enough to where you won't even have to think about it. It will become natural. Everything we learn will come naturally to you. Now let's sit here and concentrate on doing it again together."

"Okay." After they sit and watch each other for a few minutes Archon asks, "Aranae?"

"Yes, little one."

"Why did Lawrence refuse?"

Knowing what he was talking about but not how he knew it, she asked, "How do you know about Lawrence?"

"I saw it. I saw how all the Archons came to be."

"You did? How did you see it?"

"After you bit me and I fell out, I was shown images by the Light. He even told me about them." He begins to recount the images he had seen and the conversation he had with Light while he was unconscious. She listens intently. As he talks she doesn't say anything. She's in fascination of what he went through. She's never heard such stories before. It excites her more that Circle of Light actually *spoke* to him. When he's done, they watch each other for a few minutes.

Finally, she says, "For Light to even talk to you means that you are blessed beyond my understanding." She thinks about it for a moment then sighs, "Lawrence and his friends were coerced."

"I don't know that word."

"He was tricked into giving up the gift even though he was deemed worthy."

"Oh. By who?"

"The one I gave it to. Since he was what you consider a Class of Lord and Lawrence was a Class of Peasant, he felt that it was his birthright to be Archon over him because as he put it, 'the world doesn't need trash as their hero.' I tried to convince them otherwise, but Vil . . . "

Archon perks up, "Vil? As in Lord Vil?"

"Yes, actually. A distant relative of his. The Vil you know is named after the lord who became Archon. The family considers him a hero even though he didn't earn the blessings to be Archon." Aranae sounds as if she were not happy to have given him the gift. She sounds as if she were repulsed by him.

"Didn't he die?"

"Yes. The next day."

"And they consider him a hero?"

"The family had blamed me because I didn't train him. The little louse didn't want to be trained. He felt that, as Lord Vil, he knew best how to defend his class."

"That must have gone over real well with the Rings."

"That's why we are cursed. The Rings blame us for allowing ourselves to be coerced so easily and denying the one that was truly blessed to be Archon. We lived in exile for a long time. Darkness ruled this world during that time until the Rings gave us another blessed through another circle of brotherhood. From then on, we became the Cursed Brothers. Of course, I'm their Cursed Sister. Darkness had my league brothers and sisters sought out and destroyed, thinking that he had rid himself of Light's gift-givers, not knowing I was damned to live forever to do the job."

"So you truly are the last girachnid on Terra-Earth?"

"No, my children are." She sighs with remorse. "They will replace me, and when they die, we are gone. They are both males. There are no more females for them to mate with."

"Oh. I'm so sorry." And he truly is. To hear that there will be no other girachnids like her roaming Terra-Earth makes him feel a pain of sadness from within.

Neither one of them speak for a while. They just sit and study one another. The tickling feeling returns. He recognizes the feeling and hangs onto it. He becomes Rodin again. "I did it."

She happily replies, "I knew you can do it. Now all you have to do is concentrate on holding on to that form."

"Okay."

XIV

odin is able to hold his form longer. He learns to do common chores while hanging on to being Rodin. When Archon returns, she teaches him how to use his form to propel himself into the air and land on his feet nimbly. He also learns that when he lands with his fist to the ground, the ground quakes, and a massive shock wave flows around him. This can be useful to throw a surrounding horde of enemies away from him when he needs to. Even Aranae is knocked off her feet and goes belly-up. She laughs at his accomplishment while struggling to twist her body over to get her eight legs back underneath her. She sounds more childlike in her amusement, as if she hadn't had this much fun in a really long time.

Eventually, Aranae calls it quits. "Okay, little one. We've had enough fun for a day. Now, what I want you to do is put that coat of yours on and see if you can make it a part of you."

"A part of me?" he replies in confusion.

"Oh yeah. It's time for you to get us some supper, and we can't have you being seen. If you go as Rodin, you'll be naked, and if you go as Archon, you'll be mobbed and possibly targeted. Just put it on and concentrate on infusing it into your form."

Reluctant, he grabs the fur coat and throws it on. "Okay." He stands there for a moment and thinks about how he can make it happen. *Just make it a part of me,* he thinks. The coat suddenly sinks into his body, and the fur coat is gone. It becomes the free-flowing form of his body. Hanging from his back is a silvery hood that he throws over his head. Instantly, he's gone.

Aranae claps her fangs together. "Very good! You did it! Now go get us some fresh food. Remember, mine has to be alive."

Archon shivers in repulsion. "I forgot about you spiders."

"Make sure it is big. I'm starving."

His voice travels from the corridor. "Okay!"

She freezes and tells him, "No! You have to go through the caverns!"

"But I can't see!"

"Concentrate. You can see in the dark without any light."

His voice passes in front of her to the caverns leading outside the palace. "Okay. I'll go this way."

"And don't forget that unless you want yours raw, you need firewood and a way to cook it."

He yells from the tunnel, "Anything else?"

She responds bluntly, "No."

Archon enters the tunnel. He lowers his hood since there is no need to be invisible at the moment. His eyes brighten, and he finds that he can see very well. He looks around the tunnel and notices that the rock surrounding him is smooth. It shows no sign of being dug by pickaxes or other means by human hands. *It was either done by magic or this used to be an underground riverway.*

He notices a network of more tunnels forking off in three directions in front of him. *Great! Now what?* He scans the three tunnels. He notices that two of the tunnels do appear to be manmade, and the other is smooth, like the tunnel he is currently in. *Oh, I get it.* He chooses the smooth tunnel and continues to follow it until he feels the cool air of freedom. *Oh, thank the Rings! I can breathe fresh air again.*

Just before stepping out, he throws his hood back up. When he steps out, he's glad he did. The woman from over a week ago is there. *Fannie?* She seems nervous as she looks around. Either she's making sure she's alone, or she is impatiently waiting for someone. Quietly, Archon launches himself onto the wall above and hangs from it to watch her. He is curious to find out what she is up to.

Fannie walks a few steps in a circle, looking around intensely. She stops and suddenly relaxes. She removes her coat and begins to undress. *Oh no!* Archon doesn't know how to react. He doesn't understand why she's undressing, but his curiosity holds him. Her body begins to quiver and ripple. Her skin becomes a healthier almond color. Her hands grow a little fuzzy with protruding claws. Her face changes slightly. Her ears become pointed, her nose shortens as whiskers sprout from each side, and her eyes separate just a little bit. Her hair flows down into silky black curls that flow just above her backside as a cat's tail flips out where her tailbone ends. Her body loses its anatomical features except for the curves of her female body. *She is beautiful.*

Suddenly, Archon realizes what league he is looking at. *She's a morpher!*

She relaxes and begins to enter the woods.

Without wanting to let her know that she has been seen, he jumps from the wall and farther into the trees in front of her. He removes his hood and pretends to sit and study the air around him as she unwittingly catches up to him.

She is startled to see him and yelps, "Oh!"

Archon pretends to be startled as well. "Oh!" And he jumps for the trees, leaving her behind, but just in her view.

She's quick to change herself and becomes catlike to pursue him. *Now what do I do?* She nimbly moves through the trees. In his haste to lose her, he launches himself high above through the canopy of trees and crashes over a hundred yards away into a large tree. He groans, discontent of his actions. "Oh, that should hurt. Oddly enough, it doesn't."

She catches up to him and swiftly lands on top of him, pinning him down with a knife to his throat. "Who and what are you?"

Amazed with how well she is able to do this, he responds, "You move so smoothly through the trees. Can you teach me?"

This catches her off guard. "What?"

"This is my first time being out like this. I want to learn how you did that through the trees."

"Are you serious?"

"Yes. You seem like the type that could teach me about using features of my body." He catches himself. "No, wait! That's not what I meant. What I mean is, I can use my body to change too, but you have better control than I do. I was hoping you can teach me."

She looks at him, puzzled. "You do realize I'm going to slit your throat, right?"

He looks around to take in his situation. "Oh no, please don't hurt me," he mocks.

"Really?"

"Yup."

He launches himself off his back with her screaming and hanging on tightly. He laughs. "I thought you were going to slit my throat?"

"Let's land first! Then I'll be happy to slit you throat!"

He continues laughing until they start to descend. "I'm not good at landings. Any pointers?"

She's too frightened for rational thought. "We're too high! I can't fly!"

An idea hits him. "Good idea!"

"What is?"

"Just hold on."

She wraps her arms and legs around him as he puts his arms out. Suddenly, he has the wings of a bat from the insides of his arms to his torso, making room for her arms and legs. He begins to slow down his descent.

She begins to calm down. "Oh, thank goodness! Just drop me off in those trees. I can figure out where to go from here."

"You do realize you are high in the air and I can take you anywhere I want, right?"

He pulls his body up and higher away from the trees. The color drains from her face as she watches the trees grow smaller and smaller. "No! Please! Please! Whoever you are, please put me down!" She begins to cry.

"I'm not going to hurt you. You're a morpher, Fannie, and I want you to teach me how to change my form like you do."

She begs him to take her back down as she sobs. "Please, I will do what you want."

"Thank you, Fannie."

She suddenly stops crying and looks at him in surprise. "How do you know my name?"

He laughs as they begin to descend into a rocky clearing within the woods by the river. He says to her, "We've met."

"I think I'd remember you."

"I was someone else. Trust me when I say that you will remember who I am soon."

They touch down, and she is still wrapped around him and searching his expressionless eyes.

"I believe I can trust you enough to join my circle. I have a good feeling about you. I don't know why when you have fooled everyone into thinking you're human."

She slowly unwraps herself from him. She watches him with intense curiosity. She sits down on a rock that crops up from the ground beside the bank of the river. She laughs. "I'm going out on a limb here and believe you. For tonight only, though. Well, for right now, tonight only, right now. At this moment in time, right now."

He nods in agreement. "Good." *I better be careful. I think she might figure me out, and Aranae will be so upset with me.* "Okay now, I haven't had a decent meal in a long time. I can see the fish in this river, and I would really like to name a couple of them Dinner. What would you do as a morpher?"

She looks into the river. "It's too dark. You can't see anything in there."

"I can." He points across just left of him. "One there"—he points slightly below himself then farther left—"and there. I want him. He's bigger."

She says, "Well, what I would do is just make my hair blend into a line, and my fingernail would morph into a hook and attach to it."

"Umm . . . okay. You can do that?"

"I'm a morpher. I can manipulate any part of my body to do anything except detach from my body or create complex moving parts."

He nods in understanding. "Gotcha."

He concentrates on a line and a hook. He puts his arm out, and it becomes a silver rod and a thin silver line with a hook. He reaches down and scoops a worm out of the ground as if he already knows where it is, which he does. He baits the hook and throws it to the larger of the two fish. Fannie can see the hook glowing in the dark of the water. The fish takes the bait a moment later. Fannie is impressed. "Okay, but I can't do the whole glowing thing." He laughs as he stands holding the fish. He searches himself then around.

"What are you doing?" she asks.

"I'm trying to figure out where to put it," he says.

She tilts her head. "You really are new at this." She continues to laugh as he throws up his hand in defeat.

"I'm hopeless."

"Yes, you are," she says, stifling a laugh.

He sits down beside her. "I need to rest a moment. I only woke up this morning."

She asks, "Didn't sleep well?"

"Let's just say I was out for a few days."

"Okay." She laughs at him. They sit and talk for a while longer. She tells him more about how she can change form to mimic anything she wants. She explains that some animals she can only mimic but not do as they do, such as those of the Order of Arials and the Order of Aquatics. "Only Terran Orders," she explains. After a while of talking and demonstrating, she looks at him as his eyes dazzle her. "Tell me your name," she whispers.

He calmly whispers back, "If I do, you have to promise to never tell anyone." He stares at her, taking in the fascinating features of her face. *I can watch her all day. She is so beautiful. Her blue eyes, her pointed ears, her small nose, and her brilliant black hair.* Rodin's heart beats faster as they sit and watch each other with only the babbling of the river doing all the talking.

She smiles and rubs his empty face. "I promise," she whispers.

He sighs. "Okay." He shakes his head, knowing she won't believe him. "I am Archon."

She shakes her head and becomes serious. "Wait. You're what?" She stands and looks down at him in disbelief.

He stands and grabs her hands. "I am Archon. Believe me when I say that I didn't know I was chosen to become this until the moment it was given to me."

"I don't understand." She looks at him, bewildered. "What do you mean chosen?"

"Well, I was somebody else."

"Who?" she demands.

"I can't tell you that. Not yet. Not unless you want to join my circle and become one of my army. I also want you to teach me more," he tells her.

"Your circle? What is that supposed to mean?"

"It means you will be chosen as part of my circle to represent your league as a part of my army. Only then can I tell you who I was," he mumbles to himself. "And boy, will you be surprised!"

"I don't know if I'm ready for that yet. I don't even know if I would even want to do that." She stops and looks around and looks at him in realization. "Oh wow, it's getting late. I have to go home before my husband sends out an army to find me."

He freezes. "Whoa! Wait! Back up! Husband?"

She smiles at him in guilt. "Yeah, I'm married."

He toes the ground. *Oh, Millette, forgive me.* "Thank goodness," he confesses.

She crosses her arms. "And what does that mean?" She looks at him in accusation. "Are you married?" Her voice raises several octaves higher.

"Not yet. We were supposed to be at Yuletide, but apparently"—he points out the obvious—"this happened."

"Oh, I'm sorry if I led you to believe otherwise," she says.

"Me too."

"I have to go back."

"Yeah, me too. But with food for Aranae."

She asks, "Who's that? Your fiancé?"

"No, she's the one that gave me . . . this and is helping me learn. You do a much better job."

She smiles at that and says, "Thanks."

"I can carry you back if you'd like," he offers.

"No, but thanks anyway. I can get there on my own." She begins to morph herself back into the catlike form. "Will I see you again?" she asks.

He says to her, "Yes. If you go to the palace and tell the messenger at the door that you need to speak to Logan, he'll come out. When you see him, tell him that his brother sent you."

"You're his brother?"

"Well, he's one of my brothers. Just tell him that you met his brother the Archon, and he will know to help you find me."

"Okay." She winks at him and blows him a kiss. "Thank you for tonight. I really did have fun."

His expressionless face tilts. If he had any expressions, he would be blushing. "I did too, Fannie."

"It's Francine."

He echoes her name back in a whisper, "Francine," and she's gone.

Archon is beside himself with delight. *I would be in so much trouble right now if Millette knew about this,* he reminds himself. He continues to laugh joyfully as he begins to head back. He suddenly remembers Aranae. *Something big and alive.* "What do you feed a girachnid?" he mutters to himself. "Anything it wants!" He laughs in response to his own joke.

On his way back, he spots a bear looking for a place to spend the night. *It must have been kicked out of its hiding spot for the night. Lucky Aranae.* He reaches out with his arms, and suddenly, it parachutes open and wraps around the bear like a sack. The bear struggles, slashing, screaming, and biting, trying to get out. Archon sighs. "Sorry, big guy, but you're the lucky one to be put on the menu tonight." He shudders to himself. "Ew."

He steps up to a fallen tree as he throws his arm/sack over his shoulder and transforms his other arm into a large ax. He cuts logs and splits them to make firewood to cook his catch. He gathers the wood and fish into a sack from the same arm and tosses it beside the struggling bear. *I think I can get the hang of this.* The bear begins to toss around so bad it almost knocks Archon off balance. He suddenly realizes that the bear may be struggling for air. He makes the bear's sack thin enough for air to pass through. He also speaks calmness into it. The bear soon falls asleep.

He returns to the cavern with ease and very quickly by utilizing his ability to jump from tree to tree. He has yet to master stealth, so he keeps his hood up to keep anyone looking around from seeing him. He slips into the cavern and makes his way back to the chasm. When he does, Aranae is pacing and mumbling to herself in worry.

He removes his hood, and she is overjoyed to see him. "Oh, little one! You came back! Thank the Rings." Sternness comes over her voice. "What kept you? I've been worried sick about you. Do you realize how late it is, young man?"

He looks at her in his pride of a successful hunt. "No worries," he mocks her, "Mother. I have something just for you."

The bear suddenly awakens and grunts its dissatisfaction at still being in the sack. Aranae jumps for joy, forgetting her anger with him. "Is that a bear?" She begins to happily bounce about.

Archon laughs at the sight of the giddy oversized spider jumping around. "Calm down, Aranae. I caught you a large brown bear."

Aranae is even giddier. "Oh, I love brown bears! They're so big and juicy!"

He shudders in disgust. "Oh, please. Take it over there. I can't watch that."

She watches intensely at his every movement of presenting her with the bear. She keeps watching the bear sack move up, down, and around. For a moment, Archon flips it while laughing at her as she watches it closely. As soon as he releases it, the bear runs away from him and hides behind one of her legs. It looks up and realizes its predicament in horror as it runs back to Archon, using his body as a shield.

Aranae becomes happy and impatient. "Move! It's huge! I'm so hungry! I want that bear."

Archon begins to feel sorry for the bear as he watches it curl up behind him, whining as if it were begging for its life. "Awe, man! Did you have to go and look at me like that?"

Aranae asks, "You are going to let me eat that, right?"

Reluctantly, Archon gives up, and without looking back at the poor, innocent bear, he jumps to the ceiling, allowing her to have it. She sinks her fangs into the body of the bear, and it falls lifelessly to the floor. Webbing shoots from her abdomen as her large spinnerets cocoon it. Again, he shudders at the sight and drops to the floor with his fish. He sets up the firewood beside the pool.

He then stares at it for a moment. "Damn!"

From the other side, Aranae cries. "What's wrong?"

He keeps his eyes on the firewood. "I don't have any fire to cook on." He grabs an extra log and quickly widdles it down into a stick with a blade formed from his hand. He intends to use it for a spit. He brushes the shavings into the woodpile.

"Make one."

"How?"

"You're Archon. Conjure up a fire."

"I can do that?" he asks in disbelief. As soon as he says it, he thinks about setting the pile on fire. His eyes glow fiery orange and sets it ablaze. "Wow! I guess I can!"

"Good job!" she cries as she carries the bear's cocooned body up the wall to her giant web in the far corner.

Rodin scales and cleans his fish then pushes it onto the spit and holds it over the fire as he turns it. He calms down and focuses on that tickling feeling he's used to change back to Rodin. The process is almost immediate. The fur coat returns to him. He cleans the bones of the fish with his hunger. Feeling satisfied, he walks to the pool and dunks his face into the water and takes in large gulps. He sheds the fur coat and jumps in. *This bath is going to feel great. It has been so long.* He washes himself and slips the coat back on. He allows himself to transform back into Archon, feeling refreshed and rejuvenated. *I don't know why, but this is starting to feel like me.*

Tired, he lies near the fire. His mind races through today's events. He can't wait to see Byron, Slender, and Logan. He wants to tell them all about it, except the part about almost getting too close to Fannie. Rather, Francine. It doesn't take him long to doze off.

Aranae walks up to him to check up on him. She picks him up gently and stares at him as she cradles him in her forward legs. She whispers softly as if she were crying, "Will he remember us a century from now? Or a millennium?"

A voice speaks softly. *"He will never forget you. It is not in his nature."*

"I wish I can be there to witness his victory with my children standing by his side," she says as she spins a soft bedding to lay him on.

"You know that your curse is done. The five of you can return to the Rings in the Spiritual Plane."

"When?" She lays him down and cradles his cheek.

"Soon, very soon."

"He is lucky. Everything good comes to him after the horror he went through."

"Yes, he is truly blessed. Unfortunately, the Rings will test him again."

"What do you mean?"

"He will lose someone else he loves very soon."

"Poor child." She begins to sob for him.

XV

"**N**ow for some real training. You're going to love this. Focus your mind. Your body can create weapons, project deadly darts, and protect you."

"Okay."

"I'm going to conjure all sorts of demons. I want you to attack. We will start out with just one."

Aranae watches from her web in the corner. Archon stands in the center, eager and ready. A few paces from him, an undead appears. It looks at him and screams. Its scream is deafening. Archon is frozen, covering his ears from it. He allows himself to drown out the sound to a whisper.

He regains his stance, and the undead demon lunges toward him. Surprised by its quickness to react, Archon jumps over it, allowing the demon to run past him. Archon twists in the air to face it. He concentrates on creating an ax blade with his hand and swings. The demon ducks and dodges every swing. Archon has never known the undead to be so nimble. He has heard of them being sluggish and dragging in their movements.

"They are not zombies!" Aranae tells him. "The undead are the league that wear the skin of their victims given to them by the League of Trolls! Zombies are the actual victims reanimated from the dead."

"So that's why the trolls skin their victims?"

"Yes, but they skin men and kill the women and children. Only one woman is used as a queen. They have a hive mind like bees. One queen per hive."

"So like bees, if I slay the queen, they lose themselves and become weaker?"

"Exactly."

That means she has created a queen to make this one! Archon swings at the demon to ward off its attack. He leaps up to the ceiling to get a better vantage point. *Where is she?* He searches the chasm. The undead demon leaps at him taking him by surprise with its ability to leap that high. Archon shoots a line for himself to swing to another area of the chasm. Then it hits him. *If I can to that, then I can pin it down!* He fires a dart at it that opens up into a net. The undead outmaneuvers it by rolling away. *Damn this thing is fast!*

Archon scurries about the ceiling, shooting darts and swinging his blade at it to keep it away. He continues to scan the chasm. He finds what he is looking for; two red eyes glowing from behind the falls.

Without letting on that he has spotted her, Archon continues to bound around the chasm, acting in defense and in attack of the demon until he draws himself closer as if by accident. He makes a flying lunge toward the demon and turns in midair to deliver a dart directly to the center of the queen's forehead. The demons disintegrate.

"Well done, little one!" Aranae's fangs clap together. "Next one!"

Before Archon can catch his breath, a vampire appears, its face black and gray, grotesquely resembling that of a bat. It bares a set of oversized fangs and pointed teeth at him in a wicked, drooling smile. Its bright yellow eyes shine at him. The glare is almost hypnotizing. He raises his hands to block it out. That is when the demon attacks.

Archon is surprised and thrown to the farthest wall across the chasm, the wind knocked out of his lungs. Gasping for air, Archon asks, "How do I block out his hypnotizing gaze?"

"Try blocking out his evil light!" Aranae suggests.

"Right," he responds. *As if I know how to do that.*

The vampire gazes at him again, and Archon focuses for a moment. His yellow beads for eyes begin to constrict, limiting the effect of the hypnotic stare. The vampire realizes that it is now a futile attempt and begins to attack. He swings his hands at him with its fingernails extending into six-inch claws. Those claws leave a mark in Archon's form. His chest bleeds silvery fluid. He feels the pain of the strike. It burns profusely.

"You are capable of being hurt!" Aranae says to him. "A demon's formidable weapon can kill you! Watch for his claws as well as his fangs and gazes!"

Archon grabs at his chest and mutters, "Right." He shakes himself to dismiss the pain and goes into his own attack. He dodges a few more swipes and connects to the head and chest of the vampire with a few punches of his own. The vampire staggers back, and Archon jumps at it, planting both feet into its chest. The vampire crashes into the wall of chasm. At the moment of its impact, Archon fires off a dart, and it drives into the vampire's chest and out its back. A black heart is left nailed to the wall. The vampire's eyes become empty, and it falls to the ground in a foul black sludge.

"You learn quickly, little one." She claps again and climbs down to him. "Let us stop and rest."

Exasperated, Archon agrees. He bends over from the pain of his wounds. He grunts, "Oh, this hurts."

"I'm sorry. Next time I'll make it a baby so it won't hurt you so much."

Jokingly he responds, "That would be nice."

She laughs in turn. She looks down at him and lowers herself to look at his wounds. "Okay. Masters Dahlmür and Byron will be here shortly. He might as well start his training as healer now."

"How do they know to be here?"

"I just told Dahlly." She turns around to the corridor leading inside the palace. "And don't you call him Dahlly."

"No, Aranae."

"He doesn't like being called Dahlly."

"So why do you call him that?"

She laughs. "Because he doesn't like being called Dahlly." If he had an expression, Archon would be smiling.

Dahlmür's staff clicks down the corridor. Archon figures that Byron is in tow. The first to show is Byron with a worried look.

He bypasses Aranae and runs straight to Archon, staring in horror at his wounds. "What have you done, brother?" He pulls Archon to the pool.

Archon says to him, "I fought a vampire!"

Byron looks at his stomach as he begins healing it. "Is that really from a vampire?"

"Yeah. He had, like, these fangs that were, like, nya!" Archon hangs his fingers in front of his face, forgetting he doesn't have one. "And these huge claws!" He hooks his hands and fingers to represent claws. "And he was, like, ahh!" He shakes his head at him while making a face he still doesn't remember isn't there.

Byron looks at him in fascination then bursts out laughing while pointing at him. His hands, forgetting to finish healing the wound, quit glowing. He tries to say something but can't. He holds his stomach and wipes away tears. If Archon had a face, it would have displayed the look of someone dumbfounded. Byron is truly overcome with laughter. He falls backward.

Confused, Archon asks, "What the hell is wrong with you?"

Byron sits up with his tunic above his head, reenacting Archon's face with the fangs. "Nya!"

Archon suddenly becomes aware of Byron's meaning. "You bitch!" He gazes down and spots his target. His eyes glow fiery orange.

Byron, still laughing, says, "Hey. That's cool. What are you— *ahhhhhhh!*" Byron leaps up, fanning the flames between his legs. "Shit!" He jumps into the pool. He then climbs out. "You bastard! That burned! I shouldn't finish healing that when you just tried to roast my chestnuts over an open fire!"

Now it's Archon's turn to laugh. They begin laughing together, and Byron finishes healing him.

"Oh," Archon says, grabbing him to keep him from getting up. "Watch." And he's Rodin again.

"What? I told you that mask is cool."

Rodin looks at him, confused, then looks at his hands then feels his face. He realizes the joke. "Oh, you're an ass!"

Byron giggles. "I'm glad to have you back, brother." His expression softens.

So does Rodin's. "I'm glad to be back too, brother."

They embrace, each of them glad to see the other again. After a moment, they release each other and wipe the tears from their eyes and sniffle into their sleeves.

Rodin jumps up and looks to make sure they are out of earshot of Aranae and Dahlmür.

"You've got to promise me that you will never tell anyone what I'm about to tell you, except Slender, but you've got to make him swear too. If this gets to my brother, he will tell, and Millette will murder me and never marry me. Got it?"

Byron nods. "Yeah, okay. What?"

He begins to whisper to Byron, "I saw a morpher last night!"

"What?" Byron cries.

"Shhh!"

Byron whispers, "What were you doing that you saw a morpher?"

"Aranae sent me out to get us food. And anyway, I went out the cavern, and there she was."

"She?"

"Yes! She!" he puts his hands to his chest to indicate her breast size. "She was naked and gorgeous as all hell! This was *after* she took on her morpher form. Oh, and you won't believe who it is."

"No. Tell me. Who was it?"

"Fannie!"

"What?" he cries aloud.

"Shhh! I said it's a secret, moron!" he smacks his shoulder.

"Okay! I'm sorry! Ow!"

Rodin tells him about last night.

Dahlmür gazes in Archon's direction as Byron runs to heal him. "Ah, his first wound. A vampire perhaps." He turns to look at Aranae. "I guess you went straight to the hard stuff. No wonder he's hurt."

She says to him in annoyance, "Oh, stop it, Dahlly. He's better than I had expected. He learned so quickly. He has killed two demons in less than an hour."

Intrigued, Dahlmür looks at Archon and asks her, "Which two?"

"An undead and a vampire. Both of them a level 8."

"What?" he says, astonished. "Level 8? Are you sure?"

Annoyed at his line of questioning, she crosses her front arms at him and lowers herself to be face-to-face with him. "Dahlly, I conjured them myself."

"That's—"

"Incredible. I know." They both look at Archon as he is being nursed by Byron. "I'm telling you, Dahlly, that boy is so—"

"Peculiar. I know," he whispers.

She informs him, "He's mastered the change too."

"This soon?" he asks in amazement. "How can he be so far ahead like this?"

"It is like I said when I gave it to him, it is like he has always been destined to be the Final Archon since the Rings gave the gift. Everyone else were just what they are, predecessors. Not to be blessed as the *real* Archon. If you had seen how well he spotted the queen and hid that until the final moment before he vanquished her, you would have laid out on the floor. I almost fell from my web! He was just incredible to watch!"

"Calm down, Nae," he says with a finger to his mouth. They hear Byron suddenly scream out and run into the pool with the crotch of his pants on fire. Aranae and Dahlmür look back at each other and shake their heads at the little children. He whispers to her, "We will watch together. As soon as the healer is finished, bring on three orcs."

"Whoa. That's too soon," she refuses. "He's good, but you see what a level 8 vampire did to him because he was unprepared."

"Show him the gaze," he suggests.

"I hadn't even thought of that." She chuckles. "And this is the crazy part, I don't have to show him."

"What?"

"I tell him what he's capable of doing, and he does it. I bet if I told him that he could fly to the moon, that boy would actually make it."

"Blessed Rings! Let us test that theory, Nae."

Confused, she shakes her huge head. "What?"

"Let us make up something so outrageous and see if he can do it."

She looks at Rodin and sighs. "That boy will do it or die trying, I'm sure."

Dahlmür and Aranae approach the boys. They are obviously telling secrets because as soon as they are noticed, the two boys begin hushing each other. They look up at Aranae and Dahlmür innocently and smile. Dahlmür grunts, "The cats who ate the canary." The boys look at him, puzzled.

Aranae asks, "What canary?"

Dahlmür responds, "Exactly," leaving them all confused.

Rodin and Byron look at Aranae. Byron shakes his head in confusion as Rodin asks, "Wha . . .?"

Aranae shakes her head. "Don't ask me." She looks over Rodin and asks to see his stomach. He shows her, and she studies how well he is healed. "How do you feel inside?"

Rodin rubs where the injury was, "A little tender."

She looks at Byron. "You will be here from now on. It is your job to heal him. The more you practice with your arts, the better you will get at healing not just him but also everyone else around him. Including yourself."

"Yes, Aranae," Byron responds.

"Okay! Next!" She leaps to her web and perches herself to watch as Rodin changes back. "Byron, sit at the pool with Dahlly and watch. Archon, just so you know, you have a powerful fear gaze. It is most effective when you do not have the option to fight, or if you need a tactical advantage. Focus on scaring your enemies. Your power will come from your eyes, and your body will provide the fear. Also, you can manipulate the ground around you. Use it to your advantage in a fight. Use your ground-pounding tactics also. You better be ready, because there are going to be a squadron of eight orcs coming at you." Dahlmür stands as if to object, but Aranae screams out, "Now!"

Immediately, eight nasty, foul-smelling greenish creatures appear on the other side of the chasm. They are hunched over with their crooked backs, and they carry a variety of weapons, from clubs to swords. One green-eyed demon carries a bow with flaming arrows ready to fire stacked beside it. They spot Archon, and the biggest of the bunch begins to approach. *He wants to intimidate me?* The demon flexes and stretches its arms, preparing for a fight as it beats its war hammer into its hand. *I can do this, I hope.* It walks up to him nose to nose.

Archon is scared out of his wits. "If I had a nose, I bet you'd stink," he says to his intimidator. Byron laughs. "I think he wants to kiss you, brother!"

Archon chuckles. "No tongue," he tells the orc.

The orc is not in a playful mood and catches Archon with an uppercut to the chin with its hammer. Archon flies up into the air, and the orc catches him with a kick to the gut on the way down, sending him crashing into the wall. Archon is slow to get up. "Ow." He stands up and steps up to the big demon. He focuses himself. His eyes suddenly glow bright silver, and his body flares out. His face opens up into a snarling monster screaming at the orc. The orc stands in wide-eyed horror and lets itself go.

Byron jumps in horror himself and grabs onto Dahlmür. "Wow! Even I thought that was scary!"

Dahlmür grunts and shrugs him off. "Pay attention, child."

Byron looks at him, offended. "Child? Really?" He turns his attention back to Archon.

Dahlmür points out with a snicker. "Look. He scared the shit out of him. Literally." He elbows Byron.

Still in horror, the orc looks down at the ground between its legs to confirm Dahlmür's observation. Archon looks down too then back to the frightened orc. The orc stares a moment longer and screams in terror as it turns to flee. Archon reaches out, extending his arms long enough, his hand forming an oversized sledgehammer and squashes the orc beneath it.

Dahlmür and Byron share a look of surprise. Dahlmür mumbles, "Orc pancakes. Order up." Byron catches it and chuckles at him.

Archon looks at the other seven orcs. Four of them rush after him. Archon launches himself into the air and looks down at them. The group freezes as he comes down with his body twisted, his fist drawn way back.

Dahlmür mumbles to Byron, "Orc. Corner pocket."

Byron looks at him in confusion. "Who are you?" Dahlmür laughs, taking Byron off guard.

Archon slams his fist to the ground as hard as he can. A huge wave rises from the ground and throws the orcs in separate directions directly into their own corner. They each smash hard. The impact crushes their bones killing them instantly.

Byron says to Dahlmür, "Five down, three to go."

Dahlmür calls out to the orcs. "Next!"

One orc freaks out and runs headlong at Archon. Archon stands up straight, and his hands become a large bat.

Dahlmür calls out, "Swing, batter, batter!"

Archon bends at the knees to line up his swing, draws back, and fires. *Crack!* The orc is sent screaming through the air with a bashed-in jaw.

Dahlmür stands and watches the orc flying high and toward the tunnel leading out. "It's up! It's going. Going." The orc flies over the last two's heads and into the pitch-black tunnel. "It's gone!" Byron starts cheering and clapping with Dahlmür. Archon mocks running the bases as he waves at his fans (Byron and Dahlmür) and jumps onto home plate.

The last two orcs look at each other then spread out. One orc carries a sword. The other has the flaming arrows. The one with the sword points it at Archon, and a blast of icy wind blows at him.

Archon is quick to jump the wall. He realizes he has just made himself vulnerable to the other one. He twists and curls into a ball just in time to feel heat fly right by his ear. *Zip zip zip!* This orc is apparently fast to reload and fire in the same area as the first shot.

Archon bounds around the room. He thinks for a moment, *I've got to get rid of the rapid-fire orc. I can't sit still long enough to get to him without the other getting after me too.* It suddenly dawns on him what to do.

Archon draws them toward the darkest area of the cavern. The corner is pitch-black. There isn't any light here. He launches into the blackness and disappears. The two orcs freeze. They watch for any sign of him. Growing impatient, the one with a sword blasts the corner with a freezing wind.

Nothing.

Dahlmür leans into Byron. "Where did he go?"

Byron responds, "I know what he did."

A voice comes from beside them. "Does that one with the sword look like Master Wide to you?"

They look over the orc. "I don't see a resemblance," Dahlmür states.

"You'll see it," says the voice.

Archon walks up behind the one blasting the corner with the icy wind. The other orc keeps an arrow drawn and keeps on the lookout for any movement in the darkness. Archon kneels to the ground and concentrates. The ground beneath the orcs start to tremble, and a massive boulder shoots up and launches the swordsorc into the air, reenacting what happened to Master Wide when he tried to return to the school grounds.

Byron points calmly and nods in recognition. "Oh, I see the resemblance. Hi, Master Wide." He waves at the orc as it crashes into the dark corner.

The final orc is outraged. It turns and fires a flaming shot in Dahlmür and Byron's direction. Quick to react, Archon fires a dart at the arrow, knocking it to the ground just as it is within feet from them. Byron falls backward into the pool, and Dahlmür jumps to his feet, firing a yellow spark to ground in the orc's direction screaming, "Technical foul! Unsportsman-like conduct! Twenty-yard penalty!"

Archon immediately realizes he has just given away his position and drops to the ground rolling out of the way of the incoming flaming arrows. He flies to the wall as the orc continues to shoot around his position. The orc gives up and draws a hood over his head. He's now invisible. Archon is stunned. With all his senses on high alert, he scans the area waiting for any sign of it.

Aranae announces, "Little one, orc bodies give off more heat than human bodies."

"Right!" And he says suddenly, "Shit!"

Arrows fly at his perch. *Zip! Thock!* One arrow lodges into the wall next to his head. He immediately propels himself and fires darts in its direction. *Missed!* He lands softly to the ground. He remembers Francine morphing into a catlike figure and decides to do the same. He crouches down, and he's an invisible tiger. He focuses his eyes. Suddenly, he sees everything as glowing heat sources. He sees Aranae's large body perched high above in shades of white, blue, yellow, red, and orange hues. He looks over to Dahlmür and Byron, and they appear the same, but less white. He scans the chasm. *Where the hell is it?* He looks up and sees the heat shape of a figure scurrying across the ceiling in Aranae's direction with a cold object in its mouth. *A blade! It's going to attack her!* Quickly, he leaps to the wall and stalks the orc from the ceiling. The orc gives no indication that it knows it is being followed. Just when it reaches her, Archon leaps at it with a roar. His hood flies off as he grabs the orc in his jaws and tears it from the ceiling. He shreds the orc's hood when they hit the ground and they are both visible again.

Aranae is disturbed by the orc's action. "Why that little . . . I created you!" She mutters, "That bastard."

Now, Archon and the orc stand face-to-face. The orc's breath is hot and foul. Archon breathes heavily with anger. He looks at the orc in the eye. "Let's finish this!" The orc cries out in agreement.

Archon forms an ax out of his hand, and the orc draws a short sword. The orc raises his sword. Archon swings the back of his ax into his hand and prepares to fight. They launch at each other screaming out their war cries as they dodge each other when they swing out. Archon's ax shatters the orc's blade and its arm is separated from its shoulder. When they hit the ground, Archon swings around at the orc and throws his ax at it. The ax's blade sinks into its neck. The orc is frozen with a terrified look on its face as its head slumps over the ax. It falls to the ground. Dead.

Relieved that it is over, Archon calmly walks up to the disintegrating body and puts his hand to the ax as it flows back into his body.

Byron stares in wonder as Archon's form flows faster around his body. Archon sits down by the pool to rest. Byron asks him, "Are you okay?"

Archon looks up at him. "Sleep."

It is the only word he says before he passes out.

XVI

Archon awakens to loud, bickering voices. He feels exhausted as he tries to focus on the voices. *Vaniir, Galla, and Lawrence are arguing with Aranae about somebody.* He also hears Byron involved.

"No, Sir Galla. Tell him no!" Byron says.

"I agree with him. He cannot come here. I don't care who he is. He will not enter this place! This is not a part of his kingdom. Or mine, for that matter," King Vaniir says.

"I will barricade us in if he decides to attempt to enter this sanctuary," Aranae says.

Sir Galla responds, "I caution you. He will try. He'll have his guards tear the palace apart, looking for this place."

"He can try, but it won't do him any good. He won't find us," Byron tells him.

"I suggest a formal place in the woods. It will seem like the sanctuary has moved to a new location. We'll tell him that this place no longer exists and hasn't existed in centuries."

Vaniir grunts, "That's a good idea."

"The fortress in the canyon?" Sir Galla suggests.

"When?" asks Dahlmür.

Master Lawrence sighs. "He wants to meet tomorrow morning."

Byron informs Aranae, "We need to hurry."

Aranae says, "He's still out cold. We haven't had supper yet. He's going to need to eat."

Coleman speaks up. "Allow me to arrange that. How does a nice, fat bull sound?"

Archon begins to sit up and tells him, "As long as we are cooking it for us, it sounds good. If you're talking about for her, I'll pass."

They walk up to him, and Byron helps him to his feet. He uses Bryon to hold him up. He looks around and relaxes. He becomes Rodin.

Dahlmür sets a hand on his shoulder. "That was the most fascinating thing I had ever seen. You have surpassed all expectations. You've also proven yourself to be a great warrior. You should be proud."

"I'll take food over pride for now, if that's okay," Rodin says.

Byron helps him steady himself. "We'll eat. We aren't staying here for a while."

"I heard. Who's wanting to see us?" he asks.

"King Saul," Byron says.

Vaniir speaks up, "And he is in the palace. He wants to see you tomorrow morning."

"Is there something wrong with that?" Rodin asks curiously.

Aranae says, "Everything. He wants to make a show of us! He thinks that you and I somehow belong under his rule."

"I am human."

Aranae responds, "No, as a matter of fact, you're not. Not anymore. You are now directly under the Circle of Light's rule. We belong to him."

Byron lets him stand up by himself as he tries to heal his energy by allowing some of his own to flow into Rodin. Rodin notices the change in energy. He shakes his head at him to make him stop. Byron says to him, "I am well rested, brother. Take some of my energy."

Rodin looks at him and smiles. "I'm fine now. Thanks, brother."

Byron says to him, "That isn't the only problem. Vil has gone missing. He escaped the stockade and has gone into hiding."

"Let him hide. The little plague," Rodin says about it.

"He knows about this place. He can be dangerous," Sir Galla explains.

Rodin suggests, "Then it is time for us to move."

Dahlmür agrees, "Indeed." Dahlmür claps his hands together and announces, "Let's eat. I'm famished. Larry, please get the bull for the lady here, and I'll have Lana summon supper to the library upstairs and have everyone join us to discuss our moving."

Rodin looks at Byron. "You need to have our new friend summoned here right away."

Byron looks at him, puzzled, then remembers. "Oh, right. I'll do that now." He runs off as Dahlmür converses with Helana through the stone on his staff.

In no time, Coleman brings a reluctant bull into the chasm by way of the tunnel. When the bull sees Aranae, it freaks out and starts charging back to the tunnel. Rodin stands and huffs. "I'll get it." He transforms into Archon and chases after the fighting bull. After a few attempts, Archon is able to capture and calm the bull down.

Aranae is giddy with delight. She bounces up and down with excited anticipation of the large feast. Archon laughs at her. "Really? Are you that deprived?"

She stops and looks at him. "You have no idea. I send the kids out, and they bring me back animals as small as rabbits. Look at me!" She stands up on her four back legs to show off her height. "Do I look like a rabbit-eater to you?"

Rodin chuckles. "No, my lady. You look as if one *hundred* rabbits would keep you in your shapely figure."

She takes this joke as a compliment. "Why, thank you, little one! I knew I loved you for a reason. You know how to flatter a woman."

Galla, Lawrence, Vaniir, and Dahlmür laugh at her. Galla whispers to Vaniir, "She still doesn't know when she's being insulted."

"I heard that! Besides, Archon was giving me a compliment. He understands the troubles of a girachnid like me."

Archon nods to her. "Yes, I do, Aranae. You are truly a beautiful creature of all the orders."

She snatches her bull and runs to her perch. "Thank you, little one."

Dahlmür shakes his head at Archon's spectacle of complimenting her. "Oh, if you only knew, boy."

"I heard that!"

They hear a noise coming from the corridor leading to the palace. The sound of dinner trollies as well as the voices of Helana and the others with it. Archon pulls up his own boulder from the ground within the circle of boulders they sat on during his blessing. He pulls up another for Millette to sit beside him. As soon as they appear with the trollies, he whistles for them to bring them there and becomes giddy just like Aranae. "Oh, please. Please. *Please* let there be another trolley. I'm so starving."

Lawrence laughs. "Like mother like son."

Mutt jumps at him. "Hey, we're her sons!"

Biter agrees. "Yeah. Not that two-legged thing there."

Aranae gulps and calls out, "He most certainly is like my child. That makes him your brother. So I expect you to treat him as such." She returns to her bull.

"Okay," Biter responds. "Would you like me to fetch you a live rabbit, *brother*?"

For a moment, Archon is repulsed then thinks about it. "Yeah! Fresh meat! Oh, please? I'm starving!"

Not realizing he's not pulling one of his *seven* legs, Biter mutters, "You have got to be related to Mutt. You both are full of laughs." Biter walks away to the tunnel.

Archon looks at everyone. "I wasn't kidding. Freshly roasted rabbit sounds good with our feast."

Everyone laughs at him, and Biter tells him that he will be glad to bring one back for him.

Archon graciously thanks him. Repeatedly.

Millette sits next to Archon and hugs him as Archon leans into her. She looks into his eyes. "I wish I could see you again, my love."

He becomes Rodin with his fur coat draped around him. "I'm right here, my sweet darling."

Logan pretends to gag, and Slender sits on the other side of him, batting his eyes and saying, "Look into my eyes, my love. Do you see the stars that I have for you? Kiss me."

Quickly, Logan answers, "Okay," and kisses him on the lips.

Slender jumps backward and falls over. "I was kidding!"

Logan laughs. "It didn't look like you were! I got a little worried for you for a moment!" And he laughs at him some more.

"What?" Slender hops up. "You take that back!" He chases after Logan.

Millette and Rodin laugh at the sight of them. Millette says, "They've been like this every day. I think Slender and Logan actually enjoy being brothers."

"Me too."

She looks at Rodin and studies him. "My dear, when was the last time you ate?"

"Last night."

Everyone exclaims, "Last night?"

Dahlmür looks up at Aranae. "My lady, you haven't been feeding him?"

She pauses. "What? Yeah, he just said he ate last night. It was a really big fish too."

"Aranae," Dahlmür explains, "he was a human."

She replies in guilt, "Uh-oh, I forgot. It has been so long. I keep forgetting that you Terrans eat more than one meal a day." She looks at Rodin. "Little one, why didn't you remind me? I'm so sorry."

He smiles at her. "It's okay, Mother. You and I were a little preoccupied."

"I'm sorry, my child. Don't let me forget again."

Vaniir tells him, "The more you use your abilities, the more you will need to eat to regain your energy and strength."

Dahlmür grunts, "I wondered why he passed out after all that he did today. I didn't bother to make sure he was well nourished."

Slender pats Rodin on the back as he sits back down. "Oh, how did it go today?"

Rodin grabs a piece of bread he's been spying on. *Snap! Snap! Snap!* He quickly releases it in disappointment. "Well, I fought an undead, a vampire, and eight orcs. One of them reminded Byron of Master Wide."

"Wow!" Slender says in amazement. "I wish I could have seen that!"

Millette leans in and kisses his cheek. "No wonder you're worn out."

Logan bounces up and down. "I bet that was so cool! Was it fun?"

Dahlmür says, "It was for the observer."

Byron chuckles and points out. "Dahlmür here was well entertained with his own commentary."

Slender looks at Dahlmür in doubt. "That fun-stealer? I don't think so."

Galla says to them, "Back in the day, Dahlly here was the real prankster of us!" He pats Dahlmür on the back.

Logan looks at Galla. "Back in the day? Really? *Back in the day* is something Slender's father would say. Don't you mean *back in the century*, old man? Or *maminia*, maybe?"

Slender shakes his head. "What?"

Rodin laughs. "*Millennia.*"

Lawrence and Coleman laugh as Vaniir pats Galla on the back. "Gotta watch what you say around him, Galla." He winks at Logan.

Unappreciative of the wisecrack, Galla growls, "Damn kid."

They all laugh at him. Galla begins to smile and winks at Logan. Dahlmür plays it cool.

Rodin begins to recall the tale of his battles. Aranae is quick to recant his embellishments. They are all fascinated. When he tells them about how he had been hurt from the vampire, Millette quickly pulls his coat open to look at how bad his injury is.

Helana jumps. "Hey, girl! None of that at the table! Save it for the wedding night!"

Millette turns bright red in embarrassment, and Rodin explains how Byron healed him before he moved on to the orcs.

Slender scans the chasm. "Hey, where is Byron anyway?"

Rodin looks at him in guilt. "He had to run an errand."

Dahlmür groans, "We are starving. I wish he'd hurry."

That's when they hear a woman's timid voice in the corridor, pleading, "Your Majesty, please. If this is some kind of joke to get me to your chambers, I must let you know, I'm not that kind of girl."

As Byron enters with a blindfolded young peasant woman, Helana jumps to her feet. "He better not be taking you to his chambers, or our wedding is off!" She looks at him sternly.

Byron looks around at everyone innocently, "I brought her here for Archon!" He tilts his head and gives Rodin a wide-eyed signal to change. Rodin immediately changes.

Helana flips her head to Millette in surprise. "Archon? Really?"

Millette looks at her with the same surprised look and spins and glares at Archon. "Um . . ."

Her voice deepens with sternness. "Start talking, *Archon*!" She emphasizes his name to signal the seriousness of the troubles he's currently being put in.

The girl throws off the blindfold. "Archon!" She looks around the room and sees the two women glaring at her with pissed-off faces. Everyone else is shocked to see her at all. "Um, I promise it isn't what you think!"

Millette's face glows many shades of red. "Tell me what this is then, *Archon*!"

He reaches out to touch her. "Sweetie, please!"

She pulls back. "Touch me and die, *sweetie*!"

The woman looks at Archon with a hand on her hip. "I thought you wanted me to join your circle? Did you forget to ask your circle first?"

Archon looks up at Aranae. "Help?"

Aranae turns from her bull. "Huh? What? I'm sorry I wasn't paying—" She spots the woman. "A morpher! Oh! She's a morpher! Oh, thank the Rings! Somebody to help teach him!"

Archon mumbles, "That's what I said."

Millette growls through gritted teeth, "No, you didn't. You didn't say anything." Archon shrinks away from her.

The woman raises her hand. "Actually, my lady, he did. Last night when we first met."

Millette cries out, "You met last night?" She stands to walk away.

Archon bellows, "Enough!" It echoes around the chasm for a few moments. "If you would all just calm the hell down and listen for a moment, you'd understand!" He turns to Dahlmür, Helana, Slender, and Logan. "You idiots are not very observant!" They look down at their feet shamefully. "If you will open your eyes and look, you will see that this is Fannie! But no! You morons are too busy accusing us of something!"

Aranae speaks up. "Hi, Fannie. I'm Aranae. I can tell you are a morpher. Nice to meet you!"

Fannie looks at Aranae. Fear comes across her face. She begins to scream until Archon rushes to her and calms her down. She's confused by the chirps and grunting Aranae makes at her. Aranae casts her spell to help her understand. "I'm sorry." And she repeats her introduction. Fannie gives a concerned look and waves.

Rodin continues his scolding. "And her name is Francine, if any of you care to know. And yes, she is a morpher. I asked her to come here because for some reason that I don't understand, I am compelled to ask her to join us and to train *me* in ways to control this form. I was trying to do this in a way that would have been easier to explain, but apparently, we have to move. We're all getting together a day earlier, and I, all of a sudden, have to figure how to do this while you idiots curse me! Why am I the damn victim here?" Everyone is silent as he tries to catch his breath. He looks around, shrugs, and then throws his hands in the air in surrender. "I give up. You can all just kiss my ass! I'm out of here!"

After a moment, Francine looks at Archon. "I'm sorry I caused you so much trouble."

Archon nods calmly and quietly and answers, "No, Francine, it isn't you. I wanted to wait for what was supposed to be tomorrow night if you had agreed like we had said. I wanted to give you a choice, but nobody gives me any choices anymore, and I really wanted you to teach me, and I didn't want to lose that. Plus, for some reason, I have this compulsion to have you join our circle. I can't explain why. I wanted to speak to Aranae about it first. I'm so sorry."

Millette begins to cry. "I'm so sorry! I didn't mean to accuse you of anything. I just didn't know what was going on."

Helana stifles a tear. "I'm sorry too." She walks up to him and hugs him as she breaks into a sob. She wipes her eyes as she pulls away. "You really are a good man." She turns to Francine. "I'm sorry if I offended you. I really am."

Still huffing and ready to leave, Archon looks at Francine. "I've got to get out of here, Francine. Sit next to Millette." He motions her to his spot. "This is the girl I told you about. Some of the others you remember from that night we all met."

Francine looks around and gives notice to Slender, Dahlmür, Logan, and the others that helped the night she had turned in Dawlton and his men. She turns to Archon in surprise and says in recognition, "I know who you are now, my lord."

"Please. As I said that night, just call me Rodin. When I'm like this, I'm Archon. I'm glad to share this with you. If you will become one of us, of course, then again, what will your husband say?"

She smiles in guilt as her face reddens. "No husband."

Dahlmür laughs. "Well played, my lady."

Archon shakes his head. "That's good. And while we're on that subject, we are all in this together. If I find out that any of you"—he points at Dahlmür and his crew—"are hiding anything from any of us"—he points around his own crew, including Francine—"what I did to those orcs will be nothing compared to what I can do to you."

Vaniir looks at him as if he were being insulted. "You only think—"

"Would you like to try me? Because I know how to turn anyone to ashes by just looking at them. Ask Aranae. She taught me. She's the only one that seems to be on *our* side. I'm telling you now! We. Are. *All*. In this together! You shut us out, and you can take a flying leap from Trade Canyons! Because *we* will not be left out! Not just me talking here. You've been doing this to each and every one of us. And shame on you and you"—he points to Dahlmür and Vaniir—"because they are your own children."

The two of them look at each other. The other three men watch them as they shamefully look down at the ground. Byron and Helana look at them in accusation, letting them know that they aren't happy for what's been done to them as well.

Archon shrugs and sighs. "Okay, so I really do have to go. Right now, that supper trolley is more of a snack to me. I am starving, and I really do need meat to eat. Just save a loaf of bread, some cheese, that fruit looks great, and some wine. I really do need to hunt something bigger. I'll be back, I promise. While I'm gone, I don't know what the crisis is that's going on, but I'm all for moving just because of the threat that Vil poses since he's gone missing. Just work out the details."

He's in a hurry to leave before he starves to death. His body is urging him with hunger. He changes into Rodin and smiles at Francine then hugs Millette and kisses her. He looks up to Aranae. "Mother, is there anything I can get for you?"

She burps. "Oh, little one"—she burps again—"I still have some leftover."

He laughs at her. "Very well. If Mutt comes back with a rabbit, it's mine. Unless she wants it." He points up to Aranae. "I'm off! Good-bye, my love."

"Good-bye, my sweet and wonderfully sexy man!" Slender says to him.

"I love you too, Slender. You too, Byron. I still haven't told Helana about us!" He hears Byron laugh out. "Little brother, watch over everyone while I'm gone."

"Sure will!" Logan smiles.

He changes into Archon and leaves down the tunnel.

Still angry over the insult, Vaniir sneers, "That boy has some nerve threatening me."

Byron glares at him, "Shut up, Dad!" Vaniir is startled by him. "He's right! You two should be ashamed of yourselves. Now, if you want to be a part of this circle, then join us and eat."

Helana agrees with him and sits down beside Francine. The three girls start formally introducing themselves to one another and begin gossiping with one another at once. Logan and Slender sit and continue talking with Byron about what he saw during Archon's battle with the orcs. Aranae excuses herself and announces that she will be turning in after today's hard training.

The other men sit and begin to allow themselves to be accepted among the young circle.

XVII

The trolley is cleared of all food except for the items Rodin asked for. They respect Rodin's wishes and fight with Logan, forcing him to leave it alone. After everyone is full, they laugh and listen to the old men tell their stories of their lives over the centuries. Some of their stories aren't so pleasant. Some has Logan and Slender rolling on the floor, laughing.

Francine, Millette, and Helana gang up on the men with insults. At some point in their teasing, Aranae joins in, pointing out their flaws as men and how women are better at everything. They all laugh at the insults. The three young women form a close bond quickly. Byron occasionally smiles and admires Helana from across the circle, and she admires him in turn. Slender and Logan tease the two lovers.

They are laughing and teasing Logan and Millette about his sugar candy addiction when Helana and Dahlmür's staffs glow bright red. Helana is the first to respond. She mutters into the stone and nods. She turns to Vaniir. "Your Majesty, King Saul has demanded that he speaks to the Archon tonight. I told Troy that Archon's sanctuary is a day's ride to the canyons, and he says that the king is ready to go see him. Now. He also commands that you return immediately and take him there."

Byron jumps up. "Who's Troy?"

Vaniir is appalled. "Nobody demands me to do anything in *my* kingdom! Tell him that we will go tomorrow in the morning!"

Helana says to him, "Sire, King Saul is demanding to see him now. Troy is trying to transport him to my location, but Father is blocking him."

"Who's Troy?"

Vaniir turns to Dahlmür. "Keep him out of here, Dahlly! That man does not belong in here."

Helana tells him, "He's declaring an order to have you brought to him now."

"Excuse me? Prince Byron here. Who's Troy?"

"I don't care!" Vaniir stands and paces.

Galla joins him. "Let him declare that the sun rises out of his ass! He will wait until tomorrow."

"Oh, here we go again. Ignore the prince." Nobody pays any attention to him. The argument going on between Vaniir and King Saul is far more interesting.

"Father, he's really pushing me! Troy is not making this easy!" Helana breaks into a sweat.

"No worries, Lana, just concentrate. I'm trying to block out anyone from appearing in this chasm. Someone has located us. They just don't know where." Dahlmür also breaks into a sweat.

They watch as Dahlmür and Helana concentrate hard on their tasks.

Byron is still bouncing around. "Who the hell is Troy? Dammit!" But nobody is listening. "Hello! I'm speaking! Slender? Coleman? Anybody? I give up."

Why can't I get in? I thought I remembered, but now I've lost them. Someone is blocking me. Come on! Take me there! Damn Lizard! I know it is you! I can feel your power blocking me! Let me in!

I followed the others this far. I'm in this library, surrounded by all these damn books! I saw Prince Herring bring his harlot girl in here! But where the hell did he go?

I should have killed him when I had the chance. Then when each of you came looking for him, I could have killed you until I found that cursed door. Then I could have attacked and killed you all at once!

Confounded Lizard! Let me in! Ahhh! What are you doing to me! Get out of my head! No stop! No! Stop!

Ahhh!

Dahlmür is exhausted. "I broke them. Saul must have somebody working with Troy. That was more than what Troy is capable of."

Angrily, Byron sits with his head perched on his hands, mumbling, "Who's Troy?" He raises his voice an octave to mock Helana. "Oh, he's just some boy. He's a lot cuter than you." Then he speaks in his normal voice. "Oh, isn't that nice?"

Slender turns to him. "What? You really need to stop talking to yourself, brother. I'd really hate to think that one member of Archon's circle had to be committed. What would people think of the Archon then?"

Byron becomes red in the face and growls at Slender.

Helana breaks down and collapses into the nearest boulder chair. She breathes heavily. "Troy gave up. He said that King Saul has placed his guards throughout the palace to search for you. He's also upset that the queen had her healers barricade the door. They stopped his men from entering her chambers during her recovery."

Byron jumps. "You tell Saul that I don't care who he is. If he dares enter my mother's chambers again, I will cut him down myself."

Vaniir snarls. "Not if I get to him first! How dare he!" Vaniir makes his way to the corridor. "Byron, let's go!" He points to Slender, Logan, and the young women. "You stay here! Coleman, stay with them! Dahlly, you and Galla come with us! This madness will stop now!" He and the others climb up the corridor and are gone.

Aranae exhales deeply. She climbs down and announces, "Archon is coming!"

Slender looks toward the tunnel. "How do you know?"

Logan gets up, runs for the tunnel entrance, and yells "Brother!" just as Archon walks in.

"Hey, little brother. Missed me already?" He hugs him. He changes back into Rodin. He looks around and notices the others are missing and looks at everyone else. Rodin walks over to the food trolley and begins picking and eating the leftover food. He asks, "Where did the others go?"

Coleman answers, "Trouble in the palace. King Saul is forcing Vaniir to take drastic measures to avoid us being found."

"So that's who Vaniir was talking about earlier?" Rodin asks.

Coleman smiles at him. "Yes, it was."

Millette stands and hugs him. "I thought you said you went for something to eat?"

Rodin looks at her and smiles as he kisses her. "I did. It was good. I ate a whole boar. Then Mutt caught up to me with a rabbit, and I ate that."

Helana and Francine laugh. Helana asks, "Did you even cook it? 'Cause that was fast."

Rodin turns to the trolley and begins picking at some grapes. "Yeah. Sure."

Aranae says, "Little one, what did you say about honesty earlier?"

Rodin's smile turns into guilt as he begins to look around at everyone. "Actually, I don't have to cook my food anymore. My body does this weird absorption thing. I don't understand it."

Coleman says to him, "You cleaned the bones of everything." He says this as if he already knew.

Rodin nods without saying anything. Slender says, "Wow, that saves time!"

Rodin chuckles. "Yeah, it does. It's just weird. Everything is just indescribable. I can do things that I never in my life ever dreamed about." He sits next to the trolley and takes a grape and motions to throw it at Logan. Logan smiles and opens wide. Rodin tosses the grape, and it lands right in his mouth. "I have the ability to absorb the meat of my victims, well, animals, and clean off the bones, leaving their fur behind. Even the marrow inside the bones is gone. I don't understand." He looks at Aranae and asks, "How is this possible?"

She answers him with a sigh. "Little one, you have a gift. A blessing from the Rings. You are the one that will save Terra-Earth from Darkness. You will find yourself understanding your abilities as the days go on more and more. Just be patient."

Francine stands and says to him, "My—I mean, Rodin, these abilities I have are a little similar. It does take a lot of getting used to. Trust me, you will. They will become as natural to you as breathing."

He smiles at her and says, "Thank you, Francine, and again, I'm sorry for earlier."

Millette says to him, "Oh, don't worry about that. You need to worry more about getting to the canyons. You and Aranae need to be there before the morning."

Rodin looks at Coleman. Coleman nods in agreement. Rodin looks up at Aranae. "How are we supposed to do that?"

Helana stands and sighs. "I guess that would be my job."

Coleman agrees. "We need to get there as soon as possible. Preferably now."

Helana grabs her staff and stretches her neck and her arms. She concentrates on her breathing. "Okay, Lady Aranae, if you would join us. Rodin, we need Archon. You're going to have to help me with this." She looks around at everyone and invites them all around her. "Keep close to Aranae. My lady, if you would please stand above us. Mutt and Biter, just hold on to her legs."

They all gather beneath Aranae. Archon stands in front of Helana. "What do I do?"

"Hold on to the staff and concentrate on a chasm just like this. I have to focus on getting us there. Your thought will be the destination, and my thoughts will be the trip. Hang on tight, because I've had a hard time with this before, and now I'm bringing a bunch of people and a full-grown girachnid."

Slender comments, "Oh, that doesn't sound too good."

Helana begins to concentrate and squeezes her eyes shut. "I need quiet to concentrate."

Aranae announces, "As soon as we get there, move out of the way. I have a tendency to throw up."

Helana squeezes her eyes harder. "Shh!" The room begins to spin. "Archon, concentrate on the chasm!"

Archon concentrates harder. His eyes start to flash. They begin to flash with the rhythm of the staff. Helana opens her eyes in shock. "I'm not in control anymore!"

Archon's eyes and the staff continue pulsing as the room spins into a blur. Everyone looks around in confusion. The room is gone. They watch Archon and the staff in both terror and in awe. Suddenly, the pulsing slows, and the chasm spins back into view. The spinning slows down until it stops. Archon relaxes, and the staff stops flashing.

Slender runs out from under Aranae. "I'm gonna hurl!"

Everyone looks up in horror as Aranae's stomach begins to lurch. Logan screams, "She's gonna blow!" He dashes to the nearest wall. Everyone else fans out just in time for Aranae to throw up all over the floor. To Archon, it's almost a comedic scene to see a girachnid regurgitate a giant puddle in front of her.

Aranae uses one of her front legs to wipe her mouth. "Oh, I don't feel so good!"

Logan and Coleman begin to take on a shade of green. "Oh, that smell is horrible!" Logan exclaims.

Coleman nods furiously. "Hurry, my boy!" He pushes Logan away and says while gagging, "Let us go this way to the entrance for some fresh air before we start a chain reaction!" They are gone in a hurry.

Helana concentrates again, and Aranae's mess disappears. A cool breeze flows through the chasm, driving out the smell. She smiles in satisfaction. "That's better." She approaches Archon, who is scanning their surroundings. "Care to shed some light in here?"

Archon suddenly realizes that to everyone else, it is dark in this chasm. "Oh yeah." He stares around and spots the giant decorative firepots around the chasm. He stares at each one until he sets them ablaze one by one. Millette is chilled and grabs onto him for warmth. He allows himself to cover her. She's immediately grateful for the feel of his intense body heat.

Aranae climbs to the ceiling. It contains many cavernous pits and holes throughout for her to move as she pleases. Mutt and Biter climb the walls to join her and play their own game of hide-and-seek. She makes her way to the back of the extremely vast chasm and shouts, "Look out below!" Everyone moves in to see what she is talking about. Aranae suddenly drops a boulder the size of her abdomen out of the ceiling. *Boom!* It lands hard on the floor. Water falls from the hole and into another pool. Only this pool has a gulley carved out from it leading beyond the entrance of the cave. She jumps down and asks Archon, "Would you be a sweetheart and roll this to the side of the entrance, little one?"

"Of course," he obliges her. He rolls it with ease. He pushes it alongside the gulley until he finds a spot on the ground carved out large enough to rest the marble ball in next to the opening of the cavern. He looks out. He allows his sight to adjust to the darkness. He sees the falls to his right. A smaller set of falls to his left. He steps out and looks up to see a huge piece of stone protruding above the opening, providing cover to the entrance. The stone stands out far enough to split the raging falls in two. The water flowing out from the gulley becomes another set of falls, blending into the bigger set.

In the morning, I have to take a look at the whole thing, he thinks to himself. He wanders back in and looks around the chasm.

Logan and Slender come running up to him, their breathing heavy with excitement. Slender says to him between breaths, "There are a bunch of tunnels carved into the mountain from here!"

Logan says, "This place is like a fortress carved in this mountain!" He points to the falls he's just rolled the stone from. "Behind that waterfall is a huge meeting hall. It has a huge place to build a fire. Come see!" He turns to run and flails his arms for Archon to follow, but he is intercepted by Millette.

She grabs Logan and begins to calm him down. She says to Logan, "Not right now. You need to get some rest. King Saul will be here in the morning. We will find a place to rest. We'll explore afterward."

She stands looking at Archon. She stares at him, expressionless, for a few moments. She clings onto Logan's shoulders as if she were using him to keep him between her and Archon. Archon watches her in fear of what emotions and thoughts she must be going through. Her eyes begin to water. Archon's expressionless face keeps his gaze on her. She has something she wants to say, but he doesn't know exactly what it is. She backs up and looks at the ground beside her. She looks back to him as she turns away with a smile to him and takes Logan away with her. Francine joins her.

Slender pats him on the shoulder. "She's still not used to this. Don't worry, brother, she will. She keeps telling everyone that she loves you dearly." He turns and walks away to join them.

Archon becomes Rodin. His eyes are full of tears. *I'm losing her,* he thinks. *This is too much for her. Hell, this is too much for me too. I'm different from everyone else now. She doesn't want me and Archon. She wants me, Rodin, but everyone else wants Archon. I want Rodin too. Why does this have to happen? Why can't someone else do this? I know I said I will do it, but at what cost? I'm going to lose her. I can't lose Millette because of this. It is too much. I love her! I love Millette!*

The thoughts continue to spin in his head. He thinks about this so deeply he doesn't realize Slender has been gone.

He looks around and notices that it is just him and Aranae. They stand and stare. "It is hard, little one. I see it in your face. Your heart aches to be with her, but you saw the look in her eyes. She loves you, little one. I can read her heart. She just can't make out how to accept what you've become." Tears roll down his cheeks. "Come here."

He runs to her, and she scoops him up. He jumps to her head and hugs her. He cries out his pain, "She doesn't accept me, Aranae! I've lost the woman I've known my whole life. We are to be married, and she doesn't accept me anymore because of this."

She consoles him, "I know, little one. She will accept you over time. Just give her a chance. She loves you just as much as you love her." He clings to her as she carries him to her bedding high up on the far corner. The sound of the rushing falls coming from the hole in the ceiling drowns out all other sounds. It begins to soothe him until sleep takes him.

He dreams of being with Millette, happily married and living on his farm. She holds their child in her arms. He sees her from the field he is working on. She stands on the porch of the house and smiles at him. He smiles back. He walks to her as he knocks the dust of the field from his clothes. He tells her he loves her. She says she loves him. They kiss deeply. He looks down at their beautiful baby girl and smiles at her. He softly kisses the sleeping baby on her forehead.

They are happy.

He steps into the house, and everything turns wrong. The house is dark and tossed in shambles. Cobwebs are hanging from the walls. Dust and dirt cover everything. He turns around to look back at Millette, but she is gone. The sky is a dark swirling mass of clouds. His fields are nothing but dirt. Nothing growing.

He hears a voice. "Archon! Save us!" He spins to see the source of the voice.

There is nobody.

"Archon! Save us!" He turns back outside.

Nothing.

"Archon! Please save us!"

Backyard! He runs around the house. He lifts his ax in preparation for a fight.

"Archon! Please save us!"

Logan! He turns the corner. Nobody.

"Archon!"

"Archon!"

"Archon!"

The voices keep crying out to him.

Byron! Slender! Helana! Francine!

He runs back to the porch. Five skeletons stare at him with lifeless eyes.

"Archon! Please save us!" they all cry at once.

"Ha ha ha!" another voice laughs in the distance.

He looks across the field and sees a demon with a dark-green robe standing in the distance. It laughs at him, "Ha ha ha!" The figure pulls a short green sword, and in a flash, he is standing in front of Rodin.

Rodin can't see his face. His hood makes it hard to see him. He swings his ax at him. The demon blocks him. They continue to swing and block each other. Finally, they come together face-to-face. Rodin yanks back the hood. The Archon of Vil!

XVIII

oom!

Rodin bounces up and becomes Archon. *Vil!* He looks around as Aranae drops to the floor. *Voom!* He sees everyone gathered around below in the center. Their weapons are drawn. Archon perches himself in the shadows. *Voom!* A figure appears. Vaniir! He's not happy.

"Oh, just let the bastard through please, Helana. He insists on doing it himself! I just guided him here. He won't deviate from here now. The bastard!"

Helana acknowledges him and speaks into her staff. Then seven men appear. Dahlmür, Byron, Lawrence, Galla, and three other men Archon has never seen before as well as four trollies of food. *Breakfast!* Archon notices. One man wears robes like Dahlmür wears at the school. He figures this must be the wizard Dahlmür has spoken of. He laughs at the need for wizards of his type to wear such robes just to be recognized. Another man is clad in armor polished and finished with purple highlights. The last man fascinates Archon most.

He knows royalty when he sees it, and this man is nothing short of royalty. From head to toe and from the way he stands, this man must be King Saul. The man is muscular and defined. His shoulders and arms bulge with muscles Archon has never known a man has. He can see his veins branch out throughout his body. His skin is so black that he glistens from the sunlight coming in through the cavern's opening. Archon also notes sunlight shining from openings above in many places throughout the fortress. The man wears a purple tunic highlighted with gold lace. A large leather belt is strapped across his abdomen, held together by a giant gold buckle with a sun and an arrow piercing it etched on the face. His leather pants is also dyed in purple. His heavy large leather boots are lined with fur, highlighted with gold strands.

The man turns a full circle as he scans his environment, missing Archon in the shadows. *Are those jewels pierced to his forehead?* Archon sees a sizable diamond in the center of his forehead just above his brow. Two emeralds stick out on both sides and blazing red rubies to the outside of them. Brilliant large blue sapphires pierce his ears. His face is stern as he looks around. A large jewelencrusted scabbard is strapped to his side. An ivory handle tipped with more jewels stands out from it. The scabbard shows the outline of a tremendous flat blade for a sword.

He sneers at King Vaniir and speaks to him with a loud, deep voice. "Which one is Archon?"

King Vaniir looks at him with an unimpressed look on his face. "He will come to you when he's ready!" His voice is just as boisterous as King Saul's. He puffs his chest as if he were ready for any resistance.

The man looks at the wizard. "Seek him out and bring him here. Now!" His voice booms.

Grand Wizard Dahlmür tells him, "My King, if Archon wants to be hidden, he can remain undetectable to anyone. Even me." Dahlmür flashes a look at Archon.

Archon takes this as a signal to do just that. He concentrates on remaining hidden. He feels what seems like fingers groping at him. His form begins to shimmer and swirl around him faster.

The various shapes, loops, knots, and strands flow in many directions at once. Suddenly, he sees the wizard in his mind and pushes him fiercely. "Get out!"

He opens his eyes in time to see the wizard fly backward as if he were violently pushed. He hits the wall hard and lands in the gulley as he holds his hands to his ears, screaming in pain. After a moment of splashing around, he regains his composure and walks up to King Saul and bows to him.

"Archon did that to me, sire. He doesn't want to be found."

King Saul looks at the knight beside him. "Sir Drake, make him come out!"

Sir Drake draws his sword and swings at Slender, but Slender is already prepared for a fight. Chill meets his blade, and ice flows down Drake's blade. Slender looks at him. "Do that again, and I promise you that it will be the last time you use that particular blade ever."

Sir Galla laughs. "Slender, you make a knight proud!"

Sir Drake turns and points the sword at Sir Galla's direction. Sir Galla looks at him and cautions him, "If you ever point that toothpick at me again, I will skewer your ass with it! Now drop it."

Sir Drake laughs and raises his face shield on his helmet. He sneers at him and, without warning, swings at Logan.

Archon springs out and nails the knight with both feet to his back. Sir Drake lands on his stomach and slides across the floor with Archon perched on his back for the ride. He reaches down and grabs the sword from him. He slams the sword into the ground and cuts into it as he uses it as a brake, skidding them to a halt. Archon jumps off Sir Drake and throws him up like cloth and kicks him back into the air. Sir Drake hits the ceiling above, knocking stones loose as they fall to the ground with him. Archon sidesteps out of the way to let Sir Drake land flat on his face. Sir Drake is out cold.

Archon looks at the king and stands beside Vaniir. He points a finger at King Saul. "If you ever threaten my circle again, you will be lying across the rocks below!"

King Saul looks at him furiously. "How dare you talk to me in that tone! You insolent little—"

"I will talk to whomever I want any way I want!" His body flares out at King Saul as Aranae projects for him to be calm.

Grand Wizard Dahlmür pounds his staff. *Snap! Snap! Snap!* Archon backs down and looks at Logan. Millette and Francine stand in front of him to protect him from any further threats. Byron stands beside Slender with his short sword drawn. Lawrence stands with his whip at the ready. Coleman has drawn a mace. Another threat at any of them would not be a welcoming thing to do on King Saul's behalf.

King Vaniir laughs. "I told you that you were not welcome here, King Saul. If you look around, you will see that death awaits the uninvited." He points up. "Even from above."

Kind Saul looks up and sees Aranae hanging above him with Mutt and Biter on either side of her. His face goes from anger to horror in an instant as he falls flat on his back. He tries to draw his sword, but he is lying on his scabbard. His sword refuses to be drawn. He stares at Aranae in wide-eyed terror. Aranae laughs.

Mutt swings around, screaming, "Yeah! We're scary girachnids! Fear us! We will kill you!"

Biter looks around Aranae at him. "You do know he doesn't understand us, right?"

Aranae giggles. "Watch this, children. This is how you scare somebody." She slowly descends toward King Saul as she flexes her eight humongous legs at him. She stops and tilts her head at him as she claps her fangs together. A string of drool falls from her mouth.

Everyone watching and understanding the display begins to try really hard not to laugh at the scene. Logan has his face buried into Millette's tunic, stifling his laughter. Byron grabs onto Archon's shoulder and squeezes to keep from bursting. Slender begins to cross his legs. He runs off toward the opening and leans against the side as he adds his own water to the falls. Logan and Byron point him out to Archon, coughing and trying hard to cover their outbursts. Archon's head bobs up and down as his chest heaves in and out. He makes no noise. Dahlmür looks at them and stifles them with a scowl. Helana is turning red with the desire to laugh.

Aranae gets really close to King Saul. They are eye to eye to eye to eye (and so forth). Her eyes shine to cast the spell. She then says to him, "I'm Aranae. How are you, Sire?"

His response is to scream out in horror. He continues screaming until Wizard Troy calms him down. Everyone else bursts into laughter. Slender returns to his perch as he laughs so hard. Even the old men laugh and point at him. After calming down, King Saul is not amused. "I am the league king! You will treat me as your king!"

Francine steps out toward him. "I will not! You are not my king! My king is His Majesty, King Forte!"

King Saul looks at her in confusion. "King Forte is the king of the League of Morpher."

She begins to shift her face into a cat. "That would be my king, then, wouldn't it?" She quickly, and quietly remarks, "And my father."

He asks her, "What are you doing here, Morpher?"

Sir Galla clears his throat. "Sire, what if Archon is a morpher too?"

King Saul looks over Archon and responds, "No. The Light would not send us a morpher as Archon."

"Really? There has already been one as well as a Woodland in the past," Aranae states.

King Saul looks Archon in the eyes. "Show me your true form."

"This is my true form."

Aranae says to him, "That secret is between me and his circle. Not even King Vaniir knows who he once was. The one that is now Archon came to me before they discovered him or her."

King Saul's eyes flash. "Or her?"

Archon projects his displeasure of "or her" to Aranae. Everyone else shuffles around. King Saul looks at Archon and tries to stare him down. Archon watches him calmly. They remain that way for a few moments.

Finally, Byron steps in. "If you don't mind, Sire, Archon needs to eat as well as the rest of us."

Coleman and Lawrence grab a trolley each, as well as Logan and Millette. Coleman confirms his suggestion. "Prince Byron is quite right. Master Troy, if you would please wake up your fallen comrade there and have him follow us. We'll continue these discussions in the dining hall."

King Saul looks around in detest. "This . . . *cave* has a dining hall?"

King Vaniir points toward the back area. "This *fortress* has a dining hall. That way."

Lawrence leads the way. Everyone follows him toward the falls in the far back. Archon is puzzled because he doesn't see an opening leading to any dining hall. Lawrence disappears behind the falls. Coleman follows, as do the rest. Archon shrugs and follows them, fingering the falling water as he does.

The hall is immense. Archon looks up to see sunlight shining through the rocks above to light the room. Then something odd strikes him. *How is sunlight coming through without water pouring in?* He looks closer. *Light stones!* Now he understands. The light stones are in the rocks. *This must be a huge deposit of them. They left them there to light this place. The ones who carved out this fortress must have known these light stones were here.* He turns his gaze to the oversized table in the center. He notices a huge fireplace carved into the wall to the back. He looks at Millette, who is shivering. He sets his hand on her shoulder, feeling her jump away from his touch as he gazes into the fireplace. It takes a moment, but the molded and damp logs in the fireplace ignite. He makes a note to gather more wood later to keep the place warm.

Being the king that he is, King Saul immediately seats himself at the head of the table. Troy and a groggy Sir Drake sit to either side of him. King Vaniir and everyone else seat themselves at the other end. They leave the head of that end open. Aranae lies down a few distance back as she is able to gaze across the table at King Saul. Everyone turns to Archon as King Vaniir shows him the seat at the end meant for him to be head of their group. As a show of respect, Archon bows at King Vaniir and Prince Byron as well as to everyone else. He makes sure to give the commons bow to Logan, Millette, Francine, and Lawrence. He ignores the uninvited guest, King Saul.

King Saul hisses at him. "I'm growing weary of the constant disrespect I am getting here."

Aranae says to him, "Here . . . is Archon's home. As well as mine. You have yet to give *us* any respect. Respect is given, not expected. Respect is earned, not demanded. You give us a reason to respect you, and we will give it. Otherwise, as Master Slindee would say, take a long jog on that short cliff out there."

King Saul stops for a moment. He sits and looks around as everyone focuses on him. He stares at Sir Drake's condition. His highly polished armor from a few minutes ago is now dented, is beat up, and has lost its luster. Wizard Troy is still rubbing his temples from his mental attack. He realizes that he has lost the battle. He figures that if anything, his dignity should be saved. He sighs in surrender.

Archon says to him, "Your Majesty, try to understand, they are protecting me from Darkness, our true enemy. Everyone within this circle and those men are the only ones that we can trust for now. We cannot broadcast who I am, where I come from, or what League I belong to because certain people in my life may become targets to get to me. I will tell you this, my king, I am not against you." He stands and makes his way to King Saul and bows before him. "My king, I will give the gift of my identity soon enough."

King Saul smiles at him. "You are worthy of being Archon. You have shown me great strength and power. You have proven that your circle is just as important to you as your life. Your circle has proven that they are willing to return to you the same regards." He laughs and claps his hands. He stands and reaches out a hand to Archon, and Archon takes it. "I am blessed by the Rings to be able to witness your arrival! I pray they will allow me to witness your victory as well!" He sits back down and announces, "Let us eat! As Prince Byron has stated, Archon is as hungry as we are!"

Immediately, Millette and Francine graciously stand and begin passing around the plates and set the food to the table. Millette says with pleasure at the end of the whole debate, "I will be honored to serve us, my king."

King Saul says to her, "Whoever that man is under that mask is very lucky."

Knowing where the conversation may be turning, Archon says to him, "My king, that, too, is a discussion for another time, I'm afraid. Prince Byron, Logan, and Slender are the only names you may have from my circle. If you don't mind, after we are finished here, I would like to have a meeting with you and Dahlmür."

Dahlmür coughs. "Sir!"

"Sir, in private. I have matters the three of us must discuss." King Saul looks at Dahlmür in confusion. "I accept." Dahlmür is just as confused.

Archon looks around. *I can't sit here. I have to do something. I'm not up to sitting around.* He looks at Aranae and projects to her, *Mother, may we leave them to eat? I have some tasks I would like to do today.*

She breathes a sigh of relief. *I thought you'd never ask.*

Archon looks around at everyone and excuses himself. As he steps away to leave, Wizard Troy asks, "Why do you call her Mother?" *He heard that?*

Coleman laughs. "My dear boy, if you knew the man beneath that mask, you would know why. The biggest reason is that she has given Archon life. Much like she has given the two girachnid younglings over there life."

Mutt barks at him. "Yeah, we're brothers! You mess with one, you get three of us!"

Biter comments, "I'll bite your head off if you do!"

Wizard Troy accepts this with a nod. He looks at Helana. "Grand-Uncle says that you are becoming just as powerful as he is. I'm proud of you, cousin."

Byron perks up. "Cousin? You two are cousins?"

Helana responds, "Thank you, cousin. You're pretty powerful yourself."

"Why didn't you tell me you were cousins?"

Wizard Troy responds modestly, "Thanks, but you saw what Archon did to me out there."

"I said, why didn't you—oh, never mind."

Helana turns to Byron and smiles. "Why didn't I what, my love?" She bats her eyes at him.

Byron is flushed. "Never mind, my love."

Dahlmür and Vaniir grumble and cough at them, expressing their disapproval of their affectionate display.

I found it! You hid the switch to your hiding place behind a book called **Secret Caverns and Caves***? Not so clever!*

I found it! And now I am going to kill you all! I'm tired of these games we are playing. It's time for us to end this.

Big Piggy! Would you like a pork chop? Ha ha ha! No, 'cause Little Piggy ate it! So I'll gut him for you to give it back. Ha ha ha!

King Herring! Would you like a big juicy worm? Ha ha ha! No! 'Cause Prince Herring gave it to Trash! So I will kill them all and watch you and Prince Herring die as I skin you alive! Ha ha ha!

Huh? Wait? Why is it dark in here? Where is the light? A light stone? I have no need for it. I can see very well in the dark, and I don't see any of you.

Where are you? Trash? Grand Lizard? Spiders? Where did you go? You were just here. I don't understand.

You're gone, and you didn't tell me where you were going!

I need to know where you are! I have to kill you! I have someone I want you to meet! My master wants to meet you all in death!

Where are you? No!

XIX

Archon and Aranae return to the main area of the fortress. Archon sits on a stone he raises out of the ground. Aranae laughs at him and settles down next to him. He looks at her in confusion and asks, "What?"

She says to him, "When I said you could manipulate the ground beneath you I was lying, but you actually proved *me* wrong. I never knew you could do that, little one. You've proven to me that if I had told you you could fly, you would really fly."

He chuckles at her, "I can. Fly, I mean. I can fly. I can make wings like a bat or a dragon and actually use them to fly. I've already done it."

She laughs, "Dahlly would never believe you until you actually prove it."

He snorts, "Maybe later, then."

"Okay."

"I was wondering if we could go somewhere today. I'd like very much to be outside. I haven't been home in a while. There are people on my farm that I don't trust or know. I have coins hidden in the house that I would like to get before someone else does. Not for me, but it's all for Logan. Plus, I just want to get out."

"Getting *cabin fever*, as Lawrence would call it?"

"Yeah, I guess so." He looks into her eyes. "Can I take you somewhere?"

She looks down and sighs. "I really want to go out into the forest and enjoy climbing the trees again."

"Why not?"

"Little one, it is dangerous out there for us. If we were discovered, it would be disastrous."

"Please. I know a great place. It is deep in the woods. There's nobody for miles. It will be great just to get out."

Aranae thinks for a moment and tilts her head at him. "Okay, little one." She happily sighs a moan. "Oh, it will be so great to go outside!"

"May I bring Millette?"

She looks at him and pauses. She laughs, "If it will help you two, then yes."

He concentrates. After a moment, Logan's voice rings out. "Okay!" He concentrates again as Logan screams, "She's on her way!" After a few seconds, he says, "Sorry!"

Galla's voice cries out, "Confounded, boy! Why are you yelling?"

Archon shakes his head and looks at Aranae. "I should have asked Slender to do it." Aranae laughs at him.

Millette walks up to them. "You wanted something?" she asks Archon.

She is so beautiful. His heart flutters at her.

Before Archon can respond, Aranae says, "Would you like to play in the woods with us?" She is apparently overjoyed to be getting out.

Millette smiles and laughs, "Oh yes, I'd like nothing better!"

If Archon could smile, he would be at that moment. He takes her hand and looks at Aranae. "May I?"

Catching his meaning, she flattens herself to the ground. "Sure! Oh, this will be so much fun!"

They climb onto her back. Archon looks at Millette. "Hang on, my love."

He concentrates hard. His eyes begin to flash as before. The room begins to spin. The faster it spins, the faster his eyes flash. The fortress becomes a blur. Suddenly, sunlight, blue skies, and greenery begin to come into view around them. The spinning and the flashing slow to a stop. Aranae violently jumps up and runs toward a stream beside her with Archon and Millette still on her back. Her stomach lurches as she throws up into the stream. Archon and Millette cling to each other as she moves around and tries to regain her balance. Archon pats her back as she apologizes for her display. Millette tells her that everything is fine as they climb down.

Aranae climbs a tree and happily announces, "I'm going to nap up here for a few hours. I haven't laid out in the sun for such a long time. It feels so refreshing!"

Archon laughs at her. "You go right ahead. Millette and I are going to find another area of the stream and talk."

Aranae is as delighted as a young girl. "Okay. I might pick off something while you are gone. I haven't hunted for myself in years."

Archon agrees and takes Millette against him. He easily scoops her off her feet. He runs a few feet and leaps off a large outcropping of rocks. Wings of a dragon unfurl from his form, and he soars into the air with her. He hears Aranae laugh. "Wonderful!" she says as he flies farther out. Millette looks down, breathless and in amazement. The forest grows tiny beneath them as it disappears from view when they fly into a cloud. He rises above the cloud and their world is transformed into an ocean of blue skies with waves of white clouds around them. In the distance, they see a mountainside with a large waterfall flowing down from its cliffs. A large icecap that towers well over it feeds the falls. He glides toward it.

He looks down at Millette and watches her as she looks around in wonder. She smiles as a flock of birds fly below them. He hangs on to her tightly, never wanting to let her go.

This is my love. This is my heart and soul. I hold her as I would my own life. Beautiful, kind, trustworthy, and loving. She is mine, and I am hers. Just to see her smile is the best feeling to me. To have her kiss is a wondrous moment. I long for that kiss.

As he stares at her, she looks at him. She sees Rodin with the body of Archon. She smiles in recognition as if she has just realized who it is that is carrying her. She leans forward and kisses him. He smiles at her, conveying his full love to her with that single smile. She smiles back and gazes into his eyes with her desire to keep him with her forever.

Rodin floats easily down to the top of the mountain peak and settles onto the rocky bank of the river. At this altitude, there is no grass and very few brush. The side of the cliffs is yards behind them as they stare at the towering icecap looming just a short distance ahead. They look at it in wonder. They gaze at the very peak of it as the powder of ice and snow billow around it from the winds blowing at that height. He fully recovers as Rodin with the fur coat wrapped around him.

They sit on a rock, and he holds on to her. He feels her shiver and realizes that it must be cold for her way up here. Without hesitation or modesty, he removes the coat and places it around her. She kisses him and thanks him. She chuckles at him and points out his nakedness. He laughs and nods at her and states that he doesn't feel the cold anymore. She squeezes in close to him. He wraps an arm around her and pulls her closer. He gazes at the icy mountaintop, and she kisses his ear. He turns his attention back to her with a smile. She kisses him softly. He kisses her back. She stares deep into his eyes and closes them as she kisses him again. Her breathing becomes heavy. His breathing becomes heavy as they kiss deeper. She opens the fur coat and wraps him inside with her as she pushes him to lie down while she kisses him deeper and deeper, expressing her desires for that moment in time.

XX

odin lies there naked and staring up at the sky as Millette ties the lace on the neck of her tunic. He stares at her and smiles as he remembers the feelings they've just shared. They have given themselves freely to each other without holding back their love. She lies down beside him on the fur coat used as a blanket and kisses him with an affectionate smile. He returns her smile as he gazes into her eyes.

They have sealed their love for each other today. Nothing can ever break them apart.

As Millette stares at him, she becomes horrified as Rodin's expression changes from a smile to a realization of terror. He jumps up and is immediately Archon. He reaches down, screaming, "We have to go! Now! Aranae is in danger! She's screaming for help!"

Millette jumps up. "Oh, my Rings! Are you sure?"

He grabs the fur coat and throws it on himself. It immediately bonds to him. He grabs her up, runs for the edge of the cliff, and leaps into a dive, screaming, "Yes, she's under attack! She's screaming for my help! I've told the others! They are on their way too!"

Feathered wings fly open from his back. They are more streamlined, like those of a hawk. They bend backward to allow him to dive into the direction that they have left Aranae behind.

Archon's voice cuts through the fierce wind screaming in Millette's ears, "She's hurt! It's demons! A league she's never seen before! They have her surrounded! Hang on!" And he dives more steeply through the clouds. The moment the sky opens, they see her below.

A massive number of demons surround her throwing spears and tossing boulders at her. A few are pinned to the ground from her webs. A couple of the bodies have been bitten in half. He sees one on the ground thrashing around and foaming at the mouth from being injected with venom. A spear protrudes from her abdomen on one side, paralyzing one of her back legs. Another hangs from another leg on the other side, causing her to drag around in a circle.

As they get closer, they hear her screaming in pain in her struggle to fight.

Smaller figures begin to appear out of thin air and immediately attack the demons.

Slender smashes his shield down and sends a wave in the ground toward a group that has Aranae cowering against a tree. Archon watches as they fly to the air and split to the sides of her. A group of the monstrous demons break away from the main group and attack the newly joined warriors. They run at them with their heads down, swinging their spears. A small figure leaps above the pack and bombards the rushing demons with shots of arrows. Each arrow finds its mark but doesn't slow them down. Rodin realizes that their skin must be hardened and that the arrows aren't taking any effect. He mentally tells Logan to let the others know to aim for softer points, such as their eyes.

Logan leaps backward away from the charge as the others defend themselves. He fires a single shot on point to one demon, and it falls instantly. The others see this and change tactics. He sees Francine in the form of a powerful lion and asks her to meet him behind the battle lines. She slashes at the face of her attacker and retreats. She meets Archon as he sets Millette onto her back, asking Francine to take her to safety. She agrees.

Archon leaps into the air and lands with his fists together on top of one demon in the center of a group trying to overtake Aranae. The demon's head is flattened into the ground as a wave of blood and concussive winds blast the group apart. Aranae is knocked off balance as well. He looks at her and sees that one of her smaller eyes has been taken out. A deep gash is left where her eye had been. This sends rage through him. He spots his first victim in the group. A demon standing wide and towering to Aranae's height begins to stand and lumber over to him. Its huge, muscular legs are as wide as two Archons, but Archon doesn't let that deter him from his rage. When the demon gets close enough, he leaps at it and lands with his foot onto its knee with a thunderous *crack!*

The demon howls in pain as it falls, dropping its spear to its side and landing onto one knee. The demon looks at Archon in anger for what he's done. Archon reaches out as a long strand wraps around the demon's throat. Archon then tugs hard as the strand tightens, becoming thin and taut, and slices its head from its shoulders.

The other demons watch this and shrink back in momentary confusion and terror. One points at him and cries, "Archon!" The others howl as they withdraw.

Archon looks at his fellow warriors and sees that everyone is alive and uninjured. As he walks up to greet them Galla cries out as Archon hears something shoot past the back of his head. He turns in time to see a spear pierce Aranae's head. Her body falls with and thunderous *thump!*

She becomes still.

In his horror, he hears her final thoughts: *Finally, my curse has come to an end. I love you, little one.*

He turns and shoots a massive dart at a demon that stands in the distance with a smile for what he has done. The huge demon ducks his head and catches the dart in his shoulder. He screams in pain then pulls out the dart as black ooze bleeds out from the wound. He drops the dart and points at himself then at Archon and swipes his thumb across his throat. He laughs at him and runs as Biter and Mutt try to catch him. Archon reaches out to the two screaming younglings and brings them back to him.

Everyone gathers around Aranae. Byron and Helana scream out as Slender holds tight to Mutt, and Logan holds on to Biter as they try to wriggle themselves free, screaming and crying. Dahlmür places a hand to her massive head then turns and shakes his head at the other men. Lawrence and Coleman fall down into a sitting position, their legs crossed beneath them. Galla starts becoming frantic and angry, asking everyone if they have seen such demons before. Vaniir bows his head and begins to sing an ancient death prayer, asking the Rings to accept Aranae into their grace and allow her to join them in the Spiritual Realm. He asks the Circle of Light to guide her way and curse the beasts that has brought death upon her. Troy and Drake stand back in horror of the incident. Drake's face shield is down, blocking everyone's view of his expressions. His chest bounces as if he were crying for everyone's loss.

King Saul is furious. "Why were you here?" he demands at Archon, who is too shaken up to answer. "Why did you leave to come here? And why did you leave her alone here?" He pauses for a moment. "Answer me!"

Archon turns to him and explodes as his body flares out at him. "I told you to never order me to do anything! I am not yours to command!" He swings a fist in the shape of a club at him. It punches King Saul in his stomach, sending him flying backward into his two men. Archon stands for a moment, breathing heavily, then looks at the sky and screams, "No! Mother!" Then he is gone.

Everyone searches him out in confusion. Byron yells, "Brother! Please! Take us with you!" He falls to his hands and knees and cries. Helana drops beside him and holds him in comfort.

King Saul coughs and stands, holding his gut. He is confused with Byron's display. "Why do you cry, boy?"

Vaniir places a hand to his shoulder to calm him down. "My son has known Aranae since his birth. She was as close to him as his own mother."

King Saul apologizes for his outburst then looks around. "Where did he go?"

Logan and Millette step forward. Millette says to him, "We know where he went."

Logan says, "The same place he went to when our parents died."

Lawrence walks up to Logan and says, "Take me to him. I think it is time for me to tell you a story. The whole story."

Coleman warns him, "Do you think it is really time, Larry? You saw how he reacted when Vanni told them his part."

Lawrence looks at the others and smiles. "These two deserve to know the whole truth. Not just a part."

Logan asks him, "What truth do you mean?"

Lawrence turns to Millette. "My lady, I don't mean this to sound rude, but if you will, please allow Master Logan and his brother to share some time alone with me."

Millette looks at him, confused, and agrees. "Yes, Mater Lawrence." He gives her the commons bow. She returns to console Byron and the youngling girachnids.

Galla is both outraged and still in shock over Aranae's death. "You will tell us why you and Archon brought her here while they are gone! You better pray that I believe it to be a good reason!"

She bows to him. "Yes, sire."

Dahlmür and Vaniir stand wailing at Aranae's body as they continue to sing their songs of prayer. Galla and Coleman join beside them. Helana guides Byron to the group to join in song as he begins to wail with them. King Saul and his men bow their heads in respect for the dead. Francine and Millette stand beside him as Helana and Slender join Lawrence and Logan.

Lawrence tells Slender, "I'm afraid you cannot come, Squire."

Slender nods. "I understand, Master Lawrence." He looks around at everyone and whispers to him, "Do me a favor and pass a message to Rodin. Let him know that I do not trust Sir Drake. I don't know why. I just don't. And to ease my discomfort, I want him to work his magic to find out why." Slender turns to leave then whispers back, "And please keep this between us. I will discuss this with Byron later. When he feels up to it. And tell Rodin that I'm sorry about Aranae. I know how much she has meant to him these past few days."

Lawrence reaches out and squeezes his arm. "I will. Your secret is safe with us only. I didn't want to alarm anyone, but I have the same feelings. You're not alone. Keep watch over him. Troy can be trusted. King Saul is starting to see things our way, but if you see anything out of the ordinary with Drake, you let me know immediately. Understand?"

Slender gives him the commons bow. "Yes, Master Lawrence. I promise." Then he gives him the knights' salute and returns to the others and joins in their song.

Helana tries hard not to cry as Logan breaks down in tears. She holds his hand and looks at Lawrence as she sniffs away her own tears. "Are you ready? Where do we go?"

Logan chokes, "Go behind the house on the other side of the river. If you can put us about a yard away from the riverbank, we'll end"—he coughs and tries to get through his crying—"we'll end up on a patch of rocks that lead to a gravel trail where we get our firewood. There is also a raft crossing there. If the raft is gone, then he's detached and is floating up river. If the raft is there, then in his state, he's chopping down every tree in front of him. If we don't hurry, there won't be a tree left in the woods."

Master Lawrence places a hand on his shoulder. "Thank you, Master Logan." He pulls the boy in close as he holds back his own tears. He looks at the others gathered around Aranae in song and watches for a few moments as he hums with them. When he is satisfied he turns to Helana and tries not to cry himself. "Let us go, please."

After a moment of concentration, they disappear.

Ahh! No! You were supposed to kill them all! Master is not happy with me at all, and it's your fault!

You killed the gift-giver, which is good, but Archon! Who is Archon? Who did you see? Was it Prince Herring? Or was it Piggy? Which one?

You don't know? I should have been there with you. I could have seen who wasn't there and figured it out. It wouldn't have been hard at all.

We'll do that again! Next time I want them dead! Not just one of them, but all of them! They all have to die!

I don't care if Archon shows up! Kill him! Kill him! Kill him! Make him suffer with the rest of them! He doesn't have that pitiful sword called Flare! He has no weapon! It should be easy for you! Kill him! Simple!

I have a plan. That pitiful King Saul is here now. I bet he will be at the coronation ceremonies. That little showoff of a king will want to conduct the coronations himself. They will all be there. With their recent tragedy, they will not be ready for an attack. I can get inside. I can be close. With the help of you, the new League, and the help of our newfound ally, we can catch them off their guard and attack.

Yes!

It's brilliant!

We will introduce Master's Order to the world with you, the new League! The League of Ogre!

They will all die!

Liche will rise again with their deaths!

Squeal, Piggy! Die, Trash! Gasp for air, Herring! Ha ha ha!

XXI

They appear where Logan has directed them. In front of them is the river. The house can be seen on the other side. The raft is still tied to the other side. They remember that Rodin doesn't need the raft anymore. The river runs loud and furious. They know they haven't been detected. Logan uses the crossing line to balance himself as he climbs the steep bank. The others follow him and use the line as well. When they come over the bank, they can hear Rodin singing the death song, while the sound of an ax hitting a tree is his beat. When they round a bend in the trail, they see Rodin, who's fully dressed, swinging his father's ax at a large oak tree as he sings.

Tears flow freely down his face. He is not concerned with the tears soaking his tunic. He is in deep concentration of singing and swinging. His voice cracks during his song. He cries as he swings harder. The ax breaks through the tree in one hard swing. Huge splinters fly all around him. The tree falls hard as he pushes it to fall to the side of him. He is both angry and upset at the sight of the tree falling with the blow. He screams out in frustration. Rodin turns, unaware of his visitors, stopping his song long enough to curse the tree for falling and choking the ax for taking it down so quickly. He walks up to another oak tree and begins to swing and sing as he cries again.

His back is to them. He swings in fury and screams out as the ax takes down that tree in one final blow. Again, a shower of splinters flies around him as the tree crashes down in front of him. His body heaves in heavy breathing as he stares at his feet silently. Then he says softly, "I know you're there. I felt you when you got here. I don't even have to see you, Lawrence, Helana, and little brother."

He puts up an arm, and Logan rushes to him, crying. He leans onto Logan as he embraces him. They stand there, crying and holding each other.

Lawrence tries to fight it himself. He wants to release his tears, but he holds back. Helana stands in place, sobbing, tears falling from her face to the ground. She sits and puts her face into her sleeves as she bawls. Lawrence finds a stump and turns away from them so they can't see him crying as well.

Aranae's loss is unexpected and hard. Nobody really knows how hard it is to deal with death that has come so sudden. To Rodin, it is too soon. He has just begun to know her. She had treated him like a son. He had treated her like a mother. She had entered his life without warning and so quickly, but in those few days, she had admired him and loved him before they had the chance to really know each other. They shared only a few bits of their lives with each other, but it was like they had known each other for years. She gave him life as Archon. She treated him like one of her younglings. To Rodin, it was the most beautiful mother-and-son relationship he had since the death of his own mother. This makes it all the tougher, because her death reminds him of his own mother's death, and this crushes him. He finds himself lost and alone. He is left alone without a mother to love him again.

Logan hangs on to him, crying. "I'm so sorry, brother. I loved her too. I know she loved you. I know she was like the mother we had lost. To me, she was the one that looked after you so I wouldn't have to. I love you, big brother, and I'm sorry."

Rodin whispers to him, "I love you too, little brother." He scoops Logan onto his shoulder and looks around. He walks over to Helana and Lawrence and sets him down. "Help them start gathering the logs I've cut. We need to build her pyre when we get back." He walks up to a tree to the side they've missed watching him chop down. He flips the ax and begins to cut logs out of it easily.

When they are done with gathering the logs for Aranae's pyre, Rodin looks around wearily and asks, "Why didn't the others come with you?"

Lawrence replies, "I have something to show you and Logan. It will help you with some of the questions you've been asking."

Rodin asks, "And which questions are you answering this time?"

Lawrence places a pile of logs onto a third pile and takes a breath. "That is something you need to see for yourself. I cannot do it justice here."

Logan carries a small stack of logs to the pile and sets them down. He rubs the dirt from his arms and from his clothes. "Will it take long? You know Vanni wants me with him. I'm his deskipler."

Rodin says, "*Disciple.*"

Logan smiles. "Yeah, that." He turns back to Lawrence. "By the way, who is your and Coleman's . . . that word . . . anyway?"

Lawrence allows Helana to walk through as she shows off her lack of needing to carry her larger stack of logs by using her staff. He looks at her and points at her resourcefulness with a chuckle then answers Logan, "Well, Coleman doesn't have one appointed to him yet. As for me, well, mine has passed. I will show you what his legacy has left behind."

Rodin watches Helana show off again and smiles at her. He changes into Archon and scoops all three large stacks of logs into one stack at once. Helana looks at him and puffs, "Show-off." Logan and Lawrence laugh as Archon stands proud of himself for winning the contest they didn't know they are having.

When they look around them, they see that the logs are all gathered, and they are reminded why they have gathered them in the first place. They all look at the fur coat and the ax lying against a stone outcropping to the edge of the clearing. Archon becomes Rodin as he walks to them. Logan approaches with him. As they stand looking over the ax, Logan reaches around Rodin and holds him tight. He whispers, "We'll need it again. Something tells me that it will be soon."

Rodin says to him softly, "Yes, little brother, we will." Rodin picks up the ax, and with one mighty swing, the blade of the ax is imbedded into the stone, sparks showering up and around it. He looks at the others and says, "This ax is for the building of pyres. It is all it knows so very well. That and troll killings. It will be here when I need to build more pyres to honor our dead."

They bow at the meaning of his words. Helana, Logan, and Rodin look at Lawrence in reference to his speech. Lawrence bows to them. "The logs it will bring will be my honor."

After a few moments of looking at the ax and its meaning, Lawrence breathes a sigh of relief and readiness. He looks at everyone, and says to Helana, "Take these to everyone else. We have to return to the fortress. I will let you know when we are done there. Please ask that we are not disturbed until I do."

Helana bows. "Yes, Master." She raises her staff, and concentrates. Soon, she and the logs disappear.

Lawrence points at the fur coat. "Grab your things. Please escort us to the fortress, Master Archon."

Archon grabs the fur coat and puts it back on. He walks to Lawrence and Logan and looks at them. Logan grabs his hand and holds it firmly. Lawrence stands beside them. Archon's eyes begin to flash, and they return to the fortress.

They appear inside the main entrance and proceed inside. Lawrence walks to the far wall and stands in front of a torch bowl. Archon walks up and offers to light it for him. "It is pretty easy for me now. I've gotten used to these powers."

Lawrence says to him, "I'm sure you have. No telling what more you can do." Lawrence reaches in and sets them on fire. Archon is impressed with Lawrence's knowledge and nods to him. Lawrence then tips the bowl of flaming oil over. It spills into a groove that runs behind a set of statues. When the fire settles, they see that they are tributes to Archons past.

Logan is in awe. "Whoa," he gasps.

Archon looks and says, "I was wondering what these figures were. I didn't have time to look at them." After a moment of studying them, Archon says, "I know them all. I know their stories."

Lawrence looks at him and says, "Tell us."

Archon raises three stone seats facing the statues and sits in the center. Logan sits to his right while Lawrence is seated to his left. Archon begins by pointing to the first Archon and changes into Rodin. He begins to tell their stories one by one. He tells them their names, what league they are from, and describes how they became Archon. He tells their battle stories, and how they lived and died. When he reaches the Archon called Vil, Lawrence remarks about his recognition of him as well as his feelings of disappointment for not standing up to him. He expresses guilt for their curse because of him.

Rodin shakes his head and tells him how manipulative Vil was, and how he would have made sure that Lawrence was to never have been Archon. Rodin tells him how Vil did it when he experienced Vil's knowledge, he had felt Vil's deception and decision to kill Lawrence if he had become Archon that day. He also let Lawrence know that Vil had been condemned to spend eternity with Darkness within the Plane of Hell because of his deeds.

Logan asks Rodin to finish the others stories. He is excited to hear their true tales. He becomes very excited over their battles as Rodin reenacts them while he tells them. When he is finished, Logan expresses his disappointment that the stories are done.

Lawrence looks at Logan and smiles. "Now, you can tell stories of your own. You can boast to your grandchildren about how you fought with your brother, the Eternal Archon. Imagine how excited they will be for those stories."

Logan smiles at the thought. Rodin shakes his head and huffs, "Don't give him any ideas. If war breaks, I plan on keeping him safe by locking him away in the deepest and darkest dungeon I can find."

Lawrence laughs as Logan protests. "Hey!" He looks at Rodin scornfully. "I'm supposed to be King, you know!"

Rodin says to his face, "After I've set you free."

Lawrence bellows a laugh at the two of them. He exclaims, "You two remind me of myself and my sister!" He laughs harder.

Logan looks at him curiously and asks, "Whatever happened to her?"

Lawrence becomes serious. "She passed away several centuries ago. Unfortunately, I have no heirs. I am the last of the family of Bolaster of the Class of Commons left behind." He looks down sorrowfully.

Logan looks down at his feet in regret of asking such a question. Rodin says to him, "I'm sorry, Master Lawrence. We didn't know."

Lawrence looks at them and smiles. "'Tis okay. You didn't know." He walks up to the last Archon statue and raises a hand to caress its face. He looks down the line and begins to walk by each one as he inspects them. He quietly asks, "Have you ever seen such detail in sculpting before?"

Rodin looks at the statues, then to him. "No. Someone had to have had such great knowledge of each one to carve them so beautifully detailed."

Lawrence laughs to himself, "Indeed." He carefully inspects the first statue and rubs a finger over the smooth stone face. He looks at Rodin and Logan and says to them, "I guess I should tell you about the man that sculpted these statues."

Logan sits in his seat as Rodin forms the other two into a circle facing the seat in front of the center statue, and Lawrence takes that position. He begins his story.

XXII

"**A**fter the Archon named Vil died, I went into seclusion. I had become depressed and did not want to be bothered by the world ever again. I remained here in this fortress as a hermit. I only came out to hunt and gather. Nothing more. In my seclusion, I prayed to the Rings and to the Light to lift the curse from the others and allow me to live it out, but they never granted my wish. I began to curse them, and defied their knowledge. I stayed hidden in the dark so the Circle of Light would never find me.

"Years and years had passed, and I could not take it anymore. I warned them that they were going to have to fight me to keep my curse. I had decided to commit suicide, hoping their curse would be lifted if I had sacrificed my own life in their name. On the first day, I walked to the edge of the opening and threw myself to the bottom of the falls. Let me tell you, it really is a long way down. I had time to beg for their forgiveness, and ask them to take my life and end their curse. But no. As soon as I plunged into the raging, frozen waters, I found myself very much alive. This annoyed me. I thought for sure the fall would have killed me. So, determined, I tried again. I had spent the next few days climbing back up the face of the rocks alongside these falls, and standing at the edge of the opening, I jumped again. This time, I screamed my pleas with the Rings to let me die. Again, no. I plunged safely into the waters. I allowed myself to sink to the bottom with the help of the current. I sat for what seemed like hours at the bottom of the river, clinging tightly to a rock, but I never ran out of air. So, I came back up cold, angry, and defiant. I decided that one way or another, I was going to die.

"After working my way back up again, I decided to jump away from the water and onto the rocks below. On the way down, I laughed at the Light and cursed the Rings, daring them to stop me from becoming a smear of blood on those rocks. They answered with a powerful wind strong enough to push me back over the waters. I was determined to keep jumping every day until they gave up. Instead, I gave up. The Rings and the Circle of Light are persistent deities, let me tell you. They never gave up on me no matter how persistent I became.

"After many years of trying and failing miserably, I decided that I was going to starve myself to death. No food. No water. Nothing. Just me in this dark fortress, hiding in the farthest, darkest corner. Then, the Light introduced me to his newest creation and used it to find me. The light stones. Today, they can be mined just about anywhere, but they began here. The Circle found me, and forced nourishment into my body. I was forced, again, to live. I figured if I kept it up, the Light would eventually give up and let me die. No, again. Light never gave up, but I did.

"I went mad instead. Not on purpose, mind you. I had just simply gone mad. The others decided to check on me from time to time and tried to snap me out of my frenzy, but they couldn't break me. To help me cope, Dahlly tunneled long labyrinths within this fortress in hopes that I may find myself again. As I wandered around, purposely losing myself, they brought forth new Archons without me. Those last three, in fact, I never got to know who they were.

"I was headed in a bad place soon afterward. I walked the labyrinths in a daze. I got to the point that I was able to find my way through them with my eyes closed. As a matter of fact, I still can today. The Circle of Light must have gotten tired of dealing with me because one day, as I was sitting in the meeting hall, I fell asleep, and I didn't wake up for a long time.

"Now this is the part that I don't remember. It was told to me by Coleman and the man that would become my apprentice. As I lay there in what can only be described as a hibernated state, a very young man ventured up here. He didn't know why. All he knew was that, in his mind, he was driven to come up here. He didn't even know this cavern existed, but he just knew something was here. He discovered this fortress and decided to look around. He discovered me lying on the ground. The man was concerned with my well-being and tried to wake me. The moment he touched me; he went into a trance. He began babbling about what his mind was seeing.

"Coleman came to check up on me a few days later. He had the feeling something was wrong and needed to see to it. When he arrived, the stranger was babbling and writing out a set of scrolls as he sat next to me.

"Coleman sat with the man. He fed him and forced him to drink to stay alive. Coleman realized that the Light had placed in his mind the need to check up on me to be witness to the writing of the scrolls. After the scrolls were written, the man jumped up and started chiseling out these statues of the Archons. Coleman remained and cared for him during that time. The man worked relentlessly in his trance. He continued chiseling and carving day in and day out. He slept only when he passed out from exhaustion. Months went by until he finished the last statue. Then, he slept for three days.

"When he had awakened, I woke up as well. The sickness in my head was gone, and I realized that I had been in that hibernation sleep for more than ten years. The man was in his trance for eight months. Coleman explained everything to us, and showed the scrolls in proof. The man confirmed it was done by his hand but could not remember a single moment of it. When we looked at the statues, the man said he couldn't believe such knowledge was within him. We studied the scrolls, and we three agreed to never let anyone know about them until it was necessary. We didn't tell the others either since the Light chose Coleman to be the only witness. We also realized that the prophecy of our curse was coming to a close because the Light had brought me the man to take as my apprentice.

"That man spent many years after that time learning all I could offer him, until he took a wife and she became pregnant with their first child. He knew then that prophecy had to be fulfilled. He moved to the appropriate kingdom and created the appropriate village. Then he purposely set the discovery of those scrolls in motion by burying them in a cave until he could discover them again with a witness.

"I guess by now you've figured out who my apprentice was. He was Lord Bale Ganders of Yawn, founder of the village of Millington, and more importantly, your father."

They stare at Lawrence, flabbergasted. *Unbelievable!* Rodin thinks. *Full of lies! Our own father lied to us about everything we had ever known! Why?*

Lawrence lets them take this knowledge in and allows them time to process it all. After a moment, he tells them, "Do not question the whys of it all. Just take the knowledge and keep it to learn upon. The Light has done many things to make sure that the Rings' plans were put in order. We do not question the Rings. Their plans are not ours to guess. We merely take them as they come. For now, I will leave you two alone." He turns to leave. Lawrence stops in front of the first statue and stares at it. He quietly states to them, "Your father's work here is quite remarkable, isn't it?"

Logan nods as Rodin agrees. Lawrence walks away. Rodin and Logan stand in front of the last statue in wonder of the detailed work their father had done. They take turns touching the smooth surface, and pointing out the fine details in the carving. The wrinkles in the hair. The lines in the face. Up close, the figure almost seems to be alive. It is the only connection outside their house that they have of their father. The memories flood over them.

Logan cries, and Rodin comes to tears. He tries to be strong for Logan. He turns to him and holds him. Logan cries, "I miss him, Rodin!"

Rodin squeezes him tightly. "Shh! I know. I do too, Logan. I miss him and Mom."

"Why, Rodin? Why? I don't want to be Aing. I don't want you to be Archon. I want Mom! I want Dad! I want our family back!" Logan falls to his knees, crying as hard as he can. His emotions pour from him to the floor.

Rodin isn't able to bare the weight any longer, and the two of them sit on their knees, crying and holding on to each other. It is the first time since their parents' deaths that they've actually shared their grief with each other as brothers.

As the hours pass, the two brothers relax and admire their father's legacy further. Lawrence returns to them, saying, "We must go. We have a funeral to attend." Rodin and Logan stare at the statues one last time. They touch them one more time to hold the memory.

Rodin becomes Archon, and Logan smiles at him, and says, "Our father would be proud of us." Archon quips, "Yes, but Mom would flip." They laugh, knowing it is the truth. They gather themselves together and disappear.

XXIII

They find that Aranae's pyre is built, and her body lies on top. Helana and Dahlmür have placed her there. Someone had also taken the time to remove the spears from her body and disposed them. Mutt and Biter run to Logan and Archon and jump to their chests in an embrace. They give comfort to them in a show of strength and honor for Aranae.

As Archon looks around, he comes to another realization. *These men will die soon too.* He sees the grief as well as relief in their eyes. They long for death. Their curse is coming to a close. They see that Aranae is the first to be released, and they will soon join her.

We grieve as they express joy and comfort in their deaths, he notes. *I understand. Tonight, we will not grieve at a funeral. When this is over, we will celebrate the ending of a long, fulfilled life. I promise to make this celebration happy and proud.*

Archon walks to Lawrence and hugs him. He then walks to Galla and does the same. He goes to each of the Cursed Brothers, hugging them all. They look around at one another and smile, knowing the meaning of Archon's gesture.

Archon looks at his circle of friends and brothers. Then he looks at his love, Millette. He says to all of them, "I represent Aranae's gift. I am Archon. She gave me life just as she gave life to those two younglings. In a way, I am her son. I called her 'Mother' in respect of this life. I may not have chosen this life, but who chooses life anyway? The Rings give it to us all and continues to give it every day to each new child born on Terra-Earth. No matter what Order, League, Class, or Plane they are born into. The Light provides us knowledge to allow us to protect the lives the Rings have granted us, whether we are born with the knowledge, such as the deer, or it is taught to us, such as the way we, the League of Humans, teach our children."

"We also teach one another to cherish the life of others like Aranae, as well as each of us gathered here tonight. Aranae and these men we call the Cursed Brothers have lived for centuries. They have seen what it means to cherish life through the memories of people we will only meet in the Spiritual Realm when our lives come to an end. We cannot begin to understand the heartache and pain they'd suffered as they watched the men and women they grew to love die. They had to move on without them only to continue to live themselves with their memories."

"Tonight, we will not grieve for Aranae's death. Tonight, we will celebrate her life. As we celebrate her life, we will also celebrate the end of her curse. As we celebrate the end of her curse, we will celebrate the end of these men's curse, and give praise to the Rings for allowing us to know them as fathers, friends, teachers, and in the end, brothers. We thank you, Light, for giving us the knowledge of these Cursed Brothers and their sister, Aranae."

Everyone answers, "So says the Circle of Light," and the pyre is lit as everyone outside King Saul, Troy, and Drake begin to console one another.

King Saul is amazed at them and how they have come to be so close so fast. He walks over to Archon, expressing his condolences. Troy approaches Dahlmür and Helana to console them. Archon notices that Drake remains where he is. Archon makes it a point to speak to Slender again later.

XXIV

odin walks up to Millette as she smiles at him. He's happy to see her and holds her in his arms. They kiss each other and hold each other's hands. He reminds her that he loves her. She smiles and looks into his eyes and reminds him that she loves him too. They stare into each other's eyes for some time.

After what seems like an eternity, he turns to leave her at the house for the day. He has important work to do in town. He turns back to her and waves as he reaches for Thornrose's reins. She waves back. His hand searches for the reins, but he is still unable to grasp them. He turns to look at the horse, but she's gone. Confused, he looks back at Millette, but she is gone too.

The door to the house is open. He walks back up the porch and steps inside. Dirt and cobwebs are everywhere. For some reason, the scene is familiar. He looks around for her. She had just been standing there, and now she's gone. She couldn't have gone far. He knows something is familiar about the way the house is laid out.

Suddenly, the voices begin calling. "Archon! Please save us!" *Millette!*

"Archon! Please save us!" *Logan!*

One by one they call him, "Archon!'

Francine's voice joins the chorus. "Archon! Pleases save us!"

He remembers. He looks out to the field. It is nothing but a dead field of dirt. The clouds are dark and swirling. This time, there's no figure laughing in the distance. Vil is gone.

Another voice cries out, "Archon! Please save us!"

Millette's voice restarts the cries. They begin to replay again and again.

Suddenly, a new voice cries, "Save me! Please, little one!" *Aranae! No! She's in trouble!* He bolts back outside and runs to the side of the house, looking for her. He doesn't find her. "Save me, please, little one!"

He runs back to the front yard. A huge structure is now standing in the middle of the field. The wind blows the dust all around it, keeping him from having a clear view of it. The structure looks like it has collapsed all around a central structure. It is round with columns collapsed all around it. A tower maybe? He walks toward it as a figure appears standing on top of it. A laugh comes out of it. *Vil!* He raises a green sword and shoves it down between his feet. The columns rise up around it and shake then collapse back down.

Aranae's voice cries, "Save me, please, little one!"

The others cry out after her, "Archon, please save us!"

Vil laughs and drives his sword down again. Rodin runs, screaming, at the structure that's not a structure at all. It's Aranae's body! She's belly-up with Vil laughing and driving his sword into her over and over. He looks at Rodin, and suddenly, he is standing in front of him with an evil grin. He raises his sword and laughs as he swings it down at Rodin. Vil screams out his name, "Rodin!"

Millette shakes him awake. "Wake up, Rodin!"

Rodin flips his eyes open and leaps to his feet as his body changes into Archon. His arm transforms into a blade as he circles in confusion, looking for Vil. His breathing is heavy. Even without the facial expressions, they can tell something about his dream has scared him. Millette places a hand to his shoulder as she speaks calmly into him. He flinches just a little as the fog of his nightmares slip away. He sees everyone staring at him with a look of concern across their faces.

Logan runs to him and holds him tightly.

Archon releases the blade, and his arm returns as he calms down and hugs Logan back. He reaches over and hugs Millette as he becomes Rodin again.

Logan releases Rodin and smiles at him. "That was cool. Do it again." He grabs him tightly again.

Rodin laughs. "Next time, little brother." He rubs his head. Logan expresses his disappointment as he lets him go.

Vaniir walks up to him and asks out of genuine concern, "Are you all right?"

Rodin nods as everyone else relaxes. He looks to see Francine relaxing from her perched position in the trees. He laughs at her and points out her tail, which she uses for balance. Millette laughs at it also.

Francine jumps down as the tail disappears and asks her, "What? You've never seen a lion's tail before?"

Millette says to her, "On a lion, not a lady."

She shrugs, "Oh. Well, you got me there."

Helana and Millette come together with her, laughing. They announce to everyone to stay away from an area upstream so they may take care of "lady business" in private.

Jokingly, Logan asks, "Can I help with anything?"

Slender picks him up by the collar and hauls him off in the other direction, laughing at him. "You're such a pervert. You're not supposed to ask them that. You're supposed to sneak around and spy on them."

Helana screams, "Hey!"

Millette calls out, "Oh no, you don't!"

Francine adds, "I'll kill you guys if you do that!"

Byron and Logan take off as Byron says to Rodin out loud, "C'mon, brother, let's go watch them get slaughtered. We might 'accidently' see things in the process!"

Dahlmür puts his hands to his temples. "Oh, kids!"

The rest laugh as Galla says, "They're going where I was hoping to go. I hope they don't take long."

Lawrence and Coleman giggle. Coleman says to him, "They better count themselves lucky that they went before *you*!" Lawrence laughs and agrees with him.

After a while, everyone is done taking care of their morning routines. Rodin's mood is somber. The death of Aranae, and now the nightmare begin to weigh heavily on him. He tries to snap out of his mood by doing things that the others find impossible just to make them laugh. He quips his enjoyment of being able to do these things. Since King Saul feels it is beneath him to sleep with his head on the ground, had forced Troy to return him and Sir Drake to the castle. He thinks King Saul needs to lighten up and snap back to the real world. Everyone agrees with him as Vaniir points out that to King Saul, that is his idea of the real world.

Vaniir looks at Rodin as they gather together. "Master Slindee expressed your concerns about Sir Drake. We have discussed your concerns with Troy."

Rodin is in disbelief. "But he is with him!"

Dahlmür says, "Yes, but his loyalty is to the Light, and as Archon, you have his loyalty more than King Saul thinks. He is a wizard, and as wizards, we pledge our allegiances to you. Besides, just because he is with King Saul, doesn't mean he isn't working for his wise, old grand-uncle on the side."

Rodin scratches his head. "Why don't I trust him?"

Dahlmür tells him, "You have a keen sixth sense about people. You know whom you can trust and whom you can't. Just like Lady Francine. You know you can trust her, and your feelings of trust are strong enough to make her a part of your circle. That is why we do not object to her joining you if she likes."

Francine looks at Rodin. "Look, Sire, I am very grateful to you. After everything I've witnessed these past few days, I think I would very much like to join your circle. It would mean saving my league as well."

Rodin accepts her as well as Byron and Helana. Millette hugs her. Slender and Logan return with Biter and Mutt following behind them. Lawrence and Coleman join the circle.

Vaniir says to Rodin, "Thank you. From all of us. You brought honor to us last night."

Galla says to him, "I pray that we continue to do well by you and your circle." All five men bow down to Rodin and his circle in respect.

Byron rubs his head and says to them, "Gentlemen, please. You do not need to thank us. We are humbled to follow the knowledge you've given us." The circle returns the bow.

Slender says to Galla, "Tomorrow is a big day, Sire."

Galla smiles and laughs. "Oh yes! Slender is going to be a full-fledged member of the Class of Knights!"

Vaniir becomes jolly as he strokes his beard. "We must prepare for tomorrow with a celebration in private tonight!"

Rodin looks at Dahlmür and smiles. "We must prepare for another celebration as well." He turns their attention to Helana and Byron.

Dahlmür stutters, "Don't . . . eh . . . eh . . . eh . . . remind me."

Helana begins to jump up and down. Her voice squeaks. "I'm getting married!"

Byron becomes pale as a glazed look of realization comes over him. "I'm getting married?"

Logan laughs as Rodin and Slender throw their arms over him. Slender says to Rodin, "Brother, do you think he's ready?"

Rodin chuckles. "This is about as ready as he's going to get."

Logan says, "Sire, I think this is supposed to be a double wedding. Isn't it?" He looks at Millette and Rodin.

Vaniir smiles wide and looks at Millette. "Oh yeah!"

Millette grabs Helana's hands and joins her in her exuberance. "I'm getting married too!"

Rodin laughs and shakes his head. He looks at Slender. "At least I can handle the news better. Right, brother?" He pulls Byron in close. Byron looks up at him. "I'm getting married?"

Dahlmür calls everyone's attention, "Right. We need to go back to the fortress and allow Archon some time to train while we return to the castle to prepare for tomorrow."

Rodin shakes his head. "No."

Dahlmür is confused. "No what?"

Rodin says, "Sir."

Dahlmür shakes his head. "What I mean is, is there a disagreement on something?"

Rodin nods. "Yes, sir. I do not wish to return to that place for a while."

Lawrence agrees as he steps forward. "He's right, Dahlly. He shouldn't be forced to spend his days alone in the fortress."

Vaniir looks down at his feet and sighs. "He's right. Rodin needs to come with us. It's time for us to do things right by him again. We don't want him to be alone up there. How would you feel if we left you alone, and did everything without you, Dahlly? Aranae is gone. He will be completely by himself."

Dahlmür gazes over at Rodin and realizes what he was doing. Making Rodin an outcast is not his intentions. He sighs. "My apologies, Master Rodin. Let us all return to the palace."

Everyone agrees. Dahlmür and Helana begin the process of bringing them home. Slender whispers to Logan, "I might throw up on you." Logan backs up against Millette and keeps a sharp eye on him.

As soon as they appear inside the library, they all give Slender plenty of breathing room. Slender begins to lurch. He holds it in. *Brrrrrt!*. He fans his behind with a sigh of relief. Everyone shakes their heads at him. They expresses their displeasure with him. He apologizes profusely. "Sorry!" he says as they all run for the door. Mutt and Biter roll over and play dead. Slender looks at them, sternly, "Now you cut that out!" They jump up, laughing and run out the door.

They walk down the halls of the palace as a pleasant-looking servant girl approaches them. She stops in front of Vaniir, curtsies to him, allowing her long brunette curls to fall around her, and says, "Forgive me, Sire, but if that man ever lays a hand on me again, I will stab him in the chest!"

Vaniir looks at her in surprise, "You mean King Saul?"

She purses her lips and nods furiously. She says to him, "Will you please inform him about the rules of this kingdom? Because we will stop serving him."

King Vaniir looks at her curiously and asks, "What has he done?"

She is embarrassed to say. She looks around and fidgets as she tries to find the words, "Well, Sire, he . . . he asked . . . well, tried to force me to . . . um . . . service him . . . Sire"

Millette says to King Vaniir accusingly, "You let this kind of stuff happen?"

King Vaniir does not like the accusation and furiously states, "No, I do not!"

Rodin steps forward and asks, "Sire, I'm not entirely familiar with the laws of the kingdom when it comes to serving the royal palace. As Common's Leader, I ask you to familiarize me with them."

Vaniir looks at Rodin in recognition of his intent and smiles, "Well, Master Rodin, anyone employed to serve in our kingdom cannot be asked to do anything that would be considered an unwarranted act. If, for any reason, a servant feels it is necessary, they may bring their concerns to the person in charge of the facility and ask that the person be charged, removed, or service can be refused to be given to that person by the staff indefinitely."

Rodin looks at the young servant, "So you're saying that if he had proceeded to force himself upon her, then she could, say, call upon the Common's Leader and ask me to take charge?"

"Yes."

"And as long as I fairly represent the Class of Commons with a proper proposal to rectify the situation, then he would have to abide?"

"And I would have no choice but to enforce a proposal that is found just, and execute the proper punishment if the accused does not abide."

Slender smiles, "Oh, I like where this going."

Byron laughs, "Common's Leader, as Mediator, may I escort you and Glenda to his quarters?"

Rodin says, "Bring your Adviser"—he points to Helana—"and your Enforcer as well." He points to Slender. He turns to Glenda, "My lady, please lead the way." He gives her the commons bow.

She smiles and looks at King Vaniir with a satisfied look, "Thank you, Sire." Vaniir smiles his own satisfaction.

Slender is excited, "My lady, we will be glad to take care of this problem."

She bats her eyes at him, "Thank you, Master . . ?"

"Slindee."

"Slindee," she echoes affectionately as she flips her hair.

Rodin grabs Slindee by the arms with annoyance, "Leave her alone, lover boy." He turns to Glenda with a smile. "Please," he says, motioning her to lead the way.

Helana elbows Slender. "She's cute," she whispers.

Slender agrees, "Uh, huh."

Byron says, "Too bad for you. You'd probably kill the poor girl."

Glenda comments as she walks while swinging her hips, "I'd probably kill him."

Rodin and Byron pause and smile at each other as they catch her meaning. Helana comments, "I like her."

As they make their way down the palace, Rodin comes up with an idea, "Hey, wait! Where's your room?" he asks Byron.

Byron looks at him, confused, "This is no time for sightseeing."

Rodin grabs at his clothes, "No, you idiot. I can't go looking like this."

Glenda looks at Byron, "He's got a point, my prince."

Helana perks up, "Oh, I want to see our room!"

Byron begins to correct her then realizes that she's called it correctly, "Oh, yeah. Ours."

Helana looks at Glenda and smiles, "I'm getting married."

Glenda says to him, "Congratulations, my lord." Then to Helana she says, "My lady," and bows to her.

Helana becomes giddy again and grabs Byron by the arm, "Which way, my love?"

Rodin shakes his head as he raises his voice a few octaves, "Yes, show us, my love."

Slender walks up to Glenda and extends a hand to her, "I guess we follow them. Shall we?"

She smiles at him graciously and takes his hand as they follow Byron and the others. They come to a huge hall that is full of windows leading to an outdoor atrium. Across the windows are two sets of double doors. One set is at one end of the hall, the other set on their end. Byron proceeds to the doors on the far end as Rodin admires the garden out of the windows.

Byron opens the doors, "Our room, my love." He introduces Helana to a disaster zone.

Helana looks flabbergasted, "It will be when I get done with it." Byron looks at her, confused, and rubs his head.

Glenda gives a serious comment in disgrace, "Anything would be an improvement."

Rodin says jokingly, "Should we discuss terms on the upkeep of this room?"

Slender laughs as Glenda remarks in all seriousness, "Nope. His negotiations for this room are over."

Byron is not amused as he says to her, "It's clean."

Slender says, "To a blind man's standards."

Helana looks at Byron with sweet affection, "I don't care. We can improve it together." She kisses him with a smile. The rest of them look at one another and pretend to gag at their loving display.

Rodin quickly changes the subject, "Okay, clothes please." He separates the two of them to bring them back to the task at hand.

Byron looks Rodin over and shakes his head, "Damn, you're tall."

Rodin notions to Byron, "I can make anything fit, remember?"

Byron catches on and begins grabbing clothes from his chest and wardrobe. Helana walks up to Rodin and sniffs him. Then she turns to Glenda, "Show him where the bath is, please."

Rodin sniffs himself, "Bath?" he says in confusion, "I just took one last week, remember? You were all there. Unannounced, as I recall."

Slender corrects him, "No, that was almost three weeks ago. As I recall."

Helana speaks into her staff as Glenda pulls Rodin from the room. Rodin looks at Slender to save him, with no avail. Glenda yanks him out the door as he cries, "Help!"

Glenda pulls him around the corner and into another room. The room is full of steam and is very warm. He hears splashing beneath the steam. A voice cries out, "We're ready for him!" A woman's voice.

Did she say we? Rodin becomes nervous and jittery as two women in bathing gowns approach him. They take Rodin away from Glenda as they sit him down and begin removing his boots. Rodin says to one of the girls, "You know I can bathe myself."

The girl replies in jest, "And you smell like it too, Master."

The other girl stands him up, "Remove your shirt and pants, please, Sire. And please calm down. We've seen them all."

Rodin comments, "Not mine." He stands, holding tight to his pants, not allowing them to drop.

Suddenly, he hears the door open as another woman's voice calls out, "I'll take care of him, ladies. Thank you."

Millette! Oh, thank the Rings! Rodin calls to her, "Help! They want to bathe me!"

She comments, "Well, somebody better do it." The girls laugh in response. She says to them, "I think you girls scared him."

One says on the way out, "That one is full of modesty. We should be so lucky for more like him."

Millette giggles as she closes the door behind them. She says to Rodin, "Wow. This is a lot of steam. Where are you?"

Rodin replies, "I'm over here!"

She says, "Where?"

Rodin replies, "Right here?"

Millette says, "I can't find you."

Rodin replies, "Follow my voice."

Millette says, "Oh, there you are," and she appears out of the steam naked. Rodin drops his pants.

Helana sends a nice set of Byron's clothes for him to wear. Millette laughs as she compares the size of them to Rodin's tall, thin frame. He slips them on. Millette laughs as she tells him he looks silly with the pants sagging and the legs halfway down his shins. The shirt is extremely large across the body but short down his torso. The tie is a lost cause in length. Only his toes make it into the shoes. He concentrates on making everything conform to him. Millette notes how much more defined and stronger he's become. He was strong before, but with everything he's been through and with all his fight training he's been doing, he has improved his muscular frame.

She runs a finger from his chest to his abdomen. Rodin giggles as the feeling tickles him. They kiss.

Rodin and Millette walk out the door as the others are waiting for him. Byron directs a comment at Millette, "No wonder it took so long."

Helana elbows him in the gut. She walks up to Rodin and sniffs, "You smell nice."

Rodin smiles, "Thank you. I love that bath. It's indoors too. I feel better. I can take that kind of bath more often. Including the help." He looks at Millette and winks. She smiles and bats her eyes at him.

Slender sticks his head in the bathroom to look around. He comes back out and says, "I'd like to give it a go later myself."

Glenda flips her hair and says to him, "I'll be sure to show you around, Master."

Rodin shakes his head and comments, "Time to go."

They come to a room on the western side of the palace. Glenda knocks and announces, "Someone to see you, sire!"

Troy opens the door and sees the bunch smiling at him. He looks at them curiously and stops and stares at Rodin. He turns to Byron and asks, "Can I help you, my Prince?"

Byron smiles and introduces Rodin, "This is the recently elected Common's Leader. He is Master Rodin, of Millington. He has asked us to join him to meet with King Saul about a concern that had been brought to him by the royal servants in this castle. Since he is Common's Leader, he feels it was his job to follow up with any and all concerns the Class of Commons may have in this kingdom."

Rodin greets Troy and gives him the Common's Bow. Troy bows at him and asks, "What concerns bring you here, Master Rodin?"

To keep his personality separate from Archon's, Rodin decides to make himself forceful and diligent in his determination to the representation of his Class. He steps forward and walks into the room with his posture rigid and showing pride. He smiles to Sir Drake as he answers, "I am here because I have been told that someone staying within this palace has decided to disregard the laws of service provided to the Class of Commons by His Majesty,

King Vaniir. Any such breech of these laws requires me to step in and make a resolve."

Sir Drake, still wearing his beat-up armor, grumbles, "Since when do peasants have laws?"

Rodin steps up to him and looks down at him in seriousness, "Since honor was brought back to the Class of *Commons* within this kingdom by my father, the first Common's Leader, Bale of Millington."

King Saul appears from around the corner, "Did you say Bale of Millington?"

Rodin looks at him with genuine pride in recognition of his father, "Yes, I did, Your Majesty," he gives the Common's Bow to King Saul.

King Saul stands and extends a hand to Rodin, "My father spoke of your father."

Rodin looks at him in accusation, "Good things, I hope, because he has brought good things from Anglon to Trade."

King Saul smiles at him, "He wished that he had stayed and brought about his ideals to our kingdom."

Rodin sighs and looks around the room, acting as though the items within are below his standards. He tries to imagine how a lord like Vil would act to keep up the appearance that his father taught him to be respectful to his family title but uphold the honor of the Class of Commons.

He turns to King Saul, "Onto more pressing matters. I am a busy man, Sire. The staff within this palace have called upon me to solve a problem they are having since King Vaniir is taking care of something more worthy of his time," he grumbles his disbelief, "For the life of me, I have no idea what would be more important than the honor of his people." Then he continues, "But the matter has been presented to me, and I have brought with me the new Mediator, Prince Byron; his Adviser, Lady Helana; Master Slender"—he quickly corrects himself—"*soon-to-be* Knighted, Master Slindee, as Enforcer; a representative of the staff, Lady Glenda; and an arbitrator to represent her, Lady Millette. Now, the staff claims that you, Sire, have recently made unwarranted advances upon the female staff. You've asked Lady Glenda here, and a few others to... How did they say, Arbitrator?" he cues Millette.

She steps forward with her hands cupped together in front of her, "They were asked to service him, Common's Leader."

Troy interjects, "I object, Mediator!"

Byron exclaims, "Objection recognized." He looks at Millette, "Please define yourself more clearly as to the term *service*, please, Lady Millette."

Glenda is taken aback, not knowing where this mediation may go. Millette firmly states, "Yes, Mediator. At the time it was asked, King Saul was bathing. He had the bath servant girls waiting on him. There were no servant men there at his own request." Millette assumes this is so, and Glenda confirms her assumption with a nod, "He asked they bathe him, and as they were, he grabbed Glenda and tried to force sexual services as he was in the bath. When Glenda and the others refused, he became upset and demanded that peasants should serve him as he asked. They became furious by this, and as their right by law, they walked out, and formally lodged a complaint."

Rodin spins to look at King Saul, "Your Highness, did you refer to the service staff as peasants?"

Troy interjects again, "Objection, Mediator! Who can corroborate this?"

Millette stands forward, "I am Arbitrator. I represent the staff making the claims. As witness, I have brought with me one of the members of the Class of Commons that was there," she waves her hand at Glenda to point out her witness.

Byron rules, "Objection overruled, Arbitrator Troy."

King Saul sighs, "No, she is correct. I'm afraid I am guilty. This kingdom has brought honor back to the Class of Commons." He looks at Rodin in guilt, "Common's Leader, your father has done well to eliminate the Class of Peasants. As League King, I should have recognized the pride they bring to this kingdom. No wonder King Vaniir is so regarded among our League." He turns to Arbitrator Millette and says to her, "If it pleases the Commons staff, I would like to repay them for my abhorrent behavior. I am going to order that everyone serving this palace be paid back in the price of one gold coin each." He turns to Rodin, "I will also be making a sizeable donation to help the poor and hungry."

Rodin thinks for a moment then says, "Actually, sire, a contribution to Commons City to build an orphanage and the funds to feed them and teach them would be of great service to the Class of Commons within the kingdom."

Troy addresses the mediator, "I believe an agreement has been presented."

The Mediator looks at Millette, "Arbitrator, how does your witness respond?"

Glenda and Millette speak to each other on the other side of the door. Rodin listens and chuckles as he hears them discussing not only their case but also of Glenda's desire in Slender. He interrupts them with the clearing of his throat, and the two of them look at him in guilt. When Millette and Glenda return, they regain their composure. Millette looks at Byron and says, "This agreement is acceptable to the witness."

The Mediator announces, "Then the agreement has been accepted. All terms have been agreed, and this mediation is now closed. Well done, Common's Leader Rodin."

Troy and Helana tap their staffs to the floor in unison. *Snap! Snap! Snap!*

Slender rubs his temples, saying, "Oh great, he got the entire family doing it."

King Saul begins to rub his temples as he says to him, "Annoying. Isn't it?"

"You have no clue."

Helana elbows Slender in his large frame. Slender doubles over as Millette and Glenda laugh at him.

Sir Drake stands and confronts Rodin, "Will that be all?"

Even though Sir Drake is much bigger in bulk compared to Rodin, he is much shorter. Rodin looks down at him. The Archon inside tries to come out for a confrontation. He tries with all his might not to change. The power is telling him that this man is very dangerous. Rodin begins to sweat but smiles calmly and says to the Knight down his nose, "That is all. For now." Rodin quickly turns and leaves the room. Everyone else with him is confused and then bows to King Saul as they leave just as quickly.

As they hurry to catch up, Rodin addresses Glenda behind him, "Please inform the others of the agreement. I must speak to my friends in private. Immediately!" He rounds a corner and enters the first room he comes to. Luckily, the room is empty and not being used by anyone. As soon as he is inside, he becomes Archon.

Byron is the first through the door and turns back out as he stops Glenda before she gets there, "Thank you, m'lady. We will return to see you shortly." He turns from her as he rushes everyone else in and blocks Glenda from the entrance.

As they enter, they are astonished to see Archon. He looks at Slender and says, "We were right, brother. That man is dangerous!"

A look of concern crosses Slender's face, "I think it is best if we keep you away from Sir Drake."

Archon shakes his head. "I don't know who he is, but that man is not a Knight. I don't think he is Sir Drake anymore either."

Byron asks curiously, "You mean, he's a demon?"

Archon nods in confirmation, "All my senses are telling me so."

Helana says, "I've got to tell my father."

Byron tries to calm the situation down, "Just relax." He asks Archon again, "Are you sure?"

Archon points out his form, "Do I look like I'm sure?"

Millette sides with Byron, "You have been Rodin for a long time. Maybe Archon needed to be released."

Archon shakes his head, "No. As Dahlmür explained, I have a strong sixth sense about people. I'm telling you, he's a demon."

Byron digresses with him, "Fine," he sighs, "I think we need to tell my dad and the others," he begins to open the door, "Let's go. Brother, you better be right."

Archon relaxes and becomes Rodin again, "Thank you."

XXV

When they find King Vaniir, he is sitting in his courtroom, listening to his advisers. Dahlmür sits beside him as Logan sits to the other side of him, listening and watching intensely. Rodin realizes that Vaniir has fully accepted Logan as his apprentice and is teaching him how to speak and listen to the royal court.

Rodin beams at Logan with pride.

Slender whispers to him, "He will make a good King as long as he stays with Vaniir. I can tell. He's been holding Vaniir's hand ever since he got here. If you had seen the way he has been studying him, you would have thought he was Byron's younger brother."

Byron confirms Slender's observations. "He is not a little boy when he is with my father. He's almost an adult. His actions and habits do not represent his age."

They gather into a dark balcony and watch. Rodin focuses on Logan. *He's sixteen and fully grown. When did he become this man? He grew up, and I never saw it. He is serious here and playful and childlike with me. I guess I bring him his youth, and his duties make him a man. He will bring honor to our name.* He smiles as he watches Logan follow King Vaniir's lead and listen to every advice the King gives him about each subject. Even Dahlmür offers advice to him.

Byron whispers to Rodin, "My father treats him like it were me sitting there. I remember a couple of years ago, when I was in that very same chair. The only difference is, your brother wants to be there. I hated that court. To me, it was the most boring thing in the world. Dad used to have to stop everything just to wake me up and scold me for not listening."

Rodin continues to admire his brother. He watches as Logan asks questions to the person speaking to get a better understanding of their position within the court. Sometimes, King Vaniir applauds him for making suggestions that sound reasonable at the moment, and counsels him about a decision that may seem unwise. Grand Wizard Dahlmür congratulates him, or offers advice in King Vaniir's council. Not once have they scolded him. Not once has he strayed from his intentions of learning such knowledge. He sits, watches, and speaks only when necessary.

The event lasts for another few intense hours as everyone begins to drift asleep while waiting for the court to end.

Rodin awakens in time for everyone to clear the courtroom. He stirs everyone quietly. They are beginning to gather themselves to confront Vaniir and Dahlmür when King Saul barges in.

"King Vaniir! A word please!" he shouts as he approaches him with an intense look. He stops and looks at Logan. "Boy, please leave us."

Dahlmür stops him. "Master Logan will stay. He is the King's apprentice."

"I thought he was part of Archon's circle?" King Saul points out.

King Vaniir informs him, "He is," he tugs Logan close to him. "but his destiny is not with them. His destiny will be told at a later time. For now, he will remain at my side as I pass down my knowledge as King."

King Saul is disgusted by this but shakes it off as he says, "Damn prophecy! After the ceremonies tomorrow, you will fill me in on this matter. First, I want to know why you have allowed that young man of Millington to serve in this kingdom as Common's Leader and not as he is, Lord Rodin Ganders of Yawn."

Logan says to him, "Forgive us, my king, but Common's Leader Rodin has expressed his desires to continue his father's work to bring honor back to the Class of Commons and eliminate the Class of Peasants entirely from the League of Humans."

King Vaniir puts a hand on his shoulder as an expression to let him continue the talking. Rodin and Millette watch as Logan proudly stands up to King Saul in their father's name.

Millette holds Rodin close and smiles in favor of him. Slender and Byron also look on beside them. Helana sits back and continues to watch.

King Vaniir says to King Saul, "Master Logan is right, Sire. Outside this palace, nobody knows Master Rodin's heritage. Only the Common's Elders know who he really is because they helped his father establish the new Common's Council and began the title of Common's Leader to represent their kingdom, to which I am proud of Master Rodin's representation."

King Saul looks at him in disgust and scolds him. "If this is how your kingdom is going to bring about change, then count me out. And my kingdom. And all other kingdoms, for that matter. This kind of direction won't be accepted anywhere else!"

Dahlmür interjects, "Sire, I hate to be the bearer of bad news, but King Fulst of Bolt Kingdom has accepted this change, as well as King Matterhorn of Graystone Kingdom. They have actually demanded their kingdoms to make the necessary changes. The Class of Commons is well represented in those kingdoms, and their honor has been diligently restored. Even with the resistance of others, Trade Kingdom's laws in these regards have become the basis of their new laws as they make improvements to them to fit their kingdoms' needs."

King Saul looks at him in concern. "Are you sure?"

King Vaniir nods in agreement. "Absolutely, sire."

King Saul sits down in deep regret. "Have I really been that slow to see what has been going on in my own League?"

Logan surprises everyone in saying, "Sire, change can move quickly when nobody is watching. Sometimes, the things that change matter so much to so many that to make change come about, it must be made as swiftly and quietly as possible so that those that wish to stop these changes cannot interfere. You, my King, haven't been watching, because this change in particular was something that you had hoped to bring about in one swift rule. We all know this, but those that you were seeking support from had already began the process for you. We want you to be a proud King. We are proving to you that your decision on this change is just and can be made swift and easy just like we have done. Please do not scold us for moving ahead without you. Use us as your example instead. Be proud to show everyone that this change is for the good of all in the League of Humans."

King Saul looks at Logan and laughs as he grabs Logan to him and kisses him on the cheek. He stands and says to King Vaniir, "You have given this boy great knowledge, King Vaniir. He will make you proud." With that being said, King Saul rubs Logan on the head and laughs all the way out of the court.

Vaniir and Dahlmür stare at Logan. Dahlmür whispers to Vaniir, "He is so peculiar."

Vaniir agrees as he looks up to the balcony, where Rodin is watching. "Much like his brother."

Rodin's pride in his brother beams down at him. Logan smiles, and the child reemerges. "Hi, brother! Have you been watching us the whole time? I've been learning a lot from Vanny and Dahlly here!"

Dahlmür changes his mind. "So much for that." Vaniir grumbles his agreement.

A jolly voice rings out from the other side of the court in another dark balcony. "Master Logan sure has a way about him, eh, Vanny?" It is Galla. Coleman, Lawrence, and Francine laugh with exuberance.

Rodin is relieved to finally be alone with everyone. They all congregate around the court table as they discuss his issues about Sir Drake. They all agree that Sir Drake poses a threat in some way, and they will keep their eyes on him one way or another.

King Vaniir changes the subject to the celebration tomorrow and the impending weddings, at Vaniir and Dahlmür's behest. Rodin promises to keep himself separate from the others to lower suspicions. That is when they decide to hold their wedding in private among themselves. Millette agrees even though it is not their idea of their dream wedding. Francine promises to help Millette and Helana make their preparations so they can at least have a beautiful wedding in such a short time. The three ladies become overly excited and race out to find Glenda and begin the process.

Byron and Rodin are left in shock about the amount of preparation they must go through themselves. Coleman, Galla, Lawrence, Slender, and Logan decide that a huge feast for the bachelors is in order. Dahlmür and Vaniir excuse themselves from it and decide they will confer with each other through the night to discuss the celebrations for tomorrow. Vaniir begins calling his servants to order and giving out preparation instructions with promises of fair increases in wages if things go as planned.

Those for the bachelor party head to the large dining hall and begin their own celebrations.

They eat plenty, laugh plenty, and drink plenty more. The night ends when they all pass out drunk and weary.

XXVI

Rodin is the first to awaken. Being Archon allows him to recover from his late-night binge quickly, and without the hangover. For that, he is grateful. He tries to stir them awake. Even Logan is passed out from too much unnecessary drink. He decides it is best to leave them, as he wants to explore the castle and perhaps find something to eat along the way.

He reaches back for his hood then remembers that it is now a part of him as Archon. He smiles as he decides that being Archon has its advantages while snooping. He becomes Archon and throws on his hood. Once invisible, he walks out of the room, leaving the others to sleep off their late-night partying.

Once out the door, Archon jumps to the ceiling to avoid accidental contact with anyone. He spots a boy pushing an empty food cart. *He's going back to the kitchen!* He decides to follow the boy. As they go down the hall, Archon grows impatient with hunger. *Where the hell is the kitchen? On the other end of the castle?* He is following the boy around another corner when he walks into a sea of people.

What the...

People scurry about below, carrying the decorations and gifts for today's events. Flowers, ribbons, and carts whiz by him from below. A giant floral arrangement that is too tall for the room scrapes the ceiling. Archon leaps out of the way in time to avoid it. He searches the people below for the cart boy. He spots him at the far end as the boy enters a door. Archon smiles to himself as he sees someone exit from the door, pushing a full tray of food.

Breakfast!

He jumps down and ducks behind the door as another servant exits. As the door closes, he becomes Rodin, wearing the fur coat. He pulls the door open and enters. People are running everywhere, hard at work to fill trays and carts for the morning breakfast. He smells cakes and the cooking of meats roasting in the kitchen as they prepare for the grand feasts of the celebrations. He ducks behind a counter as a baker carrying a six-tiered cake with a man and woman on top that bear the uncanny resemblance of Helana and Byron passes by. He stares at it for a moment as it goes by.

He ventures farther into the kitchen until he sees a lonely tray of cheeses and breads sitting next to a window. He walks up and begins to scarf it down.

He realizes he has just cleared an entire tray of the cheeses and breads when the cook appears out of nowhere. He looks at Rodin then at the empty tray and becomes red with anger. Rodin becomes fearful when the cook finds a meat cleaver hanging nearby and poises to throw it. Rodin apologizes, becomes invisible, and jumps out the window as the meat clever flies by him.

He becomes Archon and climbs the wall of the palace, searching for a window to climb back through. He hears what sounds like a familiar voice. *Millette!* He finds the window and climbs inside, closing the shutters behind him. He looks down from his high perch and sees a group of girls below him. They are all wearing their bath gowns. The steam rising around him reminds him where he is.

The bathing room. More importantly, the women's bathing room!

Archon becomes overly joyed to be in his current situation. The girls begin to unlace their gowns as Archon watches with anticipation. Just as they begin to remove their gowns, the room is suddenly filled with too much steam. Archon is blinded.

The girls begin to scream. "Who closed the shutters?"

"I don't know!"

"Where's the window?"

"I can't see!"

"Find the shutters!"

"I am!"

Archon begins scurrying about the ceiling, looking for a way out of the steam. He finds a small vent tunnel and crawls his way through it. Finally, the steam clears, and he can see the end of the tunnel.

He emerges from the tunnel and into the hall. Below him is the door. He figures the door leads back into the room from which he came. He climbs down and enters the room. He immediately jumps back up to the ceiling to regain his view below. The steam has cleared.

Oh, good. They opened the shutters.

As the steam clears, he is horrified at the sight. *Vaniir, Saul, Troy, naked! No!*

Archon quickly searches for the door. Luckily, Vaniir and the others are leaving the bathing room. As soon as the door is opened, he flies out and back up. He runs along the ceiling only to meet a dead end that leads to their rooms. He turns to get away only to be met with the image of the men talking and walking as they begin to wrap their towels around their waist from behind. Unfortunately, Archon is in front of them. Frantically, he tries to remove himself from the horrible scene. He turns left. *Wall!* He turns right. *Wall!* He bolts left. *Smack! Wall.* The men separate and go into their respected rooms as Archon tries to shake off the pain and the images from his head. Unfortunately, for the rest of his long life, those images are permanently burned into his memories.

Archon sees two servants pushing breakfast carts into another room. He follows them to the room as one opens the door and the other pushes and pulls the carts inside. Archon's hunger drives him to follow them inside. He looks below and sees Dahlmür in a classroom surrounded by a bunch of wizard students.

Dahlmür says to the class, "It is really a very simple technique to get attention. You simply take your staff and tap the floor." *Snap! Snap! Snap!*

Is this really a required lesson for all wizards? He watches as Dahlmür points to the student below him and asks him to give it a try. The young wizard raises his staff and drops it to the floor. *Whoosh!* Archon swings out of the way just as a ball of flame leaps to where he's just been perched.

Dahlmür is disgusted. "No! Not so hard! Try it again. This time, everyone join him!"

Whoosh! Whoosh! Whoosh! Archon leaps about the ceiling frantically, trying hard not to become the Eternally Crispy Archon! He sees the servant boys reopen the door to leave and flies out just as the heat from another fireball shoots by him. *Whoosh!*

He stops to catch his breath. He begins to make his way to the end of the hall until he reaches a fork. He forgets that he's been following the servant boys and didn't see which way they've gone. In his confusion, he decides to turn right. He sees a set of double doors at the end of the hall and hopes these doors lead to a kitchen.

He enters and discovers a room with wooden crates stacked high. He hears men working at the other end. As he approaches, he realizes this storage room leads outside. They are loading most of the crates onto a carriage. As the last crate is loaded, the men walk out and begin to close the doors. Before the room goes dark, he reads the writing on one of the crates: Fireworks. Archon huffs, "Why me?"

From out of the darkness, he hears a voice cry out, "Oy! Oym een heeah!" It is the man he met the first night he came to the city. The one that butchered the Human language.

Archon says to him, "Relax. I'll come to you."

"Eets dahk, Mastah! Oy caint see!"

"Don't worry. I can find you!"

"Oy! Air we go! Oy fownd a towch!"

"A torch? No! Don't!"

"No werries, Mastah! Oy wiw woyt eet, aind we cain geet ote!"

"No! Please! Tha—"

Fssh! He lights what he thinks is a torch. He sees that he is holding a stick that has "Dahlmür's Staff! Snap! Snap! Snap!" inscribed on it. "Oh, bloody hell!"

"-t's no torch."

Archon quickly scrambles for the door, grabbing the man with him. He kicks the door open just as he hears Dahlmür's staff. *Snap! Snap! Snap!*

He tosses the man out and shoots nets over the double doors to hold them in place. He becomes invisible again as he leaps to the ceiling. The man recovers just in time to see the double doors swell from the explosion as smoke and fire burst from their seams. The doors hold well enough to hold back the explosion, but they barely hang on by their hinges.

Archon comments, "Idiot."

He gives up. As Rodin, he decides to return to the others and wait on them to rejoin the Realm of the Living. Suddenly, he hears a knock on the door, and a voice cries, "Breakfast!"

Rodin smiles and thinks, *I can at least wait while breakfast is served.*

Rodin is able to rouse up Logan and Byron. Coleman begins to recover on his own. It takes everyone a moment to shake Slender and Lawrence. Galla is left alone after several attempts and a few death threats. Slender and Logan leap out the window to release an entire night's mead from their bladders as the rest run for the lavatory. When Slender returns, he picks at what Rodin has left behind and begins to eat. Logan returns and does the same. When Lawrence gets back, he walks over to the breakfast tray and looks at Rodin as he shrugs his apologies at him. Byron doesn't bother looking at the tray and asks a servant boy to bring more food.

Slender is the first to finally break the silence. "I woke up a little while ago. Where were you, brother?" he asks Rodin.

Rodin jumps and tries his best to act innocent. "Nowhere special."

Logan says to him, "You're a terrible liar, big brother."

Rodin becomes pale. "No, really, nowhere."

Byron says to him, "You can tell us."

Rodin gives in. He sits for a moment then confesses, "I raided the kitchen while I was invisible." *May the Rings forgive me.*

A servant enters the room, complaining to another, "Blaggart says he threw a meat cleaver at the lad, and he went invisible."

The other servant replies, "I think Blaggart has been hitting the wine kegs again."

"Me too." He laughs.

"Did you hear about the fireworks storage blowing up?"

"I heard the idiot got out just in time."

"He's a damn fool, that one." And they are gone.

They all look at Rodin, who is once again eating. They all shake their heads at him.

XXVII

After they are done eating, Rodin is finally full. The others look around at the many trolleys that are brought in to keep up. Logan calls out jokingly, "I count eighteen!" He's thought it will be interesting to know just how much it will take to satisfy Rodin's hunger. They have brought him over two-dozen eggs, over a dozen strips of thick bacon, over a pound of sausage, stacks upon stacks of pancakes, and a keg of fresh berry juice. Instead of chunks and slices of cheese, they've begun ordering more by the wheel. To figure out how much bread he had (by the loaves, after a while) is too much to keep track.

Rodin dumps the last of the juice down his throat, slams the mug down, and belches long and loud. He sighs. "That was so good!"

Lawrence walks over to him and looks at him in disgust. He says to Rodin, "My Rings, boy! Where the hell does it go?"

Rodin looks at him and smiles coyly. "Ask Millette."

Lawrence replies, "No, thank you."

Byron calls for several servants to come and pick up what remains. As they enter the door one by one, they all freeze and look around in astonishment. One walks to the nearest window and looks out then looks over them in amazement. He shrugs and orders the others to start grabbing trollies as he grabs two himself. When he gets to the door, he stops and bows to Byron. He looks at everyone else in wide-eyed amazement, thanks them, and closes the door behind him, shaking his head.

Coleman says to Logan, "You have to catch up to King Vaniir and prepare." He then looks at Byron. "As do you, sire. Master Slindee as well."

Lawrence pats Rodin on the back and says to him, "Common's Leader Rodin, you will be expected to make an entrance as a duly appointed representative of the Class of Commons."

Logan goes to the window and looks at the sky in disappointment. "Awe! It's a beautiful day today. I was hoping maybe we could look around outside and enjoy the fresh air in the city. We've never been to the city before."

Lawrence says to him, "You can do that another day."

Logan protests, "C'mon! The festival is today! At least let us look around for a few hours. I promise we'll be back in time for our presentations."

Lawrence opens his mouth, but Byron interrupts him. "Ya' know, I feel like getting out today too." He looks at Rodin and Slender, who share their sentiments. "We'll be back." He smiles at Lawrence. "Promise."

Coleman says to Lawrence with a smile, "I too have work to do in the city. I'm not a collector of trinkets. I'm a seller of goods. I have a whole cart I need to empty out. Plus, I have to find Heath to see where my trade money went with the bounty Master Rodin sold me weeks ago. The scoundrel may have spent it all on booze and women." He stands and gives Lawrence a smile. "They can escort me while I look for him and sell my cart off. Then we'll return. I promise to return them unharmed and a little brighter in spirits."

Lawrence gives up and smiles at Coleman. "Go ahead. I'll let Vanny and Dahlly know what you guys are up to." Logan cries for joy as Slender quickly changes. Rodin thanks Coleman as he and Byron swiftly walk to the door. Lawrence reminds them, "No trouble, please."

Byron smiles as the rest of them give one another a mischievous grin. "Okay." He opens the door and jumps back three feet. "Ahh!"

Francine is on the other side with her fist in motion to knock. She jumps back in surprise. "Oh, blessed Rings! You scared the hell out of me!"

Millette and Helana are behind her. They look at Byron, just as surprised. The boys quickly run out with Coleman trailing behind them. Helana asks, "Where are we going?"

Coleman says, "Follow us, my dear, before our keeper changes his mind."

Rodin pulls Millette with him as Byron grabs Helana. Logan pulls the arm of Francine, who is about to protest in confusion. The door closes behind them as Lawrence cries, "No trouble!"

They walk their way through the maze of people that continue to carry the arrangements for the celebration. They stop when Slender spots Glenda carrying a large bunch of flowers. He turns to Helana and Byron and points her out. He whispers to Byron, and

Byron smiles and nods in agreement with Slender. Byron looks around and spots a man directing everyone working. He walks up to the man and begins speaking to him. The man looks around and spots Glenda as he calls her name. She hands her arrangements off to another girl and walks to them, bowing to Byron. Byron grabs her by the arm and waves to the man as he bows to him. He escorts Glenda back to the group. She smiles as soon as she sees Slender and joins them. They make their way out the main doors to the outside.

Rodin, Logan, and Millette stop and look at the city in front of them and smile in wonder. People are everywhere. The cobbled streets and stone buildings echo the horses, the carriage wheels, the thousands of boot steps, and the voices all around them. They have never seen a city so alive before. Coleman steps out to lead them. They are so fascinated with everything. A man calls out to them to clear the way as drives his team of horses pulling a carriage of crates through the crowd.

Rodin recognizes the crates but says nothing.

Coleman agrees with them to go see things on their own. He wanders off as the rest go their separate ways. Millette, Logan, and Rodin walk straight ahead and begin to visit the separate shops, vendors, and street sellers. They round a corner of the road as it opens into a square full of activity. A group of performers tell a hilarious story about a knight and his crew venturing out to plunder and siege for glory and honor. They tell about their fights with demons and the comedic situations they have along the way. Millette and Logan laugh at them as they reenact the scenes and make jokes about them. Rodin watches Millette laugh at the performers. He can watch her smile for days.

After a while, Logan complains about being hungry and thirsty. Rodin agrees. Millette reminds them that they have no money to pay the vendors, but Rodin shakes his head and pulls a small coin sack from his pocket. When asked where it came from, he smiles and tells them that he grabbed the money when he last ventured home. Logan smiles and points at a vendor with skewers of chicken for sale. Rodin walks to the vendor and signals for the three of them. He pays the man and passes the skewers between them. Millette is all smiles as she bites into hers. Rodin then walks up to a vendor selling hot cider and pays him for three mugs. They begin to look over more vendors as they eat and drink.

They continue through the city, turning corners and following the sounds of the music and shopkeepers shouting as they stay together. Logan spots a familiar cart. Coleman's. He's surrounded by people buying his wares and trinkets. He smiles as Logan runs toward him. Rodin and Millette catch up and greet him also.

Rodin asks him, "Busy?"

Coleman states matter-of-factly, "Always." He looks at Logan and says to him, "I've been meaning to offer you something." He goes into his carriage, and the sounds of him rummaging through stuff can be heard. He exclaims, "Found it!" and returns. He presents something wrapped in cloth to him. Logan puts his hands up as he accepts it.

He unwraps it and holds up a crossbow missing its string. The crossbow is made of bright yellow stone. Light stone! He inspects it curiously and asks, "You carved a crossbow from light stone?"

Coleman laughs. "My boy, that is a powerful crossbow in the right hands. That is Firebolt."

Rodin is confused. "Where's the drawstring?"

He replies, "It doesn't have one. You point and pull the trigger. It fires a bolt of lightning with every pull from the trigger. It will fire as fast as you can."

Logan comments, "I can't believe how light it is." He passes it over to Rodin to inspect it, and he agrees with him. Logan takes it and aims at a large ceramic pot across the street. He asks, "How accurate is it?"

Coleman says to him, "Only as accurate as the shooter."

Logan laughs as he pulls the trigger. A bolt fires from it, hitting the pot dead center, and it explodes. People all around scream in response to the explosion. Some begin to cheer, thinking it's a part of the celebrations. Logan looks back at Coleman, showing a full set of teeth in his broad smile.

"I'll take it!"

Rodin looks at Coleman and shakes his head at him. "Do you know how hard it's going to be for me to get that thing away from him now?"

Millette puts her hand out at Logan, motioning him to hand it over. He shakes his head at her. She puts her other hand to her hip. He shakes his head. She purses her lips and stomps the ground and gives him a firm, stern look as she squints an eye at him. He ducks his head in shame and hands it to her.

Coleman looks at Rodin and laughs. "She doesn't seem to have that problem."

Rodin says snidely, "Not her. He knows what will happen if he doesn't listen to her."

Coleman continues laughing as Rodin hands him a small stack of gold and silver coins and hugs him. Then he begrudgingly thanks him for making Logan's day. "Thanks."

Throughout the rest of their tour, Logan tries every way he can to convince Millette to give back his new toy. Repeatedly she tells him under no circumstances will he be getting the crossbow back. She remarks that he will get it back today over her dead body. He rudely comments that it can be arranged if she lets him have the crossbow. She flips her hand across the top of his head.

Rodin laughs at the two of them.

Before long, they head back to the palace as the crowd begins to disperse and the shops begin to close down to make the opening of the royal celebrations at the front court of the palace. They rejoin the others and Coleman as they begin to go back inside to prepare themselves.

XXVIII

Rodin is dressed in the finest suit he's ever been in when he makes his entrance to formally greet King Saul as Common's Leader. The entire Class of Commons that are present applauds him as the master of introductions, Sir Galla, announces his name. He gives the crowd the Common's Bow then bows to King Saul, who returns the Common's Bow to him out of respect. The people cheer more loudly when they embrace to solidify the honor.

Another name is announced as Common's Leader of Graystone Kingdom. Again, the crowd cheers as he gives the same greeting to King Saul, and they too embrace.

Bolt Kingdom's Common's Leader does the same.

After their recognitions, they stand to the side, waving at the crowd, then turn and give King Saul the Common's Bow in unison then are dismissed. Rodin bows to the two men. The two bow to him and each other. They speak among themselves as they weave through the crowd. The lady from Graystone hugs Rodin then hugs the man from Bolt as they part ways.

Rodin joins Millette, Slender, Francine, Helana, Lawrence, and Coleman in a private balcony overlooking the ceremonies. He looks around and asks, "Where's Logan?" Millette says to him, "King Vaniir wants him by his side at all times."

Rodin responds nonchalantly, "Oh."

He sits down and kisses Millette as Slender exclaims, "Oh look! There's my father!" He points at a group of knights standing around a king.

Glenda asks, "Which one's your father?"

They all look to see who it is as he says, "The Knight to the far right."

They are all startled to see that he is meaning a short skinny man weighing next to nothing, holding a shield bigger than himself.

In wide-eyed disbelief, Helana remarks, "You look nothing like him."

Slender quickly responds, "I know. I take after my mom." He points at a tall heavyset woman who waves at him and blows him a kiss.

The whole group looks from her to Slender to the Knight and back again in total disbelief. Slender waves and blows a kiss back to her. His father waves at him, and Slender waves back.

A servant calls from behind them, "Master Slindee, please gather yourself below for your coronation!"

Slender becomes excited as he grabs his sword and his shield. "I'm finally going to be a Class of Knight!" He bends down and kisses Glenda and runs out.

As soon as he is gone, another voice calls out, "Glenda! Get in here and get back to work!" She jumps up and excuses herself.

They all watch as the long procession of the Class of Lords is announced by Grand Wizard Third Class Troy. Millette says candidly, "Thirteen kingdoms and over a thousand lords."

Coleman laughs. "Wake me when it is over." Rodin smiles and nods his agreement.

Lord Norel is announced but is not present. His wife, Lady Sheila, makes her presence without him or his son to accompany her. The crowd goes silent as she waves and smiles at everyone. The birds chirping in the distance can be heard over the silence. Even King Saul is not impressed by her due to the overwhelming response she is receiving. Rodin asks if anyone has heard whether or not Lord Norel was feeling all right. He actually hoped to meet Lord Norel and introduce himself to him as Common's Leader and thank him for the support he gives to the Class of Commons at the behest of his wife and son. Rodin feels genuinely disappointment about it.

An hour goes by, and the announcements of the Class of Lords finally end, and they move on to the Class of Knights, with Sir Galla resuming the introductions with his boisterous voice. Sir Matthew represents Trade Kingdom, with Master Walter escorting him as his reward for the day that he had taken charge of the situation with Vil in the weeks prior. Rodin notices that only the head knight and their executive officers are announced for each kingdom.

Finally, Sir Galla announces the Class of Kings of the Thirteen Kingdoms and their royal families, with their anthems playing during their introductions. Lawrence and Coleman come around in time to watch. When King Vaniir is called, he enters with his

Queen, who hides behind a veil, Prince Byron and Prince...
Logan?... following behind them.

Rodin stands with Millette in disbelief. Lawrence and Coleman
are also caught off guard with this. They all stand motionless as the
crowd cheers in their acknowledgment. Logan looks up at them
and waves. Idle stares and open mouths respond back to him.
Byron points and laughs at them. King Vaniir looks up to Rodin
and winks as he looks back to Logan. King Vaniir, King Fulst, and
King Matterhorn look at the balcony where Rodin is seated. Below
Rodin is where the other Common's Leaders are seated, also with
their family and friends. The three of them march front and center
of them and give them the honor of the Common's Bow. Then, the
three men turn to the crowd and give the people the Common's
Bow.

King Vaniir announces, "Welcome, Class of Commons!" The
crowd is in a frenzy for their recognition of their new title.

King Matterhorn steps up and says, "Without the real people of
our three kingdoms, we would be nothing!" A few snide comments
and curses are heard from the higher balconies where the Class of
Lords sit. King Vaniir scorns them all.

King Fulst steps forward and cries out, "Now we call upon our
League King, who recognizes the real people that hold him to their
hearts! The one who wishes to bring honor back to his true
people!"

All three announce in unison, "The King of the League of
Humans, King Saul!"

Suddenly, the crowd grows silent as a boisterous fanfare begins.
The League banners rise up. It is a yellow sun surrounded by a
fiery orange corona with a purple heart in the center representing
the Circle of Light, surrounded by a field of circling stars
representing the Rings. Everyone everywhere around falls to their
knees as King Saul enters. His dress is by far the regalest of all. A
long deep-purple robe lined with foils of gold and silver flows
behind him. Several small boys wearing deep-purple tunics that
shimmer gold and silver carry his robe behind him, never allowing
it to drag the ground. The boys run behind him as he turns, they
drape the robe over the steps of the palace, run back in front of
him, and drop to their knees. As soon as the anthem ends, the
entire band immediately kneels.

Silence.

King Saul looks around at everyone for a moment as nobody dares to raise their heads to look. He raises both arms to the air and yells, "Everyone rise!" And they do. Silently. King Saul paces side to side, but only a few yards at a time. Again, he puts his arms out, and two of the boys race behind him to release the robe from his shoulders, while the others begin to gather and roll it up. King Saul's outfit is the same deep purple as his robe. Just like the boys' tunics, his shimmers gold and silver. It is sleeveless and tight to show off his overly muscular frame. The sunlight glistens from his well-oiled dark skin, allowing the jewels pierced to his head to glisten and shine brighter. He smiles wide at the people around him. He shouts a single word: "Welcome!" And the crowd is thrown into a frenzy.

He allows them to cheer for what seems like minutes. He throws his hands to the air and waves at them to quiet down. The crowd is slow to respond. When they do, he turns to the announcer.

"Call in the squires!"

Sir Galla begins to call the names of the squires representing each kingdom's academy to be knighted by King Saul. Eighteen are called from Trade Kingdom Academy School alone. One hundred sixty squires in all.

Rodin whispers to everyone, "This going to be a longer ceremony than the naming of the Class of Lords."

Lawrence says, "When they knight Master Slindee, I'm done." Coleman agrees.

Glenda returns excitedly, "Oh, my big handsome squire is going to be a big handsome knight!" And she bounces for joy as she tosses her head side to side. Millette comments, "She got it half-right. He *is* big." Helana laughs as they high-five each other.

King Saul steps forward as he draws his royal sword. Slender is first. He approaches him and says, "Master Slindee, do you solemnly swear to uphold the laws of the League of Humans?"

Master Slindee kneels before him with his head held high. "Yes, my king!"

"Do you swear to place the lives of everyone at higher value before yours?"

"Yes, my king!"

"Grab this blade!" King Saul stands the sword on the ground. He balances it on its tip as he holds the hilt with both hands.

Master Slindee grabs the blade and squeezes it. His blood runs down the blade and onto the ground. Then, King Saul walks up to a large firepot and places the sword to the fire. He says, "Your blood represents your oath. The blade represents the strength of your convictions. The fire represents the Light. The heat represents Light's power. With these combined, you have sealed your oath by the witness and power of the Circle of Light in front of these witnesses!" He walks back to Master Slindee and presses the hot blade onto each of his shoulders as Master Slindee bows his head. When he is finished, King Saul steps back as Sir Galla pins the Knight's Badge onto him. King Saul places both hands on his shoulders and cries, "Rise, *Sir* Slindee!"

He rises as everyone cheers him. He turns to the people and bows to the crowd. He turns to the kings and bows to them. He repeats this process to the lords and then gives the Common's Bow to the three commons leaders. He then salutes the Class of Knights.

Lawrence jumps to his feet. "I'm going to lie down. Wake me when the real fun starts."

Rodin commands Lawrence to stop as King Saul moves onto the next soon-to-be knight. Everyone is startled by him as they watch him in anticipation. He says to them, "Something is very wrong." His eyes grow wide as he cries "Go!" and leaps from the balcony. They immediately scramble into action.

As King Saul happily addresses the next squire, the crowd gasps, and some begin to scream. He freezes as he catches Archon coming at him out of the corner of his eye. *Snap!* He turns his head slowly to see that an arrow has been stopped inches from his head. He looks at Archon then back at the arrow.

Archon says to him, "Run!"

As King Saul begins to seek refuge, the skies darken. Everyone looks at the air to see a black cloud of arrows raining down toward them from behind the castle. All hell breaks loose.

XXIX

A rchon grabs King Saul and slings him through the crowd as they cram themselves through the doors of the castle. He looks up and sees a group of arrows flying toward a group of children at a playground. They scream and are paralyzed in fear while in search of their parents. He sprouts a huge set of dragon's wings and sprints to the children using his wings as a shield. Not a single arrow gets through.

Sir Slindee runs to the middle of the land. He takes Mortar and raises it high into the air as a wall forms above, blocking the arrows over them. Unfortunately, a few arrows get by. Lawrence whips his cat-o'-nines out, and they extend in front of a group of kings. All nine balls slam together. *Boom!* A fireball explodes and burns the arrows out of the air. Helana swings her staff, and a bunch splinters in midair before they reach a good part of the crowd. Together, they quickly survey the damage around them. Few are injured, and many are dead. They are able to save some in large groups at once.

The skies blacken as another wave appear in the sky. Luckily, there really isn't many people left outside for them to target. Whoever *them* may be. They all haven't heard, but they are pretty confident what *them* is. Demons.

Archon quickly scrambles to help others to safety before the second volley can cause any more havoc. He and Slender shield groups between buildings. Other groups that fend for themselves are not so lucky. This second volley of arrows takes more lives of the people out in the open. When it is clear, Slender and Archon make for the castle. There are no more survivors by the time a third wave of arrows fall.

Once inside, people yell, cry, and demand answers. Most freeze when they see Archon.

King Vaniir yells at the top of his lungs, "Quiet!"

Everyone stops running except for a few soldiers who are to meet him. They stop and look at King Saul next to King Vaniir. They forgo the need for bowing. Their leader says to them,

"Demons! They are coming through the back walls! I've never seen anything like them, sire! Trolls and orcs accompany them. We have also seen undead warriors flanking to the front gates of the city. They are moving quickly. We need more men to barricade the front gates. We need knights to help with the rear!"

King Saul looks around. "Where is Drake?"

A squire that is to be knighted today says, "I saw him, Queen Falecia, and a hooded man go toward the living quarters, sire!"

King Vaniir looks confused. "What hooded man?"

The squire responds, "I don't know him, sire. Someone else said he was a fella named Vil."

Byron, Slender, and Archon jump and say in unison, "Vil?"

Dahlmür says to Vaniir, "Galla, Lawrence, and I will handle everything in here. The three of you go with Vannii. Logan, see to King Saul and take some knights with you. Troy, go with the remaining knights and soldiers to the rear. Helana, you recruit some to take to the front. Go now!"

Everyone scrambles. Archon leads the way to the Queen's quarters, Byron and Vaniir calling out directions. They yell at people to get to the safety of the dungeons below the castle and to be prepared to escape through the tunnels in case the castle is overrun. They round the final turn and slide to a halt. Drake stands in the center of the hall. Behind him is Lord Vil with his dagger to a very sickly-looking Queen Falecia. Vaniir shoves the others behind him and draws his sword. He releases his royal robes and lets them fall behind him. He reaches up to unbutton the top three buttons of his tunic. Drake sways in readiness for Vaniir's attack. His faceplate is down, and his armor clanks and creaks from the damage caused by Archon a few days prior. Vaniir asks, "Why do you threaten my wife, Drake?" Drake says nothing.

"I've been wondering also why you continue to wear that beaten armor." Drake still sways, his sword ready, with no response.

Vaniir demands, "Remove you helmet, Knight."

Drake obliges this order. He sheathes his sword and begins to bend the helmet where it is damaged to allow it to be taken off. He slowly pulls the helmet from his head. When it is fully removed, he smiles at them. His head is grotesquely balding. Parts of his scalp have peeled away, exposing rotting flesh and bone. One side of his cheek is missing, his jawbone exposed through.

Byron gasps. "He's undead!"

Archon attempts to stand in front of Vaniir, but Vaniir blocks him and says, "I will handle this demon. You keep your eye on that boy with my wife. Slender, the moment you get an opening, kill the boy. Byron, you help save your mother."

Vil laughs as Queen Falecia cries to Byron, "Help me, son!"

Vil says to her as he pulls the dagger closer to her throat, "Shut up! I will kill you! Watch as your husband is killed!"

Drake draws his sword and begins to sway at the ready again. Archon reminds Vaniir, "He will not die until the queen is found and killed."

Vaniir snarls through gritted teeth. "He's no good without his head on his body!" He cries out and attacks Drake. Their swords collide in a fury of swings. As hefty as King Vaniir is, he can still move fluidly and gracefully. Vaniir backs off and begins swinging his sword around, showing all who watch how graceful and well-trained he truly is with a sword. Drake takes a high swing as Vaniir ducks. He swings at Drake's legs, catching him on his left shin. Drake stands and laughs as Vaniir backs up to see black ooze and ichor seep from the wound. A foul stench fills the air. Vaniir is taken aback by it. "Blessed Rings, that's bad! Not as bad as this!"

Vaniir lunges at Drake. Drake swings in defense and raises his sword to block Vaniir's swing to his head. Unfortunately for him, Vaniir does not attack his head as he has shown his intentions to be. Instead, his sword easily slices his body in half where his breastplate meats his steel breeches. Drake's face is stuck in astonishment as his top half falls away from the bottom. Vaniir immediately grabs a torch from the wall and sets his lower half on fire. His legs begin to twist and kick as Vannir drags it away to the end of the hall from which they came as he orders Byron to get Vil.

Drake's top half comes upright. He uses one arm to hold himself up onto a pile of black guts and entrails falling out around him, and he swings his sword with the other. Byron leaps over him, kicking him in the face as he goes by.

Vil backs up, pulling the queen with him, screaming, "Stop!"

Byron stops just feet from in front of him, his short sword raised to strike. Vil says to him, "I hate you! I hate what you stand for! You allowed a peasant to insult me! You allowed a peasant in your house!" He looks at Vaniir. "And you! I should have sided with Darkness when I became Archon like I had planned all those years ago and killed you and the others. Especially that peasant Lawrence!"

Vaniir squints at him in confusion. "Vil?" he asks.

Vil laughs at him. "That's right, you idiot! I am Vil! The one that was made Archon against everyone's will. The Light punished me by not allowing me to stand up to Liche. The Rings knew of my plans when I became Archon. I was to kill Liche and join with Darkness as Archon, reborn into his Order. I was going to be his ultimate ruler! My mother saw to it. She is the Darkness's Priestess. When I died as Archon, she was told by the Darkness that the day will come when I will be born to her again, and here I am. He chose the time when your foolish curses will end and the so-called Eternal Archon would rise. Darkness saw the signs when that peasant fool Lawrence took on that even more foolish Lord Bale as his apprentice. We were supposed to kill the one to be Archon, but we were too late. Damn Aranae gave the gift to that damn peasant! Isn't that right, Peasant Rodin?"

Archon freezes in place. Everyone is taken by surprise at his words. Vil laughs as Byron steps closer. "Let my mother go, Vil. She's sick. Can't you see that?"

Vil grins at him. "Oh, I can see that. I'll tell you what. Why don't everyone back up and let me face you alone? I'll let your sick mother go to your despicable father." Rodin and Slender refuse. "Oh no," Slender says.

Archon's eyes begin to smoke. "I'll kill you myself, Vil."

Vaniir says "No!" He steps between them. "Give me my wife, then we will allow my son to take your head."

Vil shoves the queen into Vaniir's arms. King Vaniir brings her behind them, crying to her and questioning her well-being.

Queen Falecia then lets out an evil laugh. "Oh look! I've caught me King Herring at last!"

They all turn and see her pulling a knife up King Vaniir's abdomen to his chest. Blood spurts from his mouth as she pulls out his insides, and he falls fall to the ground. She laughs again, "This should have been you, Little Piggy, but I can gut a herring just the same!" She tosses Vaniir's entrails behind her.

Vil cries out as he leaps for Byron. Slender throws up his shield to block him, and he is thrown back to the other end of the hall. Byron looks at what his mother has done and screams, "Dad! No!"

He looks at the woman who was his mother in confusion. "Why?"

"Why do you think, Prince Herring?"

"But . . ." Byron looks around in confusion. "You're my mother, right?" Byron's legs begin to grow week as he drops his sword and pleads with her. "What have you done, Mom?" Queen Falecia squeals a laugh. "I'm not your mother, you pathetic little prince!"

Still confused over what has happened, Byron begins to scream at his mother, "Who are you? Where's my mother?"

Archon replies, "Remember the horse and rider? She's the undead queen."

Byron looks at her and screams, "Mom! Dad! No. No. No!" He jumps up and swings his sword at her. She jumps to the ceiling and clings there. Archon jumps up and forces her back down to him.

As she comes down, she swings her knife at him as he ducks out of the way.

Slender swings Chill, and a cold blast shoots to the floor below them. The ground becomes a sheet of ice as Archon yanks Byron up to the ceiling with him. Both halves of Drake's body become ice, as does Vaniir's body. The undead queen leaps up and hangs on to the ceiling again.

Byron shouts, "I can't stand on ice!"

Slender yells, "I know! Neither can she!"

Archon catches his plan and whispers it to Byron, who quickly understands and agrees.

The undead queen begins to laugh. "Here, Piggy! Squeal for me, Piggy!" She begins crawling toward Slender. "I'm going to gut you! I'm going to skin Prince Herring! I'm going to kill Trash! Then I'm going to let the new League of Ogres destroy your friends as I sit back and devour Beauty! The one Prince Herring calls a girlfriend!"

Archon comments, "You really can come up with some disturbing names for people." And he lunges at her.

Slender ducks as she leaps from the ceiling to the end of the sheet of ice. She lands to the ground and turns around to see Archon land back onto the ceiling. She suddenly realizes that he is swinging a silver rope toward her. At the end of it is Byron, hanging on as he skates across the ice at her. It's too late for her to act. Byron hits the end of the ice and skids to a stop past her, swinging his short sword and removing her head from her shoulders. In the silence, they hear people within the building cry in celebration.

Byron hits the floor to his knees and cries out for the death of his mother and father. His short sword clangs to the ground as he lets go of it and throws his hands to his face. Slender walks to him calmly as Archon lands off the icy floor. He becomes Rodin. The two of them kneel to him and share in his grief.

After a moment, they begin to rise. Byron begins to walk toward his father, but Rodin stops him, saying to him, "We have to keep going. Your father was brave. He lived long in his curse. You know as well as I that he is happiest now. Don't grieve. Celebrate. Remember?"

Byron tries to regain himself as he nods and wipes his tears. He says to them, "We'll celebrate after we end this." They run to the end of the hall.

As they round the corner, they are met by Mutt and Biter. Biter screams, "That boy! That boy you know!"

Archon asks out of frustration, "What about him?"

Mutt begins jumping. "He has your girlfriend, Logan, and Lawrence!"

They run, letting the younglings lead the way. Slender says to them, "Where have you been?"

Biter says, "We've been trying to stop a horde of nasty undead, but they let the boy through, and he grabbed them."

Mutt says, "Yes, but by the time all the undead fell, he had gotten away with them! A few orcs are helping him!"

Just as they come to the end of the hall that leads to an opening, the wall beside them explodes. Daylight and dust are all that's left of it. Suddenly, a giant hand reaches in and grabs Byron and Rodin. Slender, Mutt, and Biter barely escape. Rodin flips into Archon and shouts to them, "Go save Millette!" And they hurry off.

Byron screams, "It's squeezing me!"

Archon wriggles himself further onto the hand and releases darts outward and into the hand. The hand lets go as an ogre screams in pain. They hit the ground and look up. This beast of a demon is huge, much bigger than what he has seen before, but they are similar demons.

Byron stands and runs to Archon. "I have a trick to show you, brother!"

Archon retorts, "Well, it better be a good one!" The beast yells as it pulls a dart from its finger then looks at them in anger. It bends down and howls at them.

Byron swings his sword as Archon yells, "That thing is too small! It will just piss him off even more!"

Byron cries out, "It's not the same sword!" Its blade suddenly extends out another three yards and slices the creature's throat while it is ducked down at them midhowl. It immediately stops and stands up as it grabs at its slit throat, trying to gasp for breath. Black blood spurts from its mouth and out from its throat. It falls to the ground beside them with a thunderous *slam!* Byron turns to Archon and smiles. "Meet Switchblade! Its blade reaches out and slices anything! I got it as a gift this morning from Coleman!"

Archon admires it and says, "Nice!" He shoves Byron away as a large spear lands in front of him. It drives deep into the ground, burying itself halfway down its shaft.

Byron looks at Archon in surprise. "Thanks!"

"No problem, brother!" he points to the castle, "We need to get Vil!"

Byron looks up and sees a group of orcs climbing to the top wall. He says to Archon, "Throw me!" Archon obliges him and tosses him up. Byron swings Switchblade, cutting down orcs as he flies by them. He flies through a window. A loud crash is heard, and he pops his head out as he rubs it. "I'm good! Go!" He waves Archon on.

Archon hears Helana's voice, "*The front gates are secured. The undeads have fallen. Thanks for killing the queen. We are on our way to join the fight at the rear walls!*"

Archon concentrates, "*The big ones are ogres. When we are done, we will explain the queen. King Vaniir is dead. Vil is Vil. Explain later. Drake was undead. Explain later. Vil has Millette, Logan, and Lawrence. Byron*"—he sidesteps another large spear and turns to look for the rude attacker—"*and Slender are helping the younglings chase them down. We need help fast! Ogres have stepped over the walls. And that's not a metaphor!*"

Helana appears in front of him with several knights. He sprouts wings and shields the group from an onslaught of arrows obviously meant for him. When he lowers the wings, he suddenly sees a charging giant running at them, meaning to run them down. Archon leaps and punches the creature in the face, knocking it out cold. Archon shakes his fist in pain "Holy Blessed Rings! For the love of Light! That freakin' hurt!" He runs on top of the ogre and extends a blade from his arm. He shoves the blade through its eye for the kill. He mumbles at it, "Jerk!" He shakes his his hand and leaps off.

Helana laughs. "Hardheads! Good to know! Thanks!"

He laughs at her. "Damn, you too!"

Another spear comes down. This one falls short of them and into the gut of the already dead ogre, spraying them with black, foul ichor. The men grunt in disgust, and Helana screams, "I just cleaned my hair!"

Archon laughs and points at another ogre that is pulling another spear from the ground about one hundred yards away, "Him!"

Helana's face turns bright red. The men ask Archon if they should stand back, and Archon nods at them, saying, "Oh yeah! They messed up the lady's hair!"

One cries, "I'm running. There's no safe distance from that!" He takes off toward the castle and begins to attack the orcs trying to retake the wall.

Another man says, "I don't blame him, but we have the unfortunate duty to help her."

Helana steps back and yanks the stone from her staff. She draws up like she is going to pitch it at the ogre. The ogre looks at her and does the same with its spear. They mimic each other as they wind up, and they both throw their weapons as hard as they can. The stone meets the spear midair and causes it to explode into thousands of splinters. It stays on course and hits the startled ogre directly in the gut, and it explodes. The impact of the explosion blows the ogre apart. An arm flies up and lands just feet in front of her.

Archon looks at the men and says, "Lesson learned. Not the hair." They all agree.

Helana turns around, and with a satisfied look, she picks up her staff and the stone returns to it. She calmly walks away.

Archon points to a figure coming at them in the distance. "It's your father!"

Dahlmür catches up to them, out of breath. "The castle is being overrun! I understand that King Vaniir is dead! Coleman and Troy are making sure that all classes are escaping through the tunnels. King Saul says that he will hold his ship at the docks till you and the others arrive!"

Helana asks in confusion, "What about you? You need to leave! We have this! Go!"

Dahlmür looks at her with a somber expression and shakes his head. He's not going anywhere. Archon lays a hand on her shoulder. "Let's bring him honor in this battle." He understands Dahlmür's meaning.

She weeps for him as she hugs him. After giving them a moment, he hugs Dahlmür and asks, "Where is Galla, sir?"

Dahlmür points to the wall to the east side of the castle over a hundred yards away. "He's holding that wall!"

Galla and his men gather together at the top of the wall and begin throwing the ladders and cutting the grapples away from them. They lean over with bows and fire a volley at the orcs and trolls falling below. He rushes ahead to a ladder left standing and faces down a couple of trolls as they jump over the top. He cuts one down before it lands. The other plants down in front of him and swings a rusty sword at him. Metal meets metal as they continue to swing and block one another. Galla stands erect and towers over the orc easily with his half-Gia size. The orc looks at him in astonishment and hurls itself over the wall. Galla laughs at it. Then another appears over the roof from the ladder.

One man hurries behind them and tosses the ladder away as another set of archers fire below.

They back away as Galla shoves the orc backward at them. The orc regains its stance and goes after Galla. Galla swings at the rusty blade coming at him. *Clank!* The sword breaks and flies over the wall. The two warriors are amazed and look down the wall in time to see the broken blade stab through the top of the head of an unsuspecting orc. They look back at each other, and Galla lets out a hearty laugh. The orc screams and leaps at him. Galla points his sword straight out, and the orc is skewered from shoulder to backside. Galla points down his sword and tries to furiously shake it off. He swings his sword over the wall, and the body of the dead orc flies off into a gang of trolls getting ready to raise another ladder.

Galla is looking at his men in triumph when something in the trees catches the corner of his eye. He looks and sees trees falling quickly in paths. Thunderous footsteps plow through them. He looks at his men and signals them back to the castle walls. "Run!"

Unfortunately, it is too late for Galla. Three charging ogres explode through the wall in his location.

As Dahlmür points to where Galla is fighting, the east wall explodes. Three ogres power through it with their shoulders down. Then all three turn in unison and plow into the walls of the castle, obliterating the entire east wing. Archon realizes he has just witnessed the end of another Cursed Brother. Dahlmür lowers his head. Archon places a hand on his shoulder and reminds him and Helana, "Celebrate."

Dahlmür smiles at him. "He loved Sir Slindee with all his heart."

Archon nods. "And Sir Slindee will make him proud. We promise."

Dahlmür says to Helana, "Make me proud too."

She holds her head high as a tear falls. "I will, Father."

Archon wastes no time. "We must hurry. Vil, your Vil, has Millette, Logan, and Lawrence prisoner!"

Without asking his meaning, Dahlmür and Helana sprint to catch up. A horde of orcs, trolls, and ogres comes through the open wall and begins attacking everyone in their way. Archon leaps at a charging ogre and rolls around onto its back. He wraps a thin strand around its neck and yanks it with one hand, setting it ablaze. The strand burns and slices through, separating head from shoulders. A giant spear lands in front of him. He looks around in the direction of the thrower and sees several gathering spears and throwing them. Archon leaps to the air, reaches his fist back, and comes down punching the ground between them. The force blows the ogres back and off their feet. They throw spears in the air as they fall. Archon makes sure they all find their marks into the bodies of the fallen ogres by whipping at them to change their course. Black blood flies everywhere with each hit. Their bodies convulse as they lie dying.

Archon turns his attention back to the castle. A horde of trolls tries to intercept him. His right arm becomes a giant club that scrapes the ground, grinding the trolls' bodies into black pulp and dirt. He spots movement at the top of the castle's central tower. He is able to zoom in and sees Vil standing face-to-face with Lawrence, Millette, and Logan behind him.

As soon as they reach the top, an arrow flies up at them, causing Vil to become distracted. He sidesteps the arrow as it lands beside him. He looks up and sees Lawrence with his cat-o'-nine tails flaming in front of him. Lawrence whips out at him, and Vil spins safely out of the way. He is determined to keep himself between them and their only way out.

Lawrence says to him, "I cannot believe I let a dirty lord like yourself become Archon!"

Vil laughs. "I can't believe I let you live, Trash!" He swings at Lawrence, but Lawrence is able to get the whip to light a flash of fire between them.

Lawrence says to him, "You will die here today!"

Vil sneers. "At least I will have the pleasure of taking the three of you with me!" He reaches behind him, and before Lawrence sees it, Vil hits the ground on one knee and throws a knife at him. Lawrence moves out of the way just in time for the knife to fly by and cut a line into the side of his face. Just as quickly, another flies through the air. Lawrence reacts, but this one cuts through his trench and slices a long line on his arm as it flies by. Vil laughs as a third blade slices the side of his calf. Lawrence has never seen this incredible speed out of Vil before. He rolls out of the way completely as a fourth one streaks by him. As soon as he rolls to his feet, another knife finds its mark in his thigh. Lawrence screams in pain as Vil cries out in triumph.

Lawrence reaches down and pulls the knife out. He screams out in pain as he pulls harder. This knife is hard to remove. He is confused and pulls with all he can stand. The knife finally comes free, and Lawrence is in pain and shock as he sees that Vil has thrown a serrated knife. It has torn out muscle and skin as he pulled it out. He stares at the grotesque blade with anger and surprise as he sees the gore hanging from it. He catches sight of Vil moving toward him behind the sight of the blade. Vil's face is contorted with rage and hatred as he begins to stalk toward Lawrence. Then he turns and sneers at Logan and Millette, who run behind Lawrence for his protection. Lawrence throws down the knife and, against all pain, stands and faces him. He grips his whip hard as Vil laughs. The laugh is the sound of evil. Vil's throat growls as he hunches over and stares Lawrence down. Vil sneers as he curls his upper lip like a beast who has decided to go for the kill against its prey. Vil cries out as he leaps at him.

Lawrence swings his whip from overhead and down onto Vil's shoulder. Flames burst out and scorch the side of his face, down his neck, and into his shoulder. Vil screams as his dagger flies from his hand harmlessly, and he falls to the ground in immense pain. Lawrence relaxes as Vil is down and disarmed. He turns to face Millette and Logan to tell them to run for the stairwell, but he stiffens, and the wind leaves his chest with a loud grunt. Blood dribbles out of his nose and mouth as he turns to face Vil.

Millette sees the handle of a throwing dagger sticking out of his back behind his heart. Millette screams as she sees Vil standing in a thrown position with an evil, satisfied look. Lawrence drops to his knees, trying to speak. Then he slumps his head down. His body falls forward.

Another Cursed Brother has fallen.

Millette screams as Logan cries out Lawrence's name.

Archon, Helana, and Dahlmür witness Lawrence's fall. Archon becomes enraged. He leaps to the air at the tower but is intercepted by the shoulder of a charging ogre. Archon hits the ground hard. He stands and shakes it off the moment he is on his feet. Archon is furious.

Dahlmür and Helana rush by him toward the castle. Both of them fire bolts at the onslaught of trolls coming at them. Small bodies explode and fly through the air. Orcs turn to them and rush at them. They both pull swords from their staffs and begin to slaughter the orcs easily. Father and daughter fight together.

Archon leaps at the ogre that's knocked him down. The ogre bats him down again and tries to stomp onto him as he rolls out of the way. The foot thunders down next to his head. Archon jumps up to his feet and swings his arm as a club at the back of its knees. The ogre falls on its back. Archon jumps onto its chest and makes his arm into a blade, meaning to stab it in the throat. The ogre quickly swipes him off, throwing him to the air. Archon lands facefirst down into the dirt. The ogre lifts him by a leg and begins to twirl him, meaning to throw him.

Vil smiles as he looks onto Millette and Logan. He begins to circle them back and forth as if he were a vicious predator trapping his prey. Millette warns him, "You hurt us, and Rodin will kill you!"

Vil laughs at this. "Don't you mean the Archon?" Logan and Millette are stunned. "Oh, I know about him. I used to be him," he nonchalantly adds as he twirls his dagger around. "In another life, of course. I was Archon, but the Circle of Light felt that the piece-of-trash peasant lying on the ground in front of you was more worthy than me, a Class of Lord! How sick! Now the Light chose another trash over a damn knight! How sick is this world becoming?" He jumps to the side at them to keep them off balance. "So I am reborn to cleanse the sickness of the League of Humans that Light loves so greatly and take over Terra-Earth as the Circle of Darkness's ruler! Other Leagues will serve him through me! That is the way it should be! All life on Terra-Earth should serve the Circles, not run around and squander it. The Light wastes knowledge by teaching his precious Leagues to do what? Serve themselves? What good is that? There's no order to that kind of thing. It causes chaos. The Circle of Darkness wishes to end chaos on Terra-Earth by ruling over it like an iron fist! My iron fist!"

Millette and Logan separate and roll on the ground as Vil launches at them. His right arm is useless from the wounds Lawrence has given him, so his swing from his left hand is sloppy and slow. He looks at Millette and chases after her. Logan sneaks up behind him and plants a foot on Vil's back, launching him past Millette. Vil hits the wall with his head and falls over.

Millette grabs Logan. "We have to hurry! Get on the wall!"

Logan climbs up then hangs on for his life when he looks down. "I'm not wearing my boots!"

Millette looks and sees that he is wearing dress shoes for the celebrations. She screams in frustration as they hear Slender below. "Jump! We'll catch you!"

Byron then screams, "No! Biter is shooting a web to you! Take this instead!" And a webbed string sticks to the wall beside him.

Logan grabs hold then looks at Millette and sticks his hand out to her. He sees Vil standing behind her, and he points at him while shouting her name, "Millette!"

She turns around and stares into his eyes, seeing nothing but pure evil intentions. Vil looks back at her and smiles at her. He swings his sword.

Logan screams as Millette is suddenly yanked out of sight over the wall. Vil looks at the direction she is pulled to and sees Archon. He points his sword at him and laughs with evil satisfaction.

As archon is raised high, he sees Logan and Millette. He begins to shout at them, but Vil rises behind her. He hears Logan cry out her name and throws a line at Millette that wraps around her waist. He pulls her away as fast as he can. He looks down at her and smiles. His foot becomes a blade that lengthens into the top of the ogre's head. The ogre stops the attempt to throw and falls face-first. Archon holds Millette as they reach the ground, and Archon takes the final few feet in a leap to avoid being smashed to the ground. He continues to smile as he holds her and sets her down into his lap as he sits with her.

Her face doesn't smile back; instead, she hands him a small pouch. "Give this to the little squirt for me." Archon looks at her, confused. She stares at him blankly. "I love you so much, Archon or Rodin. I don't care. You are still the same person inside. That is who I am in love with. Eternally."

He looks at her in confusion. "Millette?" Blood spurts from her mouth and from her nose. "Millette?" Panic comes over him as Rodin returns. He looks around and up. Rodin sees Vil pointing his sword at him and smiling. He holds his sword up as red glints off the blade in the sunlight and runs down to the hilt. Wide-eyed and breathing heavily in a desperate panic, he looks down and sees that he is too late. His sword has found her chest just below her heart. She coughs as more blood flows from her wound and her mouth. He holds her up to keep her from choking on the blood.

Rodin cries, "Millette. No!"

She grabs his hand and kisses his cheek, leaving a bloody lip print. She whispers, "I love you, baby. Please don't cry for me."

He can't help it. Tears fall, and his body quivers. He looks around anxiously and spots Helana. *"Get Byron! She's hurt! I don't know how to heal!"* He can't tell if she's heard him. His vision becomes blurry with tears. "Help!"

Millette turns his face to her. "Don't cry for me. I love you. Celebrate my life."

Rodin whispers to her, "I want us to celebrate our marriage. Please. Hang on!" He is pleading to her. He looks around and sees everyone busy with their battles. "Help! Somebody!"

Millette pulls him to face her again. "I . . . love . . . you . . . Rodin. Please . . . don't . . . cry." She coughs again. She reaches up and pulls his other cheek to her lips. This time, she doesn't let go.

He pulls back from her, trembling. He looks around in that same panic. His eyes scan around quickly. He breathes heavily and quickly. He tries to cry out for help but only lets out a faint wail. He tries to call out again but only squawks. He cries hard. He lays her down in front of him as he falls to his knees. He bends down and cries onto her chest. He sits up and inhales hard and exhales with a wail. "Help!"

He stands and screams at Helana across the field from him. As he does, he feels his breath get kicked out of him as he is kicked from behind by a charging ogre taking advantage of the situation. Anger, sadness, fear, and confusion bring him back into Archon. He begins to rise, but in his stagger, he is kicked again. Archon's mind goes blank from all the emotion that has taken him over. Even the death of his parents never affected him so much. His thoughts and body shut down as he suddenly loses all control.

Logan makes his way down the web-rope frantically. Something drips onto his arm. It's red. It takes a moment for it to register to him that it is blood. He quickly scans around himself, looking for the wound. When he sees none, he peers up and sees Vil laughing and pointing his bloodstained sword out at someone. He hears Byron and Slender's voices calling out to him to finish his descent to safety. Vil spots him and starts climbing over the wall, grabbing the rope to follow Logan down. Logan realizes the danger and begins to slip down, burning his hands along the way, until he is unable to stand the burn anymore and releases his grip. Slender catches him and places Logan onto his feet and blocks a battered sword with his own, keeping it from severing Logan's head from his neck. Logan is then shoved to the side and sandwiched between Slender and Byron.

Logan looks around to search for Millette, who should have been right behind him instead of Vil. He spots her. He watches as his brother softly places her to the ground. Her green dress begins to turn crimson in his brother's arms. Another drop of blood falls to his shoulder. He looks up to see Vil laughing and pointing his sword at him as another drop falls from the blade at him. Logan then understands. Vil has successfully attacked her. His eyes widen as his chest heaves in and out, watching his brother call out in desperation for help.

Logan begins pointing and pounding at Byron's shoulder. "Millette has been stabbed! Rodin has her over there! She's dying! We need to help her!"

Byron swings Switchblade at an oncoming horde of orcs. "I can't get away! We're under attack!" He slams Logan to the wall behind him as he brings his sword down onto a giant hand of an ogre grabbing at them.

Logan screams at Slender, "We have to get Byron to Millette! She's dying! Vil stabbed her!" He points to Rodin and Millette. "Look!"

Slender shoves him back. "Look out!" He slams Mortar to the ground and swings chill to the side. Orcs are after them from all directions.

Logan begins to sweat and panic as he watches Millette kiss Rodin's cheek. Tears begin to fall from his eyes as he realizes he has just witnessed her dying kiss. He falls to his knees. "No!" He reaches out as he wants so desperately to save her. *My sister! No! Please save her! I love her! Somebody! Please help my sister! Millette!*

Rage fills him as he picks up a sword dropped by a fallen orc. He looks up at Vil, who watches his brother pointing his sword and laughing maniacally while still clinging from the rope. He grabs the rope and begins shaking it violently, trying to make Vil fall loose. When that fails, Logan shoves the sword's pummel into his mouth and grabs on, meaning to climb up after him. He tries to scream Vil's name, but his words can't be understood with the sword clenched in his teeth. His heart races, and his blood boils hotter as he begins to ascend. He manages a few feet into the air when suddenly, a voice screams in his head, and he is tossed to the ground. Suddenly, Logan finds himself under the body of Biter when something explodes, and the death cries of over a thousand demons are carried on all around him. Then silence.

Helana gasps and screams in horror as she sees Millette give him her dying kiss. Dahlmür sees it also and looks over to Helana as she screams out for Rodin in shock. She points behind him to warn him, but he is not acknowledging her in any way. He just screams out for help. She runs at him with her sword in hand. The ogre kicks him then runs up and kicks him again just as he becomes Archon. She leaps at the ogre and sinks her sword into its neck and chants. The neck of the ogre explodes, sending its head flying backward.

Dahlmür sees Archon fly over them and sees the black nothingness that holds his eyes go completely empty. He runs out to catch Archon, but another ogre beats him to him and kicks Archon into air again. Dahlmür launches himself at it and shoves his staff into its shoulder. He chants, and its upper body explodes away from its waist. He watches Archon hit the ground, rolling and not stopping himself. He continues to roll and bounce as he hits a few boulders. He then slows to a stop. Helana begins to run to him, but Dahlmür grabs her and prevents her from approaching.

She turns to look at him and sees fear in his eyes.

Archon comes to his feet. He looks as if he has gone insane. He falls to his knees and grabs his head. He pounds the ground with his fists, and the ground shakes around him with every blow. He tries to stand but falls to his head. His body begins to look like its bubbling and boiling.

Dahlmür grabs Helana and throws her to a ditch. He turns and holds out his staff. He begins to say something into it. Suddenly, Helana sees a giant foot come down on top of him and grind him into the ground. His voice echoes in her head as she screams.

Dahlmür's call successfully goes out. It reaches everyone in every Class, League, and Order on Terra-Earth within, around, inside, and above the castle that does not belong to Darkness. They all hear it, and they all listen without question and without hesitation. One word. One command.

"Down!"

They all fall to the ground and cover themselves. Nobody dares to look to see why except four people. The ones that love him. The ones that protect him. The ones that laugh with him. The ones that cry with him. The ones that call him "Brother." They all see why.

They see Archon losing control of his body. They see him burning with pain. They see him crying out over the one he loves most. They see his body unable to contain the anguish of his soul.

They see Archon explode.

XXX

hen he explodes, Rodin falls. A shock wave goes out in a thunder and shakes Terra-Earth and the air around them. Behind it is a rain of silver darts that make up the Archon. Nothing stops them. They shred everything everywhere for miles. No trees are left standing. No stone pillars. No stone walls. More importantly, no demons. The darts pierce through them as if they were made of paper. Byron, Slender, and Logan look up to see the wall of the tower painted in Vil's blood along with what remains of the webbed roped he has descended from. They figure Vil must have flown for miles before what remains of his body finally hit the ground.

Helana jumps up and runs to him. Byron and the others race to join her. She removes her robes and cover Rodin. His clothes have exploded with whatever it is that makes the form of Archon. He lies facedown and motionless. The marks on his back where Aranae has bitten him reopen and begin to ooze. At first, they can't tell if he has survived. Then they hear him crying in his sleep. Even in his current state, the emotion of it all comes through.

Logan begins to cry and lies over him. He begins to cry out Millette's name as well. He loved her just the same as Rodin. She wanted to be his brother. He wanted her to marry Rodin and have many children. He wanted to keep Millette in their lives forever. She had been the best thing to have ever happened to the two of them. Now she's gone. Stripped away from them forever by a monster.

Francine comes running to them, asking what's happened. When Helana announces what Archon has seen and what Rodin has gone through, she collapses beside him. Helana holds tightly onto Byron and begins to cry. Coleman approaches with Glenda in tow. He asks who is under the robe. When Slender explains what Coleman can understand and Glenda cannot, Coleman falls down and grabs Logan to comfort him. Glenda runs to Slender, crying.

Slender breaks down himself. They hover over Rodin's motionless body and comfort one another.

After what seems like hours, Byron places his hands over him to begin the healing process. Helana casts a spell to make him as light as a feather so they can all easily carry him to King Saul's ship waiting at the docks of Trade Harbor. Coleman summons his carriage, and Rodin is placed inside as Logan and Francine climb inside with him. Helana and Troy summon horses for the others to ride as they escort the carriage to a ship docked at Trade Harbor, where a man with a curious look watches them drive the transport aboard with King Saul directing them to go below. He then turns to the stranger and begins to coax him to not ask questions even he cannot answer.

In the cabin below, Francine caresses Rodin's face, and she fights back her tears and asks them, "How long will it take him to come around?"

Byron chokes back from crying and says, "The first time was ten days."

Francine says to him, "Good. He deserves all the rest he can get right now." She kisses Rodin on the cheek and sniffs back more tears. She looks down and sees Logan shivering. She removes her coat and drapes it over him. She continues to stroke Rodin's hair.

Coleman comments, "If Liche is coming, then we will need him back real soon. Archon needs to expand his circle and create an army. He will have to recruit from all leagues from the Order of Terrans, and as many additional Leagues he can get along the way. From here on out, Logan, you will remain with King Saul. You know your duties. Glenda, you will stay and serve with him as his personal servant and guide. You know how the kings work better than you let on." She nods in agreement. "I will travel with all of you until I find my apprentice. I will be your guide until my time comes. While we travel, we will undoubtedly find more demons along the way. We will take another boat and head to the northern area of the mainland."

Byron says, "That's the gias' lands."

Coleman confirms, "Yes, it is. You will go there first because we need the gias to align themselves with us immediately if we are to win this war."

King Saul appears from his quarters. Troy and another man follow him. King Saul demands, "Who is this man?"

Coleman looks up at him and says, "Not right now, sire."

The unknown man says to him, "My ship! You tell us, or I toss you all over!"

Slender jumps up to challenge him. "I'd like to see you try."

An argument ensues. Everyone begins to argue and threaten one another. Logan leans over Rodin and bursts into tears. Nobody pays any attention to him. The man shouts, "I want to know who I have on my boat, or I swear on my brother's dead body; I will toss you all personally!"

Logan cries as he states without lifting his head, "Please don't swear on our daddy. Daddy didn't like anyone to swear."

The man freezes. He turns to look at Logan. He bends down to look at his face. Faint recognition comes to him, and he throws the blanket away from Rodin's face. He looks at Rodin and falls into a sitting position.

King Saul says, "That's Commons Leader Rodin of Millington!"

The man shakes his head. "No. He's my brother's son. So is this boy."

Slender covers Rodin up to his neck now that everyone has seen his face. Francine resumes stroking his hair and kissing his cheek.

Logan looks up to the man and tries to smile. "Hi. My name is Logan. This is my big brother Rodin. We're pleased to finally meet you, Uncle." He looks at the man and tilts his head as if he were trying to remember something. "Your name is Sean, right?"

The man is astonished by his discovery. "Yes. Tell me, how did this happen?"

Coleman sits down and lights a bonfire within a metal pot beside them. He sighs and looks around to the newly joined faces. He rubs Logan's shoulder and announces, "Everyone sit. Logan has a story to tell you all about a man and a Cursed Brother."

End

Thank You

I hope everyone enjoyed reading this revised edition of **Archon: Gift of Light**. I truly enjoyed the work that has been put into this project. Believe it or not, it took quite a while to get this done. There was so much that needed to be changed, corrected, and such that the time was unbelievably extensive.

I won't say I didn't like the first version, but "Yikes!" I figured if I am going to invest the time to revise this book, I might as well go "all in!"

I want to thank my wife (Cathy) for putting up with me during the process (all of it). I want to thank my sisters (Jennifer, Samantha, Melissa, and Stephanie) for helping find the mistakes. I also want to thank my sons and stepson (Cruise, Jax, and Logan) for their input, as well.

Thank you so much _____ for recreating the beautiful artwork that is my cover. You are indeed an artist!

For now:

"Have fun and Remember... SMILE!"
                    - L. S. Quail

About the Author

L.S. Quail -Writer/Author/Storyteller- is living proudly in the beautiful city of Sarasota, Florida with his wife, step-son, and *NINE!* Dogs. He has independently published the Fantasy Archon: Gift of Light and continues to write short stories on his website shortstories4u2share.com. Writing and telling stories while guzzling coffee and praying to the coffee gods that it shall never run dry is his passion. Becoming an author and storyteller as a profession is his dream. You can also visit his website at LSQuail.com to learn more about this fool with *NINE!* dogs.

Follow him below to find out more about his up and coming Science Fiction; *Chronicles of Human Being: Being, Human*, and part two of the *Archon* series.

http://www.lsquail.com
http://www.twitter.com/lsquail
http://www.facebook.com/LSQuail
http://www.shortstories4u2share.com

WRITER/AUTHOR/STORYTELLER